"Since there's a genuine attraction between us, it won't take much to convince your family we're a couple..."

"Danny, why would you want to do this?" Jordan asked, a sexy smile tugging at her lips.

He wasn't sure when the idea had come to him—this morning in her bed or the night before when they'd been going at it for hours. Danny had now discovered Jordan's wild side, and he planned to explore it to the fullest.

"After last night, do you really have to ask?"

"So this is some kind of sexual favor?"

He cocked his head to the side, then nodded. "Yeah."

Jordan laughed. "Not that I'm agreeing, but what exactly do you want in return for faking an engagement?"

"You. Naked. Any time. Any place. Any way."

Dear Reader,

When I started this book, I thought it would be a romantic comedy of errors. (What could be funnier than an accidental kidnapping and switching identities?) But Danny and Jordan had minds of their own.

While writing Danny and Jordan's story, I learned a lot about determination, courage and the importance of family. Through the eyes of love, Jordan begins to see herself for the beautiful woman she is, inside and out. In the warmth of acceptance, Danny overcomes his fears and takes a chance on love—the biggest risk of all.

I believe in the healing power of laughter and happy endings. Hoping that you are blessed with many happy endings of your own.

I wish you joy,

Mia Zachary

P.S. Please visit at www.miazachary.com.

Books by Mia Zachary

HARLEQUIN BLAZE
83—RED SHOES & A DIARY
136—YOURS IN BLACK LACE

9½ DAYS

Mia Zachary

TORONTO • NEW YORK • LONDON
AMSTERDAM • PARIS • SYDNEY • HAMBURG
STOCKHOLM • ATHENS • TOKYO • MILAN • MADRID
PRAGUE • WARSAW • BUDAPEST • AUCKLAND

DEDICATION

This book is dedicated to those who lost their lives in New York, Washington and Pennsylvania on September 11, 2001, and to those who continuously dedicate their lives to saving others.

ACKNOWLEDGMENT

Heartfelt thanks to CeeJai, without whom this story never would have been written. I appreciate the four-hour lunches and the midnight telephone plotting sessions. And to Melissa, who reminded me about author integrity and character growth. Thank you for the trans-Pacific e-mails and @**-kickings.

ISBN 0-373-79164-X

9½ DAYS

Introduction

"*I want you, right here and right now!*"

You may never have spoken those words, or had them said to you, but you must want to. You bought this book!

Inside these pages are fifty sizzling hot, superexciting fantasies to help you recapture the passion and anticipation in your love life. Some are sensual, others sexy; some are naughty and others are oh-so-nice, but all of them are red-hot fun!

Try these ideas on the spur of the moment for a delicious quickie, or take your time and make the fantasy last all night. There are only three rules: Be Safe, Be Spontaneous and Be Satisfied.

Go ahead. Turn the page. You'll soon discover fifty ways to say "*I want you, right here and right now, and here's how!*"

1

"DID YOU FIND EVERYTHING you need?"

Jordan Gregory snapped shut the book she held as her heart plunged into her stomach. Pulse tripping erratically, she turned her head toward the source of the question. Didn't it just figure? The only young, handsome employee in all of Barnes & Noble and he had to be the one to bust her.

She pressed the front cover against her chest to hide the title as heat rushed to her face. Was it possible to actually die of embarrassment? She managed to paste on a smile for the cute book clerk.

"Yes. I mean, no. I'm just browsing."

Humor gleamed in his large brown eyes as he glanced at the book jacket. Then he offered her a knowing grin. Too late she realized the title was printed on the back cover as well as the front. Damn.

"Let me know if you have any questions, ma'am."

Jordan wasn't sure if that was a criticism or a come-on, but she thanked him just the same and waited impatiently for him to move along. Her eyes darted around the bookstore. She hoped no one else in the Thursday lunchtime crowd noticed her standing in the Sex & Relationships aisle, practically drooling all over *Fifty Fast Fantasies*.

Hot blood thudded along her veins and she imagined smoke emanating from inside her jade-green suit as a heavy ache settled between her thighs. She didn't normally read books like this, let alone follow the instructions. But she wanted to experience the kind of passion and spontaneity that *Fifty Fast Fantasies* promised.

The one time she'd had sex with her ex-boyfriend, David, had been a complete disaster. Even now, Jordan shuddered to remember how clumsy and self-conscious she'd been. By the time she'd forced herself to relax, it was already over. The whole experience had left her unsatisfied and unsure of herself.

She saw the cute clerk coming around the corner again and ducked into the Reference section. There was only one other person near the crossword puzzle dictionaries and foreign-language tapes. Jordan turned her back to the woman and randomly opened the book again. Wow. She hadn't realized how many ways you could use nondairy whipped topping.

She flipped back to the table of contents. Just reading the introduction to the sexual guidebook had scorched her white silk blouse. Chapter descriptions like Ahoy Big Pirate; French Maid Service; Great! The Outdoors, and Mirror Mirror on the Wall were enough to make her spontaneously combust.

Maybe if she tried out some of these fantasies, if

she learned some tricks to make herself sexy and desirable, she could convince David to try again. Six weeks ago he had gently suggested some time apart to think about what they wanted. Jordan thought that time apart was at the heart of their problems but hadn't argued, believing the fault lay with her and her inexperience.

But she had to win David back. Fast.

Pretend to be a pirate's wench or a sexy dominatrix? The very idea was daunting. She had never imagined herself going to this kind of extreme, but desperate times required drastic actions. At this point she would do almost anything to convince David to grant her this favor. Anything to have him look at her with something more than kindness in his gaze.

Maybe then the little voice in the back of her head that whispered she was making a mistake would shut up.

"Huh. Ah. Tuh. Hot. I know that word!" Jordan looked down to see a rosy-cheeked cherub gazing at her with innocent blue eyes. "And the next word is Ss. Eh—"

Jordan moved her book out of sight before the little girl could figure out how to pronounce the letter *X.* She contorted her stiff features into a brief smile. "Isn't your mommy looking for you, sweetie?"

"Nope. She's right over there." The girl skipped toward the woman by the dictionaries. "Mama, what does 'sex' mean?"

Jordan backed away from the heat of the

woman's glare and fled the Reference section. She was never shopping at this Barnes & Noble again.

As she moved through the store, the bright covers of the fashion and gossip magazines caught her attention. She averted her eyes, but it was too late. The jolt of ugly emotions stabbed her in the gut. She wouldn't look. She wouldn't. Jordan shoved her guilty secret to the back of her mind and kept walking.

Waiting her turn near the checkout, the latest issue of *Baltimore Today* caught her eye. David was on the front beneath a headline that read, Legal Eagles: The Best 30 Lawyers In The City. He looked tall and confident in his charcoal pin-striped suit. The cream-colored shirt and red paisley tie complemented the rich cappuccino tones of his skin. Sunlight from his large office window shone on his dark curls and rivaled the brightness of his wide smile.

David was perfect. He was handsome, successful, intelligent and considerate. What more could a woman ask for?

How about a man who actually lights your fire instead of blowing it out? How about hot, sheet-soaking sex instead of chaste kisses and friendly hugs?

David had ambitions to be the youngest Partner at Chase, Behr & Lily, the law firm where they both worked. He put in a lot of hours at the office and often traveled. When he was available, they'd gone out to firm dinners, client parties or charity functions. Rarely had they spent time alone.

Jordan raised her left hand, angling the back until the fluorescent light caught the half-karat solitaire on her third finger. Everyone in her family had been delighted when she started a promising relationship with such a perfect guy. They were downright ecstatic when she'd bragged to her cousin that David had proposed.

Too bad she'd lied about the whole thing.

Her fiancé was actually her ex-boyfriend and the solitaire was only a "friendship ring." She'd bought it herself with David's credit card. He hated shopping and told her it was the only way she was certain of getting exactly what she wanted.

What she wanted was a real relationship in her life, instead of a lie that was guaranteed to ambush her at some point.

She glanced at her watch and winced. She had to get back to the office to meet with her client, Susan Brandywine. The local news anchor wanted Jordan to handle a wrongful-discharge lawsuit.

Clutching *Fifty Fast Fantasies* a little tighter in her damp grasp, she hurried over to the checkout before she changed her mind. That little voice was whispering to her again, warning that her seduction plan was not a good idea. Jordan ignored it.

TWO DAYS LATER, Jordan just wanted to go back upstairs and put on her clothes. Instead, she was parading around in a red silk nightgown and an ankle-length lace cover-up. Underneath, she wore a pair of red bikini panties. How could anyone feel sexy with these little scraps of silk creeping into places they didn't belong?

While she hoped the peignoir set made her appear sexy and provocative, she was afraid she only looked awkward and overweight. And she couldn't leave. She was trapped by family obligation and a crush of people in the Belle Fleur Atrium of Baltimore's esteemed St. Charles Hotel.

She still couldn't figure out how her older sister had talked her into playing an active role in this lingerie show. Well, that wasn't entirely true. She remembered a lot of pleading, begging and low-balance checkbook waving.

Camryn had recently ended her career as a haute couture supermodel. A chance meeting with Mason Rowling-Shays, III, heir to the department-store chain, had led to creating her own line of intimate wear, Boudoir Allure Designs. But she'd used what little money she had saved over the years to get the fledgling business off the ground.

Jordan had been more than happy to help her sister coordinate this all-important first presentation. Camryn's future depended on the success of the show. Then one of the models had to back out at the last minute and her sister was frantic for a replacement.

But Jordan wasn't about to have her soft curves measured against the willowy size-six mannequins her sister had recruited. She'd compromised by agreeing to circulate through the after-show reception in the modest red peignoir set—modest by comparison with some of Camryn's other designs.

She still felt exposed in the audacious gown with its low-cut bodice and thigh-high split. Only the hot flush of embarrassment kept her from getting frostbite as she wandered about the Atrium. But she'd never been able to refuse her family anything. So here she was, half-clothed and completely uncomfortable.

Jordan shivered as goose bumps marched along her arms. To counter the record-high temperatures outside, the hotel's overeager ventilation system blasted air in frigid gusts. The burbling of the indoor fountain mingled with the din of a hundred voices, making it impossible to do more than smile and nod as she moved about the room.

Several magazine editors stopped to admire her outfit. She obediently turned in a tight circle, allowing yet another group of fashionistas to coo over the delicate lace embroidery of her gown. One man wore a press pass and a leering smirk, not bothering to hide the fact that he'd noticed the cold air's effect through the delicate material.

Jordan tried to pull the edges of the robe across her hardened nipples, but the little cover-up wouldn't cover a damned thing. With a faltering smile, she settled for crossing her arms over her breasts. The group moved on to critique another outfit and she continued to fulfill her promise to Camryn.

Her sister was, and always would be, the golden ideal she could never attain. Growing up in Camryn's svelte shadow hadn't been easy. Chubby and shy, she'd wanted so badly to be included in her sister's charmed circle but, knowing she could never fit in, had found solace in food.

Any kind of food. Every kind of food.

She often wondered if there'd been a switch at the hospital where she was born. Her parents, sister and two brothers were all attractive, outgoing, charismatic. And then there was her. The ugly duckling in the middle…

Enough was enough. She had to go and put on a real pair of panties. The noise level and the glass of champagne she had drunk for courage had given her a slight headache. The reception didn't look as if it would be winding down any time soon, but she doubted she'd be missed.

She judged the distance to the makeshift dressing rooms and decided the exit would be closer. With one last glance at her sister, Jordan slipped through the crowd toward the bank of elevators just beyond the doors. The concourse level of the hotel was deserted. Her sequined sandals clicked like castanets as she strode across the marble floor.

Jordan ignored the open stares of two men leaving the one available elevator and stepped inside, shoulders hunched and arms across her cleavage. Though she looked down, concentrating on the pattern of the tile, she couldn't block the sound of the men's murmured appraisals of her breasts.

"Wow! Those cups really runneth over."

"I'd love to cuddle up on her pillows tonight."

She blushed, both embarrassed and yet a little flattered by the attention. It was always like this, a mixture of shame and pride that left her confused, wishing men wouldn't stare at her chest. Mercifully, the doors slid shut as she selected the button for the twelfth floor. With a bump and a groan, the elevator began its reluctant ascent. The hotel manager must have made good on his promise to have the problem fixed. No one else got on at the subsequent floors, so she was left alone with her thoughts.

Ever since buying *Fifty Fast Fantasies,* she felt as though her nerve endings had been electrified. Jordan closed her eyes and dared to stroke her hands over the silk covering her sides and down to her hips. The smooth material skimmed her bare flesh, setting off sparks that told her she was in sore need of physical affection. Her whole being seemed to be in a heightened state of awareness. The slightest stimulation made her tingle all the way to her thighs…

She opened her eyes and sighed. Her body was crying out for attention. Her seduction plan just had to work. She and David saw each other at the law firm, of course, and he was warm and caring and friendly. However, friendship and time apart was definitely not what she needed.

Suddenly the elevator jerked to a stop and Jordan fell off her open-backed sandals, bumping her shoulder against the wood-paneled wall. She looked up at the display to find both the number seven and number eight lit. Damn.

She pushed the button for the twelfth floor and waited, but nothing happened. She pressed it again, this time holding it for few seconds. Still nothing. Damn, damn, damn. She started jabbing the buttons for every other floor, one at a time, but they didn't even light up. Next, she tried pushing them two at a time—whoa.

The whole panel was now glowing like a Christmas tree, but the elevator still didn't move. Irritation gave way to alarm so she slapped one palm against the knob with the bell symbol printed on it. The shrill clanging echoed in the small space, not a good thing when she already had a headache.

The sound faded to a metallic ringing in her ears as the air conditioner suddenly shut off. Not a bad thing. At least now she wouldn't freeze to death. She would just plunge to the basement, trapped inside a cold metal box with her boobs hanging out of her sister's red silk nightgown.

Frantic now, she punched all of the buttons over and over again, searching for a pattern that would *get this damned thing moving!* The elevator jerked again and her shoulders sagged in relief. Then everything went still and silent once more.

Omigod. Omigod. She was alone. Completely alone. In a stalled elevator. With no way out and no way to call for help…

"Help! Somebody. Anybody. Help!"

The phone! Didn't these things come with phones? Shaking her head for not thinking of it sooner, she fumbled with the small handle until she felt the compartment door release. Jordan lifted the receiver with a shaking hand. She listened for a dial tone, or better yet, another voice.

"Hello?"

"Yes! I'm here." She ignored the break in her voice and gave a nervous laugh. "I mean, I'm stuck. I'm in the elevator near the Atrium, somewhere around the seventh floor."

"Are you hurt?"

She clenched the phone a little tighter. "No, just a little uneasy."

"Okay, hon. Fire department's on the way, but it could take 'em a while to get to you."

"How long is a while?" she yelped.

"Dunno. Couple of power grids have gone down already and—"

Jordan looked up as the lights overhead flickered once. Twice.

"Looks like we're next. Just sit tight and relax. Somebody'll get to you soon as they can."

Her knees buckled and her legs gave out at the same time the lights did. Relax? *Relax?* Her fingers went numb, dropping the receiver to dangle from its plastic cord, as reality slapped her in the face. She was alone. Completely alone. In a stalled elevator. With no way out. In the dark.

Don't panic. There's no need to panic. She forced a deep, calming breath in through her nose. The elevator would start moving any second now. At any moment. Really soon. Jordan hissed the breath she'd been holding through her clenched teeth.

So much for not panicking.

She gulped, even though her mouth had gone desert-dry. Her heart stammered in her chest as the blood from her head drained into it. Sitting on the floor, the hard marble tiles icy against her almost bare bottom, she gasped for air. What had happened to the air? Suddenly it was stuffy. Warm and stuffy and hard to breathe.

Omigod. Omigod. She was going to suffocate before she plunged to the basement. The more she panicked, the more she hyperventilated. And the more she hyperventilated, the more she feared she would suck all of the remaining oxygen out of the elevator.

She couldn't see her hands in front of her face as she dropped her head into her palms. Jordan had heard the term "total darkness" before, but never fully understood it until now. Squeezing her eyes shut, the first tears slipped from beneath her lashes.

Fear like she'd never known before—hot, black, airless fear—evaporated her common sense and her crying became hysterical. If she had to die, she didn't want her twisted broken body to be found wearing a red nightgown and bikini panties.

Jordan considered her last thought. Even terrified and miserable, the irony wasn't lost on her. She was dressed in intimate wear but had never actually been intimate. Oh, sure, she'd had sex, but it hadn't been worth repeating. And now she was going to die a semivirgin without ever having a real orgasm.

Omigod, she was going to die.

She cried harder, gulping in hot, stagnant air between sobs. If by some miracle she lived through this, she wasn't going to waste any more time. She'd have sex and lots of it. She would try every conceivable position. She'd play sex games and buy toys…

Well, maybe not toys. After insisting the bedroom lights stay off the one time she was with David, she probably wasn't ready for toys.

First, though, she had to get out of here. Wrapping her arms around her knees, she tipped her head back and took a deep, deep breath. "Hellllp!"

"Hang on, ma'am! We're coming to get you out."

A voice in the darkness! It sounded like salvation. It sounded like hope. It sounded like a man.

2

DANNY NAVARRO HATED the dark.

Hated it, not feared it. No, he couldn't afford to fear it. He just hated it. The way it made his breathing shallow and his pulse race. He tightened his grip on the heavy aluminum flashlight he carried. Even with the intermittent glow of the emergency-exit lights, the eighth-floor hallway was still too damned obscure for his comfort.

His boots sank into the plush carpeting as he strode past the paler darkness of the hotel-room doors. Danny shifted the weight of the toolbox in his other hand, wishing he could reach up to wipe the sweat from under his helmet. At least he wasn't in full turnout gear, wearing the heavy Nomex coat and pants. It was hot enough without the hotel's cooling ventilation.

Beside him, firefighter Mike Cornwall huffed out a breath. "Phew. Weatherman said it's one hundred five degrees with the heat index. You can't tell me there's nothing to this global-warming thing."

Danny chuckled. "Don't blame me, I stopped using aerosol years ago. The problem is all those satellites cluttering the skies."

"Uh-huh. Seems to me you were right there enjoying my digital TV dish last Super Bowl Sunday."

"Yeah, and you still owe me twenty bucks, Stonewall." He called him by the nickname Mike's six-foot-four-frame and dedication to weight lifting had earned him. "I told you not to bet against the Ravens' running game."

"Shame it's too dark to get a look at all those underwear models downstairs. I'll bet I'd leave with a pocketful of phone numbers."

Danny snickered. "I'll take odds against that bet." They reached the bank of elevators and set down their equipment. He rolled his shoulders.

"Which one is she in, Lieutenant?"

"I don't know, Mike. We'll have to open all three."

Danny pulled out a large ring of keys while Mike shone the flashlight on the call panel to find the manufacturer's brand. "It's an Otis Geared Elevonic model."

"Okay. Let's start on the left." As he turned the skeleton key to disengage the locks on the outer doors, he heard a high-pitched shriek coming from the middle elevator.

"Hellllp!"

"Hang on, ma'am! We're coming to get you out."

Grabbing a Halligan, Danny pried open the outer doors and then Mike held them apart with a length of rebar in case the power suddenly came back on. A quick sweep with the flashlight revealed the concrete wall and thick cables inside the open shaft. The elevator itself was closer to the seventh floor than the eighth. Only the top two and a half feet of the car were visible.

"Looks like you'll have to slide in and get her, L.T."

Danny carefully controlled his reaction, refusing to let it show on his face. "Me? I'm the senior here."

"Yeah, but since L.T. stands for Lady Target as well as 'lieutenant,' you're the man for the job."

He'd always wanted to be a fireman. Always. But he'd never consider himself a hero, despite the media calling him one. He was just a guy who cared about doing his job. Right now, though, it required heroic effort to control the chill of dread seeping into his limbs.

"All right. Let's get it done."

Danny took off his helmet then helped Mike get the inner doors open and propped. He grabbed the flashlight, got down to floor level and leaned his head over the edge. He shone the light around inside the elevator car and saw the red clad figure huddled in the corner.

"Oh, thank God."

The woman's voice quavered as she choked out the words. The gleam of the flashlight revealed a tear-streaked face beneath the hand she used to shield her eyes. Her lush scarlet mouth tilted in a little smile of embarrassed relief. "I wasn't panicking, though."

Danny noticed that her voice still sounded weak and smiled a little himself. "I'm sure you weren't, ma'am. Are you injured? Did you hit your head or anything?"

"No. I'm just a bit s-scared."

"It's going to be all right. The heat's caused a rolling blackout. But I'm going to get you out." He started to turn away when she called to him.

"Don't leave!"

"I'm not leaving, ma'am. I was just talking to my partner. I'll be right down to get you."

"Oh, okay. Not that I panicked."

"No, ma'am, of course not." Danny had dealt with a lot of hysterics in his nine years on the job. People were often so relieved and grateful to be rescued that they simply broke down. He wasn't about to make fun of her, since he didn't feel that comfortable himself.

He looked up at Mike. "I'll go down and give her a lift. You help her the rest of the way. She says she's not hurt, but I'll check her out just the same."

"I'm sure you will, L.T." Mike's voice had an undercurrent of innuendo as he took the flashlight to hold.

Danny ignored him as he swung his legs into the elevator car, bearing his weight on his forearms. Since this wasn't a life or death situation, he stole a second to get himself under control. None of the guys at Station 24 knew, not even Mike. A year had passed as if it were only a moment, but that moment was all too fresh in his mind.

Just as he was about to lower himself down, an elderly woman hurried out of one of the hotel rooms down the hall. "My husband! Please help us. He collapsed! He has chest pains and says it feels like another heart attack."

"L.T.?"

Mike was training to become an FF4, a firefighter paramedic. He was already grabbing his first-aid kit while he waited for Danny's response. With many of the city fire trucks assisting Baltimore Oil & Power, generators and manpower were spread thin.

"Go. I'll handle this. Call for the nearest ambulance and wait for them to take over."

"I'll be back as soon as I can."

Mike rushed off with the only flashlight, leaving Danny hanging. Literally. The idea of being stuck in the dark, cramped space for even a few minutes wasn't doing much to alleviate his sweating. But a possible heart attack was more urgent than his problem. Inhaling quietly, he ducked his head to keep from banging it on the elevator ceiling and let himself drop. His stomach lurched as he fell.

Six feet might as well have been a sixty in the darkness...

After hitting the floor, Danny turned his head from side to side, straining his eyes and willing something to come into focus. Suddenly he heard a rustle of movement and the woman collided into him. Without the flashlight, he couldn't see her. Or anything else.

Her disjointed sobs echoed in the small, hot space, further confusing senses that were denied the capacity of sight. His lungs clenched, struggling to drag breath into their shallow depths. The scar tissue on his back tightened. His pulse accelerated and he fought to steady his pounding heart…

Someone was crying. He could hear muffled weeping, but was too disoriented to identify where it came from. It was pitch-black and impossibly hot. He couldn't breathe. Dense smoke and the acrid smell of burning fuel choked what little air was left.

He crawled through puddles of water, over jagged metal and broken concrete. The darkness seemed to cave in on him. Then more explosions rocked the floor beneath him, trapping him in what already resembled the lowest level of hell…

"I'm so glad you're here."

The woman's mumbled words brought him back to the present. As she clung to him, Danny welcomed the contact with another living being and instinctively offered the comfort of his arms. Her soft lips nuzzled the side of his neck where she'd buried her face in the crook of his shoulder. He held her tightly, breathing in the floral scent of her hair.

He couldn't have let her go if he wanted to.

He didn't know how long they stood holding each other, his sense of time as confused as everything else. But slowly his attention sharpened and he became aware of *her*. He felt the warmth of her body seeping into him and driving away the chill of anxiety. Her full breasts were flattened against his chest, the hardened peaks jutting through his cotton T-shirt. Beneath his hands, he recognized the coarse texture of lace as he soothed his palms down her back.

A nightgown? In the middle of the day? She must be one of the underwear models.

She curled into him, drawing closer when she tightened her hold around his waist. He was extremely cognizant of each place their bodies touched. Her breath warmed his throat and her nearness heated his blood. In an instant, he was rock hard and more than willing to forget where they were.

The air around them pulsed with sexual energy and he knew exactly when she noticed the change. He heard the quick intake of breath. She raised her head, as if she were about to speak, but then her mouth brushed the edge of his and he was lost.

Acting on pure instinct, he captured her lips, coaxing his tongue between them. She tasted like cinnamon; she tasted like sin. His fingers sought to caress her hair, and in doing so released the clip that restrained it. The heavy mass tumbled down to flow around her shoulders. Sexy little moans and whimpers escaped her throat as he held the nape of her neck and deepened the kiss.

She trembled so hard he thought she might collapse in his arms, but instead she shimmied against him in an invitation as old as time. He ran his hands over her curvaceous hips and backside, pressing her forward to feel the effect she had on him. His hands glided up her generous body—he loved a woman he could hold on to—until they reached her silk-covered breasts.

At her gasp of surprise and pleasure, he slipped his fingers inside the nightgown to fondle the warm fullness of her flesh. She moaned as he gently rolled her hardened nipple between his thumb and index finger. Then he bent his head to take one delicate bud inside his mouth. He laved and suckled her breast in rhythm with her soft cries.

She grasped the sides of his face and drew him up until their lips met again. The feel of her tongue exploring the recesses of his mouth sent a wave of desire through his body that crested as an aching pressure in his groin. He stroked his right hand down her torso until he came across the deep split in her gown. He slid his fingers inside to touch the satiny skin beneath the silk. Her thighs parted to allow him greater access while her lips nibbled hungrily on his mouth.

She tugged at his T-shirt, pulling it free from his trousers before she drew her hands over his stomach and up to his chest. The feel of her sensual touch had his own nipples hardening in response. He moved his hand higher under the skirt of her nightgown, lifting the fabric until he could feel the edge of her panties.

He inched his fingers toward the apex of her thighs, felt the damp heat through the material as he rubbed her feminine mound. She rocked her hips back and forth over his hand while his tongue danced with hers. His erection throbbed against his zipper when her wiggling became frenzied. Seconds later, she shuddered, groaning against his shoulder as she climaxed.

Danny grinned into her hair as she tried to catch

her breath. Of all the elevators in all the world, he found himself with the most intensely responsive woman he'd ever encountered. Under his shirt, her hands slid down his belly to grope for his belt buckle.

But just as she reached to unzip him, he heard Mike's voice right above them. "Hey, L.T. I'm back."

Startled, they jerked apart as if they'd been electrocuted. As the flashlight beam arced lower, Danny fumbled to tuck in his shirt and refasten his pants. The woman hastily adjusted the front of her nightgown and pulled the skirt part back into place.

He raised his voice to draw Mike's attention. "How's the guy with the chest pain?"

"The EMTs have him stabilized for transport."

In the dim light, Danny noted that the woman's back was toward him. Even without seeing her face, he sensed her embarrassment by the shielding curve of her posture and the low angle of her head. His whisper scarcely carried across the elevator. "Are you okay?"

She nodded but refused to look at him. Despite the lack of ventilation, he felt a distinct chill that was stunning after the heat they'd generated. He could understand it, though. They were strangers, and who knows how far things might have gone if Mike hadn't returned when he did.

If he got lucky, however, later tonight they could finish what they'd started. Danny moved behind her, keeping his voice low and willing her to turn around. "When can I see you? Where can I find you?"

Her shoulders were hunched, her arms crossed tightly in front of her. She tilted her head and glanced up, as though wondering how close Mike was. She shook her head and didn't speak.

"All right. Let's get out of here and then we can talk." Danny leaned his head back and called up to Mike. "Ready when you are, Stonewall."

"Anytime, L.T."

He placed his hands on the woman's upper arms, ignoring the way she flinched as he guided her toward the front of the elevator car. "I'm going to lift you up so that Mike can catch your hands. Don't let go of him until you're all the way out to the floor. Okay?"

She angled her head away, but he heard her whispered acknowledgment. "Okay."

He grasped her waist, bending his knees as she raised her arms to the light-filled opening. Flexing his thighs, he boosted her toward the ceiling. When he saw that Mike held her securely, he shifted his hands to her bottom, trying to ignore the intimate knowledge that his hands had been under that red silk gown only moments before. He gave a gentle push and waited for Mike to help her the rest of the way.

"I've got her, L.T."

Danny balanced on the balls of his feet then lunged up to catch the edge of the eighth floor. Using sheer arm strength, he pulled himself to chest height before pivoting to swing his legs up as well. He got to his feet and saw Mike holding the flashlight, trying to check on the woman.

"Are you sure you're okay?"

"I'm fine. Really. I just need to go—"

"Wait a minute," Danny protested. When she turned in his direction, his heart slammed to a stunned halt. He completely forgot whatever else he'd planned to say. The words caught in his throat as it tightened in dismay.

Gaze downcast, the woman still refused to look at him. But he didn't need to see her eyes to know they were the golden brown color of maple syrup. Despite the gloom in the hallway, he knew that her hair had mahogany highlights and that her skin was the warm tone of caramel. He also knew he'd just made one of the biggest mistakes of his life.

Her voice sounded tight with embarrassment. "Thank you very much for helping me. I appreciate it."

Mike started to speak. "If you're sure…"

But she was already hurrying away down the dark corridor. Danny sensed his colleague turning to him, but his attention followed the elusive glimpse of red silk.

"Well, I see you managed to get some of her lipstick." Mike's voice held a note of jealous humor. Danny drew the back of his hand across his mouth and looked down to see a smear of color on his knuckles. "Did you get her name and phone number, too?"

"No, I didn't get her number."

"Too bad, L.T. She looked hot."

Danny had no intention of getting the number now. And he already knew her name. Jordan Gregory.

His brother David's girlfriend.

"Krissy Lynn. What the hell kind of name is Krissy Lynn?"

Jordan leaned back in the conference room chair and watched her newest client, Susan Brandywine, pace the expensive wool carpeting. Her hands were jammed into the pockets of her palazzo pants, the kind Katherine Hepburn always wore in the late-night movies Jordan liked to watch.

"She's blond and petite and just so gosh-darned eager." Susan batted her eyelashes exaggeratedly. "And get this, she's all of twenty-five years old. I've got sweaters older than this bubble-headed bimbo."

Jordan didn't look up from the note she jotted on a legal pad as she asked, "Aren't you judging your replacement in the same manner you claim you're being judged?"

Susan had been the female anchor on the WBNS nightly news team for ten years. After a messy and painful divorce, she began suffering from depression and put on some weight. At that point, she was shuffled from the prominent evening slot to a position reading the midday news.

The demotion fueled Susan's depression, as did the comments of the news director and station manager, who suggested she lose weight, dress more femininely and grow out her "mannish" hairstyle. Then, just before her fortieth birthday, the station decided to "go with a more up-to-date look" for midday.

Susan stopped near the window overlooking the Camden Yards baseball stadium and sighed, running a strong hand through her short dark hair. "Yeah, damn it, I guess I am. But it hurts, Jordan. It really hurts."

She made a sympathetic noise as her client continued to stare at the view. Jordan stood up and moved to the window. "I know exactly how you must feel."

Susan eyed her up and down and scoffed. "Sure you do, honey."

"You're seeing me now. Not as the almost two-hundred-pound girl with bad skin and no friends I used to be." She turned up the corners of her mouth, hoping it resembled a smile.

Susan nodded. "So as a former 'fat girl' yourself, you're in the best position to defend me."

Something inside of her twisted at the comparison, but Jordan focused on what was important. "I think we have a good chance with both the wrongful termination and the discrimination cases."

"You know, I have a journalism degree from Columbia. I started out writing copy at a couple of newspapers. Journalism requires long hours, unbeatable dedication and street smarts as well as brain smarts." Susan's expression hardened. "It does not require looking like a Barbie doll. Especially not when my male co-anchors have gray hair, paunches and bags under their eyes. What does *sex appeal* have to do with my ability to tell an audience about a multiple rush-hour fatality on the Beltway?"

Susan was a very attractive woman: literate, funny, irreverent, and she had great personal style. And yet Jordan couldn't suppress her reluctant aversion. It was like seeing herself the way she used to be, the way she'd worked so hard never to be again…

However, she wasn't about to let her personal issues affect her zealous defense of a case. "In our favor, several successful lawsuits have set a precedent. For example, Connecticut anchorwoman Janet Peckinpaugh won her 1999 case against *Post-Newsweek*. You're not too old, nor too fat, to do your job, Susan. And we're going to prove it."

From fifteen floors below, Jordan was distracted by the strident peal of a fire engine racing up Howard Street. The huge machine blared its horn at slow-moving cars until they pulled far enough toward the sidewalk for the engine to get by. She wondered if her elevator rescuer was onboard.

She also wondered what he looked like. Jordan had been too ashamed to look at him when he'd stood before her, too embarrassed to glance back as she fled. The firefighter from the elevator would never be more than a faceless memory.

3

JORDAN DOVE INTO the sea of bodies on the sidewalk and headed down Pratt Street past the Convention Center and the Garmatz Federal Courthouse. She'd conducted all of her meetings and handled her caseload on autopilot this morning, unable to concentrate.

She couldn't stop thinking about…him. He was a complete mystery, this sensual stranger. And yet some air of familiarity had prompted her to let him kiss her, fondle and stroke her in the most intimate ways. Each time she closed her eyes, she experienced again the heat of his touch and the drugging taste of his kiss. Her lips actually tingled.

Jordan startled when someone jostled her elbow. Realizing she'd been lost in thought, *again,* she hurried to cross Charles Street before the traffic light changed. Downtown was teeming with tourists, many wearing Baltimore Orioles T-shirts in anticipation of tonight's game. Exhaust fumes polluted the humid air while the sounds of crawling traffic echoed off the multistory buildings.

She waited through another red light by the Gallery mall on Light Street. She'd left her jacket at the office in deference to the heat, but the September sun seemed intent on burning a hole through her cotton shirtdress. Over the last few blocks, it felt as if her panty hose was melting and permanently adhering to her legs. Not to mention the way the waistband was strangling her. Queen-size? Yeah, right.

The early-autumn heat wave made everything hot and tight and sticky. Not unlike the heat she felt racing along her veins whenever she relived those mind-blowing moments at the St. Charles Hotel. Over the past two nights, the firefighter from the elevator had become the faceless lover of her dreams. In her midnight fantasies that first explosive orgasm was followed by several others as they made crazy, passionate love against the wood-paneled wall.

Jordan gave herself a mental shake as a truck horn blared impatiently. She had to stop this. There was probably a special area in purgatory for good girls gone bad. And she might as well get used to the idea because, if her daydreams were any indication, she was more than willing to be bad again.

She crossed the street with a determined stride, heading toward the Pratt Street Pavilion where she was meeting her college roommates, Sheris Smith and Melanie Walters, for their Monthly Monday lunch. In the tiny amphitheater between the two main buildings of the Harborplace complex, a crowd clapped and ignored the midday heat as a juggler tossed bowling pins in time to music.

The cool air inside the Pavilion was a welcome

relief, and Jordan took a moment to let her body adjust and to check her watch. Five minutes early. Which meant Melanie would arrive at exactly twelve-thirty, and they should only have to wait another fifteen minutes after that for Sheris to show up.

She opened the door to the Cheesecake Factory restaurant, gave her name to the hostess and asked for an inside table. Once seated, she settled in with a raspberry iced tea, idly gazing out the tinted glass window.

Families and couples of all ages strolled along the red brick promenade on the harbor's edge. Water taxis and duck boats carried tourists around the Patapsco River between the Inner Harbor and Fell's Point. A line of people waited to tour the USS *Constellation,* a three-masted Civil War sloop anchored at Pier One.

Looking past the facade of the World Trade Center, Jordan could see the triangular glass roof of the National Aquarium. She'd been meaning to get over there and see the new Amazon River Forest exhibit…

"Hi!" Melanie bounced toward the table at twelve-thirty on the dot and waved to several people as she walked by. Mel was a diminutive dynamo and seemed to know everybody. With her petite figure and boy-short hairstyle, she looked like a happy pixie.

She dressed like one, too. Today she wore a bright yellow-and-white-striped pants set that complemented her coffee skin. Jordan smiled. You couldn't help but smile at Melanie. She was like a walking dose of antidepressant. Her wide-set eyes always reflected her joy in life.

She stood up to trade hugs. No air kisses with Mel, who was genuine in everything she did. "I'm glad you could come today."

"Of course, Jordan! I wouldn't miss our monthly lunch! How have you been? Is that our waitress? I'm dying of thirst!"

"Try the raspberry tea. I think you'll like it." Jordan kept her voice carefully modulated since Melanie tended to make either a question or an exclamation of everything she said. "So, tell me what's new."

"Rochelle did so well in school! And can you believe it? Chris made the winning goal for his soccer team during the last game of the season! Guess what we're doing? Bill and I are taking the kids to Disney!"

"That sounds great. But I thought you were planning a vacation without the kids." Although Melanie treated her boyfriend's children like her own, Jordan knew she often wished for more adults-only time.

Melanie reached for her tea and drank half of it before answering. "Oh, that's our anniversary trip in November! Bill and I are going back to Costa Rica! I think he's finally going to propose! Have you and David talked about where you'll spend your honeymoon? You two would just love Costa Rica!"

She was saved from having to answer when she noticed heads near the restaurant entrance turning. "There's Sheris."

Sheris nodded in response to Melanie's excited wave and sauntered across the dining room. She always moved as though she owned whatever place she was in. Given her family's diversified investments, she might very well have part ownership of the restaurant.

Jordan stifled a pang of envy over her friend's casual stylishness. Jordan spent hours meticulously planning her outfits and tending to her hair and makeup. Meanwhile, Sheris managed to look gorgeous in whatever she'd thrown on before casually running a brush through her hair and walking out the door. Her dark gypsy curls fell past her shoulders, which were bared by the white peasant blouse she wore with a short leather skirt and sandals. Only Sheris could wear leather in this heat and still look cool.

"Sorry I'm late," she offered as she brushed a kiss near each of their cheeks. Sheris dropped her overstuffed Louis Vuitton bag on the floor and slid into the seat across from Jordan.

"You're right on time, actually. Are you sick?"

Sheris laughed. "No, just depressed. I came downtown early to do some pity purchasing."

Jordan glanced down but didn't see even a small shopping bag. "You didn't find anything you liked?"

"Actually I saw several things, but I restrained myself in case I'm still feeling blue tomorrow." Sheris pulled back her hair to reveal a stunning pair of Ceylon sapphire earrings that exactly matched her deep-set eyes.

Melanie angled closer to get a better look. "Wow! Those are really blue! I take it you broke things off with Grant?"

"Yeah. It seemed best." Sheris's reply sounded offhand, but the expression on her face said otherwise. She paused while the waitress brought another glass of tea and three menus.

"You know, it was so great in the beginning. I thought maybe…well, you know how it goes. I got restless, he got defensive. He wanted to buy a place together, I suggested he find a place by himself."

"I'm sorry, honey." Jordan reached over to grasp her hand.

"Me, too." Sheris offered a bright smile. "But, hey, they can't all be Bill or David now, can they?"

"Or Logan." Melanie threw out the comment while perusing the extensive lunch choices.

Sheris dropped her menu on the table. "Now what in the world made you bring up my ex-husband?"

Mel looked embarrassed. "It just slipped out? I must have heard him last night?"

"Has he still got that little radio program? I didn't realize." Sheris tried unsuccessfully to sound dismissive and bored.

Jordan pictured the full-size, full-color billboards on I-95 and the B/W Parkway coming into the city and hid her smile. If Sheris wanted to pretend to be the only person in the Baltimore metropolitan area who didn't listen to *In the Mood with McGuire,* so be it.

"Logan was just one in a long line of relationship

regrets." With that, Sheris changed the subject. "I'm going to have the Crusted Chicken Romano over Fettuccine. How about you girls?"

"Mmm. Sounds good," Melanie replied. "But I'm going to go with the Seafood Cobb Salad."

Jordan's stomach growled at the thought of fried chicken and carbohydrate-laden pasta or fat-packed avocados, shrimp and blue cheese. She stifled a sigh, knowing she couldn't afford to let down her guard. "I'll just have the baked fish and a tossed salad."

After placing their orders, they spent some time catching up on news and acquaintances. Inevitably, though, the conversation turned intimate. Sheris dabbed a spot of pasta sauce from her mouth.

"In some ways it's a relief that things ended with Grant, but I sure am going to miss the sex. That guy could go all night."

"Really?" Melanie pouted a little and searched her salad for any shrimp she'd missed. "With the kids around most of the time, I'm lucky if Bill and I manage more than thirty minutes. What about you and David?"

"Um, actually things have been a little, um…how do I say this?" Jordan leaned forward and dropped her voice to a whisper. "I bought a sex manual."

"Good for you!" Sheris grinned at her. "Which one? I have a fairly extensive collection myself."

"I got *Fifty Fast Fantasies* last week."

Sheris nodded and speared a chunk of chicken off her plate. "That's a good one. I especially enjoyed Ride Him, Cowgirl and The Butler Did It."

Jordan choked on a bite of her baked trout and felt her cheeks flame. How could Sheris be so casual about acts that embarrassed her just reading about them? She looked over to see that Melanie had reacted the same way.

Mel's eyebrows arched toward her hairline. "You, um—you acted them out? I mean, you actually—"

"Well, of course, honey. There's no reason to buy a sex book if you're just going to leave it in the drawer."

"Shh!" Jordan and Melanie both tried to silence her when two men at a nearby table looked over with undisguised interest.

"Oh, come on, girls. Our college days aren't that far behind us, are they?"

"I don't know, Sheris. My college days weren't nearly as social as yours." Jordan set down her fork. "I mean, I bought the manual. But I'm not sure I can go through with some of those fantasies."

"Nonsense. You wouldn't have even looked at a book like that, let alone bought it, if your sex life was satisfying."

"Shh!"

"Well, you wouldn't have. So obviously you're curious and curiosity is key to great sex." Sheris pushed her empty plate aside. "You have to be willing to discover things about your partner and let him find things out about you. Like, I found out that Scott was into ropes and James loved to be spanked—"

"Eeww!" Melanie wrinkled her elfin nose. "Too much information!"

"Hey, I'm not saying I always agreed to it. But you have to be willing to give if you want to get what you like in return."

Jordan considered Sheris's advice while Mel demanded exact details about costumes and props. What was it she really wanted? Sex, certainly. Affection and attention, of course. But more than anything, she wanted to feel burning desire and urgent need. She wanted to feel like she did two days ago.

Melanie was still pressing. "Well, how did you do it, Sheris? I mean, did you suggest it, or did the guys? And if it was you, how did you bring it up?"

"I don't think I can." Jordan shook her head. "What would I say? 'Hi, honey. I made dinner reservations. And afterward, would you mind wearing this slave boy outfit I bought you?' There's no way!"

"That is more my style than yours." Sheris grinned. "So don't discuss it. Just arrange the setting for your favorite fantasy and surprise him one night. My point is, Jordan, if you want a more exciting love life, you have to lose the sweetness and discover the sweat."

Jordan's mind immediately returned to the faceless firefighter. Now there was a man who'd made her sweat. And moan. And climax within seconds of his touching her. She felt heated blood rushing to her cheeks—and other places—as she remembered how incredible he'd made her feel.

She'd never felt that way with David.

It was getting harder to ignore the crushing unhappiness that pervaded her nights. Ironically, she had discovered that being in a poor relationship was lonelier than being on her own. Being single didn't feel as incomplete as having a lover she feared didn't love her at all, one she'd struggled to love in return.

Time was running and only David could help her.

LATER THAT NIGHT, Jordan stood in the bedroom of her Federal Hill row house and stripped off her business clothes. She carefully sorted the dry-clean items from the hand-wash only before pulling on a ratty pair of sweatpants and an even older T-shirt. In the bathroom, she removed the hairpins from the chignon she wore at the office and brushed her hair until it fell loosely to her shoulders. Then she creamed the artfully applied makeup from her face.

Jordan stared at herself in the mirror, carefully studying the parts without looking at the whole. A blemish was coming out on her chin. A quick squeeze and it was gone. Tiny wrinkles were developing under her eyes. She'd have to get some retinol cream. Reaching for the tweezers, she plucked several strays from her brow. Then her eyes narrowed as she focused on her hairline. Was that one gray? The tweezers quickly yanked out the offending strand.

She spent several more minutes checking for flaws before sighing heavily and turning out the bathroom light. Downstairs in the kitchen, she opened the refrigerator and tried to decide if she wanted a lettuce or a spinach salad for dinner. Neither one was really appealing tonight. She glanced across the room to the cabinet above the coffeemaker.

No. She shouldn't.

Maybe she could mix the red leaf lettuce and baby spinach together, then julienne some raw vegetables over the top. There were some tomatoes in the crisper and—she felt the contents of that cabinet calling to her.

No!

Okay, she'd skip the salad and just make vegetables crudité with some low-fat cottage cheese on the side. She slammed the refrigerator shut. It was no use. She was going to open that cabinet. She was going to reach inside and she was going to blow her diet all to hell. Like a thief sneaking into forbidden territory, Jordan rushed across the room and grabbed the bag of Dove milk chocolates. Holding it up to her face, she inhaled the addictive scent of cocoa butter and sugar.

Just a few. Only a few.

She walked down the hall to the living room, flopped onto the overstuffed couch and tucked her bare feet underneath her. After laying the bag beside her with the opening in easy reach of her hand, she picked up the issue of *Style and Grace* magazine on the far cushion. Idly flipping though the pages, Jordan unwrapped a chocolate. *She's so pretty. Not an ounce of fat anywhere on her.* Another page. Another chocolate. *Look at her thighs. They don't even meet.* Another. And another…

There was Camryn.

Her numb fingers dropped the candy she held back into the bag. Her sister looked stunning. Simply stunning. Her golden skin was bared in a flame-red slip dress with a plunging neckline. The artful lighting emphasized the high ridge of her cheek-bones, the long line of her torso and the subtle definition of her athletic legs.

Jordan looked down to see the lone chocolate left in the bag. She felt sick. Guilty and sick and weak and ugly.

Think about something else, anything else. She'd have to run an extra mile tomorrow morning. Damn it! She tossed the magazine away and got up to turn on the television. One of the cable stations was showing *Black Lace,* a movie in which the main character enticed her boss with anonymous love notes.

Yes, that was the answer. Focus on the seduction. If she could learn to act sexy and alluring, it wouldn't matter how she looked. In the fantasies, she could be anyone she wanted. In the dark, he'd never see that she wasn't perfect.

She ran upstairs and got the *Fifty Fast Fantasies* book from her bedroom. Snuggled onto the couch once more, she ran her index finger along the table of contents until she found one she could use. A scene in the movie distracted her for a second, then she gave all of her attention to the chapter called Strangers For One Night.

Pretend your lover is a handsome stranger. Why not pick him up as if he were a one-night stand? Surprise him in an unexpected location, wearing your naughtiest undies underneath. Let your "stranger" know that you don't normally do things like this, but you can't resist him. Then take him back to your place and give him a night neither of you will ever forget.

For her this to work, Jordan would have to be sensual, naughty and fun—everything the guidebook recommended. Well, at least she could fake it. When she'd found the high-school drama class, she'd found herself. As long as she put on an act, as long as she'd played a role, she'd become confident and outgoing and even somewhat popular. It hadn't taken long to figure out that the way she wanted people to see her was just another stage personality.

Her grandparents' fiftieth wedding anniversary was a little over a week away. She needed David by her side. She needed him to perpetuate her lie. Otherwise, she could already hear her cousin's snide taunts if she had to show up alone and admit that her engagement was a fraud.

She could do this. She had to do this. It would give her the chance to discover her wild side. And it would save her a week of awkward questions and embarrassment. If she could act in high school and all through college and at the office, she could do it in the bedroom.

Jordan grabbed a notepad and began making a list of things she would need to make the Strangers fantasy a reality.

4

DANNY FOLLOWED the scent of fresh garlic bread to the large kitchen at the fire station. Mondays meant Italian food and Italian food meant Tony would be making dinner. Danny greeted the half-dozen firefighters already at the table and helped himself to the steaming hot lasagna.

Mike looked up from his plate in surprise. "Hey, L.T., you got off at six. What are you still doing here?"

"I can't resist Cappelluti's cooking."

He moved toward the end of the table and took the empty seat next to Tony, who shot him a proud grin. "It's my grandmother's secret recipe."

Mike spoke around a mouthful of pasta. "I figured you had a date tonight since you're on day shift."

"It got canceled." Danny kept his attention on his food as he answered and braced himself for the gibes.

"I can't believe it!" Barb laughed. "The Lady Target got stood up?"

"Yeah, well, Lisa took it badly when I told her things were going too fast."

"Eighth date already?"

Danny looked at Andrea in confusion. "Huh?"

"None of the women you go out with seem to last past the eighth date."

"That's not true." He scoured his memory for an example of a long-term relationship, but after a moment, he came up blank.

"Told you."

Danny shrugged impatiently. "Lisa started dropping hints every time we passed a jewelry store, so I called it quits a couple of days ago."

"You did the same thing with Kelly, Sheryl…" Barb ticked off on the fingers of both hands as she quoted names.

Danny wiped a smear of sauce from his mouth. "Are you keeping tabs on me or something?"

One of the paramedics walked in and grabbed the chair beside Andrea. Frank looked around at everyone. "So, what are you guys talking about?"

"L.T.'s single again," Tony replied.

Frank nodded sagely. "Hit the eighth date with Lisa, huh?"

"Actually, it was only our seventh." Danny pushed his plate away, feeling defensive. "But who's counting?"

From the other end of the table, Jen smirked. "It's not a hard pattern to figure out, L.T. You dated two of my friends, remember?"

"You also went out with my cousin, Vicki," Frank chimed in.

"And both of them said everything was great, then you suddenly broke it off and stopped calling."

"Now wait a minute. It's not always me who breaks up—"

"She's right, L.T." Mike gestured with his fork. "About the time your girlfriends start thinking about a future, you start thinking of reasons to back away. No matter who ends it, you're still the one with commitment issues."

Danny glared down the table at his supposed friend. "Thanks very much for that psychoanalysis, Dr. Stonewall."

"Men can't commit." Barb set down her glass and addressed the other two women at the table. "Evolution programmed them to procreate and continue the species. That's why they're compelled to initiate sex with any attractive female who comes along."

Andrea and Jen murmured agreement.

Tony scoffed. "You're way off base there. L.T.'s problem is intimacy. Since he can't open up and express his true feelings, he shuts himself off from emotional involvement."

Danny sputtered indignantly. "What the hell are you babbling about?"

"I saw it on a talk show one day."

"Oh, please. You watch that stuff?" Jen tapped her index finger twice on the tabletop. "It's all about man's need to explore. Once a guy has established his territory, he starts looking around for new worlds to conquer."

Danny raised his hand. "Can I say something here?"

His request was ignored as Mike talked over the other voices. "I think the real issue is lack of trust—"

Just then the alarm blared through the station house, saving Danny from further analysis of his love life.

The dispatcher's voice sounded over the loud-speaker. Fire in progress on the two hundred block of Paca Street near Lexington Market. Everyone scrambled away from the table, running to get into their coats and boots as the drivers revved the engines on the fire trucks.

Danny felt the rush of adrenaline that always accompanied the call to duty. Part of him was tempted to grab his gear, but he'd already put in ten hours. So, instead, he chose to stay and have another piece of lasagna rather than go home to an empty apartment. As he ate, he considered the things his colleagues had said.

He loved the thrill of the chase, the excitement of the new. He loved dating and prided himself on treating women well during the time they were together. But when his girlfriends seemed to be getting too serious, he drew the line. He wasn't about to get trapped in a bitter and disappointed marriage like his parents'.

Sirens blared on the ladder and rescue trucks as they roared out of Station 24. In the quiet that followed their departure came the thoughts Danny had been avoiding all day. The combination of guilt and lust churning him up inside could be traced to the same source.

His fascination with Jordan.

She appeared to be the single-minded, career-oriented type he usually favored. Who would have guessed that beneath her perfectly made-up, professionally groomed persona, Jordan was an explosive sensualist? He hadn't stopped thinking about the contradictions in her personality for the past two days and two long nights.

He still couldn't believe his brother's prim and proper girlfriend had nearly ripped his pants off in the elevator. Did David know? It pissed Danny off that she would cheat on him with a total stranger. Was this the kind of thing Jordan did as some sort of secret thrill?

Part of him wanted to warn David, but there was no way to do it without confessing he'd brought her to orgasm while locked in the hottest kiss of his life. That memory was followed by another wave of guilt, but all he could think about was seeing Jordan again.

A COLONY OF BUTTERFLIES had taken up residence in Jordan's stomach. Her heart fluttered in the same staccato rhythm as their jagged-edged wings. Tonight was the night. Wednesday night. A night for lovers to become strangers. She'd spent the past few days setting the necessary stage and gathering her courage.

She'd talked Camryn into letting her have some of the lingerie from the debut show. She'd bought a box full of condoms and a brand-new set of black cotton bedsheets. Candles were strategically placed to form a path from the front door to the bedroom. She was still trying to figure out how to light them and look sexy doing it.

Everything had to be perfect tonight and she was so afraid it wouldn't be.

Jordan stood in front of the bedroom mirror and stared at her reflection, the corners of her mouth tightening into a frown. Her pudgy-cheeked face sat like a full moon above her double chin and nonexistent neck. Thick shoulders rolled down to full breasts, a protruding belly, wide hips and heavy legs. She saw each bowl of ice cream she'd ever eaten, every chocolate bar and slice of pound cake. In that reflection, she saw shyness and envy, loneliness and disinterest. She saw every hope, every rejection and failure.

Jordan shut her eyes. It was only a memory. She inhaled deeply, willing the tension from her neck. She had literally worked her ass off, walking several miles every day and taking aerobics classes three nights a week, until she lost the abundance of adolescent weight and slimmed down to a healthy size twelve.

When she opened her eyes, her vision cleared along with her expression and she looked again. Her face was now an elongated heart shape, emphasized by the widow's peak at her hairline and a delicate chin. Jordan turned from side to side, critically viewing herself from different angles.

Though she was tall, her body was femininely rounded at the chest and hips. The black satin camisole cupped her full breasts while hiding the stretch marks on her waist. Matching panties covered the generous curve of her backside. Not perfect, in fact far from it. But, in the darkness, it wouldn't matter.

She shrugged on the thin summer raincoat and tied the sash into a secure bow. Then she checked the time. David was a creature of habit, even more detail oriented than she, if that were possible. So allowing for the rush-hour traffic, she should be able to get to his condo just as he was leaving for his evening workout at the nearby gym.

A half hour later, that annoying little voice was back. It was telling her she was a nut for lurking outside the Harborview condominiums to ambush her ex-boyfriend. After counting the windows to make sure the lights were on in David's living room, she hid behind a screen of thick hedges and crouched down to wait. And wait.

Beads of sweat trickled between her breasts, making her very aware of the satin fabric plastered against her skin. Her thighs were cramping and no amount of position shifting eased the aching stiffness. The humid autumn breeze tickled her bare bottom where the short raincoat rode up in the back.

Several people arrived and left through the front door, but David wasn't one of them. Jordan spared another glance at her watch. He always left for the gym at precisely six thirty. What was keeping him tonight?

"I'M GAY."

Danny half-swallowed, half-choked on his

mouthful of beer. He set down the pale ale David kept in the fridge for him and even managed to get the icy bottle on the coaster this time. He stared at his brother, momentarily at a loss for words.

David stared right back from a face that was a duplicate of the one he saw in the mirror each morning. He'd sometimes wondered about his twin's love of gourmet cooking and artsy foreign films. But now, hearing David state his sexual preference out loud, he wasn't sure how he felt.

Surprise over his brother's homosexuality warred with anxiety that it could be genetic. Being identical twins meant they had more things in common than most siblings. But, thinking of the many women he'd dated in the past year, Danny felt pretty sure sexual preference wasn't one of them.

His brother stood waiting for his reaction, defensiveness in his posture and apprehension in his dark brown gaze. Not knowing how to handle the seriousness of the discussion, Danny resorted to humor. "You can't do it like that."

"It's not just like that. I've always felt that maybe I was different—"

"No, I mean, you can't just blurt it out. How about giving a brother some warning, a little lead up. You know, 'Hi, Dan. How's it going? Great weather we're having, huh? By the way, I'm gay. Don't tell Mom and Dad'."

David smiled wryly and the strain eased from his features. They shared a look of understanding as he took a seat in the armchair opposite the sofa. "I'm guessing Dad will disinherit me and see that the club revokes my membership."

"And what *will* Mother say to her friends in church and at the Valley Golf Association?"

David still looked uneasy. "What about you? Is this okay with you?"

He propped one fist under his chin and narrowed his eyes, pretending to consider it. "Well, other than the purple spots and horns, you seem the same to me."

"I mean it, Dan. This isn't easy for me." David hunched his broad shoulders and looked away.

No, it probably wasn't. And it would be harder still to tell their parents. He was proud to know David trusted him and quickly offered reassurance. "Believe me, this doesn't change anything. You're still my brother and I love you."

"I wanted to tell you before now, but I wasn't sure how you'd react."

"Thanks for the vote of confidence." He picked up his beer. "What I'm wondering is how Jordan is going to react. Do you think she'll be upset?"

David dropped his eyes and shifted in his seat. "I, um, broke it off with Jordan over a month ago."

"Are you crazy? Why would—never mind, never mind." He waved his hand as if he could erase the question.

"She's a terrific woman and I love her as a friend." David delivered his words with an attorney's caution.

"A friend?" Danny's brows furrowed in surprise.

"You've been dating for what, eight or nine months?"

David brushed at the fabric on the chair arm. "We never connected beyond friendship, if you know what I mean."

"Do we have to talk about sex?" Danny winced, not really wanting to picture his twin in the bed he hoped to occupy.

"Don't worry. We were safe the only time we were together. The point is, I couldn't keep faking my relationship with Jordan." The phone rang and David got up to answer it. "Hello? Hi, I thought it might be you calling…. My brother's here right now…I'll talk to you sometime tomorrow, okay?"

Danny took another swallow of beer, still trying to come to terms with the situation. As soon as David sat down again, he asked the question that was bugging him the most. "If you knew you were gay, why did you start dating her in the first place?"

"I didn't know. Not for certain. Not until too late… Also, I needed to be seen in a relationship, Dan. Chase, Behr & Lily is an extremely conservative law firm. I thought having Jordan on my arm advanced my chances of a partnership."

"So, you were using her." Danny sat back against the couch.

David had the good grace to look ashamed. "Not on purpose, but yes, I was. I ended it once I understood the relationship would never work. And once I found out that Chase's son is being offered the only open partnership slot, I realized I'm tired of living a lie."

"Sorry about the partnership, David. That really stinks."

"Yeah. I've spent so much time and effort trying to impress the senior partners. All for nothing." He sighed heavily. "I wanted that promotion. But not as much as I want to be accepted for who I really am. That's why I asked you to come over."

Danny pressed the issue. "You were honest with Jordan, though, right?"

"I'm sure she knows. She has to." David stood up and headed for the wet bar.

"You don't sound very sure." He followed, leaning against the bookcase as he watched his brother.

David looked up from the wine he was pouring. "I know I didn't handle this very well."

Danny scowled. "You just broke up with her and didn't bother to explain why? Jordan deserves better from you. She's gorgeous, intelligent and successful. She's sexy and—"

"And you noticed all of this after meeting her only once." David looked at him oddly.

Danny opened his mouth, then shut it again. There was no adequate way to explain his attraction.

David smiled. "Don't bother answering, little brother. Your face says it all."

JORDAN WAS AVAILABLE.

That thought prevailed in Danny's mind when he left David's condominium. His keys jingled in his pocket as he jogged down the stairs, whistling out of tune. He didn't have to feel guilty anymore about what had happened in the elevator. Jordan was single and apparently had been for several weeks.

Now he just had to figure out how to contact her before David made good on his threat to matchmake for them.

As he pushed through the front door and bounded down the steps, he heard a rustling from the shrubs behind him. Then it sounded as if someone stumbled, followed by the click of heels on the concrete walkway. He started to turn around when he felt something poke him in the back.

Then a woman's quiet voice spoke near his ear. "Hold it, mister. I've got a banana. And I'm not afraid to use it."

Danny immediately recognized Jordan's cool, clear voice. It made him think of spring water bubbling over polished rocks. His body responded and began to resemble the alleged banana. Playing along, he lowered his voice to match hers. "Okay, lady. You've got my attention. What now?"

Her breath hitched once, then she blurted out her next command. "Stay quiet and walk toward the burgundy Honda parked at the curb."

Was Jordan looking for another illicit thrill? For the chance to be with her completely, he wasn't going to protest, so he started toward her car. Then reality hit him in the gut. He'd come out of David's condo wearing a T-shirt and sweatpants, so of course she assumed...

"No! Don't turn around."

Danny suppressed a sigh of disappointment. "I think you're making a mistake. My brother—"

"I know all about your brother. This isn't—"

"You do?" He jerked his head in her direction, but her hand shot out to nudge it forward again.

"Let's not talk about him right now." Jordan cleared her throat then continued haltingly. "Since this past weekend, I haven't been able to stop thinking about us, how we left things unfinished."

The extraordinary experience in the elevator flashed across his mind. His pulse quickened with desire and growing hope. Maybe that was Jordan on the phone earlier. Maybe David had told her he was here tonight. "I'm glad you want to pick up where—"

"Don't say anything else, okay? Otherwise I won't be able to go through with this."

Danny angled his body to one side, trying to see her face. "What exactly is *this?*"

"Um, I'm kidnapping you." She sounded a little unsure of herself, but she poked him in the back with the banana once more for emphasis.

"Okay…" He started walked again. "Are we acting out one of your fantasies or something?"

Jordan laughed softly. "Fantasy number fifteen, to be exact."

He smiled, wondering if that was the end of the list or just the beginning. He'd find out soon enough. When he reached the side of the car, she clicked the keyless entry to unlock it. Before he could open the door, though, she thrust something over his shoulder.

"Would you mind putting on this blindfold?"

Danny looked down at the scarf she held in front of his face. "It's pink. It's pink with little white dots on it. What kind of kidnapper are you?"

"You're not supposed to talk. This is hard enough."

Not yet, but he was getting there. Danny obliged and tied the scarf around his eyes, then slid into the passenger seat. Reaching for the lever beneath him, he pushed back to give himself more legroom.

He felt Jordan lean over him to secure his seat belt. The scent of her hair drifted around him and his groin throbbed in reaction to the brush of her shoulder against his chest. Despite his temporary blindness, he was relaxed and curious to find out what she had planned.

"So what happens next?"

For a moment she didn't answer. Then, after a deep breath, she said, "Now I take you to my place and bring the rest of the fantasy to life."

Less than fifteen minutes later, Jordan remained in the driver's seat, drumming her fingers lightly on the steering wheel. The trip back to her house had been relatively easy since David had stayed quiet the whole time. But now that they'd arrived, anxiety stabbed at her resolve, plagued her with doubts. She didn't want a repeat of the last time they were together...

David cleared his throat. "Do you do this kind of thing a lot?"

"Actually, I never do anything like this." Her voice was small and tight as she looked over at him. "But lately I've wanted to...experiment a little."

One dark brow lifted above the blindfold. "I'm always up for some experimentation. So, are we going to sit here the rest of the night?"

"No." She laughed nervously, got out of the Honda and went around to open the passenger door.

Jordan took his arm to guide him out of the car. He misjudged the height of the curb and tripped, bumping into her. He didn't move away. They remained side by side, silent, lost in their mutual awareness. The contact sent sparks and heat rushing along her nerves until an invisible web of desire tightened in her belly. That was a good thing. If she was turned on, there was nothing to fear. Tonight would be a success.

"Can I take this thing off now?" He sounded hoarse as he pointed to the pink-and-white blindfold.

"Not yet." She led him up the walkway. "You can take it off once we start the fantasy."

He frowned briefly, obviously confused. "The kidnapping isn't the fantasy?"

Jordan swallowed the sudden lump in her throat. "No, it was just… I wasn't sure…"

David stopped and turned in her direction. Though he couldn't see the hot color lighting up her face, his voice was quiet. "You didn't think I'd go along unless you forced me?"

She dropped her chin as her confidence evaporated. This was so stupid! Why did she think she could go through with this? Some seductress she was turning out to be. David must have sensed her anguish because he slowly exhaled.

"You didn't have to do this."

Omigod. She was standing in front of her house being rejected by a man in a pink polka-dotted blindfold. He would be polite and considerate because that was his way. But he was still going to dump her again. She twisted her fingers together, fighting harder not to cry.

"All you had to do was ask."

"Huh?" She jerked her head up.

David's voice held more than a touch of gentle humor. "So what's the real fantasy, Jordan?"

He still wanted to play. The sudden warmth of relief and gratitude swept over her and she smiled, too, though he couldn't see it. She considered telling him the real reason behind her seduction plan, then realized she wanted this night of fantasy as much as she wanted his help.

"No names."

"Excuse me?"

Her pulse accelerated and her words came out in a rush. "No names, okay? No inhibitions and no regrets tonight. We're just two strangers who met and felt an immediate attraction."

His response was complete silence and for an instant her insecurities returned. Then David grinned, his wide smile sexy despite the pink scarf on his face. "When I saw you across the smoke-filled room, I thought you were the most beautiful woman in the place."

For a second, her heart turned over. He thought—

No. Jordan shook herself back into the reality of the moment. He was just getting into the fantasy. She took a deep breath and let her imagination take over. "When I walked into that hot, crowded bar tonight, I was looking for someone, but I didn't expect to find *you*. I saw you sitting by yourself and wondered why a guy like you was alone."

She was afraid her speech sounded forced, but David got right into character. "Yeah, I had the same thought about you. I couldn't believe such a hot, sexy woman was coming on to me."

That web of desire tightened and Jordan suddenly wanted him so badly her legs started to tremble. The way David was responding, maybe they should have tried this fantasy stuff before. "There was something about you, something that intrigued me. That's why I approached you. Then you looked at me and smiled and I couldn't resist giving in to a wicked impulse."

"I'd planned to buy you a drink, but your very seductive offer distracted me. Wicked impulses are the hardest to refuse."

He stood beside her on the front step. She could feel the heat of his body and even in the dimness of twilight his arousal was obvious. There was a lot to be said for the thin fabric of sweatpants. He leaned into her, pressing the length of his body to hers as he spoke softly.

"I think we'll be good together."

Jordan drew a quivering breath as she pushed open the front door. "Why don't we go inside and find out?"

5

DANNY STEPPED into the gloom of Jordan's foyer and had to fight off a brief sense of panic. Outside, he'd been able to detect the last rays of twilight through the filmy material of the scarf. Now, though, his inability to see was further hampered by unfamiliar surroundings.

"Um, this will just—umph. This will just take a second."

Danny shifted from one foot to the other, while Jordan muttered under her breath. The distinctive odor of butane wasn't doing anything to alleviate his discomfort.

"Press. Hold. Click. It's simple. So why—can't I—get this—to work?"

He smelled the accelerant and heard the strike wheel grinding and felt the scar on his back tighten. What the hell was she setting on fire? Danny yanked off the blindfold.

"You're making me nervous."

Jordan sighed and set down the fireplace lighter she was holding. "I'm a little nervous myself."

He glanced behind her to see flames dancing in

the first three of a series of small hurricane candles. The rest, though unlit, made a path up the winding staircase.

"Seems we could both use some reassurance. Come on over here." Danny opened his arms and waited.

She hesitated for just a second, then Jordan moved across the floor and into his embrace, her face tilted expectantly. In the faint light from the transom window above the front door, he saw that her lips trembled slightly and he heard the little catch of her breath. If he didn't know better, he would have thought she was nervous.

Danny lowered his head and closed his mouth over hers. He'd been dying to kiss her again, so consumed by the memory of the elevator that there was no time to sample or savor. He slanted his lips across hers in a hot, urgent need to taste and take. Jordan pulled away with a gasp. Her brows drew together for an instant as she looked up at him with a bemused expression.

"What's wrong?"

"Nothing, nothing. I just—you reminded—" She shook her head once and then smiled. "Where were we?"

A low growl of pleasure escaped him as she moved in, molding her lush body to his straining erection. He slid his hands down to cup her butt and pull her even closer. He traced her mouth with the tip of his tongue, memorizing the sinuous curve of her lower lip, the sweet fullness of the upper one.

Then he delved inside to the warm recesses of her mouth.

She tightened her hold on his back, the slick fabric of her raincoat rustling as she rubbed her pelvis across the front of his sweatpants. She took the kiss to the next level, making him feel that she was going to devour him. Her tongue mated with his in what he hoped was a preview of things to come.

Breathing hard, he leaned back just enough to ask a question. Even in the dim light, he could see the excitement in her eyes. "So, stranger, are you just going to hold me for ransom, or was there something else you wanted to do with me?"

Jordan slid out of his arms and held out her hand. He grasped it in his and followed her toward the stairs. She looked over her shoulder, a little smile on her beautiful lips. "This is my fantasy, but it's our night."

DANNY DIDN'T MIND the darkness this time. Jordan's fingers were warm in his as they walked into her bedroom and faint light from the street filtered through the thin material of the curtains. His eyes quickly adjusted and he relaxed, allowing his desire to overtake the moment.

Jordan led him past a mirrored dresser to the center of the room then moved several steps away. He wanted to reach for her again, but this was, as she'd said, her fantasy. It wouldn't be easy, but he had to keep his arousal in check and let her set the stage. Danny crossed his hands in front of him and watched to see what she would do.

She dropped her chin, as though embarrassed by his scrutiny, and reached for the belt of her raincoat. After fumbling with the knot, she began to unfasten the buttons. Actually, he thought the short coat was pretty sexy. It made her look more like a secret agent than a kidnapper, but he didn't care. It left her long, gorgeous legs exposed—

His brain shut down in midthought as Jordan lifted her shoulders and shrugged, letting the coat fall in a puddle at her feet. His mouth went dry as he stared.

She wore only a tight black lingerie top, matching black panties and her sandals. Her body was extraordinary, beautifully proportioned from her graceful neck to her full breasts, long waist and round hips. His gaze returned to and lingered on her breasts, his hands flexing with the need to feel them again.

Wait...

All she wore was lingerie. That's all she'd had on beneath the coat the entire night. Outside of the condo. In her car. On the front step of her house. He could have reached under the raincoat and her satiny skin would have been bare to his touch. The idea turned him on so much that all of the blood in his body rushed to his groin.

Jordan stepped toward him then, her demeanor uncertain, which surprised him since they'd already shared such intimacy. Maybe it was part of the fantasy. He cupped the side of her face and drew her closer. "The first time with someone new, especially a stranger, can be scary. But I promise I won't do anything you don't want."

She hesitated, then closed the distance between them. The first brush of her lips against his mouth whetted his appetite. The second had him wanting to devour her, but still he held back. Her kisses were warm and sweet and he met each one with restraint until finally she opened to him, letting his tongue explore her in lazy circles. Her fingers stroked the back of his neck while her other hand slid over his shoulders and along his chest. Then he deepened the kiss, unleashing a little of the need he felt, turning the kiss urgent and demanding.

A moan escaped her throat as her fingers slipped beneath the waistband of his pants to drag at his T-shirt, just as she had in the elevator. But this time they would finish what they started. Jordan tugged the fabric up until he was forced to break the kiss and yank the shirt over his head. She smoothed her palms over his bare chest, leaving a trail of heat in the wake of her touch.

He claimed her lips once again, kissing her with all the passion burning inside. He tasted her excitement and responded in kind. The way she arched her back and wiggled against him drove him nuts. He reached up to slide the strap of her camisole off her shoulder. She pushed it back on.

Danny tugged at it again and, while she was distracted, pulled down the other strap. When she started to protest softly, he slipped his hand inside the underwire cup to fondle her breast. The velvety orb, more than filling his palm, warmed beneath his hand.

He brushed his thumb over her nipple until it beaded into a sensitive peak. Her gasp of surprise turned into a moan of pleasure. Danny quickly unhooked the eyelets on the front of the garment, dropping it to the floor and freeing both breasts for his enjoyment. Then he bent down to take one into his mouth. The flick of his tongue on the engorged flesh made her quiver and arch closer as he suckled each breast in turn.

When he straightened up, Jordan kissed him deeply, desperately, wordlessly expressing how much she wanted him. It couldn't be as much as he wanted her. His erection threatened to poke a hole in the front of his sweatpants. He reached down between their bodies, sliding his palm along her belly until he touched the waistband of her panties. She widened her stance to give him greater access.

Jordan gasped against his mouth as he slipped one, two fingers into her heat. She was so wet, so ready. He felt her clamp down on his hand and she tightened her arm around his shoulders. He'd only begun to touch her and already she was about to explode. He knew exactly how she felt. Then she surprised him by laying her hand on top of his.

He didn't need any more encouragement than that. He moved his hands so that he could massage her clitoris with his thumb, urging her on toward release. Her hips swiveled in almost frantic circles as he pleasured her. As soon as he increased the pressure of his thumb, Jordan cried out and came apart.

Danny held her as she caught her breath, marveling at her responsiveness and dying to be inside her the next time she climaxed like that. He toed off his running shoes and walked barefoot across the thick carpet to the bed before releasing his hold on her. He tipped her chin up until she looked at him.

"This is our night, but it's your fantasy, Jordan. What do you want to do next?"

WHAT DID SHE WANT to do next? Everything!

But she didn't know how to ask, and he was waiting for her to make the choice. He was being so sweet and so patient. And he acted as if he really wanted her. Maybe it was the supposed anonymity of the Stranger fantasy. Maybe it was the darkness and the way it somehow reminded her of the elevator. Whatever the reason, it seemed circumstances, even fabricated ones, made all the difference.

The lust and excitement and curiosity she'd felt moments ago were a positive sign. If she concentrated on the type of character she wanted to be, the kind of seductress she wanted to portray, then all she had to do was believe. She was sexy. Fun. Naughty. Alluring. There was a nearly naked man in front of her and she was going to enjoy him.

Jordan launched herself at David and threw her arms around his neck, knocking him backward onto the bed.

"Hey!" His exclamation was as much laughter as protest.

With a hand on either side of her waist, he adjusted her on his body until she lay atop him, straddling his thighs. The position put her in direct contact with his erection. He let out an involuntary moan when she shifted across the evidence of his desire.

He wrapped his arms around her and swiftly claimed her lips. The kiss was wild and demanding, familiar and yet new. Heart racing, her body on fire, currents of electricity zinged along her nerve endings. She returned his kiss with reckless abandon as his mouth teased and encouraged and enticed.

Then his hands began to glide along her sides.

She froze. Could he feel the stretch marks left from her weight loss? His hands continued toward her bottom and she began to panic. He would definitely feel the cellulite on her buttocks and outer thighs. She pushed up on one elbow, intending to roll off him, but the strength of his arms held her in place.

"Relax, Jordan. Just relax."

She tried, but the core of tension remained. The reality was that not only didn't she look like the girls in the magazines; she sure as hell didn't feel like them, either. Reality sucked.

"I can't."

"In fantasies, nobody judges. Especially not strangers."

Who was he kidding? Strangers were the most

judgmental of all. She couldn't go on with this. The fantasy spell had been broken. Suddenly overcome with anxiety, loneliness and longing squeezed her heart. If they made love now, it would be awkward and embarrassing and quickly over.

"Let me go, please."

"Shh," he whispered. "No inhibitions and no regrets tonight. There won't be anything between us, not tonight."

He kept one hand on her bottom, wordlessly insisting she accept his touch, while the fingers of his other hand tangled in her hair and guided her mouth back to his. This kiss was gentle and almost tender, a slow exploration and a gesture of reassurance. The intimacy of it added to her surreal feelings of confusion and familiarity.

He rolled over with her until they'd reversed positions. His fingers gently touched her temples and cheeks as he softly claimed her mouth again. Jordan allowed herself to unwind and to kiss him back. The tip of his tongue slipped between her parted lips, inviting her to partake. With a soft moan, she surrendered to the heat building inside her once more.

His left hand caressed the tender skin along her jaw as she parted her lips for him. His other hand moved to her breast, his palm slowly caressing the soft mound until the nipple beaded. She stroked her hands across his broad shoulders, both exploring and encouraging. Shivers of desire danced along her skin everywhere his fingers caressed her.

He brushed his lips along her jaw, nibbled on the

sensitive places on her neck before kissing a path down her chest. She groaned as he suckled her nipples. The gentle, tugging pressure sent a wave of need straight to the juncture of her thighs. He continued to kiss her breasts, the top swells and the tender undersides before trailing his open mouth over her ribs and down her abdomen.

Every inch of her body felt alive with an urgent sense of need. He placed hot kisses on her belly and hips before tracing patterns along the inside of her thighs with his tongue. Moaning softly, her pulse quickened in excitement. He knelt over her, slipped his thumbs under the waistband of her panties and peeled them off. Apprehension trembled in her chest only to dissipate when his fingers probed into her damp heat.

He shifted until he could remove the panties altogether, then settled on the bottom of the bed. Jordan half gasped, half groaned at the first touch of his mouth to the damp, swollen flesh. When his tongue delved inside her, her whole being caught fire and a familiar tightening began in her womb. She lost herself in the overload of sensations as he coaxed her toward a quickly escalating climax.

"Condoms?"

"In the night-table drawer."

David left her only long enough to strip off his sweatpants and underwear and protect them. Then he lay down beside her. Her fears and insecurities resurfaced. The last time they were together, he'd been a considerate lover, trying everything to please her. And yet she'd been left feeling empty and unsatisfied. She prayed this time was different, that her body would continue to respond.

He positioned himself between her legs, supporting his weight on his elbows. Her nipples grazed the crisp hairs on his chest before her breasts flattened against the hard planes. She could feel the ridges of his sculpted abs against her belly. Anticipation formed a knot of tension, the best kind of tension, in her belly.

His leg hairs tickled her inner thighs when he shifted. He moved forward so that the smooth tip of his penis was poised at her entrance. She tried to prepare for the sensual invasion, but she was too eager, too needy. He slowly penetrated her, inch by magnificent inch, until he was completely sheathed inside her. She writhed in pleasure as her body softened and stretched to accept him.

David pushed into her once, withdrew slightly, and then returned. Crying out in need, in relief, the raw pleasure of his possession overwhelmed her. He began rocking in a deliberate, sensuous rhythm that she quickly matched. Then he drew his knees closer, slowing the pace and changing the angle of penetration. In the back of her mind were confused questions about what was happening, but her body couldn't have cared less as long as this newly discovered passion didn't stop.

He must have felt the wondrous quickening in her womb because he accelerated the tempo, increased the glorious grinding pleasure. Wild and wanton, she reveled in his hard, fast thrusts. Wrapping her legs tightly around his thighs, her hands clutched at the sweat-slick muscles of his back. The slow insistent throb became a deep pulsating tremor. He arched his hips, heightening the pleasure until they were both frenzied.

She couldn't think; she could only feel. A sensual wave crested over her, followed by tremors of ecstasy. The orgasm shuddered through her, rocking her to the core. The joy of it almost brought tears to her eyes. He continued pushing deeper and faster until at last a triumphant groan escaped his throat when he found his own release.

Too overwhelmed to speak, Jordan simply held him tight, expressing her wonder and gratitude by her embrace. She felt something shift inside of her, felt her confidence and power as a woman blooming like a rose too long untended. Delight bubbled up inside her like champagne fizz, tickling her and making her giddy. She'd hoped that fantasy sex would be all the guidebook promised, but this had been so much more.

Smiling into the darkness, Jordan considered her seduction plan a rousing success.

THE NEXT MORNING, when she heard soft jazz music begin playing, Jordan groped for the alarm clock. She smacked her hand against a rock-solid biceps instead. Opening her eyes in surprise, she turned her head. David slept beside her. He'd stayed the night this time.

He rolled onto his side, dragging the black cotton bedsheet with him. Puzzled, she stared at the shiny, raised patch of skin that marred his right shoulder. She hadn't realized he had such terrible scarring. But, then again, she'd only been naked with him once before and she'd never seen him in the light.

David fumbled for the night table and shut off the alarm before rolling onto his back. Normally she hopped right out of bed at six in the morning, eager to start her day with a three-mile run. But this morning she chose to enjoy the unfamiliar pleasure of waking up next to someone. She laid her head on his chest, closed her eyes and snuggled against his side.

Her fantasy had been more successful than she could have dreamed. Maybe pretending to be strangers and allowing their imaginations to take over had been all they needed to open up and explore their sexual relationship. Last night had been so unlike the previous time they'd made love, it was almost like being with a different person.

They'd reached for each other in the darkness, making love again, at times fast and desperate, in other moments slow and tender. She'd lost count of how many times he'd brought her to orgasm. Jordan stretched her arms over her head, basking in the warm glow of satisfaction. Some part of her, long imprisoned, had been set free and she had David to thank for opening the door.

Jordan mentally paged through the *Fifty Fast Fantasies* book, trying to decide which scenario to try out the next time. Maybe Special Deliveryman or Buried Treasure Hunt. She smiled, already making a list of props and outfits for the first one. David would look great in a brown parcel-service uniform.

He sighed in his sleep and tightened his hold around her waist. A glance at the clock had her sighing, as well. It was getting late and she was going to have to share the bathroom. Hmm. Maybe they could save time by sharing the shower. She rubbed her hand back and forth over his chest.

"Wake up, sleepyhead."

David grunted then nuzzled his chin on her forehead as he muttered, "It's my day off."

Jordan laughed softly and propped herself up on her elbow. "Well, I guess I could call in sick, but I thought you had to take depositions this morning."

He startled and his eyes flew open. Then she felt the tension steal into his body as he turned his head to look at her. Confusion tightened his features. Jordan made a comical face, teasing him.

"Did you forget all about the Gregg case?"

She could feel his heart thudding beneath her hand. His expression became somber then he sighed heavily and closed his eyes. When he opened them again, a shadow had entered his gaze. His voice was quiet, remorseful.

"I'm not David. I'm Danny."

6

HER HEART SKIPPED several beats, trying to regain its rhythm. Icy fingers crept along her skin and suddenly she felt violently ill. *Danny. Not David. Danny.* Jordan twisted away from him, throwing away the sheet as she scrambled off the bed.

Omigod. Omigod.

He sat up and called her name, but she was already running down the hallway to the bathroom. She slammed the door and bolted the lock, resting her back against the wood and gasping for breath. She eased over to the porcelain claw-foot tub on jellied legs, settling her naked bottom on the edge.

Omigod. Omigod. Omigod.

She pressed the heels of her hands into her eyes and rocked back and forth. Tears clogged her throat and her pulse hammered erratically. This had to be the most humiliating thing that had ever happened to her, if you didn't count the disastrous prom date her cousin Keisha had set up back in high school.

A soft knock sounded. "Jordan. Let me in."

"No."

"Then will you come out?"

"No."

She heard his grunt of frustration through the door. "You can't stay in there forever."

"Yes, I can."

She dropped her hands, pounding her fists against her thighs. No, she couldn't. Grabbing her bathrobe from the hook on the wall, she slipped it on before unlocking the door. David/Danny had been leaning on the door frame, but stepped back to let her pass. She glanced down long enough to see that he'd pulled on his boxer briefs. But his magnificent chest was still bare. His bare chest reminded her of last night.

"Can we please talk about this?"

"No!" She yelled over her shoulder as she stomped down the hall.

"*Jordan.*"

Danny grasped her elbow, forcing her to stop. She drew in a ragged breath to keep her stomach where it belonged. This was unbelievable and he didn't seem to grasp the enormity of the situation. She looked at him, at the face that was identical to the one she thought she'd see this morning.

"You don't understand. I had *sex* with a *total* stranger."

His brows drew together. "Wasn't that the idea of the fantasy?"

"Yes, but you're the wrong stranger!"

HER WORDS HAD all of the power of a slap in the face. Danny dropped her arm and watched her go into the bedroom.

What the hell was happening? It felt as if a lead weight was crushing his chest and that wasn't like him at all. He set the rules of his relationships, making sure things stayed nice and easy. He never got emotionally involved. And he wasn't involved now. It was just an ego thing. Jordan had no idea who he really was when she'd met him outside his brother's condo.

She hadn't wanted *him*.

He knew his anger and a disappointment was unreasonable but, damn it, he'd felt something for her last night. Her vulnerability and fear had touched a place inside him that he hadn't known existed. Instead of enjoying the sex for its own sake, he'd found himself wanting to protect and reassure her. The intensity of his feelings scared the hell out of him and the sooner he got over it the better.

He followed Jordan down the hallway.

"I can't believe this! At least I thought I was kidnapping my ex-boyfriend."

She was standing in front of her dresser trying to put on a bra without taking off her robe. One terry-cloth arm flopped against her side as she wiggled into the straps. He caught a glimpse of the swell of her breast through the gap at the neckline when she turned to him.

"What's your excuse, Danny? Do you normally go home with women you don't know? Never mind. Don't answer that."

He crossed his arms over his chest and adapted a reasonable tone. "But I did know you. Since I recognized you at the St. Charles Hotel, I thought you'd realized—"

"Omigod." Jordan started to hyperventilate and the color drained from her complexion. She strode across the room away from him then her legs seemed to melt beneath her. Concerned, he went to her as she sank onto the little divan by the window. "That was you. It was you in the elevator. Omigod. I didn't think anyone would ever know about that."

Danny crouched down beside her and took her hand. Then he felt something under his knee. When he shifted, he saw a book lying on the thick beige carpet. He didn't bother trying to read the small print. The title, *Fifty Fast Fantasies,* said it all. He wondered if any of them involved elevators.

He returned his attention to Jordan. The harsh sunlight streaming through the window made her look even paler. Without letting on what he was doing, he checked her pulse with his thumb. "I'm confused. You told me you couldn't stop thinking about last weekend, about the way we left things unfinished."

"But that wasn't what I meant." She wouldn't meet his eye, staring instead at his bare chest. Then she pulled her hand from his grasp and massaged her temples. "Omigod. I can't believe this is happening."

He sat back on his heels, careful not to touch her, but letting his voice slide into an intimate tone. "I haven't been able to forget it, either. Before last night, I would have said it was the most incredible thing that ever happened to me. After I recognized you, I was upset at first—"

"Upset?" Jordan jumped to her feet and swept past him. "I feel like I cheated on my boyfriend. And, as if that wasn't bad enough, I cheated with his brother!"

Danny stood up and went over to grab his T-shirt off the floor by the foot of the bed. He noticed for the first time that the black bedsheets didn't really go with the rose-colored scheme of the rest of the room. "David told me you two split up. So there's nothing to be ashamed of."

"Yes, we did. But I thought we could get back together temporarily. Why do you think I went to all this trouble to seduce him?"

Danny paused in the act of pulling on his shirt, then continued to slip it over his head. He watched her fling open the closet door, then rifle through the contents. All of her clothes were arranged by color, dark to light, then long to short. A woman that organized must hate to make mistakes.

He scrubbed a hand over his face and wondered what to say. She considered and rejected several outfits, finally choosing a white V-necked blouse and dove-gray business suit. He took a couple of steps toward her then stopped, shifting his weight from one foot to the other. "This is really awkward…"

She scowled at him over her shoulder while she knelt down to pick out shoes. "No kidding."

"Last night you said you knew about David. You said, quote, 'I know all about your brother,' unquote."

"That's because I thought he was talking about you again, but it was you talking about you. I mean, about him. Argh!"

What had David been saying to Jordan about him? Why? Never mind. It could wait.

"I'm sorry, Jordan. I thought you knew."

She stood up and slowly turned toward him. "Knew what? Why do you sound so strange?"

This was a hell of a mess. He felt terrible about betraying his brother's confidence, but at the same time he resented being the bearer of embarrassing news. "Jordan, David is gay."

The clothes draped over her arm slipped onto the floor as she stared at him. Though her mouth fell open, no words escaped. Her face was absolutely expressionless, but her eyes had taken on a sheen of wetness. Suddenly, she stooped down to pick up her suit and blouse, her movements jerky.

"I'm really late for work. I can't talk about this now." Her voice sounded thin as she shoved the gray suit back into the closet. "I've got to get to the office so I can leave early and go to the airport. I have to pick up my family." She pulled out a bright blue pants suit instead and tossed it on the bed. "Then I have to figure out how to explain to them that my whole engagement was a fraud."

Danny's eyes darted to her hands, to the emerald ring on her right hand…and the diamond solitaire on her left. He cursed viciously under his breath, really damned unhappy with his brother right now. He looked at Jordan's face again and felt something twist inside his chest. He reached for her, but she shifted away. Her light brown eyes were rimmed with tears and her expression was bleak.

"Get dressed, Danny, and please go."

He shoved his fists into the pockets of his sweatpants to keep from reaching for her again. "I can't."

"Excuse me?"

He frowned, no happier about the situation than she was. "You kidnapped me, remember? My car is still at David's."

THE SILENCE in Jordan's car as she drove to David's condo was like an unwelcome third passenger. Annoying and awkward. But it was preferable to dealing with the situation before she'd had time to think about everything.

Danny cleared his throat. "Jordan, we should talk."

"I don't want to talk."

"Avoiding me doesn't solve anything."

She continued to stare straight ahead, frowning as she drove. Couldn't he just leave her alone? She felt humiliated enough without rehashing every detail.

Danny kept talking. "I know you're upset about what happened, but I think we can—"

She checked her rearview mirror for traffic, then stomped on the brake. Danny jerked forward before the safety belt slapped him back against the seat.

"I *do not* want to talk about this, Danny. You're more than welcome to walk the rest of the way."

He held up both palms in acquiescence so she put the car in gear and started off again. He crossed his arms over his chest and glowered out the window for the next few blocks, but apparently the silence got to him.

"You're being unreasonable, Jordan. You made an honest mistake. No one's going to hold that against you, least of all me."

She jerked the steering wheel toward the curb and hit the brakes again. Ignoring the blare of horns behind her, she twisted in her seat toward him and pointed. "Out."

"Oh, come on. Let's be adult about this, okay? We had sex. It's not the end of the world. In fact, I thought it was pretty damned good."

"Out!"

Danny returned her glare for a moment then scowled. "Fine. You don't want to talk, we won't talk."

"Thank you."

Having finally gotten the message, he stayed quiet for the rest of the ten-minute ride. He made one last effort before he closed the door to the Honda.

"Can I call you later?"

"What for?"

Danny just looked at her for a moment, then nodded his head and got out of the car. She pressed the automatic door locks and sped off. When she glanced into the rearview mirror, Jordan saw him standing on the sidewalk, watching her leave.

She managed to get to the law firm only a half

hour late. She pushed through the glass double doors to Chase, Behr's lobby, her heels clicking on the polished slate tiles. The receptionist greeted her with a thorough once-over and a raised eyebrow.

"Whatever it is, it must be bad."

She stopped, taken aback by the amused tone of voice, and looked at Charlie. "What makes you say that?"

"Honey, look at you. I've never seen you in a ponytail before."

Jordan smoothed a hand over her hair. "I was running late."

"Okay, that explains the lack of eyeliner or lipstick, but your suit jacket is buttoned wrong and you're wearing two different shoes."

Jordan dropped her focus and, in the harsh glare of the fluorescent lighting, saw that one pump was indeed black and the other was navy. Damn. It was a good thing she didn't have a court appearance.

"I was sort of distracted this morning."

Charlie nodded sagely. "I'll say."

Jordan fixed the buttons on her turquoise jacket as she continued through the lobby past the conference rooms. After dumping her briefcase by her desk and changing into the extra pair of black shoes she kept in the file cabinet, she headed straight for David's office on the other side of the building.

He looked up as she barreled into the room. "Hey, good morning—"

"No, it really isn't. Why didn't you tell me,

David?" She closed the door to give them some privacy. "Why didn't you tell me that you're gay?"

He put down his pen and set the papers he was working on aside. "So you did know."

"Not until this morning."

His brows drew together. "How did you find out?"

"Never mind that right now." Jordan sank into one of the guest chairs across from him. "Why didn't you tell me?"

David rubbed a hand over his face. "I needed time to sort out how I feel about everything. Us, the partnership, my future. I swear, though, I never meant to lead you on or hurt you."

"But I am hurt. You lied to me."

"I was lying to myself, about how I feel and who I am. I care about you more than any woman I've ever known. You're a good friend and a wonderful person and I thought I could make it work."

There was no doubting the sincerity in his voice, the remorse in his eyes. Jordan sighed and offered him a little smile. "I guess this explains a lot. We've been together for almost a year and all this time I blamed myself for the lack of intimacy."

David stood up and came around the desk. "I'm so sorry, Jordan. It never occurred to me that you would think it was anything but *my* fault." He reached for her hand. "After that one night we were together, I realized I couldn't keep denying my homosexuality, that it wouldn't be fair to keep dating you. Can you forgive me?"

"Of course, I do." Jordan stood up to return his hug. "In the back of my mind, I must have suspected, because as much as I care about you, I knew something was missing."

David let her go and sat down in the other guest chair. "So, what happened this morning?"

She gave an exaggerated sigh while rolling her eyes. "I've got to start listening to that little voice in my head. Then the whole seduction idea could have been avoided."

"Excuse me?"

"You're not going to believe what I've done, David. It all started when I came up with this grand scheme to seduce you into doing me a favor."

He stared at her with a bemused expression. "What was the favor?"

"My family thinks we're getting married. When I picked out this ring, I let them think it was for an engagement instead of a birthday present."

"We had the same idea in mind. I figured if the partners thought we were engaged..."

"Exactly. We both had an image we wanted to maintain. Well, the problem is, my family's arriving today for the week leading up to my grandparents' anniversary party. And they all expect to meet my fiancé."

"That's not a problem. I can leave the office early a few nights this coming week. But I already have a trip scheduled for the weekend. Can you tell them I'm out of town on business until Monday night?"

"Oh, David. Thank you! It will just be for a couple of dinners and the anniversary party. Then a week or so later, I'll tell them we broke up."

"Okay, give me a copy of the schedule and I'll do what I can." He smiled at her. "See, you didn't have to seduce me after all. And I think we both would have felt pretty awkward if you had."

"Actually, what I feel is humiliated. Because I did go through with my plan. Only… I, um, kidnapped your brother by mistake."

"What?" David choked out a sputtering half-chuckle.

Jordan twisted her mouth in annoyance. "Go ahead and laugh. I'm glad one of us can."

David settled back in his chair. "This ought to be good."

Haltingly and with some embarrassment, she explained to him about the night before. She left out the more intimate details, though, and said nothing about the elevator or about how she felt about the whole situation. She hadn't sorted that out yet.

David grinned at her. "So you and my brother really hit it off? Didn't I tell you you should get together with him?"

"Get together, yes, for coffee or maybe dinner. Not an all-night session of—" Jordan broke off abruptly.

"The sex was really hot, huh?" He wiggled his eyebrows suggestively.

"You can't embarrass me any more than I already am, so don't bother trying." She crossed her arms and glared at him.

Just then the telephone rang. He excused himself and reached across his desk to answer it. "David Navarro… Hey, Dan. Perfect timing."

Her eyes widened, then she vigorously shook her head.

"Yeah, I talked to Jordan. I told her the truth and she forgave me. What's that? Hang on." He held his palm over the receiver. "Do you want to talk to him?"

She jumped to her feet, mouthing the word *no* and waving both hands in front of her as she backed toward the exit. David had a funny little smile on his face as he watched her retreat. He spoke into the phone again as she yanked the door open.

"Sorry, bro. My secretary was just reminding me about a meeting this afternoon."

She fled back to her own office before she overheard anything more.

SHE WASN'T SURE she could win the Susan Brandywine case.

She'd spent the past few hours reading through the Code of Maryland Regulations and searching Lexis for supporting court decisions. In one case she found, *Craft v. Metromedia, Inc.,* the court of appeals held that "evidence showed a particular concern with appearance in television and that reasonable appearance requirements were obviously critical to the KMBC station's economic well-being."

The question was, what was reasonable?

An additional problem was the wording of Susan's contract. Clause XIII stated that "if there is any material change in the physical appearance of performer, then employer, at its option, may refuse to pay performer compensation during the period of such incapacity, impairment or change."

Despite the fact that Susan was more than qualified to do the job as a television news anchor, it all came down to looks. Jordan intended to keep searching for a strong defense on the age issue. Maybe there was something in the box of Responses to Requests for Production of Documents the other side had delivered yesterday she could use against them.

But on a personal level, she wondered why Susan chose to sue on the weight issue. Losing excess pounds wasn't easy—she knew that from experience—but it could be done. Jordan pushed back from the desk and stretched her arms above her head. The tension across her shoulders reminded her that she'd missed her run this morning and why.

If she put her embarrassment aside, last night had been absolutely fabulous. Because of the fantasy, she'd been able to let go of her inhibitions and truly enjoy herself. And, now that she knew the truth about David, the weight of insecurity had lifted.

Since she'd calmed down, she felt badly about the way she treated Danny this morning. None of this had been his fault. In fact, she would always be grateful to him for showing her that, with a little imagination, she could have normal, utterly satisfying sex. She should probably call him to apologize.

Then again, given his reputation, he'd be over her and already dating a new woman by dinnertime.

Speaking of time, she looked at her watch. Due to the new antiterror policies, she'd have to leave now to get through the vehicle inspection and security checks in time to meet her relatives' flight. After putting on her suit jacket, she checked the buttons, grabbed her purse and headed for Baltimore Washington International Airport.

TWO HOURS AND FORTY-FIVE minutes later, Jordan stood outside of the security checkpoint for Concourse C, anxiously waiting for the plane from Atlanta to disembark. Her relatives had taken vacation time to get reacquainted prior to her grandparents' anniversary party. She hadn't seen Uncle Matt and Aunt Celeste in almost four years.

She'd have happily waited another four to see her cousin Keisha. She had never understood why her cousin was so antagonistic toward her. Keisha had always been slim and beautiful, while Jordan had been shy and dumpy, but even when she visited a few months ago, Keisha never missed an opportunity to take a stab at her.

Her anxiety increased when she saw Aunt Celeste glide down the gangway, resplendent and wrinkle-free in a hot orange tunic and pants. Not a silver hair was out of place and her makeup was flawless. Uncle Matt was dashing in a golf shirt and khakis, looking decades younger than his sixty years.

And then came Keisha, sauntering into the waiting area as if it had red carpeting. She had on stone-washed hipsters with a U-neck knit top and stacked-heel sandals. Gold hoop earrings peeked out from the riot of ringlets that framed her heart-shaped face. Keisha looked confident and sexy and Jordan despised her on sight.

Of all the days not to look her absolute best. The Atlanta branch boasted the thinnest, most graceful limbs. And, even though she'd lost a lot of weight, they still managed to make Jordan feel like the trunk of the family tree. She suddenly felt fat and plain by comparison. And she was hungry.

What was it about her cousin that made her want to devour an entire pint of Godiva white chocolate raspberry ice cream? Jordan smoothed her palms down her suit, wishing she'd had time to run home and fix herself up.

Aunt Celeste rushed toward her, arms flung wide. "Oh, my goodness! Nibbles! You look wonderful, sweetheart. Doesn't she look wonderful, Matt?"

Jordan returned the embrace but mentally cringed at hearing the hated childhood nickname again. "Hi, Aunt Celeste. Welcome back."

Matt nudged his wife aside in order to offer his own hug. "Girl, you were always pretty on the inside but I have to say, you do look fine. You must have lost, what, sixty pounds?"

She held back a sigh at the unintentional insult. When you were heavy, people always assumed the worst because they never really looked at you. "Um, actually, it was only forty—"

"Well, you look just wonderful!"

As her aunt and uncle continued to marvel about her weight loss, Jordan glanced over at her cousin. She pasted on a smile and reached out to hug her. "Hi, Keisha. How are you?"

Her cousin's gaze was dark and decidedly unwelcoming. A flicker of unease crept over her. For a second she truly believed her cousin hated her. Jordan dropped her arm and her smile at the same time.

"Keisha," Aunt Celeste admonished. "Come on over here and greet your cousin properly."

She came forward, eyes intent as they roamed Jordan's face. She bared her teeth and lowered her voice. "You know, some blush along your jawline and more concealer on your neck would go a long way to defining your chin."

Even though she'd been braced for it, her cousin's words stabbed straight through her. Jordan knew she'd never be as beautiful as her cousin, but leave it to Keisha to make the point in her own nasty way.

Unaware of the hostility, Celeste linked her arm through Jordan's left elbow then suddenly grabbed her hand. "Good gracious! Would you look at that diamond! Oh, honey, it's gorgeous and I'll bet the man who gave it to you is, too!"

Uncle Matt grinned at her. "So, when do we get to meet your David?"

"Yeah, Nibbles, where's this fiancé of yours?"

Jordan ignored her cousin's sarcastic tone with difficulty and answered her aunt's question instead.

"Oh, he had to go out of town on business. But you'll get to meet him later."

"Uh-huh." Keisha smirked.

"Well, we should probably go to baggage claim and get your luggage." She was just about to guide them in the direction of the escalator when she heard her name called.

"Jordan? Jordan?"

She turned toward the voice and her brows shot up in surprise to see a tall, broad-shouldered man striding down the concourse. Beside her, she could almost hear Keisha licking her lips as she struck a pose.

What was David doing here? He must have broken some speed records to have had time to change into jeans and a casual shirt and meet her family's plane... Wait a minute. David *never* wore jeans...

"Sorry I'm late, baby. Traffic."

He slipped his arm around her waist with a warm smile and pulled her to him. Well aware that her family was watching every move, she started to turn so his lips would brush her cheek. However, his idea of a hello kiss left her completely breathless. Jordan just stared at him, unable to form words.

The spell was broken when a disgruntled Keisha loudly cleared her throat. She glanced over to see Aunt Celeste grinning with unconcealed delight while Uncle Matt's brows shot toward his receding hairline. Danny squeezed her hip as he held out his right hand to Matt.

"Hi, I'm David Navarro. It's nice to finally meet you."

7

JORDAN STOOD under the atrium of the Wyndham Inner Harbor Hotel with her aunt and uncle, waiting impatiently for Keisha and "David." Her cousin had insisted on riding in his Jeep when they left the airport. She watched them through narrowed eyes as Keisha laughed gaily at something Danny said while he helped the porter unload the luggage.

Uncle Matt patted her arm. "Now you just get that look off your face, girl. You're the one wearing his ring."

Jordan gave him a little smile but said nothing. What did she care if Danny flirted with her sexy, skinny cousin mere hours after leaving her bed? She didn't. Not at all.

When Danny and Keisha finally joined them, Jordan led the way inside the cool expanse of the hotel lobby. Aunt Celeste marveled at the elegant marble-tiled walls and huge floral arrangements while Matt went to check them in.

Keisha sent Jordan a mischievous look then smiled at her mother. "I was just about to ask David to recommend someplace we could all go for dinner and maybe dancing afterward."

Over her dead body. Jordan wasn't about to spend the evening having to watch Miss Thing wiggle her little butt all over her "fiancé." Aunt Celeste saved her from being the one to protest.

"Not tonight, darling. It's been a long day and I think your father just wants to go up to the suite."

Keisha widened her smile. "That's okay. Now we can go on our own and not worry about how late we get back."

Danny stepped closer to Jordan and shook his head. "Sorry, but we already have plans, don't we, baby?"

Jordan found herself oddly comforted when he draped his arm across her shoulders. The heat of his body penetrated her side despite the cold air wafting through the lobby. But that didn't let him off the hook. She batted her eyelashes and cooed at him as he kissed her cheek.

"Yes, we do. I'm sure you can find some other way to entertain yourself, Keisha."

When Uncle Matt came over from the reception desk, they said their goodbyes and followed the porter toward the bank of elevators. As soon as her family was out of earshot, Jordan shrugged out from under Danny's arm.

"What in the world do you think you're doing, 'David'?"

Danny looked around and lowered his voice. "Can we go somewhere and talk about this?"

"Fine, Shula's Steak House is right there across the lobby."

"No, I think we need more privacy. Let's go to my place. It's in Mount Vernon."

Jordan hesitated for a second then realized she'd be perfectly safe with him. "Okay. I'll follow you."

After retrieving her car from the valet, she followed Danny's Jeep along Baltimore Street then turned left on Charles. For the next eight blocks, she tried to sort out the reasons for her eagerness and anxiety. She had no idea what had possessed Danny to pretend to be his brother, nor was she certain of what he might ask for in return, but she appreciated it.

She grinned, remembering the look of jealousy on Keisha's face back at the hotel.

But now she was going to be alone with Danny, knowing for the first time who he was and exactly how much he turned her on. Though her mind was determined to doing nothing more than talk, her body was already singing the "Hallelujah Chorus." Maybe she wasn't so safe with him after all.

At Center Street, the traffic light changed and she took the opportunity to gaze at Mount Vernon Place. In the middle of the four gardenlike squares filled with fountains and statuary stood a 160-foot white marble column. This was the first monument dedicated to President Washington, completed nineteen years before the one in D.C.

When the light changed to green, she drove past the Walters Art Museum and glanced appreciatively over at the Peabody Conservatory of Music across the street. Jordan followed Danny's Jeep to Madison Street and turned left. He parked in front of one of the extravagantly detailed row homes and waited for her.

As she got out of the Honda, she looked around at the elegant neighborhood. A National Register Historic District, Mount Vernon was an eclectic mix of Georgian- and Federal-style house built between the late eighteenth and early twentieth centuries.

"Nice area. How can a fireman afford to live here?" While Danny punched in the code for the entrance, she couldn't help but smile at how incongruous the modern-day keypad looked on a traditional leaded-glass front door.

"Most of these places have been divided into apartments, so it's not as expensive as you think." He held the door for her then stepped inside. "But I still couldn't afford it without the trust."

"The what?" Jordan turned away from admiring the inlaid floor and paneled walls to look at him.

Danny scratched his head, his expression self-conscious. "Um, the money David and I inherited when we turned twenty-one."

"You guys are rich?" Jordan shook her head as she followed him up the main stairs to the second floor. "I'm beginning to think I don't know anything about my supposed fiancés."

"It's not something we go around bragging about. In fact, David almost never mentions it outside of our parents' social circle."

"Hmm, I just realized I've never heard David mention your family."

"We're not that close to our parents. Especially me. I've been the black sheep ever since I didn't follow in their legal footsteps." He pulled a set of keys out of his pocket and opened the door to his apartment. "Here we are."

She walked past him into a narrow entryway leading to a living room on her left. Everything from the hardwood floor to the plush area rugs and ten-foot ceilings was a warm earth tone in color. Overstuffed chocolate suede sofas were positioned in front of the biggest entertainment center she'd ever seen. All four walls displayed black lacquer-framed 1940s movie posters above blond wood shelves filled with books, music and DVDs.

Jordan loved the living room immediately. They shared a lot of favorite novels and films. It was easy, too easy, to imagine curling up with him on the couch and watching *Pillow Talk* or *His Girl Friday*. She turned to find Danny standing close behind her, his hands in his front pockets and his lips curved into a smile.

He looked perfect in this room, his dark brown curls and mocha skin just as warm and inviting as the room itself. She felt a magnetic force drawing her toward him and purposefully stepped back. No matter how attracted she was, and despite what had happened last night, she wasn't the type for casual sex.

"All right. Why the identity switch at the airport?"

Danny shifted from one foot to the other. "Are you hungry?"

"Hungry?" She wrinkled her brow, momentarily thrown off-balance. "I thought we were going to talk?"

"We can talk while we eat, can't we?" He shrugged, his hands still in his pockets, making him look boyishly handsome.

Jordan sighed heavily. "Fine. I did skip lunch today."

"What do you feel like?" Danny turned toward the kitchen.

She watched him walk down the hall, his stride easy and fluid, and his long, lean body filling out his jeans in a way that ought to be illegal. What did she feel like? She felt like leaving. Otherwise, she might rip off his clothes.

The small galley-style kitchen was spartan but everything was top quality. Black-and-white floor tiles complemented the granite sink and Jenn-Air stove and the white dishwasher and Sub-Zero refrigerator. The stovetop, microwave and toaster oven were spotless. The only appliance that looked used was the bright red state-of-the-art blender sitting on the countertop.

"I take it you don't cook much?"

Danny stood in front of a letter sorter, rifling through a collection of restaurant carryout menus. "No, but I eat a lot. How about Japanese?"

"Sounds good. Order me some tempura, please."

As soon as he hung up the phone, Jordan crossed

her arms and tried again to initiate the conversation they were supposed to be having. "Okay, Danny. We came to your place. We've ordered dinner. Now start explaining."

"It's simple enough. David couldn't get out of the office after all, and asked me to stand in."

She cocked her head to one side. "You had me drive all the way up here just to tell me that?"

"And so you'd have dinner with me."

His grin was incredibly charming, but she had to resist. Haywire hormones made it difficult to think straight. "Thank you for standing in. You won't have to again."

"That's fine with me. I don't do engagements."

"Neither do I. That's how I got myself into this situation. But in a couple of weeks I'll tell them the engagement is off."

He dipped his head, indicating the diamond ring she wore. "Wouldn't it be best if you just told your family the truth?"

Jordan immediately recalled the stunned delight on her aunt's face, the quiet pride on her uncle's, when they'd met her fiancé. Not to mention how smugly satisfying it had been to see Keisha speechless. "No, I'd rather not."

"Mind telling me why?"

She dropped her gaze to the floor. "Oh, you know how it is. There's always one person who gets picked on in every family. You get used to it over the years."

"But I'll bet you don't like it. I know I never have, no matter how good-natured it's supposed to be." When she looked up, Danny's expression was one of genuine empathy.

"Then you'll understand why I want my family to have a better image of me. I didn't mean to lie to them about the engagement, but their attitudes have changed. Especially now that they're finally meeting David."

An odd look crossed his features, erased before she could identify it. His tone was laced with curiosity. "How are you planning to pull this off?"

"It shouldn't be too hard. He only has to pretend to find me irresistible for about five events." Sarcasm gave her voice an edge. She longed to be part of a couple, to feel that she belonged to someone. But she wanted it to be real, not just a show she put on for her family.

Danny moved toward her with predatory determination, his dark eyes gleaming. "I wouldn't be pretending."

"What are you talking about?" Her pulse quickened as she backed away. This wasn't why she had come here tonight. Was it? Her hips suddenly bumped against the edge of the countertop, trapping her.

He braced a hand on either side of her, standing close enough for her to feel the heat radiating from his body. Her pulse leaped and thudded along her veins. Danny leaned forward, lowering his voice to an intimate level.

"You need a fiancé, Jordan. You also need a partner for the fantasies that come before and after number fifteen."

She felt heat rush up into her cheeks and slither down into her belly at the same time. Had she heard him correctly? Was he offering her the chance to explore the sensuality she'd discovered last night? Maybe they could try the Cook Up Something Hot and Delicious fantasy since they were already in the kitchen.

As she drew a shaky breath, his mouth came down to claim her. His kiss was soft and searching and she was shocked by her eager response. She didn't bother denying the raw excitement coursing though her body as he pressed closer. The iron band of Danny's arm enveloped her waist and held her against the bulge in the front of his jeans.

Hot desire pooled between her thighs. She was so turned on she could barely stand up. Jordan cupped her hands to his face, exploring the velvet warmth of his mouth. A soft moan escaped her throat as his hand slid up toward her breast. Then the doorbell rang.

Danny reluctantly broke the kiss while she tried to catch her breath. He smiled at her and pushed away from the countertop. "Saved by the delivery guy. I'll be right back. Why don't you grab the drinks?"

Oddly grateful for the momentary interruption, she went to the refrigerator. The chilled air felt wonderful on her flaming cheeks. One night of great sex had turned her into a shameless wench. When she opened her eyes, all she could do was stare at the sparse contents.

There was a gallon of milk, some cartons of yogurt, an assortment of fresh fruit and beer. Lots of beer. In all different shapes, sizes and nationalities such as Japanese Kirin, Jamaican Red Stripe, Chinese Qingdao, Indian Kingfisher and Greek Mythos.

When Danny came back into the kitchen, she shot him a questioning glance. He shrugged and reached around her for two tall silver cans of Kirin. "Food tastes better when you have the right beer to go with it. Come on into the dining room."

He led her across the hall into the pages of a fine-living magazine. A circular Persian carpet covered the hardwood floor beneath a polished dark maple table. The cut-crystal chandelier gleamed softly overhead. Six skirted chairs were sheathed in a rich damask fabric that echoed the reds and golds of the rug. An oak and glass breakfront cabinet stood against one wall and a large Impressionist oil painting hung above the matching server.

"This room is gorgeous, Danny. It's much more formal than the living room, though. Did you hire a decorator?"

"No, these pieces belonged to my grandparents. I have some good memories of them, so I keep the dining room the way Grandma used to."

Danny lit the white tapers in the pewter candlesticks on the table, creating an intimate atmosphere for the cardboard carryout food boxes. Women always appreciated atmosphere. He'd already laid out the rose-patterned china along with crystal tumblers for the beer. He held Jordan's chair before he sat down across the table.

She looked beautiful. The candlelight shed a warm glow over her golden skin and drew attention to the rich shade of her hair. His attraction was undeniable. Even sitting here sharing a perfectly innocent meal, his thoughts were anything but. Somehow, he was going to convince her to let him be both her fake fiancé and her lover.

"So, what do you think?"

Jordan kept her head down as she added more crisp fried vegetables to her plate. "It smells delicious."

"That's not what I meant."

"I know." She rubbed her chopsticks together to get rid of any splinters.

"Since there's a genuine attraction between us, it won't take much to convince your family that we're a couple."

"Why would you want to do this?"

He wasn't sure when the idea had come to him—this morning in her bedroom or this afternoon on the phone with his brother. But now that he'd discovered Jordan's wild side, he planned to explore it to the fullest.

"After last night, after that kiss in the kitchen, do you really have to ask?"

"So this is some kind of a sexual favor?"

He cocked his head to the side as though considering her question, then nodded. "Yeah."

She chose a fat, battered shrimp from the tray.

"Not that I'm agreeing, but what exactly do you want in return for faking an engagement?"

"You. Anytime. Anyplace. Anyway."

Jordan made a weird gulping noise, then choked as the shrimp lodged in her throat.

Immediately calling on his training, Danny jumped up and rushed around the dining table. He yanked her to her feet, knocking her chair backward, and wrapped his arms about her midsection. His fist was positioned at her diaphragm, ready to perform the Heimlich maneuver, when she managed to cough the shrimp free by herself.

He didn't move away, however, steadying her. He liked the way she felt in his arms, the way she leaned into him so that her breast rested against his bicep. As her breathing returned to normal and the bright color drained from her cheeks, she was able to stand on her own.

Her voice was slightly hoarse as she thanked him. "You can let me go now, Danny."

"Are you sure?" He smiled at her seductively. "You might need mouth-to-mouth resuscitation."

"My hero," she said as she eased out of his embrace. "But my dinner's getting cold and we need to talk about your…your…what the hell was that anyway?"

"A proposal." As soon as the word left his mouth, he balked. "No, wait, not a proposal. I mean, this isn't a real engagement. We'll just be faking for a couple of days."

"Well, then, let's call it a proposition."

Now that was more like what he had in mind, despite her courtroom tone of voice. Fun and games and no commitments. Danny widened his smile and moved to take her into his arms again, but she planted a hand on his chest to stop him.

"How about we use the word *agreement?* Except that I haven't agreed to anything yet, Danny."

Jordan reached down to grab her chair and set it upright. Then she settled onto the seat, leaving him standing there feeling dismissed. Danny sighed and, since she was no longer in danger of asphyxiating, went back to his sushi. He picked up his chopsticks and speared a spicy tuna roll.

"Listen, Jordan, I do want to help you out, but I have to tell you that my motives are purely selfish." She looked at him in surprise. "I want to be with you again."

She dropped her focus and squirmed on her seat. But her downward-tilted head couldn't hide the faintest of smiles. That smile made him resolve to buy his own copy of the *Fifty Fast Fantasies* book he had noticed this morning. Somewhere beneath her polished exterior beat the sensual heart of a woman who had forty-nine more reasons to agree to his plan.

Jordan pushed the tempura around her plate. "So, you're saying I have to sleep with you to get your help. Why should I? Your brother already said he'd play the part."

"You don't have to. But I know you want to."

Jordan blushed and her tone became defensive. "Could you be any more arrogant?"

"Did you think I wouldn't notice the way you look at me? Let's be honest here. Last night was fantastic. There's a lot of heat between us, and since we're both adults, there's no reason not to enjoy it."

She sat back and finally looked at him. A slight frown tugged at her mouth. Danny felt the first stirrings of disappointment and waited for her to refuse his offer.

It wasn't as if he'd never been turned down before but, for once, he wasn't going to take no for an answer. Not from Jordan. Not from a woman so eager to explore her sensuality that she'd buy a guidebook and follow the instructions. After everything they'd already done together, he didn't think he was rushing her.

"Jordan, why don't we—"

"Okay."

"Um, excuse me?" Taken aback, he paused with a piece of abalone halfway to his mouth.

"I said, okay. Another night together in exchange for a few performances."

Her voice sounded resigned, but there was a glimmer of interest in her light brown eyes, which confused him. Did she really want to do this? He sure hoped so. But he had no intention of being a two-night stand.

"Uh-uh. Not just another night. If I'm going to commit to ten days, give or take, then so are you."

She didn't answer directly. "Give or take?"

"Baltimore City's firefighters work on a rotation schedule. I do two nights, then two day shifts followed by four days off."

"Oh, this won't work then—"

He chuckled. "Don't sound so relieved. I don't have to be back at the station until Sunday afternoon, so I can take David's place this weekend."

Jordan had stopped eating a while ago, but her beer glass was almost empty. Funny, he would have figured her for the white-wine type. But alcohol was alcohol when you needed to boost your courage. Even from across the table, he could see the tension in her posture and the rapid rise and fall of her spectacular chest.

"So how about it, Jordan. Are you up for the challenge? A favor in exchange for some fantasies?"

Although bright spots of color appeared on her face, he knew that she wasn't choking this time, just battling her good-girl conscience.

"We have a *Fridays After Five* behind-the-scenes tour of the National Aquarium tomorrow."

He felt a grin split his face. It wasn't, "Okay, Danny. I can't wait to get you back in bed." But it was an *agreement* just the same.

She continued as if she didn't notice his triumphant smile. "Saturday is the barbecue at my parents' house in Annapolis. Monday night we're going to Obrycki's for crabs and on Wednesday, the Orioles play the New York Yankees. And, of course, my grandparent's golden anniversary party is the night of the eighteenth."

"I work the night shift on Monday, so I can't join you for crabs. I can probably leave a little early on Wednesday, though, to go to the baseball game."

Jordan cleared her throat and folded her hands on the table. "That's only four events so you only get four...encounters."

"*Encounters?* Do you have to talk like a lawyer?"

"What's the problem? Your brother is a lawyer."

"So are both of my parents and they can't speak plain English, either." Danny rested his arm along the back of the dining chair. "Just say I get four sessions of hot, uninhibited fantasy sex. I'll even let you choose the fantasies, but remember, they'll have to be spontaneous."

Jordan stared at him, her brows arching in disbelief. "You were serious about that 'anytime' stuff?"

"Absolutely."

"I've got to go."

She shot to her feet and made a production of clearing the table. The take-out boxes were nested inside of one another before she stacked the empty plates and gathered the linen napkins. Danny caught her arm, preventing her escape to the kitchen. He took the plates from her and set them back on the table.

"Leave the dishes. I'll take care of them. Right now, I want to know which number comes next."

"What?"

"If last night was fantasy number fifteen..." He placed a hand on either of her hips and drew her close. "Then do you want to go up the list—" he slid his palms toward the underside of her breasts "—or work your way down?" He bumped her pelvis to punctuate the question.

Her breath was audible now and he felt her nipples bead against his chest through the fabric of her blouse and his shirt. Moist and pink and slightly parted, her lips begged for his kiss. Her maple syrup-colored eyes darkened as she held his gaze. Jordan's hands came up to caress his shoulders and her thigh pressed between his, teasing the placket of his jeans. She leaned closer, tilting her head up to whisper in his ear.

"You'll have to wait to find out. Our ten days don't start until tomorrow."

8

THE BEST WAY to seduce a woman was to get inside her head and figure out what she really wanted. As soon as he saw Jordan safely to her car, Danny headed for the nearest bookstore to find a copy of *Fifty Fast Fantasies.*

Twenty minutes later, he felt as though he was back at school, studying for a particularly challenging test. Then again, his homework had never been like this. His pulse thudded down his body until it became a dull throb in his groin as he stood in the Sex & Relationships section of Barnes & Noble. This stuff was hot!

As he read the chapter titles, he didn't know whether to laugh or drive straight to Jordan's house. Him Tarzan, You Tempting had possibilities if he could figure out how to rig up some vines. And Hey Lady, Check Your Oil? might be fun if he didn't mind scratching the hood of his car.

"Can I help you with anything, sir?"

He looked up from the pages to see a kid wearing a store name tag and a smirk. The clerk's attention darted to the book title and back again. Danny shook his head. "No, thanks. I found what I wanted."

The kid's grin got wider as he turned away. "That's a popular find lately."

Left alone, he flipped to the next page in the book. Jordan would look great in a French maid's uniform. He could easily picture her wearing a little black ruffled dress and a short white apron and nothing else. But something told him she hadn't bought this guidebook looking for adventurous sex.

If he'd guessed right, Jordan just wanted to shed some of her inhibitions. From what David had told him and what he'd observed around her family, she was a quiet, responsible woman who worried too much about what other people thought of her. Even last night, she'd initiated the idea for the Strangers For One Night fantasy but hadn't carried out all of the details.

Jordan didn't need props or gimmicks. All she needed was a compassionate lover to encourage her and give her the freedom to be adventurous. Danny looked at the introduction page again and read the words "Be Spontaneous." He could do that. But what about a woman who color-coded her wardrobe?

He took his copy of *Fifty Fast Fantasies* to the checkout counter and pulled out his wallet.

"I HOPE DAVID CAN JOIN us this time."

Angela Gregory looked at her daughter expectantly even as Jordan's father, Jackson, looked at his watch. Her parents had only met David once, when they'd come to the law firm to take her out for a birthday lunch. He'd had a court appearance and couldn't join them, much to her parents' disappointment.

Jordan swallowed her nervousness and smiled weakly at her mother. "I'm sure he'll be here."

The laugh lines that usually surrounded her father's light brown eyes were absent as he studied her. "If you're sure we should wait…"

"He's not even late yet, Daddy."

"Hmm." He made a noncommittal noise before wandering over to look at the USS *Torsk,* a World War II submarine anchored near the aquarium.

Mom reached for her hand and gently squeezed her fingers until Jordan looked at her. Though partly attributed to good bone structure, the majority of her mother's beauty came from a kind heart. Right now, she had an air of sadness. "Your father is only saying that David has had to cancel at the last minute several times before."

"He's a criminal attorney, Mom. Sometimes cases or clients require last-minute attention."

"I just hope that he's paying enough attention to *you.*" Her lips tightened in a familiar expression of maternal concern. Then her brow cleared and she kissed Jordan's cheek before she went to join Uncle Matt and Aunt Celeste at the sea lion pool.

Jordan stood alone, willing the tension from her muscles and releasing the breath she held. The sooner she ended this fake engagement, the better. Her parents had been so happy that she was involved with someone, but now, because of her fabrications, they believed her "fiancé" neglected her and didn't want to meet them. Her anxiety grew as she waited for Danny. She just knew something would happen to reveal her lies.

Jordan stifled a yawn. She'd come straight from the office after a long day and an even longer night. She'd lain in bed until the wee hours, skimming the guidebook and analyzing the feasibility of the most appealing scenarios.

Not that she really believed Danny's outrageous condition to their agreement. There was no way she was going to give in to what basically constituted blackmail. And yet, she found herself wondering whether she should carry a bag of props around in case the opportunity for Doctors Do Make House-calls came up.

Needless to say, she'd gotten very little sleep the night before, fantasizing about how gorgeous Danny would look in a pair of chaps and a Stetson. She wanted to see him wearing his firefighter uniform, too, since she hadn't really seen him before. Jordan focused on the man walking toward her and smiled. Danny actually looked best in jeans and a casual shirt.

As Jordan watched him approach, she felt an instant fluttering in her belly followed by a warm rush of desire. How could she ever have mistaken him for his brother, even in the dark? Danny had a relaxed air of masculine confidence that David hadn't mastered. That self-assurance was evident in his stride, in the set of his broad shoulders and the easy smile lighting his face.

His dark brown eyes met hers and held and she suddenly felt like the only woman in the world. He was looking at her as if she were *his* woman. The quiver in her belly dropped lower with each step he took to close the distance between them.

"Hi, baby."

Danny slipped his arm around her waist, his fingers stroking her back unseen beneath her jacket. When he leaned down, she didn't know what to expect and so wasn't prepared for him to seal his mouth over hers with such intensity.

What was supposed to be a sweet kiss of greeting turned into a declaration of desire when he darted his tongue between her lips. Heat gathered at her core and quickly spread, leaving her off balance and breathless when he pulled away.

She wanted him. Oh, how she wanted him. Right here and right now and… Amusement and understanding mingled in his expression as Danny shot a glance toward her family. Embarrassed, Jordan cleared her throat and faced her parents.

"Mom, Daddy. You remember, uh, David?"

Her father looked bemused, then offered his hand. "Of course, of course. How's it going?"

"Nice to see you, sir." Danny nodded to her mother. "How are you, Mrs. Gregory?"

"Fine, thank you." She eyed his cherry-red knit shirt with a smile. "I thought, coming from work, you'd be in a suit like my daughter."

Danny didn't miss a beat as he lied. "I was out of the office this afternoon, so I stopped home to change."

Afraid to give her parents time to begin a more in-depth conversation, and even more afraid "David" might trip up, Jordan hustled everyone toward the escalator. "Well, it's just after five o'clock. We should probably start the tour. Ready, everyone?"

"More than ready." Keisha's gaze slithered over Danny, a sly smile on her brightly painted mouth as she flipped her perfectly styled hair. She raked a glance over Jordan before looking away. The smirk on her cousin's face clearly issued a challenge.

Jordan narrowed her eyes at Keisha, then took Danny's hand as they all went up to the front entrance. The warmth of his skin rushed along her nerves when he gently squeezed her fingers. He quirked an eyebrow and gave her a mischievous grin.

"What about you? Are you ready?"

She gasped. Ready for what? He wouldn't try "anything" here, would he? Her parents were right in front of them, her aunt and uncle directly behind and Keisha was trying to mold herself to Danny's other side. She sent him an inquiring glance but his attention was on the sixteen floor-to-ceiling bubble tubes decorating the aquarium's lobby.

As soon as her father showed his family membership card and signed the others in as his guests, he and her mother headed for the first-floor exhibit hall. They had started to follow when Aunt Celeste touched her arm.

"Where can I powder my nose?"

Jordan pointed to the left. "If you go down that side passageway—"

Danny interrupted. "Why don't you just show her where it is? We can wait."

Celeste called out to Jordan's parents. "Angela! Jackson! We'll meet you upstairs."

Jordan continued to escort her aunt to the door of the rest rooms across from the coat check desk. Behind them, Keisha let out an exaggerated sigh of impatience. Uncle Matt cocked his thumb over his shoulder.

"I'm going to the gift shop down the hall there. Just grab me when you're ready."

Aunt Celeste frowned. "I won't be that long, Matthew."

Her husband all but rolled his eyes. "You're wearing panty hose in ninety-degree weather. I'll be in the gift shop."

Celeste made a face at him then went inside the ladies' room. Keisha crossed her arms and leaned against the wall, lost in her own sulking thoughts.

Danny held out his hand to Jordan. "Why don't you take off your suit jacket and I'll go to the coat check for you."

"Thank you. It is hot in here."

He glanced up at the air-conditioning vents and smiled knowingly. Standing behind her, he gallantly helped her remove the lightweight blazer, revealing her sleeveless peach-colored blouse. As she started to turn, Danny caressed her bare arms and leaned down to whisper in her ear. "While you're in the ladies' room, why don't you take off your panties as well?"

She angled her head to hiss at him. "Are you crazy?"

"*Anytime, anyplace,* remember?"

"There is no way—"

He brushed his lips against her earlobe. "We have a verbal contract, counselor."

Equal parts anxiety and excitement constricted her throat, making her voice sound strangled. "You can't seriously expect me to—"

From the opposite side of the hall, Keisha snapped at her. "Would you just go already?"

Danny gave her a subtle pat on the bottom. "Don't take too long, baby. I'm anxious to get started."

Inside the rest room, Jordan checked to see which stall her aunt was occupying then chose one as far away as possible. She closed the door and stared blindly at the vinyl floor tiles. Was she actually going to do this? Her heart beat erratically in her chest and her fingers trembled.

Jordan reached under her skirt and hooked her thumbs in the waistband of her blue cotton panties. How was she going to become sexy and desirable without being adventurous? The guidebook said sensual, naughty and fun, so that's what she was going to be, damn it. Wiggling her hips, she slipped them down her legs then leaned over to tug them over her heels. Now, where to put them?

She folded the panties into a small, flat square

and jammed them into her purse, grateful she hadn't followed the current trend of carrying microbags that didn't have space for more than a wallet and set of keys. She left the stall and went to wash her hands.

Aunt Celeste smiled at her in the mirror as she freshened her lipstick. "That David sure is easy on the eyes. If anyone had told me years ago that you of all people would get yourself such a fine-looking young man, I'd have thought they were crazy."

Jordan turned away from her aunt's reflection to snatch a paper towel from the holder. She didn't believe Celeste meant to hurt her, but somehow she'd managed. With one sentence, she'd reminded Jordan of both her miserable, overweight past and the fact that she didn't really have a man like "David."

Celeste ran a comb through her silver hair, unaware of Jordan's distress. "But look at you now! Just as pretty as you can be and so obviously in love. I'm happy for you, sweetheart."

Jordan merely smiled.

Celeste cocked her head to one side. "Let's go look at some fish."

When she followed her aunt out of the ladies room, the first thing she saw was Keisha's hand stroking Danny's arm. Her cousin was flirting for all she was worth, smiling and purring in his ear.

Old feelings of insecurity mingled with an unexpected stab of jealousy. Of course her cousin was the kind of woman Danny would be attracted to. Keisha was slender and sexy and beautiful. Jordan couldn't compete with her glamorous cousin.

Then she glanced at Danny's face and realized he looked bored and annoyed. To her surprise, he wasn't returning Keisha's interest at all and when he saw her, he sent Jordan a smile so genuine and welcoming that all she could do was stare.

Aunt Celeste snapped, "Now, Keisha, you let that man alone and go get your father."

Keisha's expression darkened for a moment but she grudgingly complied.

Celeste let out a long-suffering sigh. "Don't mind her, you two. For some reason that child has always wanted whatever Jordan had, be it toys or boys."

Danny put his arm around her and smiled. "Well, she can't have me. I'm spoken for."

He glanced down the hall as Uncle Matt and Keisha returned, then brushed a tender kiss on her forehead. Jordan's heart swelled with gratitude as Aunt Celeste winked at her. Even if this whole thing was a charade, she truly appreciated Danny's efforts to make their engagement seem real.

Now that the family had regrouped, Jordan led the way toward the first display, Wings in the Water. Danny tugged her hand as they walked across the lobby. "Well?"

"Well, what?"

"Did you?" He arched one eyebrow as if to ask whether she'd actually taken off her panties.

She sent him an enigmatic smile and didn't answer.

He nodded smugly. "You didn't do it."

Jordan widened her smile.

Danny stared at her in shocked amusement. "You really did? No, you didn't. Did you?"

She felt little bubbles of delight aching to burst forth into laughter. If she had to anxiously await his next move, wondering if he dared try to seduce her in front of her family, then he could suffer a little bit, too.

Standing on the balcony overlooking a two-hundred-thousand-gallon tank, they watched dozens of kite-shaped stingrays and mantas swoop gracefully around the pool below. Danny rubbed his thumb over her wrist and spoke softly so that only she would hear him.

"They look so fast and *slick* gliding through all of that *wetness*, don't they?"

A little shudder passed through her body, just as she was sure he'd intended with the sensual emphasis on certain words. Tiny bolts of electric awareness arced between them, making her ever more aware of her state of undress. The seduction had begun.

As they walked toward the escalator to the next level, they passed a large rectangular window with a concrete ledge. Keisha moved up to look inside, turned her head to try to get a better view. "What's supposed to be in here? I don't see—"

She jerked back as a mouthful of razor-sharp teeth appeared from the edge of the curved glass wall. The twelve-foot-long sand tiger shark flicked its tail and swam by. Keisha scowled in response to the family's laughter at her expense.

Staring at the gray nurse and lemon sharks,

Danny murmured in her ear. "Something that *big* and *powerful* is dangerous, but it's also kind of exciting."

Jordan laughed softly. "What an ego. You're not that big."

He winced and clutched his chest as if she'd wounded him.

Upstairs on level two, they found her parents in the Maryland: Mountains to the Sea gallery. Her father stood patiently by the Alleghany Pond display while her mother looked for painted turtles. Jordan smiled indulgently. Her father had only gotten the aquarium membership as a gift for her mom.

As Aunt Celeste dragged Uncle Matt and Keisha over to look for native diamondback terrapins in the Tidal Marsh, Danny guided her toward the Coastal Beach display. He stood close behind her, subtly rubbing his hip against her nearly bare bottom as they watched the tropical fish that traveled the mid-Atlantic current.

"I love the beach. It's so hot and sticky."

Jordan groaned, both at his lame innuendo and in response to the sensations he created. She was feeling pretty hot and sticky herself. Especially when he caressed a particularly sensitive spot at the back of her neck. It was one of the erogenous zones he'd discovered Wednesday night.

She and Danny followed the rest of the family upstairs to the Surviving Through Adaptation gallery. She barely noticed the displays of electric eels, giant octopus or lionfish. Her thoughts were on the way Danny's hands felt casually stroking her bare arm.

"Oh, look over here!" Aunt Celeste pointed excitedly at the sign for Phantoms of the Deep, a special exhibit of several different types of jellyfish.

Her mother and cousin followed, while her father and uncle headed upstairs to the Amazon River Forest, deeply engrossed in a heated discussion about the Orioles chances of winning tonight's baseball game.

Danny kept her back with a hand at the base of her spine. "Wait for a minute. Let them go through first."

Jordan slid a sideways glance at him, the hint of a smile touching her mouth. "What are you up to?"

"Nothing yet, but who knows what might happen once your family moves on."

His gaze traveled her body and she felt the look like a physical touch. A shiver of awareness battled with a twinge of apprehension. His intent couldn't have been clearer and the sensual side of her that he'd awakened the other night impatiently anticipated his touch, but the good girl in her was nervous about fooling around in a public place.

As soon as her family went upstairs, Danny led her into the darkened gallery. The walls, floor and ceiling of the alcove were pitch-black, highlighting the seven tanks against the back wall. Softly colored underlights differentiated the delicate and graceful jellyfish and emphasized the angles and planes of Danny's face.

He pulled her to him. "You have no idea how turned-on I am right now, knowing that this skirt is the only thing between me and your sexy body."

The husky edge of his voice resonated through her, even if she didn't believe his words. "I'm not—"

"Yes. You are."

Danny moved his hands up to her breasts, cupping their weight in his palms. His thumbs traced circles around her nipples, making her gasp and look around, afraid someone could see them. His head came down to capture her open mouth in a searing kiss. It was then that she felt the proof of his desire against her thigh. No longer caring if they got caught, she deepened the kiss with eager enthusiasm.

Danny slid his hands down to her waist, pushing her away slightly, before shifting his right hand to the hem of her skirt. His questing fingers delved beneath the fabric until he made contact with her bare skin. A heavy, aching need settled in her belly as his large palm caressed the curves of her bare bottom. Then he moved around her hip to touch the damp curls between her thighs.

The feel of his finger on her delicate flesh was a delightful shock, but after a few seconds, she relaxed and widened her stance. He rubbed lazy circles around her clitoris before dipping into her moist heat. She was on the edge, breathing hard against his mouth as her body tightened.

With a soft groan, she broke the kiss and tugged at her skirt. "I can't do this. Somebody could come."

"I'm hoping it will be you." He pushed a little deeper, making her wiggle against his hand.

A flame of desire ignited within her, burned away her inhibitions. He urged her on, increasing the sensual pressure until the slow, insistent throb became a deep pulsing tremor. Danny held her to his chest until her heart rate slowed and her legs stopped trembling. Then he kissed her once and adjusted her skirt back in place.

"Um, what about you?" Slightly self-conscious of her action, Jordan brushed her hand across the bulge in his jeans.

"All I wanted for now was for you to fulfill one of my fantasies. That was number six, by the way—Barely Behaving."

Instantly recognizing the scenario, Jordan let out a startled laugh. "I was wondering if you saw my book yesterday morning."

His wide smile gleamed in the multicolored lights. "I bought my own copy last night."

When they finally made it to the next level, Angela glanced over at them briefly, but Jordan wasn't fooled for a second. In that one instant, her mother's sharp eyes had taken in their intertwined hands, the bright color on her cheeks and the grin on Danny's face.

Her cousin noticed, too, but unlike her mother, Keisha was not at all pleased. Jordan knew it was petty, but she couldn't help a little jolt of satisfaction that for once *her cousin* was jealous of *her*. Reveling in the moment, Jordan planted a quick kiss on Danny's lips.

The best part of the National Aquarium was the Atlantic Coral Reef, a 335,000-gallon, circular four-level tank filled with vibrant tropical fish. As they slowly descended the series of ramps inside the silo, marveling at the vividly colored parrot fish, silver lookdowns and sparkling angelfish, Danny was so attentive and affectionate that Jordan had to keep reminding herself it was all an act.

When the tour was over, Daddy and Uncle Matt complained that looking at all of those fish had made them hungry. Her mother offered Danny a smile.

"Why don't you join us for dinner, David? We're only a few blocks from Little Italy." She turned her head. "Jackson, do you want to walk over to Velleggia's or Chiapparelli's?"

If she hadn't been focused on Danny's face, Jordan might not have seen the slight contraction of his features. Though his expression didn't change, she sensed his withdrawal. His brow crinkled in regret, but his tone held a note of insincerity.

"Sorry, everyone, but I can't make it. I've got a ton of work to do on the Gregg case."

Her father slapped him on the back. "It's Friday night, David. Surely it can wait until Monday."

Jordan had no choice but to support the fabrication. "Senior associates are expected to put in a six-day week, Daddy. If David is going to join us for the cookout, he'll have to make up the time."

"Well, if you're sure…" her mother began.

Danny smiled at her. "Thank you for the aquarium tour, Mrs. Gregory. I had a great time." He turned to give Jordan a hug. "I'll pick you up to-morrow, okay?"

She nodded and watched him walk away, confused by her sudden feeling of loneliness. It wasn't as if her real fiancé had just abandoned her. So why did it feel that way?

9

AT HALF-PAST EIGHT on a Saturday morning, Danny's Jeep was one of the few vehicles on the Baltimore city streets. On a normal day off, he would have slept until the growling in his stomach forced him out of bed. Today he'd risen with the sun, unable to get Jordan off his mind.

He had nothing to feel guilty about. This was only a fake engagement. It wasn't as if they were supposed to spend every single minute together. But he couldn't forget the way she'd looked at him as he left the aquarium. It would have been easier if she'd been angry. Instead, she'd looked crestfallen.

The idea of sharing a meal with the Gregorys had panicked him. Dinner around a single table would have been a dangerous opportunity for probing questions he wasn't prepared to answer. Sharing a meal would have made the charade all too real.

He'd never had to meet any of his other girlfriends' families. *Not* that Jordan was his girlfriend. They were barely even lovers. And yet, here he was, driving down St. Paul Street instead of sleeping.

Danny found a parking space and, recalling the

first time he'd stood on this front step, rang the door-bell. Fun and games, that's all this was. Several min-utes later, Jordan finally answered the door. She looked disheveled and annoyed. She looked beauti-ful. Her face had the sleepy glow of a woman who'd just left a warm bed and even warmer dreams.

As she poked her head through the opening, how-ever, her voice was frosty. "Do you have any idea what time it is?"

"It's *anytime*."

"Any what?"

He offered her a lazy smile. "In accordance with our agreement, counselor, let me in."

She groaned, scrubbing a hand over her face, and moved aside. "I thought you were picking me up for the barbecue."

Danny shrugged. "I am. I just didn't say how early."

"It's too early for sex." Jordan covered a yawn.

"I was afraid you were going to say that." He closed the door behind him. "Nice jammies."

That woke her up. Her eyes widened as she real-ized she had on purple jersey sleep pants and an or-ange T-shirt. She made a halfhearted attempt to cover herself with her arm then gave up the effort. "If you ever tell anybody you saw me wearing these, you're history."

"My lips are sealed." To prove it, he caught her into his arms for a fast kiss. She felt warm and soft and cuddly and he was glad he had followed his im-pulse to come over.

Jordan seemed flustered, combing her hands over her hair as she backed away from him. She gestured toward the living room. "Make yourself comfortable while I get dressed. I'll be down in a few minutes."

"You look great. Don't get dressed for my benefit. In fact, how about getting undressed?" He tried to put his hands on her hips and pull her to him, but she danced out of reach.

"The remote control is on the coffee table."

Danny affected a scowl and crossed his arms. "I think we have a breach-of-contract issue here."

"So sue me," Jordan called over her shoulder as she went up the stairs.

He sighed and wandered into the excruciatingly neat living room. Crystal lamps with embroidered silk shades cast a soft glow over the two blue velvet love seats. A stack of fashion magazines, neatly sorted by title and date, was piled on one of the end tables. Across the room, the movie cases were arranged alphabetically in the oak entertainment cabinet.

He wasn't exactly a slob, but the degree of Jordan's organization was kind of scary.

Danny flopped down on the couch and turned on the television. He surfed the channels for a minute, finally recognizing *All About Eve* on a classic movie station. By the time Bette Davis figured out that her rival had usurped her place on stage, he was wondering why Jordan was taking so long. When the credits rolled and another movie began, he decided he'd better check on her. He was just about to get up when he heard her come down the steps.

"Oh, *The Philadelphia Story*. I love Katharine Hepburn and Cary Grant in this one."

All he could do was stare. Her dark, thick hair was curled into sexy waves and she'd painted her face. Who the hell wore all of that makeup on a Saturday morning? She'd changed into a light cotton sweater and a pair of jeans. She looked ready to go to the barbecue, but a glance at the clock on the mantel told him they still had an hour and a half before they had to leave.

She sat down next to him on the love seat, her attention on the TV screen. Danny watched her more than he did the movie. Considering the type of women he usually dated, it surprised him that he preferred Jordan with crazy sleepwear and an unadorned face. She looked pretty now, but her natural beauty was better.

"I meant it when I said you looked great before."

"Yeah, right. With wild hair and a pale face and my neon jammies."

She tucked her feet beneath her and cuddled against his side. The warmth of her seeped into him as he draped his arm over her shoulders. Then he realized what he'd done. This little scene was too damned cozy. He felt discomfited by her closeness, by the casualness of the moment. This wasn't part of the deal.

Danny's pulse accelerated and he suddenly felt agitated. Remember the sex. Think about the sex. Maybe he should reach down and grope her breast. Or better still, just kiss her senseless and take her right on the couch. It had been a mistake to come over here. What the hell was he thinking?

"This is nice." Jordan smiled at him.

He suppressed a sigh and nodded his head. "Yeah."

"How about some breakfast?"

"Don't go to any trouble." Now this was really getting domestic.

She patted his stomach playfully. "Oh, it's no problem. Unlike you, I cook."

She hopped up and headed toward the kitchen. So there he was, sitting on the couch, watching a romantic comedy while the little woman cooked bacon. He felt entirely too at home, but there was no way he could leave. He'd just have to tough it out. Besides, a guy needed to eat.

Within fifteen minutes, Jordan returned from the kitchen with a covered serving tray. His stomach made itself loudly known, anticipating firehouse chow—fried eggs, sausage, potatoes. Instead Jordan lifted the cover with a flourish to reveal egg white omelets with turkey bacon and sliced tomatoes.

Yum.

Danny picked up his fork and poked at the food on his plate. She was still standing there anxiously so, not wanting to hurt her feelings, he speared a mouthful of white fluff with red and green specks and swallowed.

"Delicious. Thanks."

"I'm so glad you like it. Enjoy and finish watching the movie while I go get ready."

"Huh?" His brows drew together in confusion. "You're already dressed."

"Oh, I'm not wearing *this*."

Danny tapped the cushion of the love seat and tried the fake bacon. "Jordan, you look beautiful. Just get your plate and sit here and eat with me."

"It'll only take me a few minutes to change." Before he could stop her, she was headed back upstairs.

Knowing his arteries would thank him someday, Danny forced himself to finish breakfast. He was on his third classic film before Jordan reappeared, this time wearing a floral sundress. The short-sleeved dress ended just below the knee, showcasing her spectacular legs. She looked really pretty. In fact, she looked perfect. That was the problem.

As she grabbed what looked like a camera case from atop one of the shelves, she smiled over at him. "Are you ready to go?"

He arched one eyebrow and returned her gaze. "I don't know, Jordan. Do you think these tennis shoes go with my outfit? Maybe I should wear a different shirt."

She twisted her fingers together and unexpectedly offered him a glimpse behind her mask. For a second, she looked uncertain and nervous and very human. That absence of perfection made him want to wrap his arms around her and hold her until…until they had mind-blowing sex. Yeah, that's it.

"The barbecue today will be the first time my whole family meets David."

Danny aimed the remote to switch off the television. "What exactly have you told them about your *fiancé?*"

"As little as possible. I didn't want to get tangled up in the details." A flush appeared on her cheeks, heightening her sheepish expression. "I was able to dance around the family's questions last night at Velleggia's. We probably won't be so lucky today."

"Well, how am I supposed to act when we get there?" He ran a hand over his hair, feeling adrift and oddly resentful. As well as he knew his brother, he wasn't sure how long he could play David.

Her confident image was back in place as Jordan picked up her handbag. "Just be yourself."

DANNY PULLED up in front of the Gregory family home a few minutes past noon. The weathered gray-cedar Colonial sat on a manicured acre surrounded by mature trees. The front door and window shutters were painted a gleaming white. There was even a white picket fence. Bright green shrubs and cheery flowers lined the brick walkway. It looked like a typical single-family home in the suburbs of Annapolis.

Inside, however, chaos reigned.

The moment Jordan opened the front door, Danny was assaulted with music and voices and laughter. Danny hesitated before following her in. The activity seemed to be at the rear of the house, so when Jordan walked back to help in the kitchen, he ducked into the comparative quiet of the living room.

Similar to his parents' house, the furniture and décor were formal and yet Danny had an immediate sense that this living room was really lived in. The seat cushions all bore the indentations of the people who'd settled into them. Moisture rings showed against the dark wood of the coffee table. A tiny handprint marred the creamy paint on one wall. And everywhere he saw photographs proudly displayed.

His parents had a specially commissioned oil self-portrait over the Georgian fireplace mantel. They also had stiff photographs of David and him documenting their achievements in lengthy increments. He could still remember the way the starched collar itched his neck. As Danny looked at the candid group pictures of the Gregorys, his heart wrenched.

This picture showed the family outside of Radio City Music Hall in New York. That one portrayed them waving from the edge of the Grand Canyon. Here was a grinning, muddy bunch who'd just won a game of tug-of-war. There was a sodden, laughing group with tangled fishing rods and a tiny lake trout.

Feeling his throat close up, Danny had to acknowledge his jealousy. The joy of the moment and the pleasure of being together was evident on every face in every picture… Except one. His brows furrowed as he realized Jordan was nowhere to be seen.

"Are you ready to join the fray? Everyone is wondering where you are."

He turned to see her standing just behind him. "Where are the pictures of you? You're not in any of these."

She patted the 35mm Nikon hanging from her neck. "I'm the official event photographer. That means I have to be behind the camera."

Some instinct told him it was a responsibility she'd volunteered for, as opposed to being asked. "There must be some pictures of you as a kid?"

Jordan shook her head and affected a smile. "Nope. I got rid of all the ones I could find."

"You're telling me your parents don't have one single, solitary photograph of you?"

She pursed her lips and swept an arm across the room toward the baby grand piano. "They hide them over there."

Danny walked over to the Steinway to look at the grouping of silver frames. Far from being relegated to the corner, it looked more like a showcase. Her parents had displayed Jordan's achievements in a place of honor. The frames sat on a white linen cloth, arranged by height and angled so they could all be easily viewed.

Jordan's expression in her younger pictures was poignant. She looked ill at ease, pudgy and miserable among her slender and attractive siblings, as she received various awards. Even in her high-school-graduation photo she refused to smile. Danny leaned closer to see the gold tassel on her cap and the blue National Honor Society scarf around her neck. Her parents stood on either side of her, grinning happily and obviously proud.

"I like this picture the best." He indicated a group shot of high-school-aged kids in bright stage costumes. He recognized the play as John Waters's *Hairspray,* a musical about a heavyset girl who wants to be on a 1962 television dance program. And there was Jordan, front and center and actually grinning, dressed as Tracy Turnblad, the lead character.

"That was the senior-year production." She smiled softly, as if momentarily lost in good memories, then pointed to a different photo. "*This one* is my favorite."

Danny shifted his attention to a picture of her law-school graduation. She'd slimmed down a lot by the time this photo was taken. Her smile was beaming, her hair was swept up into some kind of braid and her makeup was flawless. She looked like an advertisement in a glossy university brochure.

Jordan turned away from the photographs. "If you've had enough of memory lane, I'll introduce you now."

Danny braced himself and followed her along the hallway deeper into the house. As with most parties, everybody gravitated toward the kitchen. This one opened onto a family room, so there had to be fifteen people positioned at the sink or stove or counter or just standing around.

"Everyone, this is David Navarro. David, you already know my mother and my aunt Celeste. The lady peeling potatoes is Aunt Geneva and the lady chopping celery is Aunt Meredith. Over here is Aunt Linda making her famous coleslaw, Aunt Joanne with the secret baked beans recipe and my cousins Whitney, Sarah and Carrie…"

Danny nodded in greeting but gave up trying to remember all of the names and hoped there wouldn't be a test later. Jordan had told him that her mother's side of the family would be here today too, however, he hadn't realized how big the Gregory-Maxwell clan was. Just as panic began to set in, someone pushed an ice-cold beer bottle into his hand.

"Thanks," he said gratefully to the only other man in the room. The guy was his height, though he had a slighter build, and he wore a sympathetic smile as he offered to shake hands.

"Hi, I'm Mason. These women can be over-whelming the first time. They'll give you the third degree, because they're not happy until they know who your first-grade teacher was, but you'll sur-vive, I promise."

Jordan gave Mason a playful slap on the arm. "I'm going to tell my sister you said that."

"Tell me what?"

At the sound of a husky female voice, Danny glanced behind him and froze in momentary shock. The classically beautiful face and sexy body of the woman next to Mason graced several posters in the locker room at the fire station. He just stared as he tried to locate what was left of his brain cells.

Mason chuckled knowingly. "Close your mouth, dude. She's already spoken for."

"Everyone reacts that way to meeting Camryn." Jordan's quiet, detached statement captured his attention. In her expression, Danny saw both love and resentment before her lashes swept down to shield her eyes. His mind instantly recalled the family photos and his heart broke for the girl she'd once been. He slipped his arm around her waist and drew her close, placing a gentle kiss on Jordan's temple.

"I reacted that same way when I first saw *you*."

Camryn grinned at him. "Welcome to the family, David."

"YOU HAVE TO ADD a whole teaspoon of chili powder, Matt. That's what gives it the kick."

"Shows what you know, Jackson. It's the hot sauce that adds the kick."

Danny smiled and took a swallow of his beer as he turned the chicken breasts over on the gas grill. Jordan's father and Uncle Matt had been arguing over who made the better barbecue sauce for almost twenty minutes now. They'd been so focused on the debate that he had taken over the cooking so the spareribs and hamburgers didn't burn to ash.

"Next you're going to tell me you use maple syrup instead of brown sugar."

"Humph. Only amateurs use maple syrup, Jackson. Us professionals use molasses and plenty of onion powder."

Jordan's father sputtered. "Powder! You can't substitute powder for freshly chopped onions! I can't talk to you." He turned and clapped a hand on Danny's shoulder. "You're doing an excellent job there, boy. Anybody would think you'd cooked for this mob before."

Danny chuckled. "I've had to feed fifteen to twenty hungry firefighters after a three-alarm blaze. It's not so different."

Jackson Gregory shot him an odd look. "When did you have time for that, what with your workload at the law firm?"

Damn. Realizing he'd screwed up, he bought himself a minute by transferring the grilled hot dogs onto a platter. "I used to volunteer at my local fire station."

Jordan's father continued to study him, then finally smiled and changed the subject. Danny silently released the breath he'd been holding. He hadn't lied—he had volunteered before entering the Maryland Fire & Rescue Institute—but he hadn't been completely honest, either. With an unexpected bitterness, he resigned himself to half-truths for the next seven days.

JORDAN LEANED BACK in her lawn chair, enjoying the late-afternoon sun on her face. She felt…content. This was the first family gathering she could remember where she had a sense of belonging. She should probably be upset because Danny was the reason for the change in everyone's attitude. But right now she couldn't drum up the energy.

Danny, on the other hand, seemed to have nothing but energy. Jordan watched him charge across the lawn with a football clutched under his right arm and three little kids hanging tightly to the left. Just before they reached the makeshift goal line, Danny mysteriously stumbled.

The ball popped out from under his arm and was quickly snatched up by her eight-year-old nephew Lukas, who sprinted in the opposite direction. No one on Danny's team bothered to stop him—they were too busy roughhousing on the grass.

Camryn reached over to squeeze her hand. "He's a great guy. I'm really happy for you."

It was nice to have someone for a change, someone her family obviously adored. It would be even nicer if it were real. A dark void of loneliness opened within her, but Jordan simply smiled. "Thank you."

Danny finally begged out of the football game, claiming age and exhaustion and beer deprivation, until the kids let him up. He got to his feet, looking grass-stained and utterly gorgeous, and headed toward the patio. Instead of coming over to her, though, he went to sit in on her grandparents' card game.

Camryn laughed as Grandma Emma and Grandma Margaret argued over who got to be Danny's bridge partner. "This one is definitely a keeper, Jo-Jo."

Sure he is. For seven more days.

Later that night, Jordan snuggled into the leather front seat of the Jeep as Danny drove north on I-97 back to Baltimore. She felt tired, both physically and emotionally. Maintaining a false impression required a lot of mental energy. "I can't believe it's after nine o'clock already."

"Get-togethers with my family are always quiet, structured and mercifully short."

She shifted her gaze out the side window, inexplicably hurt. "I'm sorry you had to put up with—"

"No, what I meant was that I liked being with your family a lot better than my own. David and I both look on those visits as an obligation instead of a pleasure."

"Well, they sure seemed to like you, too. Keisha must have spent most of the day trying to get you to notice her." She grimaced, remembering her cousin's transparent attempts at flirtation.

"She was trying too hard. I prefer women who don't feel the need to advertise." Danny glanced over with a smile and reached for her hand. "Other than having to avoid Keisha, it's been a great day."

The warmth of his touch sent a wave of longing coursing through her body. This moment felt so comfortable, so relaxed, so right. They could be any normal couple leaving a family event.

"Yes, it was a nice day, wasn't it?" One based entirely on her lies and fallacies.

"It's easy to see why your grandparents lasted fifty years. I swear your Grandpa Charles patted Grandma Emma on the butt when he thought no one was looking."

Jordan laughed. "I'm sure he did. I caught them smooching like teenagers in the study. Luckily I found them just before my brother Reece walked in. He would have teased them for the rest of the day."

"I liked your brothers, too. Despite Eric trying to

decapitate me with the volleyball. You've got a terrific family, Jordan."

"Thank you for being nice to them. I'd say today
was a success. Everybody believed you were
David."

She felt the slightest tension in his hand before
he slid his fingers away. In the silence that followed,
he abruptly flicked the turn signal and changed
lanes. He cleared his throat before he finally replied
in an animated voice.

"Good. That's what we wanted."

Yep. That's what they wanted. That's *all* they
wanted. And the rest was just physical. How else
could she explain what she was feeling? Danny had
helped her awaken her sensual side. He'd compli-
mented and flirted with her all day, making her feel
pretty and desirable. She wasn't ready for that to
end. But she wasn't sure how to ask to be with him.
Then again, she didn't have to ask. Their agreement
could work both ways.

"You know what I want now?"

"What's that?"

Jordan quietly inhaled and tentatively placed her
fingers on his denim-clad thigh. "The *anytime* we
didn't have this morning."

10

STARTLED, DANNY involuntarily jerked the steering wheel. The Jeep careened toward the next lane and, when he turned the wheel again, he overcorrected. He laughed self-consciously as another vehicle honked its horn at them.

"You sure know how to get a guy's attention."

"Watch the road so we'll get back in one piece." Jordan patted his leg in admonishment.

"Then watch where you put your hands. At least until we get to my place." Not only did she leave her hand where it was, she moved it a few inches higher, tracing sensual patterns along his thigh. He responded with a look that could have melted steel. "Tease."

Maybe she was teasing, but she seriously wanted him. Her breasts ached for the feel of his mouth; her body throbbed in anticipation of making love with him. She felt proud of taking the initiative and yet wondered if she'd have to make the decisions for the rest of tonight. She was on her way to becoming a bona fide seductress, but she didn't know exactly what to do with him.

A familiar yearning lurked on the edge of her mind. She wanted…don't be stupid. This arrangement was temporary and so were these feelings. Mentally she flipped through the pages of *Fifty Fast Fantasies,* then smiled to herself as she chose one she thought she could handle. Jordan furtively reached into her handbag.

Danny parked the Jeep in front of his building. Upstairs, she slipped off her jacket and left it with her purse in the living room. She followed him into the kitchen, where he opened the refrigerator and handed her a bottle of Jamaican lager. "Shall we retire to the veranda, my dear?"

"What a lovely idea."

Jordan stepped through the back door and onto the fire escape. She chose one of the two wrought-iron chairs and set her Red Stripe beer on the small table next to a dead ficus tree. Obviously he watered his plants as often as he cooked. The night sky had clouded over and the air was ripe with humidity. It felt hot and steamy, perfect weather for a seduction.

Danny settled onto the blue paisley cushion of the seat next to her. "So, you're initiating the 'anytime, anyplace' rule. Did you have a particular fantasy in mind, or did you just want to wing it?"

"*Wing it?* That's really romantic, Danny."

He shrugged. "Our agreement isn't about romance. So who am I supposed to play tonight?"

She stared at him, but he didn't return her gaze. His relaxed posture seemed feigned. Was he upset about pretending to be his brother at the barbecue?

She didn't understand why, since the whole thing had been his idea. Jordan ignored the edge in his voice and purposefully misinterpreted the question.

"I'm not really in the mood for international spies or plumbers. I was thinking we'd try something different."

"How different? My space suit is at the cleaners and I don't own a horse."

She laughed and made a face. "Not that different. I thought we could play Hide In Plain Sight."

Danny looked around as if he expected to see all of his neighbors watching from their own balconies. "Are you crazy? Somebody might see us."

Jordan elevated one eyebrow and cocked her head. "Oh, so it's okay for you to fondle me in a public place when my family is nearby—"

He raised an open palm to interrupt. "Okay, you're right. But we don't have any protection out here."

Jordan reached up with her right hand, leisurely trailing her fingers toward her cleavage. Danny's eyes narrowed and focused on the movement, lingering on her breasts as her hand dipped inside her dress. She grinned while retrieving the condom that she'd slipped into her bra.

"How's this for spontaneity?"

"Not bad. Not bad at all."

She liked the way his eyes crinkled when he smiled, the heat in them as he looked at her. He came over to stand in front of her, reaching down to help her to her feet. She wrapped her arms around his neck and brushed her lips over his. His hands grasped her hips and pulled her closer until her breasts flattened against his chest. A light drizzle began to fall, the droplets evaporating on the heat of her skin.

His mouth opened beneath hers, welcoming her tongue as she explored and savored the taste of him. Her pulse thudded along her veins while her whole body vibrated with need. As he deepened the kiss, she felt his fingers gathering the material of her skirt until he'd lifted the front high enough to skim the edge of her panties. His fingers slipped inside the waistband and eased them over her hips.

Her panties slid down to her ankles and she stepped out of them, never breaking contact with his mouth. She moaned as he cupped her breast through the light cotton dress, gently rubbing her pelvis across the hard heat of his erection. Dampness flooded the apex of her thighs. God, how she wanted him. She clasped the sides of his face and gave him a kiss that branded his taste onto her lips.

Danny maneuvered them until they had reversed positions, then reached between their bodies to unzip his jeans. She tugged the placket open until she could take him in her hand. His penis was long and thick and throbbing and she ached to feel him inside of her. He broke the kiss in order to protect them and sat down.

Jordan shifted her skirt out of the way and settled on his thighs facing him, her legs dangling on either side of the chair. Had anyone been watching, they would have appeared to be doing nothing more than kissing in the rain. He bent his head to nibble the side of her neck, his voice a low growl in her ear.

"Mmm, you taste delicious."

She shrugged, giggling as she tried to dislodge his mouth from the tender spot on her throat. "Didn't you eat enough at the barbecue?"

"I never get enough of you."

Jordan leaned back and speared him with a look. "Does that line actually get you anywhere?"

"You're sitting on my lap, aren't you?" His expression was just this side of arrogant.

"Good point." She tilted her head and smiled at him. "What are you going to do about it?"

"Come a little closer and I'll show you."

With Danny's hands on her waist, she gripped the cool iron of the chair back while he guided his penis to the slick wetness of her passage. He entered her in one smooth motion, merging their bodies in the gathering darkness. Her eyelids drifted shut as her head fell back and she trembled with desire. Rocking his hips, he began moving in a deliberate, sensuous rhythm. She braced her heels on the fire escape and held on for the ride.

It was raining harder now, water poured down on them in rivulets, but Jordan couldn't have cared less. She felt wild and wanton, making love outdoors where anyone who looked out of their window might catch them. The illicitness of what they were doing was as much a turn-on as the man she was with. She opened her eyes, wanting to watch his face.

A rush of ice swept through her and she faltered.

Even in the dim light, she could see the detachment. Despite the obvious physical evidence of his desire, Danny seemed more intent on pleasuring her than in sharing the excitement of the fantasy. Something told her instinctively that he was holding back in more ways than one. Suddenly the rain felt like stinging needles on her bare arms and thighs.

"I'm getting cold."

He hesitated and she wondered if her expression told him how miffed she was. "Yeah, me too. Let's go in."

Jordan started to lift herself off of him when she realized the heel of her left sandal was jammed into the grate. As she tried to pry her foot loose, Danny groaned and she suddenly realized that she was wriggling on his lap. Damn it! She was trying to end this sexual encounter, not prolong it. With a jerk, she wrenched the shoe free and stood up. In three strides she was back in the kitchen, dripping puddles onto the black-and-white tiles.

Danny grabbed a paper towel from the counter and wiped his face while she steamed, both literally and figuratively. Her clothes were soaked and plastered against her body. She was cold and she was angry and she was just about to let him have it when he looked over at her.

"Why don't you take off that dress?"

Why don't you go to hell? I'm through playing for one night. Jordan scowled at him, but didn't say it out loud.

Danny sighed and tossed the balled-up towel into the trash can. "I meant, you should get out of that wet dress and go take a hot shower."

"Oh." She felt heat stealing into her cheeks and welcomed the warmth as her teeth began to chatter.

He led her down the hall to the bathroom. After flicking on the light, he turned to her and tapped the wall. "There's a robe hanging right here and the towels are clean. I'll put your dress in the dryer for you."

Slipping past him, Jordan partially closed the door. She peeled the wet cotton from her body, handed it to him through the crack and shut the door with a resounding click. She dialed on the water and waited for it to heat. Stepping under the spray, she took off her panties and rinsed them out before hanging them over the shower rod.

Fifteen minutes later, her skin pink now instead of blue, Jordan dried off and finally noticed the bathrobe. It was a delicate yellow flannel and obviously meant for a woman. She couldn't imagine Danny in anything with lace cuffs. She stared at it, wondering how many others had worn it before, and tucked the ends of the bath towel around her chest.

She walked across the hall, uncomfortable about being in the intimate setting. Danny was reclining on the bed, his long legs crossed at the ankle, his elbow propped on the copper-and-black geometric spread. He'd stripped off his wet clothes and now wore only a towel around his waist.

"Your clothes aren't dry yet, Jordan. As soon as

they are, I'll drive you home." He got up and offered her a smile that missed his eyes by a mile. "I hope you left me some hot water."

When he walked out, she clutched the towel a little tighter, wondering what to do. There was no way she was going near that bed, but there was nowhere else to sit. So she remained standing as she looked around the dimly lit room. It was warmly decorated and yet minimalist. The furnishings were pale wood, modular with clean lines and a European feel.

Curious, she walked over to the bookcase to look at the unusual light sitting on top. She'd never seen anything like it before. The translucent rock was cool to the touch, but it cast a soft orange glow over the cream-colored walls.

"It's salt."

Jordan startled at the sound of Danny's voice behind her. "It's what?"

"It's a lamp made out of a hunk of rock salt. A stewardess friend brought it back from Germany." He opened the top drawer of the dresser and pulled out a pair of boxer briefs. Reaching beneath the damp bath towel, he struggled to put them on. "Next time, give a guy a little warning. I smacked myself in the face with your panties when I got into the shower."

He had a beautiful back—cappuccino-colored skin stretched over lean muscle. But as he moved about, the light shone in such a way that the scarring she'd noticed before looked worse.

"How did you get hurt, Danny?"

In the past, when someone asked about the scar tissue on his upper back, he'd simply said, "Line of duty," and left it at that. So he had no idea why he turned around, braced both palms on the edge of the dresser and told her, "I was assigned to Fairfax County Fire and Rescue on September eleventh."

He heard her soft intake of breath but didn't look at her, concentrating instead on the soft orange glow of the rock light. "I remember it was a beautiful Tuesday morning. The sun was shining and it was just a gorgeous day."

"You—you were at the Pentagon."

"VATF-One is one of the most experienced urban search-and-rescue squads in the country. Because of flight time, we could have been in New York City in a matter of hours. We were all ready to go up and help when that plane slammed into the Pentagon."

"Oh, Danny. Omigod."

"We thought, 'We're going to get people out alive. The Pentagon is so close we've got a great chance of finding survivors.'" He hunched his shoulders, crossing his arms over his chest, and stared at the carpet. "When we got there, pieces of the plane littered the ground near the heliport. The vehicles posted there were on fire. I'll never forget that. The Pentagon fire trucks were on fire."

Jordan made a little choking noise and he glanced over to see her hand covering her mouth beneath eyes damp with unshed tears.

"It was weird, you know. I mean, less than twenty miles from Dulles Airport the skies were absolutely silent. Until the F-16s screamed over the building. And I realized there were fighter jets, combat ready, flying over the nation's capital because we were under attack.

"Inside it was like hell. The building was unstable and it was still burning. There was so much oily black smoke filling the air, cutting me off so I couldn't see and could barely breathe. God, it was so hot in there. It smelled like burning insulation and aviation fuel. Ceilings had fallen and the walls were charred and there were bodies entangled in the wreckage."

He dropped his head into his palm and massaged his temples, wanting to erase the memories, knowing he'd always see them in his dreams.

"It was so damned dark and the heat was like nothing you can imagine. We had on full flash gear with face shields and helmet lights. We had radios, but they were useless. We kept looking, kept hoping. For hours we just kept searching for anybody who was still alive.

"There was so much debris and twisted metal and suddenly there would be... I saw horrible things. Something slammed into me, knocking me to the floor. I couldn't believe how deep the cracks were. Concrete shouldn't have spalled like that. I didn't realize that what was left of Flight Seventy-seven was right below us.

"When we got outside, my buddy rushed me over to one of the medics. A melted ceiling grid had fallen on me, ripping through my Nomex jacket. I wanted to go back. I wanted to keep searching. But they wouldn't let me. I was bleeding and dehydrated and the rest of the team was in no better shape."

He finally looked up and Jordan was by his side. Tears streamed down her cheeks as she grasped his hand in both of hers. Wanting—needing—the solace she offered, he allowed her to lead him to the bed. He lay down next to her, closed his eyes and rested his head on her shoulder.

"You never leave anyone behind. That's the code we live by, and yet that's what we had to do. It's one of the hardest things I've ever done. When the fires were finally out, there were bodies found less than twenty feet from an exit—people kept coming to me with pictures, showing me these photographs, asking if I'd seen…but I never found anyone alive that day, or any of the next six days we searched…"

His voice trailed away. Speaking the words out loud couldn't begin to convey the appalling reality of those events. The images were branded onto his memory. He opened his eyes, seeking the reassurance of the rock light even as he gratefully accepted the comfort of Jordan's fingers stroking his bare arm.

Her hand reached up to caress his face, her voice equally soft. "You're a hero."

Danny scowled and shook his head. "Heroes are the guys in the movies and on TV. I was just doing my job. I wish I'd done it better."

"That's what makes you a hero."

Jordan turned until they were lying side by side,

the towel she'd tucked around herself falling away as she moved. Her bare breasts felt like warm silk against his chest. Danny wrapped his right arm around her waist, pulling her closer, letting the heat of her body seep inside to warm him.

She cupped his face in her palm and tilted his head up until he looked at her. He saw that tears still shimmered on her lashes before she kissed his brow, his cheek, then sealed her lips over his mouth. He opened to her, letting her tongue glide over his in a slow exploration. The kiss was warm, sweet and heartrending.

Her fingers brushed his skin in a long, gliding caress, making him shiver. Her touch was raw torment. As they kissed, her hands were everywhere at once, sliding, squeezing, stroking. Comforting, giving… The sensation was almost more than he could stand.

A raging need built inside him, something he wasn't ready to acknowledge. What the hell was she doing to him? She was supposed to seduce him and then screw his brains out. But it felt more like they were making love—

His heart thundered as panic formed a knot in his gut.

Jordan draped her bare leg over his thigh and pushed herself up until she lay on top of him. Bracing her hands on either side of him, she continued to sweep feather-light touches over his mouth and jaw. Her kisses were like whispered promises that he didn't want to hear. A tremendous weight settled on his chest, threatening to crush him. Danny angled his body, intent on rolling her beneath him, but Jordan resisted.

"No."

He chuckled weakly. "You got a taste for being on top out on the fire escape, huh?"

Jordan looked at him, her brown eyes dark and unfathomable. Her expression was gentle, almost tender. "Yeah. That's it."

She leaned down to capture his lips again. Need sang in his blood as she combed her fingers over his hair and deepened the kiss. She settled her bottom on his lap so that only the thin cotton of his briefs separated her from his throbbing erection. The heat between them built gradually, but it was a warm glow as opposed to a raging fire.

A sense of urgency mingled with one of dread. He couldn't go on like this. Danny planted his hands on her hips and lifted her off him, then rolled to the edge of the bed. He closed his eyes for a second, struggling to catch his breath. Then he glanced over his shoulder with what he hoped was a smirk.

"I need to grab a condom before we go any further."

He stood up and reached into the nightstand for one of the foil packets inside, then shucked off his underwear. When he turned, Jordan had removed the towel completely and pulled down the bedspread. She lay atop the sheet, waiting for him. Waiting. For him.

Well, she had a hell of a long wait. The boundaries of their agreement had been crystal clear. Sexual favors in return for a fake engagement. That was it. He had no intention of getting involved with her. When the ten days were over, so were they.

Danny sheathed himself in the condom and climbed back onto the bed. When she opened her arms, he moved over her and ravished her mouth in a punishing kiss. He savored the softness of her lips, the faint taste of beer on her tongue, the eagerness of her response. Yeah, this was what they both wanted.

He reached between their bodies to touch the damp curls then positioned himself at her entrance and pushed into her. Jordan pressed her mouth to his throat, gasping aloud, her hands gripping his back. He pressed forward, inch by inch, shuddering with the fulfillment of it.

He rocked his hips, nestling into sleek warmth and pulling out again. Spurred on by the way she squirmed beneath him, he quickened his pace. Jordan moaned and arched her back, cupping his buttocks to urge him on. With that, he stopped being selfish and saw to her pleasure.

Incredible emotion and fierce desire combined to intensify the sensation, but he struggled for control. Thrusting heavily, he raced toward physical release. Every muscle in his body went taut as a groan escaped his throat in a slow, ragged breath. Finally, gloriously, his body convulsed inside her; her body trembled around his.

After a moment, he shifted his weight off her and

rolled onto his back. Jordan cuddled against his side, already drifting off to sleep. He reached for the bedspread and settled it over her shoulders. For a long time, Danny stared up at the ceiling, listening to the soft whoosh as Jordan's breath fanned his neck.

_11_

"RISE AND SHINE, beautiful."

A playful swat on the bottom was Jordan's Sunday morning wake-up call. She startled and rolled over to look at Danny. He wore a blue T-shirt and navy trousers, obviously dressed for work. She rubbed her eyes and tried to focus. She'd been sleeping a lot later since they met, which meant she'd been missing her runs.

"What time is it?"

"Time for breakfast. I've got to get going."

He laid her dress, panties and jacket on the bed without meeting her eye. Jordan watched him walk out, closing the door behind him. A feeling of trepidation crept over her. Not exactly the warm greeting she might have expected after the intimacy they had shared.

She got off the bed with a heavy sigh and pulled on her panties. They felt a bit snug. She sighed again. The grilled chicken, baked beans and sorbet she ate at the barbecue would be her last real meal for a while. It was back to salad for her.

Jordan stepped into the cotton sundress, slipped

her arms into the cap sleeves and reached for the zipper. Which rose an inch then stopped. And wouldn't go any farther. She hadn't eaten *that* much! She looked down and realized that the hemline was three inches higher than it had been yesterday. Her shoulders slumped. Danny had shrunk her dress in the dryer.

Rolling her eyes, she closed the dress as best she could and put her jacket on to hide the open back. When she left the bedroom, she heard a mechanical grinding sound. She followed the noise to the kitchen and found Danny measuring protein powder into the bright red blender. Banana peels and empty ice-cube trays littered the countertop.

"I wondered what you did with all of that fruit."

Jordan walked over and placed a hand on his shoulder, leaning in to give him a kiss. The muscles beneath her fingers bunched as he angled his face so that her mouth brushed his cheek. Her uneasiness increased.

She watched him toss chunks of pineapple and slices of strawberry into the mix. Then he handed her a tall frosted glass already filled with the pale orange concoction. She took a tentative sip and licked her lips. "This is really good. And here I thought you didn't cook."

"I do my share of KP at the fire station, but soy milk smoothies are the extent of my home repertoire."

At the mere mention of "fire," a wall of tension thunked down between them. The very air crackled with strained silence. Danny turned away, busying himself with the blender, but not before she saw the look in his eyes.

Though his expression was nonchalant, the stiffness of his posture said otherwise. His dark brown eyes reflected the painful shadows of his memories. He must be embarrassed. It probably hadn't been easy for Danny to bare his heart like that. Her own heart wrenched in response to his withdrawal, but she understood and would give him the space he so obviously wanted.

Jordan tried to keep her tone casual. "I'm going to miss you at the crab feast."

He lifted his glass and chugged down his smoothie, stretching out the silence. Finally he said, "Yeah, well, I was already scheduled to work tomorrow night."

She stood by, feeling helpless and rejected, while he washed out the blender and the glasses. She hated to act like one of those needy, clinging women, but she couldn't stop herself. "When are we getting together again?"

Danny still wouldn't look at her. "I'm going to try and make it to the baseball game Wednesday."

SEVERAL HOURS LATER, Jordan trudged along The Avenue at White Marsh. The design of the outdoor retail complex was reminiscent of a small-town main street, where stores and restaurants faced off in single rows across a brick-lined thoroughfare. Shade trees, boxed flower beds and small plazas with burbling fountains and comfortable benches enhanced the layout. Normally it was one of Jordan's favorite places.

Shopping bags dangled from her elbows, forearms and both hands. Sheris was equally encumbered, but that didn't stop her from pushing through the glass door of yet another boutique. Jordan groaned. Her feet hurt. She was depressed. It was going to be a long day.

Her friend didn't pull the shop-until-you-drop routine unless she was really upset. Breaking up with Matt had led to the purchase of sapphire earrings. Shane Smith's ultimatum was going to max out his daughter's platinum American Express card.

Jordan tried to adjust Sheris's bags so the weight didn't dislocate her shoulder. "Can we please sit down somewhere and talk about this?"

"What's to talk about?" She yanked a cashmere sweater from a pile on a display table. "I either pull off a miracle, or I get disinherited."

Jordan wrinkled her brow. "Did you bother to look at that? It's not your color and I don't think it's even your size."

"It's not. I'm buying it for Melanie. I figure I'd better do my holiday shopping now since I'll be broke come December."

"You could try cooperating with your dad's request." Jordan dropped the shopping bags on the floor.

"It wasn't a request! It was an order." She made her voice a deep and commanding drawl, a dead-accurate imitation. " 'You're a perpetually unemployed student. Either you stop flittin' through your life or I'm cuttin' off your credit.' "

Jordan grasped her friend's arm to stop her from picking up a rivet-studded miniskirt. "You told me that, for once, you weren't bored, discouraged or quitting. This Celebrate Celibacy program is a lucrative contract. You'll do a great job of managing this campaign, Sheris."

Her clear blue eyes darkened and the corners of her mouth turned down. "I *could have* done a great job. I could have gotten Smith and Watson Advertising running in the black if I didn't have to deal with...him!"

Jordan didn't know whether to sigh or to laugh. Logan was the best thing that had ever happened to Sheris. But neither of them had seen it during their short-lived marriage or in the years that followed. So she tried the logical approach.

"WRRS is the most popular radio station in the city. I don't think you could pull off this campaign without their help. Especially since the *In the Mood with McGuire* show is at the top of the ratings."

"I don't want to talk about this anymore."

Sheris stalked over to the cashier to pay for the cashmere sweater, a silk dress and a pair of purple snakeskin boots. Back outside, Sheris strode briskly along the sidewalk, forcing her to keep up.

"Okay, Jordan. Let's deal with *your* problem. You lied to your family, kidnapped a stranger, had fabulous sex and now you're in love. Does that about cover it?"

Jordan stumbled, barely catching herself before she crashed into a tree. Love? Who said anything about love?

No way. No way could she have fallen in love with Danny after only four days. It was probably just the brothers' similarities that were confusing her. Except…they really weren't identical other than in their looks.

Unlike with David, there had been sparks between her and Danny from the start. What she'd passed off as excitement over acting out fantasies was really a deeper connection. Oh, my God. What she'd thought was role-playing was the beginning of something real. Omigod. She was in love with him.

"Oh, look! The Scent Shop."

Jordan hefted the bags and felt a twinge in her upper back. She hurried after Sheris. "Haven't you bought enough stuff yet?"

"I could use some new lotions."

Jordan groaned in frustration, already anticipating the headache she'd end up with after helping Sheris choose between Mango Mandarin, Vanilla Grapefruit or Peach Ginger. Dragging the shopping bags, she followed her friend into the store.

"I'm in real trouble here," Jordan admitted.

"You said yesterday went great. So what's the problem?" Sheris rummaged through the samples in the discontinued product bin.

"Yes, the barbecue was a success. My family really likes him. And last night was so incredible. I really thought it was a turning point in our relationship.

But, this morning, that man couldn't have backpedaled fast enough."

Sheris pulled a face, her voice tinged with bitterness. "He's a guy. That's what guys do."

"Could you please focus?" Jordan pulled the room spray out of her friend's hand before she got covered in Berry Banana mist. "Falling in love was not part of our deal. What am I going to do?"

"Follow his lead—finish out the agreement, enjoy the sex and walk away. That tactic ensures you won't get hurt."

Jordan knew her friend was probably right, but the idea of not having Danny around caused her a sense of disquiet. She adored his sense of humor and his spontaneity. She liked the way he interacted with her family. She loved the way he looked at her, as if she were beautiful, curves and all.

"I'm not sure he's following the plan anymore."

Sheris glanced over from the display of herb-scented candles. "Come on, Jordan. His own brother calls him the Eight Date Man—"

"Thanks for reminding me about his reputation. I feel so special now."

"Fantasies for favors, honey. That's all. What makes you think he wants to change?"

Jordan recalled the intimacy of holding Danny in her arms while he shared his memories. "Last night he let me inside. He told me about an experience so deeply personal that it had to be a show of trust."

Sheris scoffed. "This guy is a player, Jordan.

Logan used to try and manipulate my sympathy, too. And then he walked out. Don't forget that."

She guessed it was possible, but for what purpose? Why would Danny entrust her with his secret if he never intended to see her again?

HE ONLY HAD TO SEE Jordan two more times and then he was off the hook. What had started out as a fantasy had become all too real.

Danny sat across the table from his parents, Robert and Gayle, and wished like hell that either his brother were here or that he could order a beer. Unfortunately, David wouldn't be back until later tonight, and he had to report for work in a few hours. Danny hated having to put up with these obligatory brunches alone and sober.

Alexis, the restaurant at the Valley Golf Association, was upscale, overpriced and perfectly suited to his parents. Late morning sunlight streamed through the atrium's two-story windows overlooking the pristine fairway. The elegant decor was enhanced by large vases of fresh flowers; the soft strains of classical music and white-jacketed waiters offered impeccable service.

Not that his parents noticed. They were too busy seeing and being seen. In fact, they hadn't bothered to notice Danny since he first sat down. That was fine with him. He had a lot to think about.

No red-blooded male would have turned down the chance to have great sex without having to commit. And, even better, it was Jordan who wanted to keep their association strictly physical. This was the perfect arrangement for a guy like him. He'd be crazy not to make the most of 'any time, any place'... But somehow it wasn't enough anymore.

Jordan was great in bed. She was even better out of it. She was smart and compassionate and she made him laugh. She was beautiful, sexy and sensual. Her carefully created image hid a mass of insecurities, so much so that she couldn't see what a terrific person she really was. Deep in his heart he knew that he liked waking up with her more than sleeping with her.

His father cleared his throat and Danny braced himself for The Lecture. "You know, son, it's still not too late to get that law degree. Hale Robards is Dean of Admissions at Howard University now. I was talking to him about you the other day on the back nine. We both agree it's high time you stopped playing fireman and got serious about your future..."

Danny just nodded and toyed with the eggs Benedict on his plate. His father especially tended to talk at him rather than to him, so no response was necessary or expected. He'd worn his uniform today just to piss them off. Neither of his parents had a clue about his job or his commitment to it. He choked down a bite of ham covered in hollandaise that had gone cold, then realized his father had stopped speaking and his mother had started The Talk.

"I saw Carol Summers at the symphony last week. Remember you used to date her? The Mozart concertos were lovely. We're so lucky to have Maestro Temirkanov conducting. Anyway, Carol asked about you. She's divorced again, you know. You should give her a call…"

Just then, some old friends of the family stopped by the table and Danny was immediately forgotten. Again. He passed the time trying to remember all of the names of all of the au pairs and nannies that had raised him and David over the years.

A little smile tugged at his mouth when he pictured Angela and Jackson's faces as they laughed over their children's exploits. During the barbecue, he must have listened to a hundred stories about the kid's goofs and tricks and triumphs. His parents never let him forget their disappointment while the Gregorys were just as proud of Eric, who worked construction, as they were of Reece, who ran an accounting firm.

When his friends had moved on, Danny's father cleared his throat again, an annoying attention-getting habit. "I'm giving a speech at the Tomorrow's Children fund-raiser the firm is sponsoring next weekend. I'll expect my family to be there."

His mother tossed her linen napkin on the table. "You dragged me to that last year and I'm not dealing with those children again. Had you bothered to consult me, I would have told you I'm attending the Women's Law Center luncheon."

"I shouldn't have to consult you. All of the other wives will be there."

Danny pushed his plate away. Same arguments;

different year. In the month that had passed since he had last endured their company, he'd forgotten how smoothly two jurists could slice pieces off each other. His mother resented the way Robert tried to make all of the decisions. His father hated the fact that Gayle had never settled for the role of wife.

As they launched into a hushed but bitter conversation, Danny suddenly remembered why he wanted nothing to do with marriage or family. He stood up, physically interrupting his parents' argument. "Well, it's been pleasant as always."

"Watch your tone, Daniel."

"Sorry, Mom. But you know how much I enjoy listening to you two admire and flatter each other." He pushed his chair under the table. "I'll see you next month."

JORDAN WALKED through her front door at three o'clock and toed off her shoes with a grateful sigh. The sandals had low heels but, after trailing Sheris into almost every shop on The Avenue, her feet ached just the same. She wandered barefoot into the living room and flopped down on the sofa. She was seriously considering a nap when the telephone rang.

"Hello?"

"Are you going to be there for a while?"

She recognized Danny's voice over the cellular connection and the fatigue instantly dropped away. "Yes, I just got in from shopping with a friend."

"Good. I'll be there in fifteen minutes."

Jordan dashed upstairs to freshen up. She splashed water on her face, combed her hair and reapplied her lipstick, though she figured it would get smeared off again in a couple of minutes. She was debating whether to change her clothes when the doorbell chimed.

Danny stood on the front step, just staring at her. His expression was one of…relief? His eyes roamed over her face as though he hadn't seen her in a year. Then, in the space of a heartbeat, Jordan found herself backed against the wall of the entryway. One strong arm curled around her waist while the other hand was braced beside her head. The look in his eyes literally made her quiver.

Danny claimed her mouth with a reckless passion. His kiss was raw, primitive, the act of a man declaring his objective. She wrapped her arms over his shoulders, returning the kiss with equal fervor but with different purpose. She took her time, countering his eagerness with a slow exploration, soothing her hands over his short curls.

He made a rough, impatient sound in his throat as he held her closer, molding his pelvis to her thigh. Her fingers sought the tender skin at the base of his neck, gently massaging away the corded tension. He cupped her breast through the thin material of her blouse, pinching her nipple until it beaded. Jordan stroked her palms along his back, sensing the heat and strength of the taut muscles.

Danny broke the kiss abruptly. He closed his eyes and rested his forehead on hers. She reached up and lightly caressed his cheek, trying to tell him without words that she understood. Inhaling sharply, he tilted his head back until their eyes met. The deep brown depths were turbulent with emotion, though his features seemed set in stone.

He reached down to pick up a bag that she hadn't seen him bring in. The logo on the plastic was for a western apparel shop downtown. When he handed it to her, she suppressed a sigh and peered at the contents. A cream Stetson and a pair of fringed suede panties. Jordan glanced up at him. Was he serious?

Danny offered her a cocky grin. "I thought we'd give fantasy number twenty-seven a try."

A twinge of disappointment pierced her heart. Was this his way of reestablishing the rules, of keeping their relationship superficial? Last night must have scared him more than she realized. "Are you sure this is what you want, Danny?"

"It'll have to do. I was looking for a French maid outfit but didn't see any I liked."

Fine. She would play Ride Him, Cowgirl if this was the only way he'd let her be with him.

Jordan took the outfit into the powder room to change. It didn't occur to her until halfway back to the living room that she was bare except for the panties. Danny would see her in the harsh afternoon sunlight. He would see her stretch marks and her cellulite and her vulnerability. And she no longer cared.

He was already undressed, standing in the center of the room wearing his boxer briefs and an attitude. Whatever sassy comment he might have made seemed to die away. A softness came over his features and his mouth curved with warmth. The tension visibly dropped away from his shoulders.

"You're beautiful, Jordan. Lose the hat."

She laughed softly and tossed the Stetson onto the coffee table. Then she moved into his open embrace, welcoming his kiss. A wild shudder of pleasure raced through her as their tongues met and mated. Without breaking contact, they stripped off their underwear. Danny guided them over to the sofa, easing her down onto the smooth cotton material.

While he protected them, she trailed her fingers over his tan skin from the column of his long neck over the wide expanse of his shoulders to the rock-solid muscle of his chest. She caressed the well-defined planes of his abs before moving on to his narrow hips and lean, toned thighs. Danny gulped in a draft of air when her fingers wrapped around his penis.

He rolled on top of her, supporting his weight on his elbows. A heavy, aching need settled in her chest, making her tremble with desire. Her eyelids fluttered but she refused to close them. She watched his face, saw the arrogance in his expression as he positioned himself at her entrance. The sudden tensing of his arms and thighs was her only warning before he plunged into her.

Passion built within her like a storm. She arched her back, crying out with each powerful thrust. Danny slipped his palms beneath her, pulling her closer still. She squeezed his waist with her thighs to encourage him as he rocked them toward release. The delicate inner shivers rippled through her and her body wept. A moment later, Danny groaned with the force of his own climax. His heart pounded in rhythm with her own as his ragged breath warmed her face. Then he shifted his weight until he lay beside her, one arm draped across her hips.

Something between them had changed. Her instinctive response to him was too powerful, the emotions too strong, to question. And though Danny didn't seem willing to face it, she welcomed it head-on.

12

"Oh, LOOK. There's David." Camryn pointed. "I thought you said he couldn't make it?"

Jordan swiveled her head toward the entrance of the restaurant. As "David" spotted them and walked into Obrycki's Crab House, she knew it really was David. He wore a blue oxford-cloth shirt and a pair of khakis with a pleat so sharp you could cut your finger on it. What she didn't know, however, was why he'd shown up.

"Um, I guess his plans changed. I'll be right back." She scrambled out of her seat and hurried to David's side, hoping she looked pleased instead of panicked.

"Hi, Jordan."

"Hi. Why are you here?"

David arched one brow. "If this is the way you greet your fiancé, I doubt if anybody is buying your engagement."

"I didn't mean it that way." Glancing back at the table, she pasted on a bright smile and lowered her voice. "I'm just wondering what you're doing here."

David replied in a stage whisper. "You gave me

a schedule, remember? I'm supposed to be eating crabs and admiring you."

"That was before Danny took your place. I told everyone he's working tonight. What are we going to do?"

He shrugged. "If Danny can act like me, there's no reason I can't act like him."

"You can't act like him." Jordan frowned. "*You* have to act like him pretending to be you, without giving away that you really are you."

"No wonder you do so well in court." David grinned at her. "Can we stop this now? I'm hungry and your family is beginning to stare."

He leaned down to kiss her. It was sweet and entirely appropriate, and yet she found herself bothered by the tame greeting. She took his hand but felt none of the sparks Danny's touch provoked. "We'd never have pulled this off for an entire week."

David squeezed her fingers. "I shouldn't have come tonight, huh?"

Jordan was instantly contrite. "No, I'm glad you did. I appreciate it. You're a good friend."

"All right, then. Tell me who everybody is."

"Clockwise from the empty seat, my sister Camryn and her boyfriend, Mason. Then my brother Reece, Uncle Matt, my father and mother, my aunt Celeste, and finally my brother Eric and cousin Keisha. 'You' met all of them the other day at my parent's house."

They took their seats at the brown kraft-paper-covered table and Jordan watched anxiously as

David greeted everyone. The difference between the Navarro brothers was so obvious to her, she figured her family could tell them apart as well. Her mother was definitely looking at David oddly.

A tuxedo-clad waiter came over to ask about their drinks and he started to order a glass of wine until Jordan shot an elbow into his side. He picked up on her cue immediately and ordered a bottle of beer instead.

Her father spoke from across the table. "Charles and Emma send their regrets that they couldn't join us."

David glanced at her, silently asking who they were talking about. "My grandparents had other plans tonight."

"That's okay. I look forward to meeting them on Saturday." Jordan kicked his ankle. "Meeting them again, I mean. I didn't get to spend much time with them on Saturday."

Eric laughed. "Grandpa thinks you spent *too* much time with him. He's still griping that you didn't let an old man beat you at canasta."

Jordan knocked her fork to the floor. Gentleman that he was, David leaned down to pick it up for her, just as she'd hoped. She bent over, too. Grabbing his arm, she whispered in his ear. "Try and avoid talking about the barbecue."

"What if someone else brings it up?"

"Just be vague."

David smirked. "That shouldn't be difficult."

They sat up at the same time and he placed her fork back on the table.

When her uncle asked how it was going at work, David regaled then with anecdotes about some of his cases while Jordan sat next to him, sweating. Things went well until the waiter returned to take their dinner order. Everyone chose the steamed crabs. Except David, who asked for New England clam chowder, shrimp cocktail and a garden salad.

In the silence that followed, he smiled sheepishly. "Crabs aren't that filling and I didn't have much for lunch."

"All you Navarro men ever think about is food," Jordan muttered.

Unfortunately, Camryn overheard the comment and leaned around her to look at David. "Oh, there are more like you?"

"I have a twin brother—"

Jordan nailed his ankle again.

On the other side of David, Keisha narrowed her eyes speculatively. "A twin. Really?"

Uh-uh. We're not going there. Jordan affected a loud cough to distract attention. "We still have to decide what we're giving Grandpa and Grandma. Any ideas?"

As the family began offering and rejecting suggestions, she knocked her fork on the floor a second time. When David bent down, she muttered, "I told you to be vague. Do not talk about Danny."

"How was I supposed to know you never mentioned your fiancé had a brother?"

Jordan huffed out a breath. "I was trying to keep the details to a minimum."

"Well, what other details did you leave out?"

Aunt Celeste poked her head under the table. "Would you two care to join us? We're down to a pair of gold-plated golf clubs or a day at the Golden Gateway Spa."

All three of them sat back up. As Jordan replaced her fork, Mason grinned over at her. "You sure are clumsy tonight, girl. You'd better leave that thing on the floor."

Heat rushed to her cheeks as she joined in the laughter.

David sampled a mouthful of chowder before suggesting, "If they like golf, how about a weekend on the Gold Coast of Florida? My parents go down to The Breakers on Palm Beach twice a year."

Her mother raised her voice to address him. "I think it's about time for us to meet your parents, don't you, David?"

Just then the platters of steamed crabs arrived, saving Jordan from having to drop her fork again. The hot-red crustaceans were unceremoniously dumped into the center of the table. Then the waiter handed out crab mallets and paring knives. She simply stared as David accepted one of the large paper bibs with Baltimore's Famous emblazoned above a smiling mascot.

No self-respecting Marylander wore a crab bib. Bibs were for tourists.

Reece snickered. "Are you the same guy who walked around with barbecue sauce and grass stains all day Saturday?"

"I've got on a nicer shirt this time."

Once the crabs cooled to a manageable temperature, the serious eating began. While David munched his salad and shrimp, everyone else at the table ripped open the hard top shells with their bare hands. Jordan was in the process of breaking her crab into sections to get the backfin meat when David practically jumped out of his seat.

He knocked his fork to the floor. She was a beat late in getting the message, so he grasped her arm and pulled her down with him. "Your cousin is flirting with me."

Jordan sighed. "Keisha is like that. Just ignore her."

"I can't. She's fondling my thigh."

"When we sit up, stab her with your fork."

The rest of the meal was uneventful, except for David occasionally flinching and squirming in his chair, until her father said, "So, you two, have you set a date for the wedding?"

To keep him from answering, Jordan knocked a crab into his lap. They both bent down to retrieve it and David sighed.

"Danny *should* have been with you tonight. I'm spending more time under this table than at it."

THE FOURTEEN-HOUR second shift was always the most active. Even the smallest of fires seemed worse at night and this one, Danny thought, was going to be a bitch.

Built in 1851, Stephenson Mill was originally a

machine-manufacturing plant. Now the complex housed artist studios and furniture refinishers. The place was so big you could probably fit two football fields into it. When the ladder company from Station 24 arrived, only a light-to-moderate smoke condition was showing at the roof, with no flames in sight.

Mike stood next to him on the A side of the building as they unloaded equipment and grabbed their air packs. "This doesn't look too bad, L.T."

No, it didn't. But the hair was rising on the back of his neck just the same. "Wait for it, Stonewall. No way to know how long it's been burning."

Battalion Chief Forsyth, who was Incident Command for tonight, decided the initial attack would be an interior one. The windows had metal grilles and four guys from Rescue 1 had to aggressively tackle the roll-up metal door to gain access. When they finally carved an opening, the first crew went in to scout out the fire.

Danny forced a deep breath into his lungs and led his company inside.

"I can't see a thing in here, L.T."

"Shake it off, Mike."

The first floor was a confusing maze of dark, smoky rooms. Danny's pulse tripped along his veins and he had to swallow against the nausea. Beneath his face shield, sweat dripped from his forehead. Despite the intense heat, a chill of dread crawled down his spine. The squad marked each door with a chalk X so nobody wasted time repeating their efforts.

After checking the whole floor, Ladder 24 climbed one of the only two sets of stairs to the next level. With no windows on the upper floors, the heat was trapped inside. Firefighters from Station 17 attacked the fire on the second floor but they were losing it. The solid oak floors were probably soaked with oil from a century and a half of machinery use. Cork insulation in the ceiling added to the smoke.

Danny jumped into the assault, battling flames and smoke and fear. The scar tissue on his back itched like mad and sweat ran into his eyes, further obscuring his vision. Another company joined them and it seemed as if they were finally getting the fire under control. Then, just when he thought they had it boxed in, explosions erupted like bombs from somewhere to his left.

"Shit! That smells like propane!"

What had been a modest fire was now a raging, seething inferno of boiling smoke. His heart thundered in his chest as he aimed the hose at flames that seemed to be leaping out of nowhere. His throat tightened up and he felt as though he was choking. Then he realized he'd started to hyperventilate and made every effort to steady his breathing.

Over the radio, he heard the Bat Chief shouting. "I want all personnel down off the upper floors! I want a head count. Everybody down!"

Danny ordered his men out, still ineffectually sweeping the hoses over the flames as they backed toward the direction of the stairs. Toxic smoke flooded the labyrinthine, windowless building as they raced down the steps. Danny felt an ominous vibration and looked up. A smoldering heat duct plummeted toward them. "The wall is coming down!"

He pushed Mike in front of him and urged the rest of the company to run faster. He spared another glance at the ceiling and his heart stopped. A flaming floor joist was about to break free of the level above him. He lunged down the last flight of steps and crashed into the wall.

It was pitch-black and impossibly hot. He couldn't breathe. He could hear muffled weeping and it sounded like Jordan, but he couldn't find her. The darkness was caving in on him...

He came to a few seconds later. Danny dragged himself to his feet and found his helmet. A jackhammer pounded the inside of his head, making him light-headed and dizzy. Stumbling, he ran out of the building. One of the paramedics grabbed him and started cleaning the cut on his forehead.

By now the fire had gone to five alarms—twenty engines, eight ladders and several rescue and utility trucks were parked in front of the mill. As the various fire companies regrouped on the pavement, the Bat Chief started yelling instructions. "Okay, we're gonna fight this from an outside defensive perimeter. Get the master streams going and let's surround and drown. In the meantime, take a roll call and—"

"Mayday! We're running out of air!" Everything stopped, even time. For several seconds the firefighters stood listening to the voices on the radio, frozen in horror. "We're buddy breathing and we can't find our way off the second level! Mayday!"

Forsyth turned to the closest crew of firefighters. "See if you can find them. We've got to get this done. The fire is out of control. We don't have a lot of time."

The four men ran back into a building that was now bursting into flames, disappearing into the smoke to rescue their colleagues. In the meantime, the master streams were going full bore. Wide, fixed jets of water arced into the air from the snorkels on top of the aerial ladder and pumper trucks.

But the fire kept on burning.

Flames boiled from the roof, leaping into the sky. Though another alarm had shown up, all the firefighters could do at this point was minimize the exposure to other buildings.

After what seemed like a lifetime, Sharp and Mozelewski staggered out and collapsed on the pavement. Danny's gaze flew to the entrance, waiting for Barry and Cassadine. It seemed that everyone held their breath, and waited. But nothing came out of the door except black oily smoke.

"What are conditions like up there? How bad?" The Bat Chief demanded.

Sharp answered, his voice husky and shaking. "We didn't even make it across the first floor."

Forsyth held his gaze for a moment, an agonizing and final understanding passing between them. Then the Battalion Chief sighed heavily and nodded his head. "That's it. No more."

"They're still up there!"

"What do you mean, no more?"

A dozen firefighters, including Mike, lined up, ready to go. They started shouting and pushing toward the warehouse entrance. Danny remained where he was, sick with the knowledge that there was no way in hell he was going back in there.

The Bat Chief moved in front of them, making himself an obstacle. "We've already lost four. We're not going to lose any more! I'm calling it."

It was like somebody collectively kicked them all in the stomach. Danny's shoulders slumped and he dropped his head as the air horns of every fire truck started giving successive short blasts in a code that meant "all out." They were abandoning the mill and the men still trapped inside.

Lyons. Blackmon. Barry. Cassadine. Gone.

Danny looked down at his helmet, at the emblem that read Pride Protecting People, and tears welled in his eyes.

Hours later, after leaving the hospital with a concussion, he reached for the phone. He just wanted to hear Jordan's voice. He started dialing, then realized how late it was and hung up the receiver.

He sat back against the suede couch, staring blindly at flickering images on the TV screen. All he could see was the face of Blackmon's new wife. Only twenty-three years old, John had just gotten married a couple of months ago. Now his bride was a widow. Suddenly her face was replaced with Jordan's in his mind.

Danny ran to the bathroom and threw up.

13

JORDAN LIKED BASEBALL about as much as she enjoyed watching grass grow. But the law firm had season tickets and she'd promised her brothers, who were rabid Orioles fans, that she'd get them into this game.

The New York Yankees were apparently Baltimore's archrivals and this late-season game was part of the pennant race. Whatever a pennant race was. Down on the field, some player hit a white ball with a fat stick, then another player started running around the diamond. She stared morosely at the action and felt several hundred of her brain cells implode.

At least it was a beautiful night in a charming setting. Oriole Park had been built on the site of an old rail yard. The Baltimore & Ohio Railroad warehouse had been incorporated as part of the new 110-million-dollar structure. The Camden Yards ballpark design reflected nineteenth-century architecture, including an arched brick facade, a sunroof over the upper deck, an asymmetrical playing field and Maryland bluegrass turf.

It was amazing what you could learn by reading the fifteen-page program instead of watching the game.

Jordan took a sip of her cola, barely resisting the urge to dump it over Danny's head. She hadn't seen him since Sunday afternoon. He hadn't called since then, either, except to confirm tonight's game time. Had he thought about her? Had he missed her? It was so difficult to tell when he was busy chatting and laughing with Keisha.

When they'd taken their seats in the terrace box, her cousin had made certain she sat on the other side of Danny. Keisha put on a great show of complaining about the heat. She'd taken off her jacket to reveal a low-cut crop top that exposed her flat belly above her equally low-cut jeans. Jordan scrunched down in the hard, uncomfortable seat and hoped her cousin choked on the hot dog Danny bought her.

"Do you want one, too, Jordan?"

"No, thanks…David."

He shrugged and took his seat, his body angled away from her. She couldn't see his face, but she sure as hell saw the calculating gleam in Keisha's eye. Her cousin giggled and grinned, occasionally touching Danny's forearm as she talked. With music playing over the chatter of the crowd, it was too noisy to hear what they were saying. However, body language didn't require words.

Reece turned in the seat next to her. After glancing over her shoulder, he looked directly into her eyes. "Is there anything you need to talk about, Jo-Jo?"

"What do you mean?"

Her brother's voice had an edge. "Your fiancé seems to be distracted tonight."

Jordan looked down and toyed with the straw in her cup. "Oh, he's under pressure at work—"

"He works a lot."

"We're not joined at the hip, Reece." Her laughter was forced. "I mean, you didn't expect to see him every night this week, did you?"

"I wouldn't mind seeing more of the guy I met on Saturday. I don't know who was at the crab house, and I don't know who that is beside you." He leaned closer and lowered his voice. "Does David have some kind of personality disorder?"

Before she could think of a reply, Eric jumped up and screamed, "Did you see that play? Grandma could have caught that fly ball!" and Reece's attention was back on the game.

At the sound of Danny's chuckle, she glanced to the right. Keisha had gotten a blob of hot-dog mustard on her cheek and he was wiping it off. Jordan looked away as tears pricked her eyes, focusing on whatever was happening down on the field so she wouldn't lose control.

The initial stab of jealousy was consumed by the heat of her anger, then drowned in a wave of misery. Jordan crunched the ice in her soda cup and attempted to count the number of people in the stadium wearing red shirts. The distraction didn't work.

She felt bereft and isolated and the craving for

chocolate was so strong that it hurt. Her heart contracted in anguish as she realized what she had to do.

After warm goodbye hugs from her brothers and an awkward parting from "David," Jordan and her cousin walked to the Honda. Then they sat and waited in traffic with forty thousand other baseball fans trying to make their way out of downtown. Keisha fiddled with the radio and squirmed in the passenger seat, until finally she turned to Jordan and broke the silence.

"David is so handsome. And he's got a great body."

Jordan answered quietly. "Yes, he does."

"He's got a great sense of humor, too. I laughed the whole night."

She concentrated on inching the car forward a couple of feet, determined not to let Keisha get a rise out of her.

"I told David I was thinking about moving back to Maryland. He thought it was a great idea."

Jordan saw an opening and zipped into the left lane. "I think Camryn's going to rent her place and move in with Mason. Maybe you could take over the mortgage."

Keisha stared at her, seemingly confused by her even temper and tone of voice. "I still can't believe *you're* engaged. I wouldn't want to tie myself down to only one person. Though a guy like David might make me change my mind."

"David" had Jordan changing her mind about a few things, too. The traffic was a little thinner on

Charles Street, so she relaxed her grip on the steering wheel. "I'm curious about something, Keisha. Do you really want him? Or do you only want him because he's mine?"

Her cousin looked away and laughed. "I don't know what you're talking about. I mean, it's obvious your fiancé likes me, but I've got more boyfriends than I know what to do with. Guys ask me out all the time."

That had been true back in high school, too. Boys were always asking Keisha out on dates, but the dates never seemed to turn into relationships. She worked hard at her good-time-girl image, always claiming the boys were madly in love with her but "why settle for one when you could have them all?"

As she pulled up to the entrance of the Wyndham Hotel, Jordan gazed over at her cousin. For the first time it occurred to her that, though Keisha was stunningly pretty, she wasn't happy. She spoke quietly, sympathetically. "I hope you find what you're looking for."

Surprise replaced the usual calculating animosity in Keisha's eyes. Then the moment passed and she opened the car door. "Don't worry about me, cuz. I always get what I want."

Jordan watched her cousin sashay toward the glass doors, smiling and flirting with the valet as she passed by. Keisha threw a glance over her shoulder and winked before going into the lobby.

DANNY HEARD THE KNOCK at his apartment door and glanced at his watch. He didn't usually get visitors this late. Unless it was the stewardess with the great legs and adventurous libido. He opened the door to find Jordan, her features set and determined.

"Can I come in? This won't take long."

"Sure." He stood aside to let her pass. "Do you want something to drink?"

"No, thank you. I want to talk about what happened tonight."

Here it comes. He braced himself to deal with a jealous scene. Or a plea to take their agreement to the next level. Well, he'd handled this before. He'd be kind, remind her that they didn't have any sort of commitment, and let her down as gently as he could.

"Have a seat while I turn off the TV." He grabbed the remote and shut down the movie he'd been watching. When he turned, though, she was still standing. Great, it was going to be that kind of talk. "I realize you're upset, Jordan. I'm sorry I didn't pay more attention to you at the game."

"What you did was embarrass me in front of my family."

"I don't understand."

"Of course you don't." A note of irritation crept into her voice.

Danny immediately got defensive. "No, I really don't. All I did was talk to someone for a few minutes."

"It was a few hours, Danny. And I'm not the only one who noticed."

"It was a perfectly innocent conversation. Keisha's actually a nice person when she wants to be. I think you got the wrong impression."

Jordan's eyes seemed to be focused just over his shoulder. "I'd appreciate it if you wouldn't lead my cousin on."

"I wasn't—"

"Keisha tends to blow things out of proportion, Danny. She has a habit of confusing sex with love and then getting hurt."

"Are you talking about your cousin or about yourself?" She held his gaze until he shifted from one foot to the other and glanced away. "I'm sorry. That was uncalled-for."

"I know the difference. All too well."

Her quiet dignity made him feel like a first-class jerk. He *hadn't* been flirting with Keisha, but that didn't excuse him. Danny scratched his chin. "I guess I didn't hold up my end of the deal tonight."

"The thing is—the thing is, I think we both know this isn't working out the way we'd planned." The look on her face was an odd combination of resignation and hope.

Danny suppressed a sigh. This was familiar territory. She was about to ask for something he just couldn't give her. Wanting to put it off as long as possible, he turned in the direction of the kitchen. "Are you sure I can't get you something to drink?"

"The deal is off, Danny. I'm ending our agreement."

Her voice was stronger now, decisive. He heard the words, but they didn't register at first. Jordan was breaking up with him? She was ending it? Her eyes searched his, waiting for a response. He just stared at her, uncomprehending. Then her expression cleared and she offered him a polite smile.

"Okay. Well, I'll be going. Take care of yourself."

This was what he'd wanted. Sort of. But now he wasn't so sure. A chill danced over his skin and his heart slammed against his chest at the thought of her walking out the door. He caught her arm to keep her from leaving.

"Wait a—just wait!"

"Why, Danny?" Her tone was gentle, with just a trace of huskiness.

He dropped her arm, feeling as if a pit had opened up beneath him. If he took one step, he'd be trapped. But he wouldn't go back on what he'd promised. "What about your grandparents' party?"

"I'll go alone. Everybody is used to my fiancé having to work odd hours or suddenly go out of town." She sighed and he suddenly realized the strain her lies had caused. "Or I'll tell them we broke our engagement. Or… I don't know. I'll tell them something."

"You don't have to do that. I'll still take you."

"Listen, it's obvious you're not interested in playing the part anymore. And I'd rather be spared the public embarrassment of having to watch you romance my cousin. All I ask is that you wait until we've 'officially broken up' before you call her, okay?"

Danny rubbed his forehead. Christ, what a jerk he'd been. He'd only intended to put some distance between them—he honestly hadn't meant to hurt her. "I'm not going to call her at all. Come on, sit down and tell me what this is about."

Jordan reluctantly allowed him lead her over to the sofa. She dropped onto the nearest cushion, clenching her hands in her lap. He sat down beside her and lightly touched her hand. "Now, tell me, what makes you think I would choose Keisha over you?"

Her laugh was devoid of humor. "Why wouldn't you? She's slim and beautiful, easygoing and un-complicated. Exactly the kind of woman your brother said you always date."

That was true enough. He tended to gravitate to independent women who didn't mind a casual rela-tionship. But since he'd met Jordan, his tastes had changed without him realizing it. Keisha did abso-lutely nothing for him. "No man in his right mind would prefer your cousin."

She shrugged and wouldn't look at him. "It wouldn't be the first time."

"Will you tell me about it?"

She didn't want to. She hated to even remember. It had been the worst moment in a long history of tricks Keisha had played on her. Danny took her hand and she felt the warmth travel all the way to her heart. Maybe this was a turning point. Maybe, if she shared something personal and painful, the way he had, maybe he would open himself to her.

"His name was Aaron Lawrence. He was the most popular boy in school. All of the girls had a crush on him." Including Jordan, who never would have dreamed he'd look twice at her. "I guess I should have questioned a guy like him asking me to the Senior Prom."

"He didn't take you?"

"No, he took me…" She paused, then went on. "My mom bought me a beautiful evening gown. She had it tailored so it fit me perfectly…so it hid my belly and thighs. Aunt Celeste owned a salon and she treated me like a princess. She styled my hair and did my nails and makeup. I was so excited because this was my first dance."

"What happened?"

"Aaron was really nice at first. He was attentive and seemed like he was really interested in me." Jordan laughed bitterly. "Halfway through the night I was entertaining fairy tales about him, stupidly thinking that this could lead to something, that he saw who I was inside of my big, fat body."

"Jordan—"

"You saw the photos, Danny. You know what I looked like then. Would you have asked me to a dance?" She didn't wait for an answer, because she knew he wouldn't admit the truth. "He led me outside the gymnasium and kissed me. My first kiss at my first dance. It was sweet initially, but then he got more aggressive and I tried to pull away."

Danny's hand tightened around hers. "Please tell me he didn't…"

"No, it didn't go that far. He just— He just put his hand inside my dress and squeezed my breast. I pushed him away just as some of his friends came out and asked if he'd gotten anywhere with me yet. Aaron laughed and told them, not yet but he'd get lucky later."

Danny shook his head. "What a bastard."

"I just stared at him. Then I finally got the courage to ask why he thought I would have sex with him. He said…" She cleared her throat. "He said, 'everyone knows fat girls are easy.' Keisha wouldn't date him unless he asked me to the prom as a favor."

Danny slipped his arm around her shoulders, pulling her to his side. "I'm so sorry. I'm so sorry she did that to you."

"I was devastated. I knew Keisha didn't like me, but I never thought she'd do anything like that. And, by the time I got back inside, all of Aaron's friends were laughing about it. Everyone was laughing at me. I've never felt so horrible in my life."

Danny held her for a moment, slowly rocking from side to side. Then he stood up and held out his hand to her. When she took it, he pulled her to her feet.

"Come with me."

When he led her across hall toward the bathroom, she stopped in confusion. "What are we going to do in here?"

He tugged her hand until she stepped inside. "Turn around, Jordan."

She did so automatically, but then realized she was fully exposed to the mirror above the sink. Damn it, what was he trying to do? She attempted to turn away, but Danny moved behind her, his hands on her shoulders to hold her in place. "Look."

"I don't want to play."

"This isn't a game, not for you."

The slight pressure of his grip implied that he wasn't going to let it drop, so she did as he asked. Defiant, unhappy and irritated, her expression clearly indicated what she was thinking— *Let's get this over with.* The image in the mirror changed and there she was. The heavyset, ugly duckling she used to be. She averted her eyes.

"Do you know what I see, Jordan?"

"What?" Her tone was curt.

Placing his fingertips under her chin, Danny tilted her head up until their eyes met in the glass. "I see one of the most beautiful women in the world."

"Don't—"

"I see an intelligent mind and a sharp wit. Eyes that notice the best in people. A mouth that smiles easily and is quick to laugh. When I look at you, I see a heart that's compassionate and kind. An enchanting spirit. I see a woman who is beautiful on the inside, and always has been."

His deep, rich voice soothed her. The sincerity of his words touched her, breaking through her fragile control. Hot tears welled in her eyes and spilled over. Danny wrapped his arms around her, resting his cheek against her temple. She raised her hands to clutch his forearms as she cried.

For so long, she'd believed she had to be perfect to be loved. She'd wished for someone to accept her, thinking that would make her feel whole. But in fact what she needed was to accept herself, to realize she was worthy of affection no matter what she weighed or how she looked. Danny had shown her that.

"And on the outside you're beautiful, too. Except for your flushed cheeks and runny nose." He placed a kiss on her brow.

Embarrassed, she reached for a tissue and wiped her face. Danny caressed her upper arms, smiling at her in the mirror. "Your eyes gleam like the brightest stars. Your hair shimmers with fire and light, just like in the shampoo commercials."

Jordan burst out laughing.

"What? I'm praising your gorgeousness. Where was I?" He pretended to contemplate her features. "Your skin is as soft as a baby's butt. Your lips are like the petals of a rose."

He leaned forward and she turned her head to meet him. His hot mouth covered hers in a kiss that was both tender and demanding. When they came up for air, Danny grinned at her. "And they sure can kiss."

Their eyes met in the mirror and her heart turned over in response. She watched as he cupped the fullness of her breasts in his palms. He slowly circled his thumbs around her nipples and she gasped softly at both the sight and the sensation. As his hands glided down her torso, she leaned her head back against his shoulder. Her eyes drifted shut and she smoothed her palms along the hard sinews of his thighs. Desire danced along her nerves as his hands moved over her hips.

Danny bent his head to nuzzle the side of her neck and she felt the hard ridge of his erection against her bottom. "You've got a great body. Real women have curves. You're like a fantasy come true."

And with those words, Jordan was reminded of the true nature of their relationship. She opened her eyes and her hands dropped away from him. Disappointment washed over her and she felt an acute sense of loss. Fun and games were all she could ever expect from him. She broke out of his embrace and turned to face him.

"Fantasy number forty-two. Mirror, Mirror on the Wall, isn't it?"

His dark brown eyes widened and he stepped back, bumping the edge of the tub. He looked as if he'd been slapped. For a second there was such vulnerability in his expression it broke her heart. "This isn't one of your fantasies, Jordan…"

Danny startled, as if he hadn't realized the impact of what he'd said. Then the shutters came down and she watched him completely withdraw. "I've been honest with you from the start. We can't put on costumes or take on roles and make any of this real."

Resignation settled on her shoulders. She offered him a gentle smile, her voice soft as she spoke. "I know we can't."

She turned out of the bathroom. Her chest ached under the weight of melancholy and pain and regret. But she was strong, stronger than she'd ever realized, strong enough to walk away.

Danny followed her into the hall. "What about Saturday?"

He was trying to put the decision of where they went from here on her. If he didn't know by now how she felt, then he never would. She loved him. But the next move was his. Jordan opened the front door. "It's late. I've got to go."

14

DANNY GRABBED his gift off the passenger seat, locked the Jeep and strode across the parking garage to the stairs. Last night had been one of the longest of his life. He doubted he'd slept for more than an hour or two, tossing and turning and trying to figure out what he'd done wrong. He'd finally gotten up to sit out on the fire escape and watch the sun rise.

He'd always been in control of his relationships before, always been the one to set the boundaries. Jordan was the first woman who'd ever walked out on him. He knew he was in trouble because her rejection hurt. Not only had it been a blow to his ego, but he'd also felt in danger of losing something special. There was something about Jordan that both attracted and scared the hell out of him.

As he walked into the building where Chase, Behr & Lily was located, he pictured her face, her disappointed expression. He'd wanted to comfort her last night, to show her how desirable she was. Instead, she thought he wanted to try out another fantasy when he'd actually wanted to make love.

But was he in love? Or was it just the novelty of

the situation? They'd known each other for less than two weeks. They'd seen each other six times and had sex three. He couldn't possibly have fallen for her. Could he? No, more likely he was responding to the challenge. Women liked to be chased. They liked to believe they had the upper hand. So he would pour on the charm, add an element of romance.

This wasn't love. It was all part of the ultimate game. And he played to win.

"Mmm, mmm, mmm." Charlie, the law firm receptionist, hummed into the phone. "You should see what's waiting up here for you."

Jordan tucked the handset between her shoulder and chin as she sorted the papers on her desk. "More chocolates from that one court reporter?"

"Well, he does look rich and delicious and I'd nibble him in a heartbeat." Charlie hummed some more. "Where has David been hiding this brother?"

Danny was here? Her brow crinkled in confusion. What was he doing here? "I'll be right up."

Jordan smoothed her hands over her plum-colored suit and combed her fingers through her hair, suddenly questioning her choice to leave it loose. She started to reach for the compact in her desk drawer then stopped herself. It didn't matter how she looked. She looked just fine. Jordan left her office and walked down the hallway to the lobby.

Wow. Danny did look good enough to nibble. It was the first time she'd seen him wearing something other than jeans or his uniform. He had on a pair of khakis, a button-down shirt, a summer blazer and a hesitant expression. And flowers. Which fantasy was that move from? Stop it. That isn't nice.

"Hi, Danny."

He greeted her with a wide smile. "How are you, pretty lady?"

"I'm fine. And you?"

"Good."

They sounded like two strangers on a bus. Well aware of the awkwardness beneath the pleasantries, she nodded. "Good."

Danny held out the flowers. "I saw these and immediately thought of you."

That was a line if ever she'd heard one. But she loved romantic gestures and these really were lovely. She accepted the bouquet, breathing in the scent of bright pink lilies, orange snapdragons and Shasta daisies. "Thank you very much."

"I was wondering if you were free for lunch? I'm in the mood for seafood myself."

"Oh. I'm sorry." She touched his arm with genuine regret. "I can't today. I have a client meeting in twenty minutes."

"That's okay. I guess I should have called first." He offered her a little smile. "How about dinner then? I'll let you pick the beer."

Jordan winced. "We've got an important trial coming up. I'm going to be working late for the next week or so."

A perplexed expression crossed his face, as if he didn't know what to do next. She thought she heard

him sigh in frustration. Danny took his hand out of
his pocket and scratched his temple. "So, um, what
time is your grandparents' party?"

Jordan's brows rose in surprise. She thought he'd
be thrilled to have his freedom. But he acted as
though there'd never been any question of his taking her. Men. There was just no figuring them out.

"It starts at six-thirty for a seven-o'clock dinner."

"I'll be at your house around six, then."

She cradled the flowers in her arm and shifted un-
comfortably. He'd probably think she was making
up excuses. "I'm going to change at the hotel. I've
got to be there early to help with the place cards and
the thank-you bags."

His jaw clenched and this time he did sigh. Then
he recovered with another winning smile. "Okay.
See you there."

Danny leaned in to kiss her and she offered her
cheek. He barely managed to hide his exasperation. She watched him walk to the elevator before
she allowed the smile of delight to spread across her
face. He'd asked her to lunch, an encounter that
didn't involve either her family or sex. A date. A
rendezvous.

A sign of hope?

As she walked past the reception desk, Charlie
made a tsking sound. "Hard-to-get does not become
you, honey."

Jordan laughed and pulled one of the lilies from
the bouquet. She handed it to Charlie. "Buzz me
when my eleven-thirty gets here."

JORDAN WALKED into the conference room after Susan Brandywine and closed the door behind them. She set her notes and files on the table and drew a deep breath. "Before we get started, I owe you an apology."

Susan frowned in confusion as she took a seat at the conference table. "For what?"

"I allowed my personal opinions to cloud my professionalism and I'm very sorry for that." Jordan clenched and unclenched her hands together but willed herself to maintain eye contact. "You see, I'm as guilty of judging you as any skinny person. More guilty, in fact, because I know what you've been through." Her voice caught. "I felt that if I could lose weight, so should you."

"I understand, Jordan. I really do." Susan looked at her with a blend of sadness and sympathy. "I struggled with my weight for years, making myself sick with one fad diet after another. But now, I'm very proud of who I am and what I've accomplished in my life. This is my body, and I like it just the way it is."

Jordan sat down next to Susan and took her hand. "I admire your courage. Despite losing weight, I'm a long way from acceptance. It's only recently that I've begun to face my issues. I'm still working on it."

"I appreciate your honesty." Susan briefly squeezed Jordan's fingers, then reached into her briefcase for a notepad and pen. "All right. Where do we go from here?"

"I can try to get a settlement. The station may be willing to spend make-it-go-away money in order to avoid the expense of going to trial. And that way you'd have something to tide you over until you can get another job."

Susan scoffed. "This lawsuit may keep me from ever getting another anchor job, but I want to see it through." She rested her elbows on the table and laced her fingers. "Regardless of how many ways women are discriminated against, obesity is the worst because it's the most accepted and the least questioned. I want to fight for my self-respect and maybe set a precedent for other women in entertainment."

Jordan pulled several sheets of paper from the file. "Okay, then. I did find supporting case law. Television anchor Holly Bertram filed a discrimination and breach-of-contract suit against WMTU-TV.

"She contended that middle age forced her out and that because of her weight she didn't get the anchor positions she sought." Jordan shuffled the papers until she found the one she wanted. "Now, Bertram did lose her age claim, but she won on the injury and retaliation claims. A federal jury awarded…are you ready? Five million dollars."

Susan gasped. "Are you serious? And you think we can apply her case to my situation?"

"I found this buried in the production of documents. It's a memo from Bob Milton, the station manager, to Paul White, the news director. Milton says some pretty nasty things about your weight gain." She handed the document over. "He also outlines the steps they should take to get rid of you."

Susan covered her mouth with one hand and tears glistened in her eyes as she read the damning statements.

"This is the key to winning the case, Susan. They can try to prove breach of contract based on Clause XIII of your contract, but this memo clearly shows malicious intent. Someday we might see a case in which it's successfully argued that looks and gender are bona fide occupational qualifications for television news anchors, but until then…"

A triumphant smile spread across Susan's face. "Until then, we've got WBNS by the balls."

As HE STRODE through the lobby of the Wyndham Hotel, Danny tugged at the jacket of his borrowed tuxedo. He hated stuffing himself into a monkey suit, especially tonight. He was wearing his brother's tux to meet the woman who was supposed to be his brother's fiancée. Thankfully, this would be the last night he had to answer to his brother's name. Would it also be the last night he saw Jordan?

His pulse tripped along his nerves. His stomach was tied in tiny knots. He was really looking forward to spending time with the Gregorys tonight. He'd promised Grandma Emma a dance and Eric had challenged him to sing karaoke. But, as for the most important member of the family, he had no idea where he stood with Jordan.

He'd tried flowers, compliments, charm, surprise visits and late-night phone calls. All of which had been met with reserve. Was she stringing him along or had she really lost interest? The uncertainty was making him nuts. Danny paused beneath the flower-strewn lattice at the entrance of the Liberty Ballroom, feeling unsure of himself.

The floor-to-ceiling windows overlooked the night skyline of downtown Baltimore and the Inner Harbor. Crystal chandeliers glowed above tables set with creamy linen and topped with tall vases of peach roses, yellow tulips and sprays of fern. His eyes scanned the ballroom, looking for familiar faces.

Waiters in white dinner jackets offered trays of hors d'oeuvres to the hundred or so people milling about. Near the windows, a photographer snapped group portraits of various family and friends. Meanwhile, a cameraman circulated through the gathering, interviewing guests for a keepsake video.

Then he saw her. And she took his breath away.

Jordan was stunning. Tonight she wore a lime-green cocktail dress that left a whole lot of golden-brown skin on display. The satin material caressed her generous curves like a lover. The strapless bodice showcased her cleavage while the short hemline bared her legs to the thigh. That surprised him most of all.

Danny looked at her with a mixture of lust and pride. Her hair fell loosely around her bare shoulders as if inviting his fingers to stroke the silky tresses. Her light brown eyes were lined with dark green shadow, her lips glistened a deep rose. He'd never seen her look more sexy, more confident or more beautiful. Finally he forced his trembling legs to move.

When he reached her side, he simply followed his instincts and took her into his arms. He claimed her mouth and kissed her eagerly, thoroughly, telling her without words how much he wanted her. When he broke the kiss a moment later, Jordan gave a self-conscious laugh, pretending to fan herself.

"Hello to you, too."

He smiled at her, his hands still on her waist. "You are just gorgeous."

"All right, that's enough, young man. Stop drooling over the girl and greet the rest of us."

Startled, Danny glanced around him and realized several members of Jordan's family stood nearby, watching them. With a grin, he shook hands with Matt and Reece, accepted a kiss from Celeste and even gave Keisha a hug. He was both touched and saddened by the warm welcome he received. They were good people and he'd come to hate lying to them.

Celeste looked him over then gave him an exaggerated wink. "You certainly do clean up nice. Save me a dance later so I can make my husband jealous."

Jordan looped her arm through his and leaned against him. "Watch it, lady. Uncle Matt won't be the only one jealous."

Danny sighed and addressed the other two men. "Don't you hate it when they fight over you?"

"Doesn't anybody want to dance with me?" Reece sulked.

"With those two left feet?" Jordan laughed. "No way, little brother."

Just then a bell chimed lightly and the maître d' invited everyone to be seated for dinner. Danny took Jordan's hand and followed her to one of the round tables near the dance floor and brass-railed stage. Crystal buckets held chilling bottles of champagne and the place cards were replicas of Charles and Emma's wedding announcement.

As he held Jordan's chair, Danny couldn't resist leaning down to plant a kiss on her shoulder. Camryn beamed at them from across the table. "Get a room, you two."

"As long as it's not the one we booked. I have plans for later." Mason leaned over to give her a smacking kiss.

"You're supposed to get married before you have the honeymoon, you know."

"Daddy!" Camryn blushed hotly. "He hasn't asked me yet."

The entrées were served and Danny was pleasantly surprised again. Jordan was eating, and not just her salad. She didn't deny herself a single bite of the Fillet of Beef with Wild Mushroom Medley or the Ocean Trout in Filo with Tomatoes and Olives. He pushed his plate closer so that she could spear one of the baby potatoes.

Danny indicated the head table. "Who are the people sitting with your grandparents?"

"You met my mom's parents at the barbecue. They've got their backs to us. The others are Grandpa and Grandma's oldest friends." Jordan subtly pointed to each couple as she named them.

Danny watched the older folks laughing and gesturing and felt a pang of envy. It must be wonderful to share an evening like this with people who'd known you for several decades. He tried to picture what Jordan would look like in another forty years. She'd probably be as beautiful then as she was now.

She caught him staring and smiled. "What are you thinking?"

He couldn't tell her the truth, not here, not yet. "I was just wondering if Charles and Emma are playing footsy under the table. She keeps glancing at him with a funny little smile."

Jordan looked over at her grandparents and giggled. "I think Grandma just put her hand on his thigh."

Eric made a face. "Ugh. You don't think they still…?"

"And why shouldn't they? Some things get better with age." Jordan's father wiggled his eyebrows at her mother.

Angela playfully swatted his shoulder. "Behave yourself, Jackson."

Danny felt a tightening in his chest and had to swallow a sudden lump in his throat. These people were so obviously in love as couples, and just as obviously loved each other as a family. The Gregorys shared a warmth and a closeness that was missing from his own life, except for his relationship with David.

Horrified, he recognized the sting of tears behind his eyes. Because he couldn't deny it any longer. He had fallen deeply, irrevocably in love. With the other women he'd dated, he'd always held a part of himself back. But with Jordan, he didn't want to hold back anymore. He wanted to matter to her, as she'd come to matter to him. He wanted to have a place in her life, to be a real couple, and to be included in this family.

The power of his emotions left him both stunned and disoriented. His first reaction was panic. He'd never been in love before so how could he be sure of what was happening?

Then he felt Jordan's hand on his thigh under the table, saw her very subtle wink, and a sense of calm settled over him, a sense of rightness. Danny reached over to cup her cheek and draw her to him. The kiss he gave her this time was sweet and tender, a prelude to the things he'd say to her later.

Danny's kiss rocked her to the core. In his eyes, she saw a tenderness and a longing that had never been there before. Lightning struck her heart. She had prayed that he would come around, that he'd realize they had something special, and it seemed her prayers had been answered. If that kiss was anything to go by, ten days wasn't long enough for him, either.

For the rest of the meal it was all she could do not

to dance on the tabletop and shout with joy. But this was her grandparents' night and she wouldn't take attention away from them. With difficulty, Jordan concentrated on the game of Anniversary Trivia they were playing.

"Okay, it's my turn." She picked up the small white card above her plate and read the question. "True or false? The first time Emma saw Charles, he was wearing a banana suit."

Her father laughed. "That's true."

Eric turned his head in surprise. "It is?"

"Yep," Jackson replied. "Dad was the banana in his elementary school play about nutrition."

Danny murmured in her ear. "What is it with your family and bananas? If you're not wearing them, you're using them as fake weapons."

Jordan chuckled and whispered back, "Did you read the one fantasy called Strawberry Fields For Hours? We could plan a whole fruit-themed night."

"I'm next." Her mother read from her trivia card. "To further their love of learning, which of the following classes have Charles and Emma taken? Citizen's Police Academy, Ceramics and Pottery or Tai Chi?"

After dinner, Jordan was extremely tempted by the slice of orange-vanilla wedding cake, but decided she'd indulged herself enough for one night. Instead she fed pieces of cake to Danny while they watched a video montage of photographs taken of her grandparents through the years.

"They look very happy together," Danny whispered.

"I think they are."

As the lights came up, the DJ started playing upbeat tunes and encouraging people to come out to the floor. Before she could ask Danny to dance with her, though, Aunt Celeste had already grabbed him. But she made sure he was all hers for the first slow song, a romantic ballad about falling in love forever. Jordan melted into his embrace as they danced, hips swaying and thighs brushing.

It felt so good, so right to be in his arms. She closed her eyes, focusing on the music and the magic of the evening. Danny must have been caught up in it, too. When the tempo changed to something faster, he continued to hold her for a moment before reluctantly letting her go.

"Save all of the other slow songs for me, too, okay?"

Jordan beamed at him. "It's a deal."

The DJ had set up a karaoke machine on the stage, so in between dance numbers, the guests were treated to an impromptu talent show. Emma and Charles even stepped up to the microphone, delighting everyone with a hit from the latest pop song princess.

Emma started off with, "Oh baby, baby. There's something you just gotta know." Then Charles chimed in with, "I love you baby. I'm never going to let you go." Jordan winced and covered her eyes when they tried some moves from the video. Beside her, Danny howled with laughter. "Wow. That belly-dancing class they took really paid off."

A few songs later, Eric stepped onto the stage. Instead of singing, though, he made an announcement. "Ladies and gentlemen, you're really in for a treat tonight. My sister Jordan and her fiancé, David, have agreed to a duet."

Jordan looked at Danny with an expression of mock horror. "I didn't agree to that. Did you agree to that?"

Eric continued. "I've chosen a special song for them because it's one of my grandparents' favorites. Jordan, David, come on up here!"

Jordan felt hot color rush to her cheeks as Danny took her hand and led her forward. She hadn't performed in public since the *Hairspray* musical back in high school. She tugged on Danny's hand. "Can you even sing?"

"I never sing except in the shower. The water drowns out the worst of it."

"Oh, great…"

She laughed, but to her surprise, when the music intro began, Danny's rich tenor confidently belted out the first line. Jordan grabbed the other microphone, waited for her cue and came in with the next verse of a famous Motown hit. Although Danny sang with more enthusiasm than talent, they ended the duet to thunderous applause.

As they held hands and took their bows, Jordan decided this was the best night of her life.

15

HE'D DANCED with almost every woman at the party in the past two hours. Danny loosened his bow tie and rested his forearms on the railing of the balcony outside the ballroom. A slight breeze blew off the Inner Harbor, cooling him off as he undid the top button of his shirt.

"Are you having a good time?"

He angled his head to see Keisha swaying toward him, a half-empty glass of champagne in her hand. Danny straightened. "Yeah, I'm just a little worn-out from all of that dancing."

"Well, I hope you recover quickly. You haven't danced with me once tonight." When she came over and leaned back against the rail, he could tell this wasn't her first glass of wine.

"I think I'm done for the night—"

"You danced with everyone else. Why not me? Why won't you dance with me?"

Her voice took on a definite edge, one that was best avoided. Danny pushed away from the railing with the intention of going back inside. She came after him.

"You know what they say, don't you? Good on the dance floor, better in bed."

He rubbed his head, dropping his gaze in embarrassment. He had no clue how to respond to that. She shifted in front of him to block his path. He tried to go around her again.

"Excuse me, Keisha. I'm going back in."

She grabbed the loose ends of his bow tie and pulled, forcing him to lower his head. She planted her lips on his in a smooth, expert kiss. It left him completely unmoved. In fact, it confirmed his feelings for Jordan that a great kiss from a gorgeous woman had no effect on him at all. Danny gently pushed her away and yanked his tie from her fist.

Keisha glared at him, her voice rising. "What's wrong with you? Men always find me attractive. They always want *me*. How can you choose Jordan over me?" She locked both arms around his neck and kissed him again, this time hard and angry and desperate.

"What the hell are you doing?"

Danny finally succeeded in breaking away just as Reece came out on the balcony. Startled and off balance, Keisha dropped her champagne. The sound of glass shattering against concrete distracted Danny for a second. When he turned back, Reece's fist flew toward his face. Pain exploded in his head and his eye began to swell almost instantly. Keisha ran past them to the ballroom door.

"You son of a bitch," Reece growled through clenched teeth. "I knew there was something going on."

"I swear, it's not what it looks like." Danny's fingers tentatively explored the bruise developing on his cheek.

"Neither are you. I don't know what's going on, but you'd better leave." Reece shoved him back a step. "Stay the hell away from both my cousin and my sister."

On the one hand, he felt compelled to stay and defend himself against Reece's anger. But it was more important to get to Jordan before her cousin did. Given the animosity between the two, Keisha's ploy would be like throwing gasoline on a lit match. Danny went back inside with Reece hard on his heels.

At their appearance, several people pointed and stared. He heard a series of whispers ripple through the gathering crowd. Danny's eyes urgently sought any sign of Jordan. A moment later, she pushed past some of the guests to get to his side. Her gaze swept over him, taking in his black eye and unbuttoned shirt.

He seized her hand and drew her close. "We have to talk. Right now."

Reece glared at him. "You can't talk your way out of this."

Jordan reached up with her index finger to tilt his chin. "What happened to your face?"

"It's nothing—"

"Danny!"

"Danny?" Reece shifted his attention to his sister. "Why did you call him…?" He turned back to Danny. "Who are you?"

Jordan clapped a hand over her mouth, her eyes

darkening as she realized what she'd said. Danny pulled her aside, trying to put some distance between them, her brother and the rest of the guests drawn to the scene they were making. He had to explain. He had to tell her how he felt, but his words came out as jumbled as his thoughts.

"This wasn't supposed to happen. It took me completely by surprise. I didn't mean for—"

Jordan squeezed his fingers to get his attention. "*What* is going on?"

Reece lowered his voice so that only she would hear him. "I went outside for some air and caught him kissing Keisha."

"What?" She dropped Danny's hand.

"I didn't kiss Keisha. She kissed me." He pressed his palms against his temples. "Oh God, this is such a mess!"

"I can not believe—"

"Listen to me," Danny insisted, "I can't *pretend* anymore."

Jordan blinked in confusion at the swift change of subject. "You promised me, Danny. We agreed."

"To hell with that agreement! I know we made a deal, but now I can't do this—"

"Jo-Jo, is everything all right?"

Charles Gregory's quiet inquiry broke through the tension. Jordan turned to her grandfather with tears in her eyes. Danny reached for her hand, but she was twisting her fingers together as she always did when she was upset.

"No, Grandpa, it isn't."

"Jordan, wait. I didn't tell you—"

Reece interrupted him. "The only thing you need to tell her is how sorry you are!"

Beside him, Jordan took a deep breath. "No. I'm the one who should apologize—"

Danny tried again. "*Please,* wait a minute. Let me explain."

Grandpa Charles touched her face. "Is there something you need to tell us?"

"I lied to you. I lied to everyone."

"Don't," Danny pleaded. "You don't have to tell them. If you'll just hear me out, I can make this right."

Jordan ignored him. She looked around at the faces in the crowd and he could feel her start to tremble. "We're not really engaged. We never were." She closed her eyes for a second then continued. "This isn't David Navarro. It's his twin brother, Danny."

"Not engaged?" "Who did she say he was?" Strident voices overlapped as everyone seemed to ask questions at once. "Why did you lie?" "Why did you fool us?"

Reece's angry voice rose above the rest. "We're not the only ones he made fools of. This guy's been messing around on Jordan—"

"Reece, no!"

"He was flirting with Keisha the other night and I caught them out on the balcony just now."

There was a collective gasp and the eyes that had been merely confused a moment ago now looked on

Danny with hostility. Jordan began to cry softly. In an instant, her mother was at her side, trying to comfort her.

Danny reached for Jordan, but she shied away from his touch. "Give me a chance to talk to you. I just need a minute."

"I never would have believed you'd do something like that. But, then, you're not who we all thought you were, are you?" Angela glared at him. She led her daughter to one of the tables where several other women formed a shield around them. Then a hush came over the crowd as both her father and uncle stepped forward.

"Is this true what Reece said?" As Matt questioned him, Danny thought he detected a hint of sympathy. If anyone would believe the kiss wasn't his fault, it might be Jordan's uncle.

"I can explain everything, Mr. Gregory. But I have to talk to Jordan first."

Jackson held up his hand. "Danny, is it? I think it might be best if you left now, son. We can sort this all out later." Though his words were quiet, his voice sounded harsh.

He couldn't believe this was happening. His stomach churned with nausea in response to the cold look Jordan's father gave him. It couldn't end, not like this. Danny shouldered his way through the crowd before anyone could stop him. Kneeling down beside the table where Jordan sat, he put a hand on her arm.

"There are so many things I need to say to you,

I don't know where to begin. I've never been in love before. I didn't recognize it at first because I didn't know it could happen so fast—"

Jordan pulled her arm aside and turned her head, refusing to look at him. "Leave me alone, Danny."

He knew she was hurt and offended by that damned kiss, but why wouldn't she listen? Was she punishing him for breaking their agreement or had he misread her feelings? His throat constricted along with his heart. He'd exposed himself completely only to have her turn him away.

Something inside him was dying, something he belatedly recognized as hope.

Getting to his feet, he looked about him and saw only the silent accusations of strangers. He didn't realize how badly he wanted to belong until now, when the woman he'd fallen in love with and the family he'd come to cherish had shunned him. Feeling miserable and empty and alone, Danny walked out of the ballroom.

IT HAD BEEN just like the senior prom. Only worse. Because this time she loved the guy who'd humiliated her. Jordan lay on one of the twin beds, staring at the ceiling, in the room she and Camryn had shared. She'd come home to Annapolis, to the comfort of her family, rather than spend the night alone.

She'd asked Danny to play a role and he'd turned in an award-winning performance. Only days ago, he'd convinced her that no man would choose her cousin over her. And all the while her scheming

bitch of a cousin had been laughing at her—
again—because Keisha knew who Danny really
desired.

What had he said? "This wasn't supposed to happen. It took me completely by surprise. I've never
been in love before." Jordan pounded her clenched
fists against the mattress. *Stupid, stupid, stupid!*
Hadn't Keisha warned her that she always got what
she wanted? She'd gotten the best of Jordan again.

Yet, oddly enough, a part of her felt sorry for her
cousin. Because she doubted that Danny really cared
about Keisha, either. An eight date man who
changed his girlfriends along with his underwear
wasn't capable of love.

She covered her eyes with both hands, grateful
for the temporary relief of the darkness. Her
thoughts were spinning and twisting around in her
head so fast they were giving her a headache.

Regret and embarrassment washed over her, but
anger was her foremost emotion. Why would he
kiss Keisha in such a public place, why would he
take the chance, unless he *wanted* to get caught?
Why else would he have done such a despicable
thing? His actions were at exact odds to the sensitive, caring person she'd lost her heart to.

Danny had shown her, through his words and
his touch, that she was beautiful in her own way.
With him, she'd discovered that she was sexy and
passionate, sensual and desirable. For the first
time in her life, she was proud of her full breasts
and rounded hips and curvaceous figure. She

would always be grateful to Danny for that, even though he apparently hadn't meant a single word he'd said.

There were moments when Danny had let her inside and allowed her to see the pain and the tenderness. He'd seemed to truly enjoy being with her and her family. That's what made this whole situation so confusing. Was he so afraid to open his heart, to let her love him, that he would purposely sabotage their developing relationship?

Someday she would find a man who meant the pretty things he said, a man without ulterior motives for his actions. One day she'd find a man who genuinely cared for her and whose affection would last for more than nine and a half days.

A knock came softly just before the door opened and Camryn walked in. Jordan rolled over onto her side as her sister stretched out on the other bed. Camryn's eyes roamed the room, noting the familiar and the changes. "I'm glad Mom kept the rosebud wallpaper, but I kind of miss the lace canopies and the teen idol posters."

"We shared a lot of dreams in this room, didn't we?" Jordan smiled, remembering. "And all of yours came true."

She was quiet for a moment. "Yes, they did. At least for a while."

"You really miss your modeling career."

She rolled over to face Jordan, resting her head on her arm. "I don't miss living on bottled water and cigarettes, terrified of gaining six ounces and losing a job. I don't miss constantly being judged by my appearance. That judgment can be extremely harsh."

"I know all about being judged."

Her sister got up and came to sit on her bed. "I know you do, honey. I know you always envied me and Keisha to some extent. But the way you look—or don't look—should never be the measure of your happiness. And it shouldn't be the foundation for love." Camryn reached for her hand.

"What I came up here to say, Jo-Jo, is don't beat yourself up for believing in a dream when the reality was beyond your control. I know how much you must be hurting right now. But you'll survive and be stronger for it." Camryn stood up and gave her a little smile. "I also came to tell you that Daddy called a family meeting."

Jordan's heart sank and her stomach fluttered with sudden anxiety. It was time to face the consequences of her lies.

She padded down to the kitchen a few minutes later, hesitating in the doorway as her parents and brothers turned to look at her. On their faces, she saw concern and curiosity, but thankfully no anger. Camryn squeezed her shoulder before moving past her into the family room. Bracing herself, Jordan took a seat on one of the sofas, next to her grandparents.

"I'm glad everyone is here. I owe all of you an apology, but especially you two." She touched her grandmother's hand. "I'm so very sorry for ruining your party last night."

Grandpa reached over to pat her knee. "Thank

you, darling. But what none of us understand is how this all happened?"

Her mother spoke from across the room. "We let it be last night because we were all tired and upset. But now we'd like to know why you lied to us."

Jordan twisted her mouth in a smile of self-derision even as tears stung her eyes. "It seems so damned stupid now."

"Most things do in hindsight." From his seat on the carpet, Eric squeezed her calf in a show of support.

"It all started because I wanted Keisha to stop teasing me. I know that sounds incredibly childish, but—"

"We know how cruel your cousin can be." Her parents shared a look. "However, we felt we should let you sort it out. I see now that was our mistake."

"It was mine, too, Mom. When I began seeing David, I—I made more of the relationship than there was. And when Keisha came up from Atlanta in May, I let things go too far. She was taunting me about my weight and bragging about all of her boyfriends… To shut her up, I said that David had proposed."

Grandpa cleared his throat. "Your cousin is in the other room and she has something to say to you. Reece, will you please ask them to join us?"

A moment later, Celeste, Matt and Keisha walked in. Jordan noticed her aunt and uncle's tight expressions. However, they both put an arm around their daughter as they settled on the other couch. Her cousin's eyes were red-rimmed and her skin had a grayish pallor, as though she were hungover. She glanced at Jordan and then averted her gaze.

"I'm sorry, Grandpa. I'm sorry, Grandma. I, um, apologize for last night."

"You owe your cousin an apology, too, young lady."

"I know." She dropped her chin, staring at the floor. "Sorry, Jordan."

Uncle Matt scowled at her. "Keisha Marie Gregory, we talked about this."

"I said I was sorry!"

"That's not good enough." Aunt Celeste's voice was stern. "Your behavior was inexcusable."

Eric made a harsh sound. "Keisha, do you realize what you've done? And for what?"

"Oh, that's right. Take her side, as always."

"This isn't about taking sides," Aunt Celeste said. "You've hurt people with your thoughtlessness and antagonism in the past, but this time you went too far."

An accusing silence settled over the room, then Grandma tilted her head. "Jordan, honey, I still don't understand why you felt you had to lie. You know we love you, no matter what."

"Every member of this family is part of a couple. Each of you belongs to and is with somebody, while I had no one." Twisting her fingers in her lap, she cleared her throat. "Whether you realized it or not, you all treated me differently when you thought I was getting married."

"They've always treated you different," Keisha muttered bitterly.

"Excuse me?"

"I've spent most of my life in your shadow. It didn't matter that I was prettier or thinner or more popular—everyone always loved you more!"

Jordan frowned in confusion. "Keisha, what in the world are you talking about?"

"I was jealous, okay? I was jealous. You upstaged me all the time! I made the cheerleading squad, but everyone was more excited that you were on some national debate team." Keisha jumped up from the sofa and began pacing the room.

"Then there was the time I was first runner-up in the Miss Maryland pageant. But all I heard about was, 'Jordan made the Honor Society.' Even my college graduation was overshadowed because you were accepted into law school."

Angela spoke quietly, her voice tinged with remorse. "Keisha, we never meant to exclude you. We're just as proud of your accomplishments—"

"Yeah, right. Everybody thinks I get more attention, but Jordan always had what I really wanted—everyone's respect."

Eric snorted. "I think you've blown things out of proportion—"

"No, she's right." Camryn spoke up quietly. "There were times when I was jealous of you, too, Jordan. You never seemed to realize that you're the star this family revolves around."

She couldn't believe what she was hearing. The two people she envied most in the world had been consumed by jealousy because of her? She never would have guessed that her cousin looked on her as competition. Jordan stood up and walked across the room. She gently touched Keisha's arm but made no other move toward reconciliation.

"If I hurt you, it was unintentional. But this is a problem you'll have to resolve yourself."

Keisha's resentful expression crumbled. Her voice broke as she tearfully met Jordan's eyes. "Danny—it wasn't Danny's fault. All he ever was was nice to me. He didn't—he pushed me away last night. I tried to kiss him, I tried to make him want me, but he pushed me away."

A mantle of sadness dropped onto Jordan's shoulders. Danny had told her the truth. He really had chosen her over her cousin. But she'd refused to listen when he tried to explain.

Omigod. Had he been trying to tell her he'd fallen in love with *her?*

For a moment joy bubbled up inside her and she was filled with hope. Until she remembered how often he'd retreated in the face of any sign of real emotion. It was a false hope, one that would only set her up to be hurt again.

Grandpa caught her attention. "Last night you said you weren't engaged to David. Now, you're saying you weren't engaged to Danny, either?"

"No." Jordan shook her head slowly. "It was all a lie, one that snowballed until I got buried under it."

"So how did Danny end up getting involved?" Camryn asked.

"Mom and Dad had met David at the law firm.

So when I needed a fiancé these past two weeks, the only solution was to convince Danny to play the role."

"I don't know, Jo-Jo. From what I saw of you together, it seemed as if you and Danny really were in love."

Her father's statement brought a stab of pain. Jordan thought they might have a chance, but Danny had made it clear all along that he was willing to give her his body but not his heart. Despite his declaration of love, and the truth about that kiss, he would always keep her at arm's length.

"Whatever happened between us, whatever I thought Danny and I had, that's all over now."

16

"I TRIED CALLING, but she wouldn't pick up the damned phone." Danny stalked past the tall windows in the living room of his brother's condo, oblivious to the beauty of the Sunday morning sky.

"Well, maybe she was in the shower or something. Try again," David suggested in a rational tone.

He turned and prowled in the other direction. "I did. She still wouldn't pick up the phone, so I drove to her house. I stood there like an idiot, ringing the bell and knocking, but she never came down."

"Jordan might not have been home, Dan."

"Her car was there. She was home. She's blowing me off."

David drummed his fingers on the armchair. "Would you please sit down? You're making me dizzy trying to follow you around the room."

He dropped onto the couch, barely resisting the urge to kick the coffee table. Frustration and anger churned inside his gut over the injustice of it all. How could she believe he would stoop so low as to kiss Keisha at their grandparents' party? How could Jordan think he would kiss her cousin at all?

"Damn it, she didn't give me the chance to explain. She turned her back and believed the worst of me."

His twin looked at him with sympathetic and all too observant eyes. "I can understand that you're hurt—"

"I'm not hurt." Danny shifted on the couch. "I'm just ticked off that it had to end this way. You know I prefer to walk away still friends."

"Jordan isn't like the other women you've dated, and you know it."

He forced a laugh past the tightness in his throat. "Yeah, this was one for the books, huh? I hope the next woman comes without baggage. I mean, her family was a lot to deal with."

Even as he said it, the truth sliced at his heart. The Gregorys' rejection hurt him terribly. He understood their rallying around Jordan, but he'd wanted somebody to stand by him, too. He wanted someone to believe him, or at least to hear him out. Ever since he had walked away, a cold, lonely void had grown inside him. He was going to miss Jordan. He was going to miss all of them.

He injected a lighthearted tone into his voice. "I called Marlee to set up dinner for next week. And the jazz festival is coming up. I figure Valerie will want to go."

David stared at him with an expression of wonder and disappointment. His dark brows drew together in a frown. "Why are you making dates with these women? Aren't you going to try and win Jordan back?"

"Hey, it wasn't going to work out anyway." Danny affected a shrug. "She wanted more than I could give her. So this was as doomed as all of my other relationships."

A hard light flared in David's eyes. "Was it? Or were you following your usual pattern?"

"You think I should have hung around, waiting for things to turn sour? We always swore we'd never end up like Mom and Dad."

David's expression softened, but his tone of voice was firm. "At least they're together and still trying. You, on the other hand, are going to end up alone with nothing except memories and shadows. Jordan is a very special woman. She's your chance to reach for the light."

Danny slumped deeper into the couch and dropped his chin. "This wasn't real, David. It wouldn't have lasted. Nothing ever does. It either blows apart or dies a slow, agonizing death. Either way, the pain is too hard to live with."

"Take it from someone who learned this lesson the hard way, and at Jordan's expense. You can't go through life denying what you know in your heart. The fact that you don't like it doesn't make it any less true. You love her. Now, what are you going to do about it?"

DANNY HAD NO IDEA what to do about Jordan, so he didn't do anything. Sure, he picked up the phone to call her numerous times, but then hung up the receiver again. He'd even driven past her house, slow-

ing down to stare at the lights in the windows and
wanting to see her so badly it hurt.

But her rejection felt too much like all of the
times he'd reached out to his parents, only to find
himself rebuffed or ignored. To keep from thinking
about Jordan, Danny retreated to the straightfor-
ward demands of his job, even taking extra shifts on
what were supposed to be his days off.

It seemed that Tuesday night at the fire station
might be quiet. There had been few calls during the
day and the second shift was pretty relaxed as a result. Having spent the past two nights tossing and
turning, Danny crashed out on one of the beds upstairs. Sleep eluded him for the longest time until he
finally dropped into an exhausted slumber.

Around seven o'clock he was awakened by the
strident peal of the alarm bell. Instantly going from
sleep to full alert, he swung his legs over the side
of the bed and into his steel-toed rubber boots. In
the same motion he pulled up his bunker pants and
snapped the suspenders in place. Danny stuffed his
arms into his turnout coat as he raced for the stairs.
The thunderous rumbling of the diesel engines
filled the station and the bay doors were already
opening.

The first rush of adrenaline hit his system as he
jumped onto Ladder 24, listening to the dispatcher
announce what they were facing. Fire in progress,
commercial building, corner of Pratt and Howard
streets. The second rush was a spiked fist in the gut.
Oh, no. Had he heard the address right? No. Danny

fumbled beneath his protective clothing for the cell phone in his trouser pocket.

Mike Cornwall yelled at him over the sirens as the fire truck roared along Pratt Street past King Boulevard. "Who the hell are you calling?"

"That address. It's the CB&L building. Jordan works there."

Danny stuck his index finger in his ear, listening for the connection to go through. Her home phone rang and rang, with no answer. He knew David was out with friends, leaving him free of worry about his brother. But where was Jordan?

Oh God, he hoped she wasn't working late tonight. She'd said there was an important trial coming up, but she must have left the office by now. Please let her have left. He dialed the direct line to her office and got a busy signal. Shit!

Danny banged his fist on the roof and yelled at the chauffer, the firefighter driving the big ladder truck. "Move this thing!"

Mike leaned forward. "What's up, L.T.?"

He swallowed against the nausea, practically choking on the words. "Her office line is busy. I think she's still in there."

Sirens screamed into the night, the sound reverberating off the skyscrapers and empty streets. Every fiber of his being hummed with dread as they got closer to the CB&L building. Through the tinted-glass windows, he could see the orange light of dancing flames on the middle floors.

The law firm was on the fourteenth.

Ladder 24 was the second company to arrive on the scene. Protocol dictated that they lay down supply lines to the first engine, which had only tank water to attack the fire. But Danny couldn't wait for the third-on-scene company to perform the necessary search and rescue. He grabbed an SCBA tank from the equipment rack and donned his mask, then leaped off the truck and sprinted for the building.

He had to find Jordan. Now.

"You know we're going to catch hell for this, don't you?"

Danny glanced over to see Mike running at his side. Too grateful to speak, he simply nodded his head and ran on.

The lights were out, indicating that power had been lost. Several hoses snaked across the marble floor of the lobby. Mike almost tripped when the pressurized water rammed through the one and a half inch diameter line. Danny yanked the flashlight from his utility belt and turned it on.

A firefighter from Engine 32 came out of the stairwell, helping a distraught woman and reassuring the three other civilians with him. Shit. There were still people in the building. Danny and Mike reached the bank of elevators and he frantically flipped through his ring until he found the right key. "Where's the focal point, Stonewall?"

Mike listened to the radio on his shoulder. "Twelfth floor. Some kind of office supply and photocopy business."

He overrode the elevator doors. As they stepped

inside, Mike pulled his mask onto his face. Danny shoved the key into the slot marked Fire Service and pressed the call button for twelve. His stomach plummeted as the car ascended. It was an unspoken rule that firefighters never discussed their fears with anyone, not even each other. But Mike had been his friend and partner long enough to read his face in the golden glow of their flashlights.

"Don't sweat it, L.T. I'm sure she's fine."

When the elevator opened onto the twelfth floor, Danny saw that it was fully engaged. Flames licked the walls and spread up across the ceiling. Thick smoke billowed throughout this floor, giving the fire scene a murky, ethereal appearance. Hose crews from another company were already battling the blaze. Mike looked over at him and, by unspoken agreement, he punched the button to shut the elevator doors again.

"Fourteen, Mike. Head straight for fourteen."

The smoke was thick up here, too, making an already dark area completely obscure. Playing their flashlights over the floor in front of them, they found the reception desk. Danny knew that Chase, Behr & Lily took up the whole floor, but he had no idea where Jordan's office was located.

"Split up. You take this hallway. I'll take the other."

Mike nodded. "Let's do it, L.T. We've only got another fifteen minutes of air."

His pulse stuttered along his veins as he jogged down the passageway, flinging open doors to look

for Jordan or anyone else that might have been overcome by the smoke. His hope grew with each empty
office he found, but there were still too many left to
check. He fervently prayed that Jordan wasn't anywhere in here. Every moment that slipped away
could mean a moment off of her life.

Then he heard it. The ominous whistling noise.
The shrill sound warning him that he only had a
quarter tank of air left. Fear as he'd never known it
before slammed into him like a freight train. He
couldn't leave, not yet, not until he was sure. He
began panting into his mask to conserve precious
oxygen as he rushed toward yet another closed office door.

But the exertion was too much. Darkness crept
along the edge of his consciousness. No. Not yet,
damn it. Not now. He…had to…find… Fairy lights
danced in front of his eyes and Danny knew he was
in danger of blacking out. His strength ebbed and he
felt himself sinking…

*He couldn't see. He could barely breathe. But he
knew there were bodies all around him, trapped in
the wreckage of the building and the plane, and he
was helpless to save them.*

Jordan. He had to save Jordan. His heart thundered in his chest and in his mind he cried out to her.

*It was a nightmare of intense heat and unrelent-
ing fear. Oily black smoke filled the air, surrounding him. Oh God, he couldn't breathe.*

Danny struggled against the terror. He couldn't
give in, not this time. He had to be strong. If he got

a second chance, he wouldn't waste it, he wouldn't take it for granted. He'd been wrong, so wrong. Jordan had offered him the gift of her love and he'd been too afraid to reach for it, too afraid of it slipping through his hands. He couldn't lose himself in the fear. He wouldn't lose her.

There was no way out. Fires raged in a seething inferno of boiling smoke. They'd already lost four in that warehouse. He was out of air. Tears welled in his eyes. The darkness was coming and he couldn't find the light...

Jordan.

As if from a great distance, he heard a voice yelling for him. "There's nobody here! We have to get out. L.T.? L.T.!"

Mike dragged him to his feet. Then he hazily realized his partner had him in a fireman's carry. Somehow he held on until they made it back to the elevator. Mike overrode the doors and tossed him inside. Danny propped himself against the wall and ripped the shield off his face. Mike replaced it with his mask. Danny gasped for breath as the pure, sweet oxygen filled his starving lungs.

Stonewall looked at him with a combination of humor and concern. "Man, the dumb-assed things we do for love."

From behind the air mask, Danny managed a weak grin. By the time the elevator reached the lobby, he felt steadier on his feet. Again a silent look of understanding passed between him and his partner so that Danny walked outside unassisted. As they approached the nearest fire engines, the Battalion Chief came gunning for them.

"I told you we'd catch hell," Mike muttered.

Danny leaned against the bumper of the truck, his eyes scanning the onlookers huddled behind the police barricade. Suddenly, through the crowd, the darkness and the commotion, he saw her. His relief at knowing Jordan was all right almost brought him to his knees.

He shoved past the Bat Chief in mid-harangue and ran toward Jordan. She cried out his name when he reached for her. As her hands cupped his cheeks, he felt her love touch his soul. Overwhelmed by the intensity of his feelings, Danny buried his face in her shoulder and held on, knowing he'd never again let her go.

DANNY HAD TO GO BACK and help battle the fire, so Jordan had been left to come home alone with only concern to keep her company. That was hours ago. She'd fallen asleep on the sofa, not waking until well after midnight.

She got up and changed out of her suit into an old pair of sweatpants and a T-shirt. It didn't matter anymore if Danny saw her looking less than perfect. She knew now that she didn't have to be perfect for him, that she was beautiful in his eyes. Jordan paced the living room of her row house, anxiously waiting for him to show up. The thick carpeting bore the imprint of her bare feet as she wandered the house.

As though her thoughts conjured his presence,

the doorbell rang. She ran to answer it. Danny stood on her doorstep, simply gazing at her with an expression of tenderness and longing. He'd showered and changed clothes, but the specter of tonight's fire still enveloped him.

Jordan wrapped her arms around him, sensing that he needed comfort and reassurance. "It's all right, Danny. I'm okay."

"I thought you were still in the office." His rich voice was husky with emotion. "I thought I would lose you."

"It's okay now. Come inside."

Holding hands, they moved to the sofa where Danny settled her onto his lap. She slipped one arm behind his neck while he hugged her around the waist and nuzzled her cheek. They sat in silence, simply touching and physically expressing their joy at being together again. Jordan brushed a kiss over his temple and heard his soft intake of breath.

Danny tightened his arms around her. He closed his eyes and she noticed his lower lip quiver before he pressed them into a firm line. When he sighed again, she felt some of the tension ease from his muscles. Without relinquishing his hold, Danny finally spoke.

"I didn't realize how empty my life was before you came into it. I've never let myself get close to any woman, always pushing them away before they could disappoint or hurt me. I didn't let myself care when it was over. I made sure I was the one to walk away."

Jordan caressed his upper back, encouraging him to continue. When he looked at her, there were shadows in his eyes.

"I withdrew even more after September eleventh. That day made me realize how fragile life is, how quickly someone you love could be lost. I refused to take a chance on any relationship, knowing that the pain would be unbearable. But I've learned the hard way that you can't go through life without taking the biggest risk of all. That's not really living."

Danny's voice broke, breaking her heart along with it. The emotion evident on his face mirrored everything she was feeling. "So, I'm taking the chance. I'm saying it out loud, without hesitation and without fear. I love you, Jordan. With all my heart, I love you and I always will."

This was everything she'd hoped for, all that she'd once wanted. To be part of a couple, to have someone in her life as a friend and a partner. She'd always believed that having a man accept and love her would make her whole. But instead, she'd discovered that giving love was what made her complete.

"I love you, Danny. I love you so much."

Danny held on to her, gently rocking and whispering words of comfort in her ear. After a moment she stopped crying and he brushed the tears from her face. Jordan leaned closer and pressed her mouth to his in a slow, sensual kiss.

"You may not have realized, Danny, or wanted to admit it, but you've shown me your love in so many ways. It's in the way you look at me, the way you smile, the way you touch me. And now it's my turn to show you."

Jordan smiled gently as she stood up and took his hand to lead him toward the stairs. In her bedroom, she walked over to the night table and switched on the small bedside lamp. Returning to stand proudly before Danny, she stripped off her clothes, knowing that her flaws were exposed, but not caring.

He gathered her into his arms, holding her tightly in his embrace. She could feel his heart beating in time with her own. She kissed him hungrily and he opened to her. His tongue traced sensual patterns inside her mouth as he glided his hands over her body.

Jordan broke the kiss and went over to lie down on her bed. Danny quickly shed his clothes and joined her, easing her back onto the smooth linen sheets before covering her body with his own. He claimed her mouth as she stroked her palms along the muscles of his bare back.

Heat, warm and penetrating, increased the fierce desire arcing between them until the kiss became eager and urgent. When Danny positioned himself between her legs, she spread her thighs, draping her calves over his, urging him to claim her completely. He began thrusting heavily and she lifted her body to meet him. The slow, insistent throb became a deep pulsating need until the orgasm shuddered through her. A moment later Danny's body tensed and he cried out his release.

Afterward, she lay cuddled against his side, her

head resting on his chest, his arm draped over her back. She planted a kiss on his warm skin then raised her head to look at him. "Thank you for loving me, Danny. And thank you for helping me learn to love myself."

"My pleasure. The homework assignments have been a lot of fun." He wiggled his brows suggestively, then his expression softened. His rich voice was hoarse with feeling. "I love you very much, Jordan."

His kiss was gentle and sweet. As she began to drift off to sleep, Danny reached over for the lamp and turned out the light.

Epilogue

"HEY, PRETTY LADY."

Jordan smiled as she heard Danny's voice on the other end of the phone. "Hi, sweetheart."

"Go do the hair-and-makeup thing and put on a dressy outfit. I'll come pick you up in about thirty minutes."

She looked down at the hole in the right knee of her jeans, then at the yellow latex glove on her left hand. Her Saturday morning had been spent on routine housecleaning. When the phone rang, she'd been scrubbing the grout between the kitchen tiles.

"I need more than a half hour to get ready."

"Sorry, you can't have it. I'm initiating our *anytime* agreement. See you in thirty."

"Danny—"

He'd already hung up. Jordan set down the receiver and smiled. Anytime, huh? She pulled off her glove and quickly put away the cleaning supplies. Although the agreement she and Danny made was supposed to have ended over a month ago, they still took pleasure in being spontaneous and acting out the occasional fantasy.

She glanced at her watch and made a dash for the stairs. They were more than halfway through the *Fifty Fast Fantasies* book. Which one had he chosen this time and why did she have to dress up? Could it be A Rise from the Boss? Or maybe it was Dropping His Legal Briefs? Her pulse fluttered in anticipation. Whatever the fantasy, it would be acted out with the man she loved.

Exactly thirty minutes and twenty seconds later, Jordan opened the door for Danny. She grinned when he whistled appreciatively. Turning in a circle, she modeled her cream wool sweater dress and the purple boots Sheris had given to her. She'd left her hair down the way he liked it and kept her makeup to a minimum.

"You look beautiful, Jordan. Love the boots."

"You're looking pretty fabulous yourself." She eyed the muted pin-striped charcoal suit that fit his broad shoulders and lean build like a second skin. "So, where are we going and what happens when we get there?"

Danny reached into his jacket pocket. When she saw the items he removed, she burst into giggles. He grinned at her as he held up a silk necktie and a medium-sized banana. "You know the routine, darling. Stay quiet and walk toward the Jeep."

"You're kidnapping me?"

He closed the front door behind them and brandished the fruit at her. "No funny business, lady. I don't want to have to use this."

Danny helped her into the vehicle and then he

carefully secured his necktie over her eyes. Jordan heard him open the other door, slide into the driver's seat and start the engine. Though she couldn't tell how far they traveled, the time passed quickly with laughter and flirting and kisses at traffic lights. Before she knew it, Danny had stopped the Jeep.

"Where are we?"

"This fantasy is different from anything we've done before. And, I have to admit, I'm a little nervous."

"Really? Ooh, must be kinky." Jordan wiggled her brows beneath the necktie. "What's this one called?"

She felt Danny take her left hand and suddenly her heart fluttered when he slipped a ring onto the third finger. Omigod. Jordan ripped off the blindfold and stared. The square-cut solitaire nestled between two rows of smaller diamonds glittering in the October sunlight.

"Oh. My. God."

"The name of this fantasy is Be My Bride. No more faking, Jordan. This ring is real and so is my love. Will you marry me?"

"Yes. Absolutely. Yes, yes, yes!"

A wide smile spread across her face as she felt tears sting her eyes. In his gaze she saw all the love she felt reflected. Jordan reached over the gearshift to give him a hard, passionate kiss. Danny leaned back a moment later and looked at her with a tender expression.

"If you're ready, then let's go inside."

She smoothed her palms over her hair and turned in the seat. She had just grabbed the door handle when she saw where they were. A gasp of surprise escaped her and all she could do was stare.

They were parked next to the curb outside her family's church in Annapolis. The tears that had only threatened before trickled down her cheek. She looked at the people standing on the front steps. There was her mother and father, and beside them, stood both sets of grandparents. Her sister, Mason and her brothers were here as well. And Aunt Celeste, Uncle Matt and Keisha had flown up from Atlanta. She saw David, grinning down at them and waving, standing with his new partner. And next to him were two people who could only be her future in-laws.

Danny opened the car door and passed her a handkerchief. He waited patiently while she repaired her face, then held out his hand. "I love you, Jordan. Let's go make nine and a half days last forever."

She smiled even as her eyes filled again, and Danny smiled back. Jordan took his hand and walked with him toward the chapel.

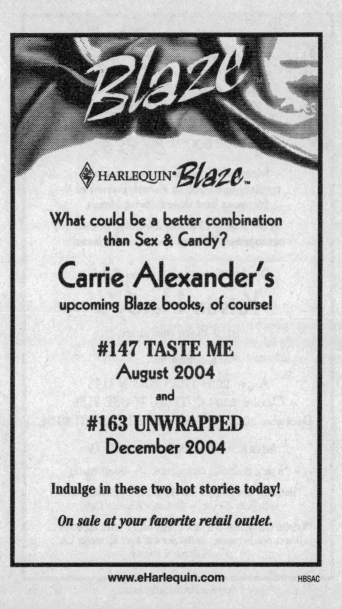

The world's bestselling romance series.

DRAGONFLIGHT

The men who rode the dragons were a
breed apart. Chosen when the dragons
were first hatched, they became
soulmates for life with the huge,
magnificent beasts they controlled –
the green, blue, brown, and bronzes –
beautiful – terrible – the only creatures
who could defend the planet Pern
from the blood-red star.

But without the Queen the dragons
would become extinct – only the
gigantic, golden Queen could breed
the new flights. And the Queen was
fading ... dying ... leaving behind
one last, huge, golden egg ...

and published by Corgi Books

DRAGONFLIGHT

Anne McCaffrey

CORGI BOOKS

DRAGONFLIGHT
A CORGI BOOK 0 552 08453 0

Originally published in Great Britain
by Rapp & Whiting Ltd.

PRINTING HISTORY
Rapp & Whiting edition published 1969
Corgi edition published 1970
Corgi edition reissued 1973
Corgi edition reprinted 1973
Corgi edition reprinted 1975
Corgi edition reprinted 1979
Corgi edition reprinted 1980 (twice)
Corgi edition reprinted 1981
Corgi edition reprinted 1982
Corgi edition reprinted 1983
Corgi edition reprinted 1984
Corgi edition reprinted 1986
Corgi edition reprinted 1987
Corgi edition reprinted 1989
Corgi edition reprinted 1990

This book is set in 10pt Baskerville (Monotype)

Corgi Books are published by Transworld Publishers
Ltd., 61–63 Uxbridge Road, Ealing, London W5 5SA, in
Australia by Transworld Publishers (Australia) Pty. Ltd.,
15–23 Helles Avenue, Moorebank, NSW 2170, and in New
Zealand by Transworld Publishers (N.Z.) Ltd., Cnr. Moselle
and Waipareira Avenues, Henderson, Auckland.

Printed and bound in Great Britain by
Cox & Wyman Ltd., Reading, Berks.

Contents

DEDICATORY NOTE

Dear God,
   Yes, there is a Virginia who helped
me create this planet and the marvels
thereon. And for whom I thank you.
                                    AMJ

Introduction

When is a legend legend? Why is a myth a myth? How old and disused must a fact be for it to be relegated to the category 'Fairy-tale'? And why do certain facts remain incontrovertible while others lose their validity to assume a shabby, unstable character?

Rukbat, in the Sagittarian sector, was a golden G-type star. It had five planets, and one stray it had attracted and held in recent millenia. Its third planet was enveloped by air man could breathe, boasted water he could drink, and possessed a gravity that permitted man to walk confidently erect. Men discovered it and promptly colonized it. They did that to every habitable planet, and then – whether callously or through collapse of empire, the colonists never discovered and eventually forgot to ask – left the colonies to fend for themselves.

When men first settled on Rukbat's third world and named it Pern, they had taken little notice of the stranger-planet, swinging around its adopted primary in a wildly erratic elliptical orbit. Within a few generations they had forgotten its existence. The desperate path the wanderer pursued brought it close to its stepsister every two hundred (Terran) years at perihelion.

When the aspects were harmonious and the conjunction with its sister planet close enough, as it often was, the indigenous life of the wanderer sought to bridge the space gap to the more temperate and hospitable planet.

It was during the frantic struggle to combat this menace dropping through Pern's skies like silver threads that Pern's tenuous contact with the mother planet was broken. Recollections of Earth receded further from Pernese history with each successive generation until memory of their origins degenerated past legend or myth, into oblivion.

To forestall the incursions of the dreadful Threads, the

Pernese, with the ingenuity of their forgotten Terran fore-bears, developed a highly specialized variety of a life-form indigenous to their adopted planet. Such humans as had a high empathy rating and some innate telepathic ability were trained to use and preserve this unusual animal whose ability to teleport was of great value in the fierce struggle to keep Pern bare of Threads.

The winged, tailed, and fiery-breathed dragons (named for the Earth legend they resembled), their dragonmen, a breed apart, and the menace they battled, created a whole new group of legends and myths.

Once relieved of imminent danger, Pern settled into a more comfortable way of life. The descendants of heroes fell into disfavor, as the legends fell into disrepute.

Part I – Weyr Search

Drummer, beat, and piper, blow,
Harper, strike, and soldier, go.
Free the flame and sear the grasses
Till the dawning Red Star passes.

LESSA WOKE, cold. Cold with more than the chill of the ever-lastingly clammy stone walls. Cold with the prescience of a danger stronger than the one ten full Turns ago that had then sent her, whimpering with terror, to hide in the watch-wher's odorous lair.

Rigid with concentration, Lessa lay in the straw of the redolent cheeseroom she shared as sleeping quarters with the other kitchen drudges. There was an urgency in the ominous portent unlike any other forewarning. She touched the awareness of the watch-wher, slithering on its rounds in the courtyard. It circled at the choke limit of its chain. It was restless, but oblivious to anything unusual in the predawn darkness.

Lessa curled into a tight knot of bones, hugging herself to ease the strain across her tense shoulders. Then, forcing herself to relax, muscle by muscle, joint by joint, she tried to feel what subtle menace it might be that could rouse her, yet not distress the sensitive watch-wher.

The danger was definitely not within the walls of Ruath Hold. Nor approaching the paved perimeter without the Hold where relentless grass had forced new growth through the ancient mortar, green witness to the deterioration of the once stone-clean Hold. The danger was not advancing up the now little-used causeway from the valley, nor lurking in the craftsmen's stony holdings at the foot of the Hold's cliff. It did not scent the wind that blew from Tillek's cold shores. But still it twanged sharply through her senses, vibrating every nerve in Lessa's slender frame. Fully roused, she sought to identify it before the prescient mood disolved. She cast outward, toward the Pass, farther than she had ever pressed. Whatever threatened was not in Ruatha . . . yet. Nor did it have a familiar flavor. It was not, then, Fax.

9

Lessa had been cautiously pleased that Fax had not shown himself at Ruath Hold in three full Turns. The apathy of the craftsmen, the decaying farmholds, even the green-etched stones of the Hold infuriated Fax, self-styled Lord of the High Reaches, to the point where he preferred to forget the reason he had subjugated the once proud and profitable Hold.

Relentlessly compelled to identify this oppressing menace, Lessa groped in the straw for her sandals. She rose, mechanically brushing straw from matted hair, which she then twisted quickly into a rude knot at her neck.

She picked her way among the sleeping drudges, huddled together for warmth, and glided up the worn steps to the kitchen proper. The cook and his assistant lay on the long table before the great hearth, wide backs to the warmth of the banked fire, discordantly snoring. Lessa slipped across the cavernous kitchen to the stable-yard door. She opened the door just enough to permit her slight body to pass. The cobbles of the yard were icy through the thin soles of her sandals, and she shivered as the predawn air penetrated her patched garment.

The watch-wher slithered across the yard to greet her, pleading, as it always did, for release. Comfortingly, she fondled the creases of the sharp-tipped ears as it matched her stride. Glancing fondly down at the awesome head, she promised it a good rub presently. It crouched, groaning, at the end of its chain as she continued to the grooved steps that led to the rampart over the Hold's massive gate. Atop the tower, Lessa stared toward the east where the stony breasts of the Pass rose in black relief against the gathering day.

Indecisively she swung to her left, for the sense of danger issued from that direction as well. She glanced upward, her eyes drawn to the red star that had recently begun to dominate the dawn sky. As she stared, the star radiated a final ruby pulsation before its magnificence was lost in the brightness of Pern's rising sun. Incoherent fragments of tales and ballads about the dawn appearance of the red star flashed through her mind, too quickly to make sense. Moreover, her instinct told her that, though danger might come from the northeast, too, there was a greater peril to contend with from due east. Straining her eyes as if vision would bridge the gap between peril and person, she stared intently eastward. The watch-wher's thin, whistled question reached her just as the prescience waned.

Lessa sighed. She had found no answer in the dawn, only discrepant portents. She must wait. The warning had come and she had accepted it. She was used to waiting. Perversity, endurance, and guile were her other weapons, loaded with the inexhaustible patience of vengeful dedication.

Dawnlight illumined the tumbled landscape, the unplowed fields in the valley below. Dawnlight fell on twisted orchards, where the sparse herds of milchbeasts hunted stray blades of spring grass. Grass in Ruatha, Lessa mused, grew where it should not, died where it should flourish. Lessa could hardly remember now how Ruatha Valley had once looked, sweetly happy, amply productive. Before Fax came. An odd brooding smile curved lips unused to such exercise. Fax realized no profit from his conquest of Ruatha . . . nor would he while she, Lessa, lived. And he had not the slightest suspicion of the source of this undoing.

Or had he, Lessa wondered, her mind still reverberating from the savage prescience of danger. West lay Fax's ancestral and only legitimate Hold. Northeast lay little but bare and stony mountains and the Weyr that protected Pern.

Lessa stretched, arching her back, inhaling the sweet, untainted wind of morning.

A cock crowed in the stable yard. Lessa whirled, her face alert, eyes darting around the outer Hold lest she be observed in such an uncharacteristic pose. She unbound her hair, letting the rank mass fall about her face concealingly. Her body drooped into the sloppy posture she affected. Quickly she thudded down the stairs, crossing to the watch-wher. It cried piteously, its great eyes blinking against the growing daylight. Oblivious to the stench of its rank breath, she hugged the scaly head to her, scratching its ears and eye ridges. The watch-wher was ecstatic with pleasure, its long body trembling, its clipped wings rustling. It alone knew who she was or cared. And it was the only creature in all Pern she had trusted since the dawn she had blindly sought refuge in its dark, stinking lair to escape the thirsty swords that had drunk so deeply of Ruathan blood.

Slowly she rose, cautioning it to remember to be as vicious to her as to all, should anyone be near. It promised to obey her, swaying back and forth to emphasize its reluctance.

The first rays of the sun glanced over the Hold's outer wall, and, crying out, the watch-wher darted into its dark nest. Lessa crept swiftly back to the kitchen and into the cheeseroom.

From the Weyr and from the Bowl,
Bronze and brown and blue and green,
Rise the dragonmen of Pern,
Aloft, on wing, seen, then unseen.

F'LAR, ON bronze Mnementh's great neck, appeared first in the skies above the chief Hold of Fax, so-called Lord of the High Reaches. Behind him, in proper wedge formation, the wingmen came into sight. F'lar checked the formation automatically; it was as precise as on the moment of their entry to *between*.

As Mnementh curved in an arc that would bring them to the perimeter of the Hold, consonant with the friendly nature of this visitation, F'lar surveyed with mounting aversion the disrepair of the ridge defenses. The firestone pits were empty, and the rock-cut gutters radiating from the pits were green-tinged with a mossy growth.

Was there even one Lord in Pern who maintained his Hold rocky in observance of the ancient Laws? F'lar's lips tightened to a thinner line. When this Search was over and the Impression made, there would have to be a solemn, punitive Council held at the Weyr. And by the golden shell of the queen, he, F'lar, meant to be its moderator. He would replace lethargy with industry. He would scour the green and dangerous scum from the heights of Pern, the grass blades from its stoneworks. No verdant skirt would be condoned in any farmhold. And the tithings that had been so miserly, so grudgingly presented, would, under pain of firestoning, flow with decent generosity into the Dragonweyr.

Mnementh rumbled approvingly as he vaned his pinions to land lightly on the grass-etched flagstones of Fax's Hold. The bronze dragon furled his great wings, and F'lar heard the warning claxon in the Hold's Great Tower. Mnementh dropped to his knees as F'lar indicated he wished to dismount. The bronze rider stood by Mnementh's huge wedge-shaped head, politely awaiting the arrival of the Hold Lord. F'lar idly gazed down the valley, hazy with warm spring sunlight. He ignored the furtive heads that peered at the dragonman from the parapet slits and the cliff windows.

F'lar did not turn as the rush of air past him announced the arrival of the rest of the wing. He knew, however, when F'nor, the brown rider who was coincidentally his half brother, took the customary position on his left, a dragon length to the rear. From the corner of his eye, F'lar glimpsed F'nor twisting to death with his boot heel the grass that crowded up between the stones.

An order, muffled to an intense whisper, issued from within the great Court, beyond the open gates. Almost immediately a group of men marched into sight, led by a heavy-set men of medium height.

Mnementh arched his neck, angling his head so that his chin rested on the ground. Mnementh's many-faceted eyes, on a level with F'lar's head, fastened with disconcerting interest on the approaching party. The dragons could never understand why they generated such abject fear in common folk. At only one point in his life span would a dragon attack a human, and that could be excused on the grounds of simple ignorance. F'lar could not explain to the dragon the politics behind the necessity of inspiring awe in the holders, Lord and craftsman alike. He could only observe that the fear and apprehension showing in the faces of the advancing squad which troubled Mnementh was oddly pleasing to him, F'lar.

'Welcome, bronze rider, to the Hold of Fax, Lord of the High Reaches. He is at your service,' and the man made an adequately respectful salute.

The use of the third person pronoun could be construed by the meticulous to be a veiled insult. This fit in with the information F'lar had on Fax, so he ignored it. His information was also correct in describing Fax as a greedy man. It showed in the restless eyes that flicked at every detail of F'lar's clothing, at the slight frown when the intricately etched sword hilt was noticed.

F'lar noticed, in his own turn, the several rich rings that flashed on Fax's left hand. The overlord's right hand remained slightly cocked after the habit of the professional swordsman. His tunic, of rich fabric, was stained and none too fresh. The man's feet, in heavy wher-hide boots, were solidly planted, weight balanced forward on his toes. A man to be treated cautiously, F'lar decided, as one should the conqueror of five neighboring Holds. Such greedy audacity was in itself a revelation. Fax had married into a sixth . . . and had legally inherited, however unusual the circumstances, the seventh. He was a lecherous man by reputation. Within these seven Holds, F'lar anticipated a profitable Search. Let R'gul go southerly to pursue Search among the indolent if lovely women there. The Weyr needed a strong woman this time; Jora had been worse than useless with Nemorth. Adversity, uncertainty: those were the conditions that bred the qualities F'lar wanted in a Weyrwoman.

'We ride in Search,' F'lar drawled softly, 'and request the hospitality of your Hold, Lord Fax.'

Fax's eyes widened imperceptibly at mention of a Search.

'I had heard Jora was dead,' Fax replied, dropping the third person abruptly as if F'lar had passed some sort of test by ignoring it. 'So Nemorth has laid a queen, hmmm?' he continued, his eyes darting across the rank of the wing, not ing the disciplined stance of the riders, the healthy color of the dragons.

F'lar did not dignify the obvious with an answer.

'And, my Lord –' Fax hesitated, expectantly inclining his head slightly toward the dragonman.

For a pulse beat, F'lar wondered if the man was deliberately provoking him with such subtle insults. The name of the bronze riders should be as well-known throughout Pern as the name of the dragon queen and her Weyrwoman. F'lar kept his face composed, his eyes on Fax's.

Leisurely, with the proper touch of arrogance, F'nor stepped forward, stopping slightly behind Mnementh's head, one hand negligently touching the jaw hinge of the huge beast.

'The bronze rider of Mnementh, Lord F'lar, will require quarters for himself. I, F'nor, brown rider, prefer to be lodged with the wingmen. We are, in number, twelve.'

F'lar liked that touch of F'nor's, totting up the wing strength, as if Fax were incapable of counting. F'nor had phrased it so adroitly as to make it impossible for Fax to protest the return insult.

'Lord F'lar,' Fax said through teeth fixed in a smile, 'the High Reaches are honored with your Search.'

'It will be to the credit of the High Reaches,' F'lar replied smoothly, 'if one of its own supplies the Weyr.'

'To our everlasting credit,' Fax replied as suavely. 'In the old days many notable Weyrwomen came from my Holds.'

'Your Holds?' asked F'lar, politely smiling as he emphasized the plural. 'Ah, yes, you are now overlord of Ruatha, are you not? There have been many from that Hold.'

A strange, tense look crossed Fax's face, quickly supplanted by a determinedly affable grin. Fax stepped aside, gesturing F'lar to enter the Hold.

Fax's troop leader barked a hasty order, and the men formed two lines, their metal-edged boots flicking sparks from the stones.

At unspoken orders, all the dragons rose with a great churning of air and dust. F'lar strode nonchalantly past the welcoming files. The men were rolling their eyes in alarm as the beasts glided above to the inner courts. Someone on the high Tower uttered a frightened yelp as Mnementh took his position on that vantage point. His great wings drove phosphoric-scented air across the inner court as he maneuvered his great frame onto the inadequate landing space.

Outwardly oblivious to the consternation, fear, and awe the dragons inspired, F'lar was secretly amused and rather pleased by the effect. Lords of the Holds needed this reminder that they still must deal with dragons, not just with riders, who were men, mortal and murderable. The ancient respect for dragonmen as well as dragonkind must be reinstilled in modern breasts.

'The Hold has just risen from table, Lord F'lar, if . . .' Fax suggested. His voice trailed off at F'lar's smiling refusal.

'Convey my duty to your lady, Lord Fax,' F'lar rejoined, noticing with inward satisfaction the tightening of Fax's jaw muscles at the ceremonial request.

F'lar was enjoying himself thoroughly. He had not yet been born on the occasion of the last Search, the one that ill-fatedly provided the incompetent Jora. But he had studied the accounts of previous Searches in the Old Records that had included subtle ways to confound those Lords who preferred to keep their ladies sequestered when the dragonmen rode. For Fax to refuse F'lar the opportunity to pay his duty would have been tantamount to a major insult, discharged only in mortal combat.

'You would prefer to see your quarters first?' Fax countered.

F'lar flicked an immaginary speck from his soft wherhide sleeve and shook his head.

'Duty first,' he said with a rueful shrug.

'Of course,' Fax all but snapped and strode smartly ahead, his heels pounding out the anger he could not express otherwise.

F'lar and F'nor followed at a slower pace through the double-doored entry with its great metal panels, into the Great Hall, carved into the cliffside. The U-shaped table was being cleared by nervous servitors, who rattled and dropped tableware as the two dragonmen entered. Fax had already reached the far end of the Hall and stood impatiently at the open slab door, the only access to the inner Hold which, like all such Holds, burrowed deep into stone, the refuge of all in time of peril.

'They eat not badly,' F'nor remarked casually to F'lar, appraising the remnants still on the table.

'Better than the Weyr, it would seem,' F'lar replied dryly, covering his speech with his hand as he saw two drudges staggering under the weight on a tray that bore a half-eaten carcass.

'Young and tender,' F'nor said in a bitter undertone, 'from the look of it. While the stringy, barren beasts are delivered up to us.'

'Naturally.'

'A pleasantly favored Hall,' F'lar said amiably as they reached Fax. Then, seeing Fax impatient to continue, F'lar deliberately turned back to the banner-hung Hall. He pointed out to F'nor the deeply set slit windows, heavy bronze shutters open to the bright noonday sky. 'Facing east, too, as they ought. That new Hall at Telgar Hold actually faces south, I'm told. Tell me, Lord Fax, do you adhere to the old practices and mount a dawn guard?'

Fax frowned, trying to parse F'lar's meaning.

'There is always a guard at the Tower.'

'An easterly guard?'

Fax's eyes jerked toward the windows, then back, sliding across F'lar's face to F'nor and back again to the windows.

'There are always guards,' he answered sharply, 'on all the approaches.'

'Oh, just the approaches,' and F'lar turned to F'nor and nodded wisely.

'Where else?' demanded Fax, concerned, glancing from one dragonman to the other.

'I must ask that of your harper. You do keep a trained harper in your Hold?'

'Of course. I have several trained harpers.' Fax jerked his shoulders straighter.

F'lar affected not to understand.

'Lord Fax is the overlord of six other Holds,' F'nor reminded his wingleader.

'Of course,' F'lar assented, with exactly the same inflection Fax had used a moment before.

The mimicry did not go unnoticed by Fax, but as he was unable to construe deliberate insult out of an innocent affirmative, he stalked into the glow-lit corridors. The dragonmen followed.

'It is good to see one Holder keeping so many ancient customs,' F'lar said to F'nor approvingly for Fax's benefit as they passed into the inner Hold. 'There are many who have abandoned the safety of solid rock and enlarged their outer Holds to dangerous proportions. I can't condone the risk myself.'

'Their risk, Lord F'lar. Another's gain,' Fax snorted derisively, slowing to a normal strut.

'Gain? How so?'

'Any outer Hold is easily penetrated, bronze rider, with trained forces, experienced leadership, and well-considered strategy.'

The man was not a braggart, F'lar decided. Nor, in these peaceful days, did he fail to mount Tower guards. However, he kept within his Hold, not out of obedience to ancient Laws, but through prudence. He kept harpers for ostentation rather than because tradition required it. But he allowed the pits to decay; he permitted grass to grow. He accorded dragonmen the barest civility on one hand and offered veiled insult on the other. A man to be watched.

The women's quarters in Fax's Hold had been moved from the traditional innermost corridors to those at the cliff-face. Sunlight poured down from the three double-shuttered deep-casement windows in the outside wall. F'lar noted that the bronze hinges were well oiled. The sills were the regulation spear-length; Fax had not given in to the recent practice of diminishing the protective wall.

The chamber was richly hung with appropriately gentle scenes of women occupied in all manner of feminine tasks. Doors gave off the main chamber on both sides into smaller sleeping alcoves, and from these, at Fax's bidding, his women hesitantly emerged. Fax sternly gestured to a blue-gowned woman, her hair white-streaked, her face lined with disappointments and bitterness, her body swollen with pregnancy. She advanced awkwardly, stopping several feet from her lord. From her attitude, F'lar deduced that she came no closer to Fax than was absolutely necessary.

'The Lady of Crom, mother of my heirs,' Fax said without pride or cordiality.

'My Lady – ' F'lar hesitated, waiting for her name to be supplied.

She glanced warily at her lord.

'Gemma,' Fax snapped curtly.

F'lar bowed deeply. 'My Lady Gemma, the Weyr is on Search and requests the hospitality of the Hold.'

'My Lord F'lar,' the Lady Gemma replied in a low voice, 'you are most welcome.'

F'lar did not miss the slight slur on the adverb or the fact that Gemma had no trouble naming him. His smile was warmer than courtesy demanded, warm with gratitude and sympathy. Judging by the number of women in these quarters, Fax bedded well and frequently. There might be one or two Lady Gemma could bid farewell without regret.

Fax went through the introductions, mumbling names until he realized this strategy was not going to work. F'lar would politely beg the lady's name again. F'nor, his smile brightening as he took heed which ladies Fax preferred to keep anonymous, lounged indolently by the doorway. F'lar would compare notes with him later, although on cursory examination there was none here worthy of the Search. Fax preferred his women plump and small. There wasn't a saucy one in the lot. If there once had been, the spirit had been beaten out of them. Fax, no doubt, was stud, not lover. Some of the covey had not all winter long made much use of water, judging from the amount of sweet oil gone rancid in their hair. Of them all, if these were all, the Lady Gemma was the only willful one, and she was too old.

The amenities over, Fax ushered his unwelcome guests outside. F'nor was excused by his wingleader to join the other dragonmen. Fax peremptorily led the way to the quarters he had assigned the bronze rider.

The chamber was on a lower level than the women's suite and was certainly adequate to the dignity of its occupant. The many-colored hangins were crowded with bloody battles, individual swordplay, bright-hued dragons in flight, firestones burning on the ridges, and all that Pern's scarlet-stained history offered.

'A pleasant room,' F'lar acknowledged, stripping off gloves and wher-hide tunic, throwing them carelessly to the table. 'I shall see to my men and the beasts. The dragons have all been fed recently,' he commented, pointing up Fax's omission in inquiring. 'I request liberty to wander through the crafthold.'

Fax sourly granted what was traditionally a dragonman's privilege.

'I shall not further disrupt your routine, Lord Fax, for you must have many demands on you, with seven Holds to supervise.' F'lar inclined his body slightly to the overlord, turning away as a gesture of dismissal. He could imagine the infuriated expression on Fax's face and listened to the stamping retreat. He waited long enough to be sure Fax was out of the corridor and then briskly retraced his steps up to the Great Hall.

Bustling drudges paused in setting up additional trestle tables to eye the dragonman. He nodded pleasantly to them, looking to see if one of these females might possibly have the stuff of which Weyrwomen are made. Overworked, underfed, scarred by lash and disease, they were just what they were – drudges, fit only for hard, menial labor.

F'nor and the men had settled themselves in a hastily vacated barrackroom. The dragons were perched comfortably on the rocky ridges above the Hold. They had so arranged themselves that every segment of the wide valley fell under their scrutiny. All had been fed before leaving the Weyr, and each rider kept his dragon in light but alert charge. There were to be no incidents on a Search.

As a group, the dragonmen rose at F'lar's entrance.

'No tricks, no troubles, but look around closely,' he said laconically. 'Return by sundown with the names of any likely prospects.' He caught F'nor's grin, remembering how Fax had slurred over some names. 'Descriptions are in order and craft affiliation.'

The men nodded, their eyes glinting with understanding. They were flatteringly confident of a successful Search even as F'lar's doubts grew now that he had seen all of Fax's women. By all logic, the pick of the High Reaches should be in Fax's chief Hold, but they were not. Still, there were many large craftholds, not to mention the six other High

Holds to visit. All the same . . .

In unspoken accord F'lar and F'nor left the barracks. The men would follow, unobtrusively, in pairs or singly, to reconnoiter the crafthold and the nearer farmholds. The men were as overtly eager to be abroad as F'lar was privately. There had been a time when dragonmen were frequent and favored guests in all the great Holds throughout Pern, from southern Nerat to high Tillek. This pleasant custom, too, had died along with other observances, evidence of the low regard in which the Weyr was presently held. F'lar vowed to correct this.

He forced himself to trace in memory the insidious changes. The Records, which each Weyrwoman kept, were proof of the gradual but perceptible decline, traceable through the past two hundred full Turns. Knowing the facts did not alleviate the condition. And F'lar was of that scant handful in the Weyr itself who did credit Records and ballad alike. The situation might shortly reverse itself radically if the old tales were to be believed.

There was a reason, an explanation, a purpose, F'lar felt for every one of the Weyr Laws from First Impression to the Firestones, from the grass-free heights to ridge-running gutters. For elements as minor as controlling the appetite of a dragon to limiting the inhabitants of the Weyr. Although why the other five Weyrs had been abandoned F'lar did not know. Idly he wondered if there were Records, dusty and crumbling, lodged in the disused Weyrs. He must contrive to check when next his wings flew patrol. Certainly there was no explanation in Benden Weyr.

'There is industry but no enthusiasm,' F'nor was saying, drawing F'lar's attention back to their tour of the crafthold.

They had descended the guttered ramp from the Hold into the craftholds proper, the broad roadway lined with cottages up to the imposing stone crafthalls. Silently F'lar noted moss-clogged gutters on the roofs, the vines clasping the walls. It was painful for one of his calling to witness the flagrant disregard of simple safety precautions. Growing things were forbidden near the habitations of mankind.

'News travels fast,' F'nor chuckled, nodding at a hurrying craftsman, in the smock of a baker, who gave them a mumbled good-day. ''Not a female in sight.'

His observation was accurate. Women should be abroad at this hour, bringing in supplies from the store-houses, washing in the river on such a bright warm day, or going out to the farmholds to help with planting. Not a gowned figure in sight.

'We used to be preferred mates,' F'nor remarked caustically.

'We'll visit the Clothmen's Hall first. If my memory serves me . . .'

'As it always does . . .' F'nor interjected wryly. He took no advantage of their blood relationship, but he was more at ease with the bronze rider than most of the dragonmen, the other bronze riders included. F'lar was reserved in a close-knit society of easy equality. He flew a tightly disciplined wing, but men manoeuvered to serve under him. His wing always excelled in the Games. None ever floundered in *between* to disappear forever, and no beast in his wing sickened, leaving a man in dragonless exile from the Weyr, a part of him numb forever.

'L'tol came this way and settled in one of the High Reaches,' F'lar continued.

'L'tol?'

'Yes, a green rider from S'lel's wing. You remember.'

An ill-timed swerve during the Spring Games had brought L'tol and his beast into the full blast of a phosphine emission from S'lel's bronze Tuenth. L'tol had been thrown from his beast's neck as the dragon tried to evade the blast. Another wingmate had swooped to catch the rider, but the green dragon, his left wing crisped, his body scorched, had died of shock and phosphine poisoning.

'L'tol would aid our Search,' F'nor agreed as the two dragonmen walked up to the bronze doors of the Clothmen's Hall. They paused on the threshold, adjusting their eyes to the dimmer light within. Glows punctuated the wall recesses and hung in clusters above the larger looms where the finer tapestries and fabrics were woven by master craftsmen. The pervading mood was one of quiet, purposeful industry.

Before their eyes had adapted, however, a figure glided to them, muttering a polite if curt request for them to follow him.

They were led to the right of the entrance, to a small office, curtained from the main hall. Their guide turned to them, his face visible in the wallglows. There was that air about him that marked him indefinably as a dragon-

22

man. But his face was lined deeply, one side seamed with old burn marks. His eyes, sick with a hungry yearning, dominated his face. He blinked constantly.

'I am now Lytol,' he said in harsh voice.

F'lar nodded acknowledgment.

'You would be F'lar,' Lytol said, 'and you F'nor. You both have the look of your sire.'

F'lar nodded again.

Lytol swallowed convulsively, the muscles in his face twitching as the presence of dragonmen revived his awareness of exile. He essayed a smile.

'Dragons in the sky! The news spread faster than Threads.'

'Nemorth has laid a female.'

'And Jora dead?' Lytol asked concernedly, his face cleared of its nervous movement for a second. 'Hath flew her?'

F'lar nodded.

Lytol grimaced bitterly. 'R'gul again, huh?' He stared off in the middle distance, his eyelids quiet but the muscles along his jaw taking up the constant movement. 'You have the High Reaches? All of them?' Lytol asked, turning back to the dragonman, a slight emphasis on 'all.'

F'lar gave an affirmative nod again.

'You've seen the women.' Lytol's disgust showed through the words. It was a statement, not a question, for he hurried on. 'Well, there are no better in all the High Reaches.' His tone expressed utmost disdain. He eased himself down to the heavy table that half-filled one corner of the small room. His hands were clenched so tightly around the wide belt that secured the loose tunic to his body that the heavy leather was doubled.

'You would almost expect the opposite, wouldn't you?' Lytol continued. He was talking too much and too fast. It would have been insultingly rude in another, lesser man. It was the terrible loneliness of the man's exile from the Weyr that drove him to garrulity. Lytol skimmed the surfaces with hurried questions he himself answered, rather than dip once into matters too tender to be touched – such as his insatiable need for those of his kind. Yet he was giving the dragonmen exactly the information they needed. 'But Fax likes his women comfortably fleshed and docile,' Lytol rattled on. 'Even the Lady Gemma has learned. It'd be

23

different if he didn't need her family's support. Ah, it would be different indeed. So he keeps her pregnant, hoping to kill her in childbed one day. And he will. He will.'

Lytol's laughter grated unpleasantly.

'When Fax came to power, any man with wit sent his daughters down from the High Reaches or drew a brand across their faces.' He paused, his countenance dark and bitter memory, his eyes slits of hatred. 'I was a fool and thought my position gave me immunity.'

Lytol drew himself up, squaring his shoulders, turning full to the two dragonmen. His expression was vindictive, his voice low and tense.

'Kill that tyrant, dragonmen, for the sake and safety of Pern. Of the Weyr. Of the queen. He only bides his time. He spreads discontent among the other Lords. He –' Lytol's laughter had an hysterical edge to it now. 'He fancies himself as good as dragonmen.'

'There are no candidates then in this Hold?' F'lar said, his voice sharp enough to cut through the man's preoccupation with his curious theory.

Lytol stared at the bronze rider. 'Did I not say it? The best either died under Fax or were sent away. What remains is nothing, nothing. Weak-minded, ignorant, foolish, vapid. You had that with Jora. She –' His jaw snapped shut over his next words. He shook his head, scrubbing his face to ease his anguish and despair.

'In the other Holds?'

Lytol shook his head, frowning darkly. 'The same. Either dead or fled.'

'What of Ruath Hold?'

Lytol stopped shaking his head and looked sharply at F'lar, his lips curling in a cunning smile. He laughed mirthlessly.

'You think to find a Torene or a Moreta hidden at Ruath Hold in these times? Well, bronze rider, all of Ruathan Blood are dead. Fax's blade was thirsty that day. He knew the truth of those harpers' tales, that Ruathan Lords gave full measure of hospitality to dragonmen and the Ruathan were a breed apart. There were, you know' – Lytol's voice dropped to a confiding whisper – 'exiled Weyrmen like myself in that Line.'

F'lar nodded gravely, unwilling to deprive the man of such a sop to his self-esteem.

24

'No, there is little, very little left in Ruatha Valley.' Lytol chuckled softly. 'Fax gets nothing from that Hold but trouble.' This reflection restored Lytol to a semblance of normal behavior, and his face twisted into a better humor. 'We of this Hold are now the best clothmen in all Pern. And our smithies turn out a better tempered weapon.' His eyes sparkled with pride in his adopted community. 'The conscripts from Ruatha tend to die of curious diseases or accidents. And the women Fax used to take . . .' His laugh was nasty. 'It is rumored he was impotent for months after.'

F'lar's active mind jumped to a curious conclusion. 'There are none of the Blood left?'

'None!'

'Any families in the holdings with Weyr blood?'

Lytol frowned, glanced in surprise at F'lar. He rubbed the scarred side of his face thoughtfully.

'There were,' he admitted slowly. 'There were. But I doubt if any live on.' He thought a moment longer, then shook his head emphatically. 'There was such resistance at the invasion and no quarter given. At the Hold Fax beheaded ladies as well as babes. And he imprisoned or executed any known to have carried arms for Ruatha.

F'lar shrugged. The idea had been a probability only. With such severe reprisals, Fax undoubtedly had eliminated the resistance as well as the best craftsmen. That would account for the poor quality of Ruathan products and the emergence of the High Reaches' clothmen as the best in their trade.

'I wish I had better news for you, dragonman,' Lytol murmured.

'No matter,' F'lar reassured him, one hand poised to part the hanging in the doorway.

Lytol came up to him swiftly, his voice urgent.

'Heed what I say about Fax's ambitions. Force R'gul, or whoever is Weyrleader next, to keep watch on the High Reaches.'

'Is Fax aware of your leanings?'

The haunted, hungry yearning crossed Lytol's face. He swallowed nervously, answering with no emotion in his voice.

'That would not signify if it suited the Lord of the High Reaches, but my guild protects me from persecution. I am

25

safe enough in the craft. He is dependent on the proceeds of our industry.' He snorted, mocking. 'I am the best weaver of battle scenes. To be sure,' he added, cocking one eyebrow waggishly, 'dragons are no longer woven in the fabric as the comrades of heroes. You noticed, of course, the prevalence of growing greens?'

F'lar grimaced his distaste. 'That is not all we have noted, either. But Fax keeps the other traditions. . . .'

Lytol waved this consideration aside. 'He does that because it is basic military sense. His neighbors armed after he took Ruatha, for he did it by treachery, let me tell you. And let me warn you also' – Lytol jabbed a finger in the direction of the Hold – 'he scoffs openly at tales of the Threads. He taunts the harpers for the stupid nonsense of the old ballads and has banned from their repertoire all dragonlore. The new generation will grow up totally ignorant of duty, tradition, and precaution.'

F'lar was not surprised to hear that on top of Lytol's other disclosures, although it disturbed him more than anything else he had heard. Other men, too, denied the verbal transmissions of historic events, accounting them no more than the maunderings of harpers. Yet the Red Star pulsed in the sky, and the time was drawing near when they would hysterically re-avow the old allegiances in fear for their very lives.

'Have you been abroad in the early morning of late?' asked F'nor, grinning maliciously.

'I have,' Lytol breathed out in a hushed, choked whisper. 'I have. . . .' A groan was wrenched from his guts, and he whirled away from the dragonmen, his head bowed between hunched shoulders. 'Go,' he said, gritting his teeth. And, as they hesitated, he pleaded, '*Go!*'

F'lar walked quickly from the room, followed by F'nor. The bronze rider crossed the quiet dim Hall with long strides and exploded into the startling sunlight. His momentum took him into the center of the square. There he stopped so abruptly that F'nor, hard on his heels, nearly collided with him.

'We will spend exactly the same time within the other Halls,' he announced in a tight voice, his face averted from F'nor's eyes. F'lar's throat was constricted. It was difficult suddenly for him to speak. He swallowed hard, several times.

26

'To be dragonless . . .' murmured F'nor pityingly. The encounter with Lytol had roiled his depths in a mournful way to which he was unaccustomed. That F'lar appeared equally shaken went far to dispel F'nor's private opinion that his half brother was incapable of emotion.

'There is no other way once First Impression has been made. You know that,' F'lar roused himself to say curtly. He strode off to the Hall bearing the leathermen's device.

Honor those the dragons heed,
In thought and favor, word and deed.
Worlds are lost or worlds are saved
From those dangers dragon-braved.

Dragonman, avoid excess;
Greed will bring the Weyr distress;
To the ancient Laws adhere,
Prospers thus the Dragonweyr.

F'LAR WAS amused . . . and unamused. This was their
fourth day in Fax's company, and only F'lar's firm control
on self and wing was keeping the situation from exploding
into violence.

It had been a turn of chance, F'lar mused, as Mnementh
held his leisurely glide toward the Breast Pass into Ruatha,
that he, F'lar, had chosen the High Reaches. Fax's tactics
would have been successful with R'gul, who was very conscious of his honor, or S'lan or D'nol, who were too young
to have developed much patience or discretion. S'lel would
have retreated in confusion, a course nearly as disastrous
for the Weyr as combat.

He should have correlated the indications long ago. The
decay of the Weyr and its influence did not come solely
from the Holding Lords and their folk. It came also from
within the Weyr, a result of inferior queens and incompetent
Weyrwomen. It came from R'gul's inexplicable insistence
on not 'bothering' the Holders, on keeping dragonmen
within the Weyr. And yet within the Weyr there had been
too much emphasis on preparation for the Games until the
internal competition between wings had become the be-all
and end-all of Weyr activity.

The encroachment of grass had not come overnight, nor
had the Lords awakened one morning recently and decided
in a flash not to give all their traditional tithe to the Weyr.
It had happened gradually and had been allowed, by the
Weyr, to continue, until the purpose and reason of the
Weyr and dragonkind had reached this low ebb, where an
upstart, collateral heir to an ancient Hold could be so

contemptuous of dragonmen and the simple basic precautions that kept Pern free of Threads.

F'lar doubted that Fax would have attempted such a program of aggression against neighboring Holds if the Weyr had maintained its old prominence. Each Hold must have its Lord to protect valley and folk from the Threads. One Hold, one Lord – not one Lord claiming seven Holds. That was against ancient tradition, and evil besides for how well can one man protect seven valleys at once? Man, except for dragonman, can be in only one place at a time. And unless a man was dragon-mounted, it took hours to get from one Hold to another. No Weyrman of old would have permitted such flagrant disregard of ancient ways.

F'lar saw the gouts of flame along the barren heights of the Pass, and Mnementh obediently altered his glide for a better view. F'lar had sent half the wing ahead of the main cavalcade. It was good training for them to skim irregular terrain. He had issued small pieces of firestone with instructions to sear any growths as practice. It would do to remind Fax, as well as his troops, of the awesome ability of dragonkind, a phenomenon the common folk of Pern appeared to have all but forgotten.

The fiery phosphine emissions as the dragons belched forth gasses showed the pattern well flown. R'gul could argue against the necessity of firestone drills, he could cite such incidents as that which had exiled Lytol, but F'lar kept the tradition – and so did every man who flew with him, or they left the wing. None failed him.

F'lar knew that the men reveled as much as he did in the fierce joy of riding a flaming dragon; the fumes of phosphine were exhilarating in their own way, and the feeling of power that surged through the man who controlled the might and majesty of a dragon had no parallel in human experience. Dragonriders were forever men apart once First Impression had been made. And to ride a fighting dragon, blue, green, brown, or bronze, was worth the risks, the unending alertness, the isolation from the rest of mankind.

Mnementh dipped his wings obliquely to slide through the narrow cleft of the Pass that led from Crom to Ruatha. No sooner had they emerged from the cut that the difference between the two Holds was patent.

F'lar was stunned. Through the last four Holds he had

been sure that the end of the Search lay within Ruatha.

There had been that little brunette whose father was a clothman in Nabol, but ... And a tall, willowy girl with enormous eyes, the daughter of a minor Warder in Crom, yet ... These were possibilities, and had F'lar been S'lel or K'net or D'nol, he might have taken the two in as potential mates, although not likely Weyrwomen.

But throughout he had reassured himself that the real choice would be found to the south. Now he gazed on the ruin that was Ruatha, his hopes dispersed. Below him, he saw Fax's banner dip in the sequence that requested his presence.

Mastering the crushing disappointment he felt, he directed Mnementh to descend. Fax, roughly controlling the terrified plunging of his earthbound mount, waved down into the abandoned-looking valley.

'Behold great Ruatha of which you had such hopes, he enjoined sarcastically.

F'lar smiled coolly back, wondering how Fax had divined that. Had F'lar been so transparent when he had suggested Searching the other Holds? Or was it a lucky guess on Fax's part?

'One sees at a glance why goods from the High Reaches are now preferred,' F'lar made himself reply. Mnementh rumbled, and F'lar called him sharply to order. The bronze one had developed a distaste bordering on hatred for Fax. Such antipathy in a dragon was most unusual and of no small concern to F'lar. Not that he would have in the least regretted Fax's demise, but not at Mnementh's breath.

'Little good comes from Ruatha,' Fax said in a voice that was close to a snarl. He jerked sharply at the bridle of his beast, and fresh blood colored the foam on its muzzle. The creature threw its head backward to ease the painful bar in its mouth, and Fax savagely smote it a blow between the ears. The blow, F'lar observed, was not intended for the poor, protesting beast but for the sight of unproductive Ruatha. 'I am the overlord. My proclamation went unchallenged by any of the Blood. I am in my rights. Ruatha must pay its tribute to its legal overlord. . . .''

'And hunger the rest of the year,' F'lar remarked dryly, gazing out over the wide valley. Few of its fields were plowed. Its pastures supported meager herds Even its orchards looked stunted. Blossoms that had been so profuse on trees in Crom, the next valley over, were sparse, as if reluctant to flower in so dismal a place. Although the sun was well up, there seemd to be no activity in the farmholds or none near enough to be observed. The atmosphere was one of sullen despair.

'There has been resistance to my rule of Ruatha.'

F'lar shot a look at Fax, for the man's voice was fierce, his face bleak, auguring further unpleasantness for Ruathan rebels. The vindictiveness that colored Fax's attitude toward Ruatha and its rebels was tinged with another strong emotion which F'lar had been unable to identify but which had been very apparent to him from the first time he had adroitly suggested this tour of the Holds. It could not be fear, for Fax was clearly fearless and obnoxiously self-assured. Revulsion? Dread? Uncertainty? F'lar could not label the nature of Fax's compound reluctance to visit Ruatha, but the man had not relished the prospect and now reacted violently to being within these disturbing boundaries.

'How foolish of the Ruathans,' F'lar remarked amiably. Fax swung around on him, one hand poised above his sword hilt, eyes blazing. F'lar anticipated with a feeling close to pleasure that the usurper Fax might actually draw on a dragonman! He was almost disappointed when the man controlled himself, took a firm hold on the reins of his mount, and kicked it forward to a frantic run.

'I shall kill him yet,' F'lar said to himself, and Mnementh spread his wings in concord.

F'nor dropped beside his bronze leader.

'Did I see him about to draw on you?' F'nor's eyes were bright, his smile acid.

'Until he remembered I was mounted on a dragon.'

'Watch him, bronze rider. He means to kill you soon.'

'If he can!'

'He's considered a vicious fighter,' F'nor advised, his smile gone.

Mnementh flapped his wings again, and F'lar absently stroked the great, soft-skinned neck.

'I am at some disadvantage?' F'lar asked, stung by F'nor's words.

'To my knowledge, no,' F'nor said quickly, startled. 'I have not seen him in action, but I don't like what I have heard. He kills often, with and without cause.'

'And because we dragonmen do not seek blood, we are

not to be feared as fighters?' snapped F'lar. 'Are you ashamed of being what you were bred?'

'I, no!' F'nor sucked in his breath at the tone of his leader's voice. 'And others of our wing, no! But there is that in the attitude of Fax's men that . . . that makes me wish some excuse to fight.'

'As you remarked, we will probably have that fight. There is something here in Ruatha that unnerves our noble overlord.'

Mnementh and now Canth, F'nor's brown, extended their wings, flapping to catch their riders' attention.

F'lar stared as the dragon slewed his head back toward his rider, the great eyes gleaming like sunstruck opals.

'There is a subtle strength in this valley,' F'lar murmured, gathering the import of the dragon's agitated message.

'A strength, indeed; even my brown feels it,' F'nor replied, his face lighting.

'Careful, brown rider,' F'lar cautioned. 'Careful. Send the entire wing aloft. Search this valley. I should have realized. I should have suspected. It was all there to be evaluated. What fools have dragonmen become!'

The Hold is barred,
The Hall is bare,
    And men vanish.
The soil is barren,
The rock is bald.
    All hope banish.

LESSA WAS shoveling ashes from the hearth when the agitated messenger staggered into the Great Hall. She made herself as inconspicuous as possible so the Warder would not dismiss her. She had contrived to be sent to the Great Hall that morning, knowing that the Warder intended to brutalize the head clothman for the shoddy quality of the goods readied for shipment to Fax.

'Fax is coming! With dragonmen!' the man gasped out as he plunged into the dim Great Hall.

The Warder, who had been about to lash the head clothman, turned, stunned, from his victim. The courier, a farmholder from the edge of Ruatha, stumbled up to the Warder, so excited with his message that he grabbed the Warder's arm.

'How dare you leave your Hold?' The Warder aimed his lash at the astonished Holder. The force of the first blow knocked the man from his feet. Yelping, he scrambled out of reach of a second lashing. 'Dragonmen indeed! Fax? Ha! He shuns Ruatha. There!' The Warder punctuated each denial with another blow, kicking the helpless wretch for good measure, before he turned breathless to glare at the clothman and the two underwarders. 'How did he get in here with such a threadbare lie?' The Warder stalked to the Great Hall door. It was flung open just as he reached for the iron handle. The ashen-faced guard officer rushed in, nearly knocking the Warder down.

'Dragonmen! Dragons! All over Ruatha!' the man gibbered, arms flailing wildly. He, too, pulled at the Warder's arm, dragging the stupefied official toward the outer courtyard, to bear out the truth of his statement.

Lessa scooped up the last pile of ashes. Picking up her equipment, she slipped out of the Great Hall. There was a

33

very pleased smile on her face under the screen of matted hair.

A dragonman at Ruatha! An opportunity: she must somehow contrive to get Fax so humiliated or so infuriated that he would renounce his claim to the Hold, in the presence of a dragonman. Then she could claim her birthright.

But she would have to be extraordinarily wary. Dragonriders were men apart. Anger did not cloud their intelligence. Greed did not sully their judgment. Fear did not dull their reactions. Let the dense-witted believe human sacrifice, unnatural lusts, insane revels. She was not so gullible. And those stories went against her grain. Dragonmen were still human, and there was Weyr blood in *her* veins. It was the same color blood as that of anyone else; enough of hers had been spilled to prove that.

She halted for a moment, catching a sudden shallow breath. Was this the danger she had sensed four days ago at dawn? The final encounter in her struggle to regain the Hold? No, Lessa cautioned herself, there was more to that portent than revenge.

The ash bucket banged against her shins as she shuffled down the low-ceilinged corridor to the stable door. Fax would find a cold welcome. She had laid no new fire on the hearth. Her laugh echoed back unpleasantly from the damp walls. She rested her bucket and propped her broom and shovel as she wrestled with the heavy bronze door that gave into the new stables.

They had been built outside the cliff of Ruatha by Fax's first Warder, a subtler man than all eight of his successors. He had achieved more than all the others, and Lessa had honestly regretted the necessity of his death. But he would have made her revenge impossible. He would have found her out before she had learned how to camouflage herself and her little interferences. What had his name been? She could not recall. Well, she regretted his death.

The second man had been properly greedy, and it had been easy to set up a pattern of misunderstanding between Warder and craftsmen. That one had been determined to squeeze all profit from Ruathan goods so that some of it would drop into his pocket before Fax suspected a shortage. The craftsmen who had begun to accept the skillful diplomacy of the first Warder bitterly resented the second's grasping, high-handed ways. They resented the passing of the Old Line and, even more so, the way of its passing. They were unforgiving of the insult to Ruatha, its now secondary position in the High Reaches, and they resented the individual indignities that Holders, craftsmen and farmers alike, suffered under the second Warder. It took little manipulation to arrange for matters at Ruatha to go from bad to worse.

The second was replaced and his successor fared no better. He was caught diverting goods – the best of the goods, at that. Fax had had him executed. His bony head still rolled around in the main firepit above the great Tower.

The present incumbent had not been able to maintain the Holding in even the sorry condition in which he had assumed its management. Seemingly simple matters developed rapidly into disasters. Like the production of cloth. Contrary to his boasts to Fax, the quality had not improved, and the quantity had fallen off.

Now Fax was here. And with dragonmen! Why dragonmen? The import of the question froze Lessa, and the heavy door closing behind her barked her heels painfully. Dragonmen used to be frequent visitors at Ruatha – that she knew and even vaguely remembered. Those memories were like a harper's tale, told of someone else, not something within her own experience. She had limited her fierce attention to Ruatha only. She could not even recall the name of queen, or Weyrwoman from the instructions of her childhood, nor could she recall hearing mention of any queen or Weyrwoman by anyone in the Hold these past ten Turns.

Perhaps the dragonmen were finally going to call the Lords of the Holds to task for the disgraceful show of greenery about the Holds. Well, Lessa was to blame for much of that in Ruatha, but she defied even a dragonman to confront her with her guilt. If all Ruatha fell to the Threads, it would be better than remaining dependent to Fax! The heresy shocked Lessa even as she thought it.

Wishing she could as easily uuburden her conscience of such blasphemy, she ditched the ashes on the stable midden. There was a sudden change in air pressure around her. Then a fleeting shadow caused her to glance up.

From behind the cliff above glided a dragon, its enormous wings spread to their fullest as he caught the morning updraft. Turning effortlessly, he descended. A second, a third, a full wing of dragons followed in soundless flight and patterned descent, graceful and awesome. The claxon rang belatedly from the Tower, and from within the kitchen there issued the screams and shrieks of the terrified drudges.

Lessa took cover. She ducked into the kitchen where she was instantly seized by the assistant cook and thrust with a buffet and a kick toward the sinks. There she was put to scrubbing the grease-encrusted serving utensils with cleansing sand.

The yelping canines were already lashed to the spitrun, turning a scrawny herdbeast that had been set to roast. The cook was ladling seasonings on the carcass, swearing at having to offer so poor a meal to so many guests, some of them of high rank. Winter-dried fruits from the last scanty harvest had been set to soak, and two of the oldest drudges were scraping roots to be boiled.

An apprentice cook was kneading bread and another carefully spicing a sauce. Looking fixedly at him, Lessa diverted his hand from one spice box to a less appropriate one as he gave a final shake to the concoction. She innocently added too much wood to the wall oven to insure the ruin of the breads. She controlled the canines deftly, slowing one and speeding the other so that the meat would be underdone on one side, burned on the other. That the feast should result in fast, with the food presented found inedible, was her whole intention.

Above, in the Hold, she had no doubt that certain other measures, undertaken at different times for this exact contingency, were being discovered.

Her fingers bloodied from a beating, one of the Warder's women came shrieking into the kitchen, hopeful of refuge there.

'Insects have eaten the best blankets to shreds! And a canine who had littered on the best linens snarled at me as she gave suck. And the rushes are noxious, and the best chambers full of debris driven in by the winter wind. Somebody left the shutters ajar. Just a tiny bit, but it was enough,' the woman wailed, clutching her hand to her breast and rocking back and forth.

Lessa bent with great industry to shine the plates.

Watch-wher, watch-wher,
In your lair,
Watch well, watch-wher!
Who goes there?

'THE WATCH-WHER is hiding something,' F'lar told F'nor
as they consulted in the hastily cleaned great chamber. The
room delighted to hold the wintry chill, although a generous
fire now burned on the hearth.

'It was but gibbering when Canth spoke to it,' F'nor
remarked. He was leaning against the mantel, turning
slightly from side to side to gather some warmth. He
watched his wingleader's impatient pacing.

'Mnementh is calming it down,' F'lar replied. 'He may
be able to sort out the nightmare. The creature may be
more senile than sane, but . . .'

'I doubt it,' F'nor concurred helpfully. He glanced with
apprehension up at the web-hung ceiling. He was certain
he'd found most of the crawlers, but he didn't fancy their
sting. Not on top of the discomforts already experienced in
this forsaken Hold. If the night stayed mild, he intended
curling up with Canth on the heights. 'That would be a
more reasonable suggestion than Fax or his Warder have
made.'

'Hmmm,' F'lar muttered, frowning at the brown rider.

'Well, it's unbelievable that Ruatha could have fallen
to such disrepair in ten short Turns. Every dragon caught
the feeling of power, and it's obvious the watchwhere has
been tampered with. That takes a good deal of control.'

'From someone of the Blood,' F'lar reminded him.

F'nor shot his wingleader a quick look, wondering if he
could possibly be serious in the light of all information to
the contrary.

'I grant you there is power here, F'lar,' F'nor conceded.
'But it could as easily be a hidden male bastard of the old
Blood. And we need a female. But Fax made it plain, in his
inimitable fashion, that he left none of the old Blood alive
in the Hold the day he took it. Ladies, children, all. No,

no.' The brown rider shook his head, as if he could dispel the lack of faith in his wingleader's curious insistence that the Search would end in Ruath with Ruathan blood.

'That watch-wher is hiding something, and only some-one of the Blood of its Hold can arrange that, brown rider,' F'lar said emphatically. He gestured around the room and toward the window. 'Ruatha has been overcome. But she resists . . . subtly. I say it points to the old Blood *and* power. Not power alone.'

The obstinate expression in F'lar's eyes, the set of his jaw, suggested that F'nor seek another topic.

'I'll see what may be seen around fallen Ruatha,' he mumbled and left the chamber.

F'lar was heartily bored with the lady Fax had so courteously assigned him. She giggled incessantly and sneezed constantly. She waved about, but did not apply to her nose, a scarf or handkerchief long overdue for a thorough washing. A sour odor, compounded of sweat, sweet oil, and rancid food smells, exuded from her. She was also pregnant by Fax. Not obviously so, but she had con-fided her condition to F'lar either oblivious to the insult to the dragonman or directed by her Lord to let drop the information. F'lar deliberately ignored the matter and, except when her company was obligatory on this Search journey, had ignored her, too.

Lady Tela was nervously jabbering away at him about the terrible condition of the rooms to which Lady Gemma and the other ladies of the Lord's procession had been assigned.

'The shutters, both sets, were ajar all winter long, and you should have seen the trash on the floors. We finally got two of the drudges to sweep it all into the fireplace. And then that smoked something fearful till a man was sent up.' Lady Tela giggled. 'He found the access blocked by a chimney stone fallen aslant. The rest of the chimney, for a wonder, was in good repair.'

She waved her handkerchief. F'lar held his breath as the gesture wafted an unappealing odor in his direction.

He glanced up the Hall toward the inner Hold door and saw the Lady Gemma descending, her steps slow and awkward. Some subtle difference about her gait attracted him, and he stared at her, trying to identify it.

'Oh, yes, poor Lady Gemma,' Lady Tela babbled, sighing deeply. 'We are so concerned. Why my Lord Fax insisted on her coming I do not know. She is not near her time, and yet . . .' The lighthead's concern sounded sincere.

F'lar's incipient hatred for Fax and his brutality matured abruptly. He left his partner chattering to thin air and courteously extended his arm to the Lady Gemma to support her down the steps and to the table. Only the brief tightening of her fingers on his forearm betrayed her gratitude. Her face was very white and drawn, the lines deeply etched around mouth and eyes, showing the effort she was expending.

'Some attempt has been made, I see, to restore order to the Hall,' she remarked in a conversational tone.

'Some,' F'lar admitted dryly, glancing around the grandly proportioned Hall, its rafters festooned with the webs of many Turns. The inhabitants of those gossamer nests dropped from time to time, with ripe splats, to the floor, onto the table, and into the serving platters. Nothing replaced the old banners of the Ruathan Blood, removed from the stark brown stone walls. Fresh rushes did obscure the greasy flagstones. The trestle tables appeared recently sanded and scraped, and the platters gleamed dully in the refreshed glows. Those unfortunately, were a mistake, for brightness was much too unflattering to a scene that would have been more reassuring in dimmer light.

'This was such a graceful Hall,' the Lady Gemma murmured for F'lar's ears alone.

'You were a friend?' he asked politely.

'Yes, in my youth.' Her voice dropped expressively on the last word, evoking for F'lar a happier girlhood. 'It was a noble line!'

'Think you *one* might have escaped the sword?'

The Lady Gemma flashed him a startled look, then quickly composed her features, lest the exchange be noted. She gave a barely perceptible shake of her head and then shifted her awkward weight to take her place at the table. Graciously she inclined her head toward F'lar, both dismissing and thanking him.

He returned to his own partner and placed her at the table on his left. As the only persons of rank who would dine that night at Ruatha Hold, Lady Gemma was seated on his right; Fax would be beyond her. The dragonmen and

Fax's upper soldiery would sit at the lower tables. No guild-men had been invited to Ruatha.

Fax arrived just then with his current lady and two underleaders, the Warder bowing them effusively into the Hall. The man, F'lar noticed, kept a good distance from his overlord – as well a Warder might whose responsibility was in this sorry condition. F'lar flicked a crawler away. Out of the corner of his eye he saw the Lady Gemma wince and shudder.

Fax stamped up to the raised table, his face black with suppressed rage. He pulled back his chair roughly, slam-ming it into the Lady Gemma's before he seated himself. He pulled the chair to the table with a force that threatened to rock the none too stable trestle-top from its supporting legs. Scowling, he inspected his goblet and plate, fingering the surface, ready to throw them aside if they displeased him.

'A roast, my Lord Fax, and fresh bread, Lord Fax, and such fruits and roots as are left.'

'Left? Left? You said there was nothing harvested here.'

The Warder's eyes bulged and he gulped, stammering, 'Nothing to be sent on. Nothing *good* enough to be sent on. Nothing. Had I but known of your arrival, I could have sent to Crom . . .'

'Sent to Crom?' roared Flax, slamming the plate he was inspecting onto the table so forcefully that the rim bent under his hands. The Warder winced again as if he himself had been maimed.

'For decent foodstuffs, my Lord,' he quavered.

'The day one of my Holds cannot support itself *or* the visit of its rightful overlord, I shall renounce it.'

The Lady Gemma gasped. Simultaneously the dragons roared. F'lar felt the unmistakable surge of power. His eyes instinctively sought F'nor at the lower table. The brown rider, all the dragonmen, had experienced that inexplicable shaft of exultation.

'What's wrong, dragonman?' snapped Fax.

F'lar, affecting unconcern, stretched his legs under the table and assumed an indolent posture in the heavy chair.

'Wrong?'

'The dragons!'

'Oh, nothing. They often roar . . . at the sunset, at a flock of passing wherries, at mealtimes,'' and F'lar smiled amiably at the Lord of the High Reaches. Beside him his tablemate gave a little squeak.

'Mealtimes? Have they not been fed?'

'Oh, yes. Five days ago.'

'Oh. Five . . . days ago? And are they hungry . . . now?' Her voice trailed into a whisper of fear, her eyes grew round.

'In a few days,' F'lar assured her. Under cover of his detached amusement, F'lar scanned the Hall. That surge had come from nearby. Either in the Hall or just without it. It must have been from within. It came so soon upon Fax's speech that his words must have triggered it. F'lar saw that F'nor and the other dragonmen were surreptitiously searching every face in the Hall. Fax's soldiers could be disqualified and the Warder's men. And the power had an indefinably feminine touch to it.

One of Fax's women? F'lar found that hard to credit. Mnementh had been close to all of them, and none had shown a vestige of power, much less – with the exception of Lady Gemma – any intelligence.

One of the Hall women? So far he had seen only the sorry drudges and the aging females the Warder had as housekeepers. The Warder's personal woman? He must discover if that man had one. One of the Hold guards' women? F'lar suppressed an intense desire to rise and search.

'You mount a guard?' he asked Fax casually.

'Double at Ruath Hold!' he was told in a tight, hard voice, ground out from somewhere deep in Fax's chest.

'Here?' F'lar all but laughed out loud, gesturing around the sadly appointed chamber.

'Here!' Fax changed the subject with a roar. 'Food!'

Five drudges, two of them women in such grimy brown-gray rags that F'lar hoped they had had nothing to do with the preparation of the meal, staggered in under the emplattered herdbeast. No one with so much as a trace of power would sink to such depths, unless . . .

The aroma that reached him as the platter was placed on the serving table distracted him. It reeked of singed bone and charred meat. Even the pitcher of *klah* being passed smelled bad. The Warder frantically sharpened his tools as if a keen edge could somehow slice acceptable portions from this unlikely carcass.

The Lady Gemma caught her breath again, and F'lar saw her hands curl tightly around the armrests. He saw the convulsive movement of her throat as she swallowed. He, too, did not look forward to this repast.

The drudges reappeared with wooden trays of bread. Burnt crusts had been scraped and cut, in some places, from the loaves before serving. As other trays were borne in, F'lar tried to catch sight of the faces of the servitors. Matted hair obscured the face of the one who presented Lady Gemma with a dish of legumes swimming in greasy liquid. Revolted, F'lar poked through the legumes to find properly cooked portions to offer Lady Gemma. She waved them aside, her face ill concealing her discomfort.

As F'lar was about to turn and serve Lady Tela, he saw Lady Gemma's hand clutch convulsively at the chair arms. He realized then that she was not merely nauseated by the unappetizing food. She was seized with the onslaught of labor contractions.

F'lar glanced in Fax's direction. The overlord was scowling blackly at the attempts of the Warder to find edible portions of meat to serve.

F'lar touched Lady Gemma's arms with light fingers. She turned her face just enough so that she could see F'lar out of the corner of her eye. She managed a socially correct half-smile.

'I dare not leave just now, Lord F'lar. He is always dangerous at Ruatha. And it may only be false pangs . . . at my age.'

F'lar was dubious as he saw another shudder pass through her frame. The woman would have been a fine Weyrwoman, he thought ruefully, if she were younger.

The Warder, his hands shaking, presented Fax the sliced meats, slivers of overdone flesh, portions of almost edible meats, but not much of either.

One furious wave of Fax's broad fist and the Warder had the plate, meats and juice, square in the face. Despite himself, F'lar sighed, for those undoubtedly constituted the only edible portions of the entire beast.

'You call this food? *You call this food?*' Fax bellowed. His voice boomed back from the bare vault of the ceiling, shaking crawlers from their webs as the sound shattered the fragile strands. *"Slop! Slop!"*

F'lar rapidly brushed crawlers from the Lady Gemma, who was helpless in the throes of a very strong contraction.

'It's all we had on such short notice,' the Warder squealed, bloody juices streaking down his cheeks. Fax threw the goblet at him, and the wine went streaming down the man's chest. The steaming dish of roots followed, and the man yelped as the hot liquid splashed over him.

'My Lord, my Lord, had I but known!'

'Obviously. Ruatha can*not* support the visit of its Lord. You must renounce it,' F'lar heard himself saying.

His shock at such words issuing from his mouth was as great as that of everyone else in the Hall. Silence fell, broken by the splat of crawlers and the drip of root liquid from the Warder's shoulders to the rushes. The grating of Fax's boot heel was clearly audible as he swung slowly around to face the bronze rider.

As F'lar conquered his own amazement and rapidly tried to predict what to do next to mend matters, he saw F'nor rise slowly to his feet, hand on dagger hilt.

'I did not hear you correctly?' Fax asked, his face blank of all expression, his eyes snapping.

Unable to comprehend how he could have uttered such an arrant challenge, F'lar managed to assume a languid pose.

'You did mention, my Lord,' he drawled, 'that if any of your Holds could not support itself and the visit of its rightful overlord, you would renounce it.'

Fax stared back at F'lar, his face a study of swiftly suppressed emotions, the glint of triumph dominant. F'lar, his face stiff with the forced expression of indifference, was casting swiftly about in his mind. In the name of the Egg, had he lost all sense of discretion?

Pretending utter unconcern, he stabbed some vegetables onto his knife and began to munch on them. As he did so, he noticed F'nor glancing slowly around the Hall, scrutinizing everyone. Abruptly F'lar realized what had happened. Somehow, in making that statement, he, a dragonman, had responded to a covert use of the power. F'lar, the bronze rider, was being put into a position where he would *have* to fight Fax. Why? For what end? To get Fax to renounce the Hold? Incredible! But there could be only one possible reason for such a turn of events. An exultation as sharp as pain swelled within F'lar. It was all he could do to maintain his pose of bored indifference, all he could do to turn his attention to thwarting Fax, should he press for a duel. A

43

duel would serve no purpose. He, F'lar, had no time to waste on it.

A groan escaped Lady Gemma and broke the eyelocked stance of the two antagonists. Irritated, Fax looked down at her, fist clenched and half-raised to strike her for her temerity at interrupting her lord and master. The contraction that rippled across the swollen belly was as obvious as the woman's pain. F'lar dared not look toward her, but he wondered if she had deliberately groaned aloud to break the tension.

Incredibly, Fax began to laugh. He threw back his head, showing big, stained teeth, and roared.

'Aye, renounce it, in favor of her issue, if it is male ... and lives!' he crowed, laughing raucously.

'Heard and witnessed!' F'lar snapped, jumping to his feet and pointing to his riders. They were on their feet in an instant. 'Heard and witnessed!' they averred in the traditional manner.

With that movement, everyone began to babble at once in nervous relief. The other women, each reacting in her way to the imminence of birth, called orders to the servants and advice to each other. They converged toward the Lady Gemma, hovering undecidedly out of Fax's range like silly wherries disturbed from their roosts. It was obvious they were torn between their fear of their Lord and their desire to reach the laboring woman.

He gathered their intentions as well as their reluctance and, still stridently laughing, knocked back his chair. He stepped over it, strode down to the meat stand and stood hacking off pieces with his knife, stuffing them, juice dripping, into his mouth without ceasing to guffaw.

As F'lar bent toward the Lady Gemma to assist her out of her chair, she grabbed his arm urgently. Their eyes met, hers clouded with pain. She pulled him closer.

'He means to kill you, bronze rider. He loves to kill,' she whispered.

'Dragonmen are not easily killed, brave lady. I am grateful to you.'

'I do not want you killed,' she said softly, biting at her lip. 'We have so few bronze riders.'

F'lar stared at her, startled. Did she, Fax's lady, actually believe in the Old Laws? He beckoned to two of the Warder's men to carry her up into the Hold. He caught

44

Lady Tela by the arm as she fluttered past him in their wake.

'What do you need?'

'Oh, oh,' she exclaimed, her face twisted with panic; she was distractedly wringing her hands. 'Water, hot, clean. Cloths. And a birthing-woman. Oh, yes, we must have a birthing-woman.'

F'lar looked about for one of the Hold women, his glance sliding over the first disreputable figure who had started to mop up the spilled food. He signaled instead for the Warder and peremptorily ordered him to send for the birthing-woman. The Warder kicked at the drudge on the floor.

'You ... you! Whatever your name is, go get her from the crafthold. You must know who she is.'

With a nimbleness at odds with her appearance of extreme age and decrepitude, the drudge evaded the parting kick the Warder aimed in her direction. She scurried across the Hall and out the kitchen door.

Fax sliced and speared meat, occasionally bursting out with a louder bark of laughter as his thoughts amused him. F'lar sauntered down to the carcass and, without waiting for invitation from his host, began to carve neat slices also, beckoning his men over. Fax's soldiers, however, waited till their Lord had eaten his fill.

Lord of the Hold, your charge is sure
In thick walls, metal doors, and no verdure.

LESSA SPED from the Hall to find the crafthold birthing-
woman, her mind seething with frustration. So close! So
close! How could she come so close and yet fail? Fax should
have challenged the dragonman. And the dragonman was
strong and young, his face that of a fighter, stern and controlled. He should not have temporized. Was all honor dead
in Pern, smothered by green grass?

And why, oh, why, had the Lady Gemma chosen that
precious moment to go into labor? If her groan hadn't
distracted Fax, the fight would have begun, and not even
Fax, for all his vaunted prowess as a vicious fighter, would
have prevailed against a dragonman who had Lessa's
support. The Hold must be secured to its rightful Blood
again. Fax would not leave Ruatha alive!

Above her, on the High Tower, the great bronze dragon
gave forth a weird croon, his many-faceted eyes sparkling
in the gathering darkness.

Unconsciously she silenced him as she would have done
the watch-wher. Ah, that watch-wher. He had not come
out of his den at her passing. She knew the dragons had been
at him. She could hear him gibbering in his panic. They'd
drive him to his death.

The slant of the road toward the crafthold lent impetus
to her flying feet, and she had to brace herself to a sliding
stop at the birthing-woman's stone threshold. She banged
on the closed door and heard the frightened exclamation of
surprise within.

'A birth. A birth at the Hold,' Lessa cried in time to her
thumping.

'A birth?' came the muffled cry, and the latches were
thrown up on the door. 'At the Hold?'

'Fax's lady and, as you love life, hurry, for if it is male,
it will be Ruatha's own Lord.'

That ought to fetch her thought Lessa, and in that instant the door was flung open by the man of the house. Lessa could see the birthing-woman gathering up her things in haste, piling them into her shawl. Lessa hurried the woman out, up the steep road to the Hold, under the Tower gate, grabbing the woman as she tried to run at the sight of a dragon peering down at her. Lessa drew her into the Court and pushed her, resisting, into the Hall.

The woman clutched at the inner door, balking at the sight of the gathering there. Lord Fax, his feet up on the trestle table, was paring his fingernails with his knife blade, still chuckling. The dragonmen in their wher-hide tunics, were eating quietly at one table while the soldiers were having their turn at the meat.

The bronze rider noticed their entrance and pointed urgently toward the inner Hold. The birthing-woman seemed frozen to the spot. Lessa tugged futilely at her arm, urging her to cross the Hall. To her surprise, the bronze rider strode to them.

'Go quickly, woman, Lady Gemma is before her time,' he said, frowning with concern, gesturing imperatively toward the Hold entrance. He caught her by the shoulder and led her, all unwilling, toward the steps, Lessa tugging away at her other arm.

When they reached the stairs, he relinquished his grip, nodding to Lessa to escort her the rest of the way. Just as they reached the massive inner door, Lessa noticed how sharply the dragonman was looking at them. At her hand on the birthing-woman's arm. Warily, she glanced at her hand and saw it, as if it belonged to a stranger – the long fingers, shapely despite dirt and broken nails, a small hand, delicately boned, gracefully placed despite the urgency of the grip. She blurred it.

The Lady Gemma was indeed in hard labor, and all was not well. When Lessa tried to retire from the room, the birthing-woman shot her such a terrified glance that Lessa reluctantly remained. It was obvious that Fax's other ladies were of no use. They were huddled at one side of the high bed, wringing their hands and talking in shrill, excited tones. It remained to Lessa and the birthing-woman to remove Gemma's clothing, to ease her and hold her hands against the contractions.

There was little left of beauty in the gravid woman's

face. She was perspiring heavily, her skin tinged with gray. Her breath was sharp and rasping, and she bit her lips against outcry.

'This is not going well,' the birthing-woman muttered under her breath. 'You there, stop your sniveling,' she ordered, swinging around to point at one of the gaggle. She lost her indecision as the requirements of her calling gave her temporary authority over those of rank. 'Bring me hot water. Hand those cloths over. Find something warm for the babe. If it is born alive, it must be kept from drafts and chill.'

Reassured by her tyranny, the women stopped their whimpering and did her bidding.

If it survives, the words echoed in Lessa's mind. *Survives to be Lord of Ruatha. One of Fax's get?* That had not been her intention, although ...

The Lady Gemma grabbed blindly for Lessa's hands, and despite herself, Lessa responded with such comfort as a strong grip would afford the woman.

'She bleeds too much,' the birthing-woman muttered. 'More cloths.'

The women resumed their wailing, uttering little shrieks of fear and protestation.

'She should not have been made to journey so far.'

'They will both die.'

'Oh, it *is* too much blood.'

Too much blood, thought Lessa. *I have no quarrel with her. And the child comes too early. It will die.* She looked down at the contorted face, the bloodied lower lip. *If she does not cry out now, why did she then?* Fury swept through Lessa. This woman had, for some obscure reason, deliberately diverted Fax and F'lar at the crucial moment. She all but crushed Gemma' hands in hers.

Pain from such an unexpected quarter roused Gemma from her brief respite between the shuddering contractions that seized her at shorter and shorter intervals. Blinking sweat from her eyes, she focused desperately on Lessa's face.

'What have I done to you?' she gasped.

'Done? I had Ruatha almost within my grasp again when you uttered your false cry,' Lessa said, her head bent so that not even the birthing-woman at the foot of the bed could hear them. She was so angry that she had lost all discretion, but it would not matter, for this woman was close to death.

The Lady Gemma's eyes widened. 'But ... the dragon-man ... Fax cannot kill the dragonman. There are so few bronze riders. They are all needed. And the old tales ... the star ... star ...' She could not continue, for a massive contraction shook her. The heavy rings on her fingers bit into Lessa's hands as she clung to the girl.

'What do you mean?' Lessa demanded in a hoarse whisper.

But the woman's agony was so intense that she could scarcely breathe. Her eyes seemed to start from her head. Lessa, hardened though she had become to all emotion save that of revenge, was shocked to the deeper feminine instinct of easing a woman's pain in her extremity. Even so, the Lady Gemma's words rang through her mind. The woman had not, then, protected Fax, but the dragon-man. The star? Did she mean the Red Star? Which old tales?

The birthing-woman had both hands on Gemma's belly, pressing downward, chanting advice to a woman too far gone in pain to hear. The twisting body gave a convulsive heave, lifting from the bed. As Lessa tried to support her, Lady Gemma opened her eyes wide, her expression one of incredulous relief. She collapsed into Lessa's arms and lay still.

'She's dead!' shrieked one of the women. She flew, screaming from the chamber. Her voice reverberated down the rock halls. 'Dead ... ead ... ead ... ddddd,' echoed back to the dazed women, who stood motionless in shock.

Lessa laid the woman down on the bed, staring amazed at the oddly triumphant smile on Gemma's face. She retreated into the shadows, far more shaken than anyone else. She who had never hesitated to do anything that would thwart Fax or beggar Ruatha further was trembling with remorse. She had forgotten in her single-mindedness that there might be others motivated by a hatred of Fax. The Lady Gemma was one, and one who had suffered far more subjective brutalities and indignities than Lessa had. Yet Lessa had hated Gemma, had poured out that hatred on a woman who had deserved her respect and support rather than her condemnation.

49

Lessa shook her head to dispel the aura of tragedy and self-revulsion that threatened to overwhelm her. She had no time for regret or contrition. Not now. Not when, by affecting Fax's death, she could avenge not only her own wrongs but Gemma's!

That was it. And she had the lever. The child ... yes, the child. She'd say it lived. That it was male. The dragonman would have to fight. He had heard and witnessed Fax's oath.

A smile, not unlike the one on the dead woman's face, crossed Lessa's as she hurried down the corridors to the Hall.

She was about to dash into the Hall itself when she realized she had permitted her anticipation of triumph to destroy her self-discipline. Lessa halted at the portal, deliberately took a deep breath. She dropped her shoulders and stepped down, once more the colorless drudge.

The harbinger of death was sobbing in a heap at Fax's feet.

Lessa gritted her teeth against redoubled hatred for the overlord. He was glad the Lady Gemma had died, birthing his seed. Even now he was ordering the hysterical woman to go tell his latest favorite to attend him, doubtless to install her as his first lady.

'The child lives,' Lessa cried, her voice distorted with anger and hatred. 'It is male.'

Fax was on his feet, kicking aside the weeping woman, scowling viciously at Lessa. 'What are you saying, woman?'

'The child lives. It is male,' she repeated, descending. The incredulity and rage that suffused Fax's face was wonderful to see. The Warder's men stifled their inadvertent cheers.

'Ruatha has a new Lord.' The dragons roared.

So intent was she on achieving her purpose that she failed to notice the reactions of others in the hall, failed to hear the roaring of the dragons without.

Fax erupted into action. He leaped across the intervening space, bellowing denials of the news. Before Lessa could dodge, his fist crashed down across her face. She was swept off her feet, off the steps, and fell heavily to the stone floor, where she lay motionless, a bundle of dirty rags.

'Hold, Fax!' F'lar's voice cut across the silence as the

Lord of the High Reaches lifted his leg to kick the unconscious body.

Fax whirled, his hand automatically closing on his knife hilt.

'It was heard and witnessed, Fax,' F'lar cautioned him, one hand outstretched in warning, 'by dragonmen. Stand by your sworn and witnessed oath!'

'Witnessed? By dragonmen?' cried Fax with a derisive laugh. 'Dragonwomen, you mean,' he sneered, his eyes blazing with contempt, one sweeping gesture of scorn dismissing them all.

He was momentarily taken aback by the speed with which the bronze rider's knife appeared in his hand.

'Dragonwomen?' F'lar queried, his lips curling back over his teeth, his voice dangerously soft. Glowlight flickered off his circling blade as he advanced on Fax.

'Women! Parasites on Pern. The Weyr power is over, dragon woman, over!' Fax roared, leaping forward to land in a combat crouch.

The two antagonists were dimly aware of the scurry behind them, of tables pulled roughly aside to give the duelists space. F'lar could spare no glance at the crumpled form of the drudge, yet he was sure, through and beyond instinct sure, that she was the source of power. He had felt it as she entered the room. The dragon's roaring confirmed it. If that fall had killed her ... He advanced on Fax, leaping away to avoid the slashing blade as Fax unwound from the crouch with a powerful lunge.

F'lar evaded the attack easily, noticing his opponent's reach, deciding he had a slight advantage there. He told himself sternly that wasn't much advantage. Fax had had much more actual hand-to-hand killing experience than had he whose duels had always ended at first blood on the practice floor. F'lar made due note to avoid closing with the burly Lord. The man was heavy-chested, dangerous from sheer mass. F'lar must use agility as a weapon, not brute strength.

Fax feinted, testing F'lar for weakness or indiscretion. The two crouched, facing each other across six feet of space, knife hands weaving, their free hands, spread-fingered, ready to grab.

Again Fax pressed the attack. F'lar allowed him to close, just close enough to dodge away with a backhanded swipe.

He felt fabric tear under the tip of his knife and heard Fax's snarl. The overlord was faster on his feet than his bulk suggested, and F'lar had to dodge a second time, feeling the scoring of Fax's knife across his heavy wher-hide jerkin.

Grimly the two circled, looking for an opening in each other's defense. Fax plowed in, trying to turn his weight and mass to advantage against the lighter, faster man by cornering him between raised platform and wall.

F'lar countered, ducking low under Fax's flailing arm, slashing obliquely across Fax's side. The overlord caught at him, yanking savagely, and F'lar was trapped against the other man's side, straining desperately with his left hand to keep the knife arm up. F'lar brought up his knee, timing a sudden collapse with that blow. He ducked away as Fax gasped and buckled from the pain in his groin. F'lar danced away, sudden fire in his left shoulder witness that he had not escaped unscathed.

Fax's face was red with bloody anger, and he wheezed from pain and shock. But F'lar had no time to follow up the momentary advantage, for the infuriated Lord straightened up and charged. F'lar was forced to sidestep quickly before Fax could close with him. F'lar put the meat table between them, circling warily, flexing his shoulder to assess the extent of his injury. The slash felt as if it had been scored by a brand. Motion was painful, but the arm could be used.

Suddenly, Fax seized up a handful of fatty scraps from the meat tray and hurled them at F'lar. The dragonman ducked, and Fax closed the distance around the table with a rush. Instinct prompted F'lar to leap sideways as Fax's flashing blade came within inches of his abdomen. His own knife sliced down the outside of Fax's arm. Instantly the two pivoted to face each other again, but Fax's left arm hung limply at his side.

F'lar darted in, pressing his luck as the Lord of the High Reaches staggered. But F'lar misjudged the man's condition and suffered a terrific kick in the side as he tried to dodge under the feinting knife. Doubled with pain, F'lar rolled frantically away from his charging adversary. Fax was lurching forward, trying to fall on him, to pin the lighter dragonman down for a final thrust. F'lar somehow got to his feet, attempting to straighten up to meet Fax's stumbling charge. His very position saved him. Fax overreached his mark and staggered off balance. F'lar brought his right hand over with as much strength as he could muster, and his knife blade plunged through Fax's unprotected back until he felt the point stick in the chest plate.

The defeated Lord fell flat to the flagstones, the force of his descent dislodging the dagger from his chest bone so that an inch of the bloody blade re-emerged from the point of entry.

A thin wailing penetrated the haze of pain and relief. F'lar looked up and saw, through sweat-blurred eyes, women crowding in the Hold doorway. One held a closely swathed object in her arms. F'lar could not immediately grasp the significance of that tableau, but he knew it was very important to clear his thoughts.

He stared down at the dead man. There was no pleasure in killing the man, he realized, only relief that he himself was still alive. He wiped his forehead on his sleeve and forced himself erect, his side throbbing with the pain of that last kick and his left shoulder burning. He half stumbled to the drudge, still sprawled where she had fallen.

He gently turned her over, noting the terrible bruise spreading across her cheek under the dirty skin. He heard F'nor take command of the tumult in the Hall.

The dragonman laid a hand, trembling in spite of an effort to control himself, on the woman's breast to feel for a heartbeat. . . . It was there, slow but strong.

A deep sigh escaped him, for either blow or fall could have proved fatal. Fatal, perhaps, for Pern as well.

Relief was colored with disgust. There was no telling under the filth how old this creature might be. He raised her to his arms, her light body no burden even to his battle-weary strength. Knowing F'nor would handle any trouble efficiently, F'lar carried the drudge to his own chamber.

He put the body on the high bed, then stirred up the fire and added more glows to the bedside bracket. His gorge rose at the thought of touching the filthy mat of hair, but nonetheless and gently, he pushed it back from the face, turning the head this way and that. The features were small, regular. One arm, clear of rags, was reasonably clean above the elbow but marred by bruises and old scars. The skin was firm and unwrinkled. The hands, when he took them in his, were dirt-encrusted but all the same, well-shaped and delicately boned.

F'lar began to smile. Yes, she had blurred that hand so skillfully that he had actually doubted what he had first seen. And yes, beneath grime and grease, she was young. Young enough for the Weyr. And no born drab. She was not young enough, happily, to be Fax's seed. One of the previous Lords' by-blows? No, there was no taint of common blood here. It was pure, no matter whose line, and he rather thought she was indeed Ruathan. One who had by some unknown agency escaped the massacre ten Turns ago and bided her time for revenge. Why else force Fax to renounce the Hold?

Delighted and fascinated by this unexpected luck, F'lar reached out to tear the dress from the unconscious body and found himself constrained not to. The girl had roused. Her great, hungry eyes fastened on his, not fearful or expectant; wary.

A subtle change occurred in her face. F'lar watched, his smile deepening, as she shifted her regular features into an illusion of disagreeable ugliness.

'Trying to confuse a dragonman, girl?' he chuckled. He made no further move to touch her but settled against the great carved post of the bed. He crossed his arms on his chest and then shifted suddenly to ease his sore arm.

'Your name, girl, and rank.'

She drew herself upright slowly, her features no longer blurred. Deliberately she slid back against the headboard so they faced each other across the length of the high bed.

'Fax?'

'Dead. Your name!'

A look of exulting triumph flooded her face. She slipped from the bed, standing unexpectedly tall. 'Then I reclaim my own. I am of the Ruathan Blood. I claim Ruath,' she announced in a ringing voice.

F'lar stared at her a moment, delighted with her proud bearing. Then he threw back his head and laughed.

'This? This crumbling heap?' He could not help but mock the disparity of her manner and her dress. 'Oh, no. Besides, fair lady, we dragonmen heard and witnessed Fax's oath renouncing the Hold in favor of his heir. Shall I challenge the babe, too, for you? And choke him with his swaddling clothes?'

Her eyes flashed, her lips parted in a terrible smile.

'There is no heir. Gemma died, the babe unborn. I lied.'

54

'Lied?' F'lar demanded, angry.

'Yes,' she taunted him with a toss of her chin. 'I lied. There was no babe born. I merely wanted to be sure you challenged Fax.'

He grabbed her wrist, stung that he had twice fallen to her prodding.

'You provoked a dragonman to fight? To kill? *When he is on Search?*'

'Search? What should I care for a Search? I have Ruatha as my Hold again. For ten Turns I have worked and waited, schemed and suffered for that. What could your Search mean to me?'

F'lar wanted to strike that look of haughty contempt from her face. He twisted her arm savagely, bringing her to his feet before he released his pressure. She laughed at him and had scuttled to one side and was on her feet and out the door before he could realize what she was about and give chase.

Swearing to himself, he raced down the rocky corridors, knowing she would have to make for the Hall to get out of the Hold. However, when he reached the Hall, there was no sign of her fleeing figure among those still loitering there.

'Has that creature come this way?' he called to F'nor, who was, by chance, standing by the door to the Court.

'No. Is she the source of power, after all?'

'Yes, she is,' F'lar answered, galled all the more by her escape. Where had she gone to? 'And of the Ruathan Blood, at that!'

'Oh-ho! Does she depose the babe, then?' F'nor asked, gesturing toward the birthing-woman who occupied a seat close to the now blazing hearth.

F'lar paused, about to return to search the Hold's myriad passages. He stared, momentarily confused, at his brown rider.

'Babe? What babe?'

'The male child Lady Gemma bore,' F'nor replied, surprised by F'lar's uncomprehending look.

'It lives?'

'Yes. A strong babe, the woman says, for all that he was premature and taken forcibly from the dead dame's belly.'

F'lar threw back his head with a shout of laughter. For all her scheming, she had been outdone by Truth.

At that moment he heard the unmistakable elation in

Mnementh's roar, followed by the curious warble of the other dragons.

'Mnementh has caught her,' F'lar cried, grinning with jubilation. He strode down the steps, past the body of the former Lord of the High Reaches and out into the main court.

He saw the bronze dragon was gone from his Tower perch and called him. An agitation drew his eyes upward. He saw Mnementh spiraling down into the Court, his front paws clasping something. Mnementh informed F'lar that he had seen her climbing from one of the high windows and had simply plucked her from the ledge, knowing the dragonman sought her. The bronze dragon settled awkwardly onto his hind legs, his wings working to keep him balanced. Carefully he set the girl on her feet and carefully he formed a cage around her with his huge talons. She stood motionless within that circle, her face turned toward the wedge-shaped head that swayed above her.

The watch-wher, shrieking terror, anger, and hatred, was lunging violently to the end of its chain, trying to come to Lessa's aid. It grabbed at F'lar as he strode to the two.

'You've courage enough to fly with, girl,' he admitted, resting one hand casually on Mnementh's upper claw. Mnementh was enormously pleased with himself and swiveled his head down for his eye ridges to be scratched.

'You did not lie, you know,' F'lar said, unable to resist taunting the girl.

Slowly she turned toward him, her face impassive. She was not afraid of dragons, F'lar realized with approval.

'The babe lives. And it is male.'

She could not control her dismay, and her shoulders sagged briefly before she pulled herself erect again.

'Ruatha is mine,' she insisted in a tense, low voice.

'Aye, and it would have been had you approached me directly when the wing arrived here.'

Her eyes widened. 'What do you mean?'

'A dragonman may champion anyone whose grievance is just. By the time we reached Ruath Hold, my lady, I was quite ready to challenge Fax given any reasonable cause, despite the Search.' This was not the whole truth, but F'lar must teach this girl the folly of trying to control dragonmen. 'Had you paid any attention to your harper's songs, you'd know your rights. And' – F'lar's voice held a vindictive edge that surprised him – 'the Lady Gemma might not now lie dead. She, brave soul, suffered far more at that tyrant's hand than you.'

Something in her manner told him that she regretted Lady Gemma's death, that it had affected her deeply.

'What good is Ruatha to you now?' he demanded, a broad sweep of his arm taking in the ruined Court yard and the Hold, the entire unproductive valley of Ruatha. 'You have indeed accomplished your ends, a profitless conquest and its conqueror's death.'

F'lar snorted. 'As well, too. Those Holds will all revert to their legitimate Blood, and time they did. One Hold and One Lord. Anything else is against tradition. Of course, you might have to fight others who disbelieve that precept: who become infected with Fax's greedy madness. Can you hold Ruatha against attack . . . now . . . in her condition?'

'Ruatha is mine!'

'Ruatha?' F'lar's laugh was derisive. 'When you could be Weyrwoman?'

'Weyrwoman?' she breathed, staring at him in shocked amazement.

'Yes, little fool. I said I rode in Search . . . it's about time you attended to more than Ruatha. And the object of my Search is . . . you!'

She stared at the finger he pointed at her, as if it were dangerous.

'By the First Egg, girl, you've power in you to spare when you can turn a dragonman, all unwitting, to do your bidding. Ah, but never again, for I am now on guard against you.'

Mnementh crooned approvingly, the sound a soft rumble in his throat. He arched his neck so that one eye was turned directly on the girl, gleaming in the darkness of the Court.

F'lar noticed with detached pride that she neither flinched nor blanched at the proximity of an eye greater than her own head.

'He likes to have his eye ridges scratched,' F'lar remarked in a friendly tone, changing tactics.

'I know,' she said softly and reached out a hand to do that service.

'Nemorth has laid a golden egg,' F'lar continued persuasively. 'She is close to death. This time we must have a strong Weyrwoman.'

'The Red Star?' the girl gasped, turning frightened eyes to F'lar. That alone surprised him, for she had never once evinced any fear.

'You've seen it? You understand what it means?' He saw her swallow nervously.

'There is danger . . .' she began in a bare whisper, glancing apprehensively eastward.

F'lar did not question by what miracle she appreciated the imminence of danger. He had every intention of taking her to the Weyr by sheer force if necessary. But something within him wanted very much for her to accept the challenge voluntarily. A rebellious Weyrwoman would be even more dangerous than a stupid one. This girl had too much power and was too used to guile and strategy. It would be a calamity to antagonize her with injudicious handling.

'There is danger for all Pern. Not just Ruatha,' he said, allowing a note of entreaty to creep into his voice. 'And *you* are needed. Not by Ruatha.' A wave of his hand dismissed that consideration as a negligible one compared to the total picture. 'We are doomed without a strong Weyrwoman. Without you.'

'Gemma said all the bronze riders were needed,' she murmured in a dazed whisper.

What did she mean by that statement? F'lar frowned. Had she heard a word he had said? He pressed his argument, certain only that he had already struck one responsive chord.

'You've won here. Let the babe' – he saw her startled rejection of that idea and ruthlessly qualified it – 'Gemma's babe – be reared at Ruatha. You have command of all the Holds as Weyrwoman, not ruined Ruatha alone. You've accomplished Fax's death. Leave off vengeance.'

She stared at F'lar with wondering eyes, absorbing his words.

'I never thought beyond Fax's death,' she admitted slowly. 'I never thought what should happen then.'

Her confusion was almost childlike and struck F'lar forcibly. He had had no time or desire to consider her prodigious accomplishment. Now he realized some measure of her indomitable character. She could not have been above ten Turns of age herself when Fax had murdered her family. Yet somehow, so young, she had set herself a goal and managed to survive both brutality and detection long enough to secure the usurper's death. What a Weyrwoman she would be! In the tradition of those of Ruathan Blood. The light of the paler moon made her look young and vulnerable and almost pretty.

'You can be Weyrwoman,' he repeated with gentle insistence.

'Weyrwoman,' she breathed, incredulous, and gazed around the inner Court bathed in soft moonlight. He thought she wavered.

'Or perhaps you enjoy rags?' he said, making his voice harsh, mocking. 'And matted hair, dirty feet, and cracked hands? Sleeping in straw, eating rinds? You are young . . . that is, I assume you are young.' His voice was frankly skeptical. She glared at him coolly, her lips firmly pressed together. 'Is this the be-all and end-all of your ambition? What are you that this little corner of the great world is *all* you want?' He paused, then with utter contempt added, 'The Blood of Ruatha has thinned, I see. You're afraid!'

'I am Lessa, daughter of the Lord of Ruath,' she countered, stung to responding by the Blood insult. She drew herself erect, her eyes flashing, her chin high. 'I am afraid of nothing!'

F'lar contented himself with a slight smile.

Mnementh, however, threw up his head and stretched out his sinuous neck to its whole length. His full-throated peal rang out down the valley. The bronze communicated his awareness to F'lar that Lessa had accepted the challenge. The other dragons answered back, their warbles shriller than Mnementh's male bellow. The watch-wher which had cowered at the end of its chain lifted its voice in a thin, unnerving screech until the Hold emptied of its startled occupants.

'F'nor,' the bronze rider called, waving his wingleader to him. 'Leave half the flight to guard the Hold. Some nearby Lord might think to emulate Fax's example. Send one rider to the High Reaches with the glad news. You go directly to the clothmen's Hall and speak to L'to . . . Lytol.' F'lar grinned. 'I think he would make an exemplary Warder and Lord Surrogate for this Hold in the name of the Weyr and the baby Lord.'

The brown rider's face expressed enthusiasm for his mission as he began to comprehend his leader's intentions. With Fax dead and Ruatha under the protection of dragonmen, particularly that same one who had dispatched Fax, the Hold would be safe and flourish under wise management.

'She caused Ruatha's deterioration?' he asked his leader.

'And nearly ours with her machinations,' F'lar replied, but having found the admirable object of his Search, he could now be magnanimous. 'Suppress your exultation, brother,' he advised quickly as he took note of F'nor's expression. 'The new queen must also be Impressed.'

'I'll settle arrangements here. Lytol is an excellent choice,' F'nor said, although he knew that F'lar needed no one's approval.

'Who is this Lytol?' demanded Lessa pointedly. She had twisted the mass of filthy hair back from her face. In the moonlight the dirt was less noticeable. F'lar caught F'nor looking at her with an all too easily read expression. He signaled F'nor with a peremptory gesture to carry out his orders without delay.

'Lytol is a dragonless man,' F'lar told the girl, 'no friend to Fax. He will ward the Hold well, and it will prosper.' He added persuasively with a quelling stare full on her, 'Won't it?'

She regarded him somberly, without answering, until he chuckled softly at her discomfiture.

'We'll return to the Weyr,' he announced, proffering a hand to guide her to Mnementh's side.

The bronze one had extended his head toward the watch-wher, who now lay panting on the ground, its chain limp in the dust.

'Oh,' Lessa sighed, and dropped beside the grotesque beast. It raised its head slowly, crying piteously.

'Mnementh says it is very old and soon will sleep itself to death.'

Lessa cradled the repulsive head in her arms, stroking the eye ridges, scratching behind its ears.

'Come, Lessa of Pern,' F'lar said, impatient to be up and away.

She rose slowly but obediently. 'It saved me. It knew me.'

'It knows it did well,' F'lar assured her brusquely, wondering at such an uncharacteristic show of sentiment in her.

He took her hand again, to help her to her feet and lead her back to Mnementh.

In one split second he was knocked off his feet, sprawling across the stones and trying to roll to his feet again, to face his adversary. The force of the initial blow, however, had dazed him, and he lay sprawled on his back, startled to see the watch-wher, its scaly body launched – straight at him.

Simultaneously he heard Lessa's startled exclamation and Mnementh's roar. The bronze's great head was swinging around to knock the watch-wher aside, away from the dragonman. But just as the watch-wher's body was fully extended in its leap, Lessa cried out.

'Don't kill! Don't kill!'

The watch-wher, its snarl turning into an anguished cry of alarm, executed an incredible maneuver in mid-air, turning aside from its trajectory. As it fell to the stone yard at his feet, F'lar heard the dull crack as the force of its landing broke its back.

Before he could get to his feet, Lessa was cradling the hideous head in her arms, her face stricken.

Mnementh lowered his head to tap the dying watch-wher's body gently. He informed F'lar that the beast had guessed Lessa was leaving Ruatha, something one of her Blood should not do. In its senile confusion it could only assume Lessa was in danger. When it heard Lessa's frantic command, it had corrected its error at the expense of its life.

'It was truly only defending me,' Lessa added, her voice breaking. She cleared her throat. 'It was the only one I could trust. My only friend.'

F'lar awkwardly patted the girl's shoulder, appalled that anyone could be reduced to claiming friendship with a watch-wher. He winced because the fall had reopened the knife wound in his shoulder and he hurt.

'In truth a loyal friend,' he said, standing patiently until the light in the watch-wher's green-gold eyes dimmed and died out.

All the dragons gave voice to the eerie, hair-raising, barely audible, high keening note that signified the passing of one of their kind.

'He was only a watch-wher,' Lessa murmured, stunned by the tribute, her eyes wide.

'The dragons confer honor where *they* will,' F'lar remarked dryly, disclaiming the responsibility.

Lessa looked down for one more long moment at the repulsive head. She laid it down to the stones, caressed the clipped wings. Then, with quick fingers, she undid the heavy buckle that fastened the metal collar around the neck. She threw the collar violently away.

She rose in a fluid movement and walked resolutely to Mnementh without a single backward glance. She stepped calmly to Mnementh's raised leg and seated herself, as F'lar directed her, on the great neck.

F'lar glanced around the Court at the remainder of his wing which had reformed there. The Hold folk had retreated into the safety of the great Hall. When his wingmen were all astride, he vaulted to Mnementh's neck, behind the girl.

'Hold tightly to my arms,' he ordered her as he took hold of the smallest neck ridge and gave the command to fly.

Her fingers closed spasmodically around his forearm as the great bronze dragon took off, the enormous wings working to achieve height from the vertical takeoff. Mnementh preferred to fall into flight from a cliff or tower. Dragons tended to indolence. F'lar glanced behind him, saw the other dragonmen form the flight line, spread out to cover the gaps of those still on guard at Ruatha Hold.

When they had reached a sufficient altitude, he told Mnementh to transfer, going *between* to the Weyr.

Only a gasp indicated the girl's astonishment as they hung *between*. Accustomed as he was to the sting of the profound cold, to the awesome utter lack of light and sound, F'lar still found the sensations unnerving. Yet the uncommon transfer spanned no more time than it took to cough thrice.

Mnementh rumbled approval of this candidate's calm reaction as they flicked out of the eerie *between*. She had not been afraid or screamed in panic as other women had. F'lar did feel her heart bounding against his arm that pressed against her ribs, but that was all.

And then they were above the Weyr, Mnementh setting his wings to glide in the bright daylight, half a world away from nighttime Ruatha.

Lessa's hands tightened on his arms, this time in surprise as they circled above the great stony trough of the Weyr. F'lar peered at Lessa's face, pleased with the delight mirrored there; she showed no trace of fear that they hung a thousand lengths above the high Benden mountain range. Then, as the seven dragons roared their incoming cry, an incredulous smile lit her face.

The other wingmen dropped into a wide spiral, down,

down, while Mnementh elected to descend in lazy circles. The dragonmen peeled off smartly and dropped, each to his own tier in the caves of the Weyr. Mnementh finally completed his leisurely approach to their quarters, whistling shrilly to himself as he braked his forward speed with a twist of his wings, dropping lightly at last to the ledge. He crouched as F'lar swung the girl to the rough rock, scored from thousands of clawed landings.

'This leads only to our quarters,' he told her as they entered the corridor, vaulted and wide for the easy passage of great bronze dragons.

As they reached the huge natural cavern that had been his since Mnementh achieved maturity, F'lar looked about him with eyes fresh from his first prolonged absence from the Weyr. The huge chamber was unquestionably larger than most of the halls he had visited in Fax's procession. Those halls were intended as gathering places for men, not the habitations of dragons. But suddenly he saw his own quarters were nearly as shabby as all Ruatha. Benden was, of a certainty, one of the oldest dragonweyrs, as Ruatha was one of the oldest Holds, but that excused nothing. How many dragons had bedded in that hollow to make solid rock conform to dragon proportions! How many feet had worn the path past the dragon's Weyr into the sleeping chamber, to the bathing room beyond where the natural warm spring provided ever-fresh water! But the wall hangings were faded and unraveling, and there were grease stains on lintel and floor that could easily be sanded away.

He noticed the wary expression on Lessa's face as he paused in the sleeping room.

'I must feed Mnementh immediately. So you may bathe first,' he said, rummaging in a chest and finding clean clothes for her, discards of former occupants of his quarters, but far more presentable than her present covering. He carefully laid back in the chest the white wool robe that was traditional Impression garb. She would wear that later. He tossed several garments at her feet and a bag of sweetsand, gesturing to the hanging that obscured the way to the bath.

He left her then, the clothes in a heap at her feet, for she made no effort to catch anything.

Mnementh informed him that F'nor was feeding Canth and that he, Mnementh, was hungry, too. *She* didn't trust F'lar, but she wasn't afraid of himself.

'Why should she be afraid of you?' F'lar asked. 'You're cousin to the watch-wher who was her only friend.'

Mnementh informed F'lar that he, a fully matured bronze dragon, was no relation to any scrawny, crawling, chained, and wing-clipped watch-wher.

'Then why did you accord him a dragon tribute?' F'lar asked.

Mnementh told him haughtily that it was fitting and proper to mourn the passing of a loyal and self-sacrificing personality. Not even a blue dragon could deny the fact that that Ruathan watch-wher had not divulged information he had been enjoined to keep, though the beast had been sorely pressed to do so by himself, Mnementh. Also, in managing, by some physical feat, to turn aside its attack on F'lar, at the cost of its own life, it had elevated itself to dragonlike bravery. Of course, the dragons had uttered a tribute at its passing.

F'lar, pleased at having been able to tease the bronze one, chuckled to himself. With great dignity Mnementh curved down to the feeding ground.

F'lar dropped off as Mnementh hovered near F'nor. The impact with the ground reminded him he had better get the girl to dress his shoulder for him. He watched as the bronze one swooped down on the nearest fat buck in the milling herd.

'The Hatching is due at any hour,' F'nor greeted his brother, grinning up at him as he squatted on his haunches. His eyes were bright with excitement.

F'lar nodded thoughtfully. 'There will be plenty to chose from the males,' he allowed, knowing F'nor was tauntingly withholding choicer news.

They both watched as F'nor's Canth singled out a doe. The brown dragon neatly grabbed the struggling beast in one claw and rose up, settling on an unoccupied ledge to feast.

Mnementh dispatched his first carcass and glided in again over the herd, to the pens beyond. He singled out a heavy ground bird and lifted with it in his claws. F'lar observed his ascent, experiencing as always the thrill of pride in the effortless sweep of the great pinions, the play of the sun on the bronze hide, the flash of silvery claws, unsheathed for landing. He never tired of watching Mnementh in flight or admiring the unconscious grace and strength.

'Lytol was overwhelmed by the summons,' F'nor remarked, 'and sends you all honor and respect. He will do well at Ruatha.'

'The reason he was chosen,' grunted F'lar, nonetheless gratified by Lytol's reaction. Surrogate Lordship was no substitute for loss of one's dragon, but it was an honorable responsibility.

'There was much rejoicing in the High Reaches,' F'nor continued, grinning widely, 'and honest grief at the passing of Lady Gemma. It will be interesting to see which of the contenders takes title.'

'At Ruatha?' F'lar queried, frowning down at his half brother.

'No. At the High Reaches and the other Holds Fax conquered. Lytol will bring his own people to secure Ruatha and to give any soldiery pause before they might attempt that Hold. He knew of many in the High Reaches who would prefer to make a change of Hold, even though Fax no longer dominates the High Reaches. He intended to make all haste to Ruatha so that our men will soon rejoin us.'

F'lar nodded approval, turning to salute two more of his wing, blue riders, who dropped with their beasts to the feeding ground. Mnementh went back for another fowl.

'He eats light,' F'nor commented. 'Canth's still gorging.'

'Browns are slow to get full growth,' F'lar drawled, watching with satisfaction as F'nor's eyes flashed angrily. That would teach him to withhold news.

'R'gul and S'lel are back,' the brown rider finally announced.

The two blues had the herd in a frenzy, stampeding and screaming in fright.

'The others are recalled,' F'nor continued. 'Nemorth is all but rigid in death.' Then he could no longer contain himself. 'S'lel brought in two. R'gul has five. Strong-willed, they say, and pretty.'

F'lar said nothing. He had expected those two would bring in multiple candidates. Let them bring hundreds if they chose. He, F'lar, the bronze rider, had in his one choice the winner.

Exasperated that his news elicited so little response, F'nor rose.

'We should have backtrailed for that one in Crom and the pretty . . .'

'Pretty?' F'lar retorted, cocking one eyebrow high in disdain. 'Pretty? Jora was pretty,' he spat out cynically.

'K'net and T'bor bring contenders from the west,' F'nor added urgently, concerned.

The wind-torn roar of homecoming dragons crackled through the air. Both men jerked their heads skyward and saw the double spirals of two returning wings, twenty strong.

Mnementh tossed his head high, crooning. F'lar called him in, pleased the bronze one made no quarrel at recall, although he had eaten very lightly. F'lar, saluting his brother amiably, stepped onto Mnementh's spread foot and was lifted back to his own ledge.

Mnementh hiccuped absently as the two walked the short passage to the vaulted inner chamber. He lumbered over to his hollowed bed and settled himself into the curved stone. When Mnementh had stretched and comfortably laid down his wedge-head, F'lar approached him. Mnementh regarded his friend with the near eye, its many facets glinting and shifting, the inner lids gradually closing as F'lar scratched the eye-ridge soothingly.

Those unfamiliar with it might find such a regard unnerving. But since that moment, twenty Turns before, when the great Mnementh had broken through his shell and stumbled across the Hatching Ground to stand, weaving on weak legs, before the boy F'lar, the dragonman had treasured these quiet moments as the happiest of a long day. No greater tribute could man be paid than the trust and companionship of the winged beasts of Pern. For the loyalty that dragonkind gave their chosen one of mankind was unswerving and complete from the instant of Impression.

Mnementh's inner content was such that the great eye quickly closed. The dragon slept, only the tip of his tail erect, a sure sign that he would be instantly on the alert if the need arose.

By the Golden Egg of Faranth
By the Weyrwoman, wise and true,
Breed a flight of bronze and brown wings,
Breed a flight of green and blue.
Breed riders, strong and daring,
Dragon-loving, born as hatched
Flight of hundreds soaring skyward,
Man and dragon fully matched.

LESSA WAITED until the sound of the dragonman's footsteps proved he had really gone away. She rushed quickly through the big cavern, heard the scape of claw and the whoosh of the mighty wings. She raced down the short passageway, right to the edge of the yawning entrance. There was the bronze dragon circling down to the wider end of the mile-long barren oval that was Benden Weyr. She had heard of the Weyrs, as any Pernese had, but to be in one was quite a different matter.

She peered up, around, down that sheer rock face. There was no way off but by dragon wing. The nearest cave mouths were an unhandy distance above her, to one side, below her on the other. She was neatly secluded here.

Weyrwoman, he had told her. His woman? In his weyr? Was that what he had meant? No, that was not the impression she got from the dragon. It occurred to her suddenly that it was odd she had understood the dragon. Were common folk able to? Or was it the dragonman Blood in her Line? At all events, Mnementh had implied something greater, some special rank. They must mean her, then, to be Weyrwoman to the unhatched dragon queen. Only how did she, or they, go about it? She remembered vaguely that when dragonmen went on Search, they looked for certain women. Ah, certain women. She was one, then, of several contenders. Yet the bronze rider had offered her the position as if she and she alone qualified. He had his own generous portion of conceit, that one, Lessa decided. Arrogant he was, though not the bully Fax had been.

She could see the bronze dragon swoop down to the

running herdbeasts, saw the strike, saw the dragon wheel up to settle on a far ledge to feed. Instinctively she drew back from the opening, back into the dark and relative safety of the corridor.

The feeding dragon evoked scores of horrid tales. Tales at which she had scoffed, but now ... Was it true, then, that dragons did eat human flesh? Did ... Lessa halted that trend of thought. Dragonkind was no less cruel than mankind. The dragon, at least, acted from bestial need rather than bestial greed.

Assured that the dragonman would be occupied awhile, she crossed the larger cave into the sleeping room. She scooped up the clothing and the bag of cleansing sand and proceeded to the bathing room. It was small but ample for its purpose. A wide ledge formed a partial lip to the uneven circle of the bathing pool. There was a bench and some shelves for drying cloths. In the glowlight she could see that the near section of the pool had been sanded high so a bather could stand comfortably. Then there was a gradual dip approaching the deeper water that slapped the very rock wall on the farther side.

To be clean! To be completely clean and to be able to stay that way. With a distaste at touching them no less acute than the dragonman's, she stripped off the remains of the rags, kicking them to one side, not knowing where to dispose of them. She shook out a generous handful of the sweetsand and, bending to the pool, wet it.

Quickly she made a soft mud with the sweet soap, and she scoured hands and bruised face. Wetting more sand, she attacked her arms and legs, then her body and feet. She scrubbed hard until she drew blood from half-healed cuts. Then she stepped, or rather jumped, into the pool, gasping as the warm water made the sweetsand foam in her scratches. She ducked under the surface, shaking her head to be sure her hair was thoroughly wetted. Then briskly she rubbed in more sweetsand, rinsing and scrubbing until she felt her hair might possibly be clean. Years, it had been. Great strands floated away in tangles like immense crawlers with attenuated legs, toward the far edge of the pool and then were drawn out of sight. The water, she was glad to note, constantly circulated, the cloudy and dirty replaced with clear. She turned her attention again to her body, scrubbing at ingrained dirt until her skin smarted. It was a ritual cleansing of more than surface soil. She felt a pleasure akin to ecstasy for the luxury of cleanliness.

Finally satisfied her body was as clean as one long soaking could make her, she sanded her hair yet a third time. She left the pool almost reluctantly, wringing out her hair and tucking it up on her head as she dried herself. She shook out the clothing and held one garment against her experimentally. The fabric, a soft green, felt smooth under her water-shrunken fingers, although the nap caught on her roughed hands. She pulled it over her head. It was loose, but the darker-green overtunic had a sash that she pulled in tight at the waist. The unusual sensation of softness against her bare skin made her wriggle with voluptuous pleasure. The skirt, no longer a ragged hem of tatter, swirled heavily around her ankles, making her smile in sheer feminine delight. She took up a fresh drying cloth and began to work on her hair.

A muted sound came to her ears, and she stopped, hands poised, head bent to one side. Straining, she listened. Yes, there were sounds without. The dragonman and his beast must have returned. She grimaced to herself with annoyance at this untimely interruption and rubbed harder at her hair. She ran fingers through the half-dry tangles, the motions arrested as she encountered snarls. She tried patting her hair into place, pushing it defiantly behind her ears. Vexed, she rummaged on the shelves until she found, as she had hoped to, a coarse-toothed metal comb. With this she attacked her unruly hair and, by the dint of much yanking and groaning as she pulled ruthlessly through years of tangles, she was able to groom the mass.

Now dry, her hair suddenly had a life of its own, crackling about her hands and clinging to face and comb and dress. It was difficult to get the silky stuff under control. And her hair was longer than she had thought, for, clean and unmatted, it fell to her waist – when it did not cling to her hands.

She paused, listening, and heard no sound at all. Apprehensively, she stepped to the curtain and glanced warily into the sleeping room. It was empty. She listened and caught the perceptible thoughts of the sleepy dragon. Well, she would rather meet the man in the presence of a sleepy dragon than in a sleeping room. She started across the floor and, out of the corner of her eye, caught sight of a strange woman as she passed a polished piece of metal hanging on the wall.

Amazed, she stopped short, staring, incredulous, at the face the metal reflected. Only when she put her hands to her prominent cheekbones in a gesture of involuntary surprise and the reflection imitated the gesture did she realize she looked at herself.

Why, that girl in the reflector was prettier than the Lady Tela, than the clothman's daughter! But so thin. Her hands of their own volition dropped to her neck, to the protruding collarbones, to her breasts, which did not entirely reflect the gauntness of the rest of her. The dress was too large for her frame, she noted with an unexpected emergence of conceit born in that instant of delighted appraisal. And her hair . . . it stood out around her head like an aureole. It wouldn't lie contained. She smoothed it down with impatient fingers, automatically bringing locks forward to hang around her face. As she irritably pushed them back, dismissing a need for disguise, the hair drifted up again.

A slight sound, the scrape of a boot against stone, caught her back from her bemusement. She waited, momentarily expecting him to appear. She was suddenly timid. With her face bare to the world, her hair behind her ears, her body outlined by a clinging fabric, she was stripped of her accustomed anonymity and was therefore, in her estimation, vulnerable.

Sternly she controlled the desire to run away, the irrational shock of fearfulness. Observing herself in the looking metal, she drew her shoulders back, tilted her head high, chin up; the movement caused her hair to crackle and cling and shift about her head. She was Lessa of Ruatha, of a fine old Blood. She no longer needed to resort to artifice to preserve herself, so she must stand proudly bare-faced before the world . . . and that dragonman.

Resolutely she crossed the room, pushing aside the hanging on the doorway to the great cavern.

He was there, beside the head of the dragon, scratching its eye ridges, a curiously tender expression on his face. It was a tableau completely at variance with all she had heard of dragonmen.

She had, or course, heard of the strange affinity between rider and dragon, but this was the first time she realized that love was part of that bond. Or that this reserved, cold man was capable of such deep emotion. He had been brusque enough with her over the old watch-wher. No wonder it had thought he had meant her harm. The dragons had been more tolerant, she remembered with an involuntary sniff.

He turned slowly, as if to loath to leave the bronze beast. He caught sight of her and pivoted completely around, his eyes intense as he took note of her altered appearance. With quick, light steps he closed the distance between them and ushered her back into the sleeping room, one strong hand holding her by the elbow.

'Mnementh has fed lightly and will need quiet to rest,' he said in a low voice, as if this were the most important consideration. He pulled the heavy hanging into place across the opening.

Then he held her away from him, turning her this way and that, scrutinizing her closely, a curious and slightly surprised expression fleeting across his face.

'You wash up . . . pretty, yes, almost pretty,' he allowed with such amused condescension in his voice that she pulled roughly away from him, piqued. His low laugh mocked her. 'How could one guess, after all, what was under the grime of . . . ten full Turns, I would say? Yes, you are certainly pretty enough to placate F'nor.'

Thoroughly antagonized by his attitude, she asked in icy tones, 'And F'nor must be placated at all costs?'

He stood grinning at her till she had to clench her fists at her sides to keep from beating that grin off his face.

At length he said, 'No matter, we must eat, and I shall require your services.' At her startled exclamation, he turned, grinning maliciously now as his movement revealed the caked blood on his left sleeve. 'The least you can do is bathe wounds honorably received in fighting your battle.'

He pushed aside a portion of the drapery that curtained the inner wall. 'Food for two!' he roared down a black gap in the sheer stone.

She heard a subterranean echo far below as his voice resounded down what must be a long shaft.

'Nemorth is nearly rigid,' he was saying as he took supplies from another drapery-hidden shelf, 'and the Hatching will soon begin, anyhow.'

A coldness settled in Lessa's stomach at the mention of a Hatching. The mildest tales she had heard about that part of dragonlore were chilling, the worst dismayingly macabre. Numbly she took the things he handed her.

'What? Frightened?' the dragonman taunted, pausing as he stripped off his torn and bloodied shirt.

With a shake of her head, Lessa turned her attention to the wide-shouldered, well-muscled back he presented her, the paler skin of his body decorated with random bloody streaks. Fresh blood welled from the point of his shoulder, for the removal of his shirt had broken the tender scabs.

'I will need water,' she said and saw she had a flat pan among the items he had given her. She went swiftly to the pool for water, wondering how she had come to agree to venture so far from Ruatha. Ruined though it was, it had been hers and was familiar to her, from Tower to deep cellar. At the moment the idea had been proposed and insidiously prosecuted by the dragonman, she had felt capable of anything, having achieved, at last, Fax's death. Now it was all she could do to keep the water from slopping out of the pan that shook unaccountably in her hands.

She forced herself to deal only with the wound. It was a nasty gash, deep where the point had entered and torn downward in a gradually shallower slice. His skin felt smooth under her fingers as she cleansed the wound. In spite of herself, she noticed the masculine odor of him, compounded not unpleasantly of sweat, leather, and an unusual muskiness that must be from close association with dragons.

Although it must have hurt him when she cleansed away clotted blood, he gave no indication of discomfort, apparently oblivious to the operation. It annoyed her still more that she could not succumb to the temptation of treating him roughly in return for his disregard of her feelings.

She ground her teeth in frustration as she smeared on the healing salve generously. Making a small pad of bandage, she secured the dressing deftly in place with other strips of torn cloth. She stood back when she had finished her ministrations. He flexed his arm experimentally in the constricting bandage, and the motion set the muscles rippling along his side and back.

When he faced her, his eyes were dark and thoughtful.

'Gently done, my lady. My thanks.' His smile was ironic.

She backed away as he rose, but he only went to the chest to take out a clean, white shirt.

A muted rumble sounded, growing quickly louder.

Dragons roaring? Lessa wondered, trying to conquer the ridiculous fear that rose within her. Had the Hatching started? There was no watch-wher's lair to secrete herself in here.

As if he understood her confusion, the dragonman laughed good-humoredly and, his eyes on hers, drew aside the wall covering just as some noisy mechanism inside the shaft propelled a tray of food into sight.

Ashamed of her unbased fright and furious that he had witnessed it, Lessa sat rebelliously down on the fur-covered wall seat, heartily wishing him a variety of serious and painful injuries that she could dress with inconsiderate hands. She would not waste future opportunities.

He placed the tray on the low table in front of her, throwing down a heap of furs for his own seat. There were meat, bread, a pitcher of *klah*, a tempting yellow cheese, and even a few pieces of winter fruit. He made no move to eat, nor did she, though the thought of a piece of fruit that was ripe instead of rotten set her mouth to watering. He glanced up at her and frowned.

'Even in the Weyr, the lady breaks bread first,' he said and inclined his head politely to her.

Lessa flushed, unused to any courtesy and certainly unused to being first to eat. She broke off a chunk of bread. It was like nothing she remembered having tasted before. For one thing, it was fresh-baked. The flour had been finely sifted, without trace of sand or hull. She took the slice of cheese he proffered her, and it, too, had an uncommonly delicious sharpness. Much emboldened by this indication of her changed status, Lessa reached for the plumpest piece of fruit.

'Now,' the dragonman began, his hand touching hers to get her attention.

Guiltily she dropped the fruit, thinking she had erred. She stared at him, wondering at her fault. He retrieved the fruit and placed it back in her hand as he continued to speak. Wide-eyed, she nibbled, disarmed, and gave him her full attention.

'Listen to me. You must not show a moment's fear at whatever happens on the Hatching Ground. And you must not let her overeat.' A wry expression crossed his face. 'One of our main functions is to keep a dragon from excessive eating.'

73

Lessa lost interest in the taste of the fruit. She placed it carefully back in the bowl and tried to sort out what he had not said but what his tone of voice implied. She looked at the dragonman's face, seeing him as a person, not a symbol, for the first time.

His coldness was caution, she decided, not lack of emotion. His sternness must be assumed to offset his youth, for he couldn't be that much her senior in Turns. There was a blackness about him that was not malevolent; it was a brooding sort of patience. Heavy black hair waved back from a high forehead to brush his shirt collar. Heavy black brows were too often pulled together in a glower or arched haughtily as he looked down a high-bridged nose at his victim; his eyes (an amber, light enough to seem golden) were all too expressive of cynical emotions or cold hauteur. His lips were thin but well-shaped and in repose almost gentle. Why must he always pull his mouth to one side in disapproval or in one of those sardonic smiles? Handsome he must be considered, she supposed candidly, for there was a certain compelling air about him that was magnetic. And at this moment he was completely unaffected.

He meant what he was saying. He did not want her to be afraid. There was no reason for her, Lessa, *to* fear.

He very much wanted her to succeed. In keeping whom from overeating what? Herd animals? A newly hatched dragon certainly wasn't capable of eating a full beast. That seemed a simple enough task to Lessa. The watch-wher had obeyed her and no one else, at Ruath Hold. She had understood the great bronze dragon and had even managed to hush him up as she raced under his Tower perch for the birthing-woman. Main function? *Our* main function?

The dragonman was looking at her expectantly.

'Our main function?' she repeated, an unspoken request for more information inherent in her inflection.

'More of that later. First things first,' he said, impatiently waving off other questions.

'But what happens?' she insisted.

'As I was told, so I tell you. No more, no less. Remember those two points. Turn out fear and do not let her overeat.'

'But . . .'

'You, however, need to eat. Here.' He speared a piece of meat on his knife and thrust it at her, frowning until she managed to choke it down. He was about to force more on

74

her, but she grabbed up her half-eaten fruit and bit down into the firm sweet sphere instead. She had already eaten more at this one meal than she was accustomed to having all day at the Hold.

'We shall soon eat better at the Weyr,' he remarked, regarding the tray with a jaundiced eye.

Lessa was surprised, for in her opinion this was a feast.

'More than you're used to? Yes, I forgot you left Rutha with bare bones indeed.'

She stiffened.

'You did well at Ruatha. I mean no criticism,' he added, smiling at her reaction. 'But look at you,' and he gestured at her body, that curious expression crossing his face, half-amused, half contemplative, 'No, I should not have guessed you'd clean up pretty,' he remarked. 'Nor with such hair.' This time his expression was frankly admiring.

Involuntarily she put one hand to her head, the hair crackling over her fingers. But what reply she might have made him, indignant as she was, died a-borning. An unearthly keening filled the chamber.

The sounds set up a vibration that ran down the bones behind her ear to her spine. She clapped both hands to her ears. The noise rang through her skull, despite her defending hands. As abruptly as it started, it ceased.

Before she knew what he was about, the dragonman had grabbed her by the wrist and pulled her over to the chest.

'Take those off,' he ordered, indicating dress and tunic. While she stared at him stupidly, he held up a loose white robe, sleeveless and beltless, a matter of two lengths of fine cloth fastened at shoulder and side seams. 'Take it off, or do I assist you?' he asked with no patience at all.

The wild sound was repeated, and its unnerving tone made her fingers fly faster. She had no sooner loosened the garments she wore, letting them slide to her feet, than he thrown the other over her head. She managed to get her arms in the proper places before he grabbed her wrist again and was speeding with her out of the room, her hair wipping out behind her, alive with static.

As they reached the outer chamber, the bronze dragon was standing in the center of the cavern, his head turned to watch the sleeping room door. He seemed impatient to Lessa; his great eyes, which fascinated her so, sparkled iridescently. His manner breathed an inner excitement of great proportions, and from his throat a high-pitched croon issued, several octaves below the unnerving cry that had roused them all.

Rushed and impatient as they both were, the dragon and dragonman paused. Suddenly Lessa realized they were conferring about her. The great dragon's head was suddenly directly in front of her, his nose blotting out everything else. She felt the warm exhalation of his breath, slightly phosphorus-laden. She heard him inform the dragonman that he approved more and more of his woman from Ruatha.

With a yank that rocked her head on her neck, the dragonman pulled her along the passage. The dragon padded beside them at such speed that Lessa fully expected they would all catapult off the ledge. Somehow, at the crucial stride, she was perched on the bronze neck. the dragonman holding her firmly about the waist. In the same fluid movement they were gliding across the great bowl of the Weyr to the higher wall opposite. The air was full of wings and dragon tails, rent with a chorus of sounds, echoing and reechoing across the stony valley.

Mnementh set what Lessa was certain would be a collision course with other dragons, straight for a huge round blackness in the cliff-face, high up. Magically, the beasts filed in, the greater wingspread of Mnementh just clearing the sides of the entrance.

The passageway reverberated with the thunder of wings The air-compressed around her thickly. Then they broke. out into a gigantic cavern.

Why, the entire mountain must be hollow, thought Lessa, incredulous. Around the enormous cavern dragons perched in serried ranks, blues, greens, browns, and only two great bronze beasts like Mnementh, on ledges meant to accommodate hundreds. Lessa gripped the bronze neck scales before her, instinctively aware of the imminence of a great event.

Mnementh wheeled downward, disregarding the ledge of the bronze ones. Then all Lessa could see was what lay on the sandy floor of the great cavern: dragon eggs. A clutch of ten monstrous, mottled eggs, their shells moving spasmodically as the fledglings within tapped their way out. To one side, on a raised portion of the floor, was a golden egg, larger by half again the size of the mottled ones. Just beyond the golden egg lay the motionless ocher hulk of the old queen.

Just as she realized Mnementh was hovering over the floor in the vicinity of that egg, Lessa felt the dragonman's hands on her, lifting her from Mnementh's neck.

Apprehensively she grabbed at him. His hands tightened and inexorably swung her down. His eyes, fierce with amber fire locked with hers.

Remember, Lessa!'

Mnementh added an encouraging note, one great compound eye turned on her. Then he rose from the floor. Lessa half-raised one hand in entreaty, bereft of all support, even that of the sure inner compulsion that had sustained her in her struggle for revenge on Fax. She saw the bronze dragon settle on the first ledge, at some distance from the other two bronze beasts. The dragonman dismounted, and Mnementh curved his sinuous neck until his head was beside his rider. The man reached up and absently, it seemed to Lessa, caressed his mount.

Loud screams and wailings diverted Lessa, and she saw more dragons descend to hover just above the cavern floor, each rider depositing a young woman until there were twelve girls, including Lessa. She remained a little apart from them as they clung to one another. She regarded them curiously, contemptuous of their tears, although her heart was probably beating no less rapidly than theirs. It did not occur to her that tears were any help. The girls were not injured in any way that she could see, so why such weeping? Her contempt of their bleating made her aware of her own temerity, and she took a deep breath against the coldness within her. Let *them* be afraid. She was Lessa of Ruatha and did not need to be afraid.

Just then, the golden egg moved convulsively. Gasping as one, the girls edged away from it, back against the rocky wall. One, a lovely blonde, her heavy plait of golden hair swinging just above the ground, started to step off the raised floor and stopped, shrieking, backing fearfully toward the scant comfort of her peers.

Lessa wheeled to see what cause there might be for the look of horror on the girl's face. She stepped back involuntarily herself.

In the main section of the sandy arena, several of the handful of eggs had already cracked wide open. The fledglings, crowing weakly, were moving toward – and Lessa gulped – the young boys standing stolidly in a semi-circle. Some of them were no older than she had been when Fax's army had swooped down on Ruath Hold.

The shrieking of the women subsided to muffled gasps and sobs as one fledgling reached out with claw and beak to grab a boy.

Lessa forced herself to watch as the young dragon mauled the boy, throwing him roughly aside as if unsatisfied in some way. The boy did not move, and Lessa could see blood seeping onto the sand from dragon-inflicted wounds.

A second fledgling lurched against another boy and halted, flapping its damp wings impotently, raising its scrawny neck and croaking a parody of the encouraging croon Mnementh often gave. The boy uncertainly lifted a hand and began to scratch the eye ridge. Incredulous, Lessa watched as the fledgling, its crooning increasingly more mellow, ducked its head, pushing at the boy. The child's face broke into an unbelieving smile of elation.

Tearing her eyes from this astounding sight, Lessa saw that another fledgling was beginning the same performance with another boy. Two more dragons had emerged in the interim. One had knocked a boy down and was walking over him. oblivious of the fact that its claws were raking great gashes. The fledgling who followed its hatch-mate stopped by the wounded child, ducking its head to the boy's face, crooning anxiously. As Lessa watched, the boy managed to struggle to his feet, tears of pain streaming down his cheeks. She could hear him pleading with the dragon not to worry, that he was only scratched a little.

It was over very soon. The young dragons paired off with boys. Green riders dropped down to carry off the unacceptable. Blue riders settled to the floor with their beasts squealing, crooning, flapping wet wings as they staggered off, encouraged by their newly acquired Weyrmates.

Lessa turned resolutely back to the rocking golden egg, knowing what to expect and trying to divine what the successful boys had or had not done that caused the baby dragons to single them out.

A crack appeared in the golden shell and was greeted by the terrified screams of the girls. Some had fallen into little heaps of white fabric, others embraced tightly in their mutual fear. The crack widened and the wedge head broke through, followed quickly by the neck, gleaming gold. Lessa wondered with unexpected detachment how long it would take the beast to mature, considering its by no means small size at birth. For the head was larger than that of the male dragons, and they had been large enough to overwhelm sturdy boys of ten full Turns.

Lessa was aware of a loud hum within the Hall. Glancing up at the audience, she realized it emanaged from the watching bronze dragons, for this was the birth of their mate, their queen. The hum increased in volume as the shell shattered into fragments and the golden, glistening body of the new female emerged. It staggered out, dipping its sharp beak into the soft sand, momentarily trapped. Flapping its wet wings, it righted itself, ludicrous in its weak awkwardness. With sudden and unexpected swiftness, it dashed toward the terror-stricken girls. Before Lessa could blink, it shook the first girl with such violence that her head snapped audibly and she fell limply to the sand. Disregarding her, the dragon leaped toward the second girl but misjudged the distance and fell, grabbing out with one claw for support and raking the girl's body from shoulder to thigh. Screaming, the mortally injured girl distracted the dragon and released the others from their horrified trance. They scattered in panicky confusion, racing, running, tripping, stumbling, falling across the sand toward the exit the boys had used.

As the golden beast, crying piteously, lurched down from the raised arena toward the scattered women, Lessa moved. Why hadn't that silly clunk-headed girl stepped aside, Lessa thought, grabbing for the wedge-head, at birth not much larger than her own torso. The dragon was so clumsy and weak she was her own worst enemy.

Lessa swung the head around so that the many-faceted eyes were forced to look at her . . . and found herself lost in that rainbow regard.

A feeling of joy suffused Lessa; a feeling of warmth, tenerness, unalloyed affection, and instant respect and admiration flooded mind and heart and soul. Never again would Lessa lack an advocate, a defender, an intimate, aware instantly of the temper of her mind and heart, of her desires. How wonderful was Lessa, the thought intruded into Lessa's reflections, how pretty, how kind, how thoughtful, how brave and clever!

Mechanically Lessa reached out to scratch the exact spot on the soft eye ridge.

The dragon blinked at her wistfully, extremely sad that she had distressed Lessa. Lessa reassuringly patted the slightly damp, soft neck that curved trustingly toward her. The dragon reeled to one side and one wing fouled on the hind claw. It hurt. Carefully Lessa lifted the erring foot, freed the wing, folding it back across the dorsal ridge with a pat.

The dragon began to croon in her throat, her eyes following Lessa's every move. She nudged at Lessa, and Lessa obediently attended the other eye ridge.

The dragon let it be known she was hungry.

'We'll get you something to eat directly,' Lessa assured her briskly and blinked back at the dragon in amazement. How could she be so callous? It was a fact that this little menace had just seriously injured, if not killed, two women.

She couldn't believe her sympathies could swing so alarmingly toward the beast. Yet it was the most natural thing in the world for her to wish to protect this fledgling.

The dragon arched her neck to look Lessa squarely in the eyes. Ramoth repeated wistfully how excedingly hungry she was, so long confined in that shell without nourishment.

Lessa wondered how she knew the golden dragon's name, and Ramoth replied: Why shouldn't she know her own name since it was hers and no one else's? And then Lessa was lost in the wonder of those magnificently expressive eyes.

Oblivious to the descending bronze dragons, oblivious to the presence of their riders, Lessa stood caressing the head of the most wonderful creature of all Pern, fully prescient of troubles and glories, but most immediately aware that Lessa of Pern was Weyrwoman to Ramoth the Golden for now and forever.

Part II – Dragonflight

> Seas boil and mountains move,
> Sands heat, dragons prove
> Red Star passes.
> Stones pile and fires burn,
> Green withers, arm Pern.
> Guard all passes.
> Star Stone watch, scan sky.
> Ready the Weyrs, all riders fly;
> Red Star passes.

'IF A QUEEN isn't meant to fly, why does she have wings?' asked Lessa. She was genuinely trying to maintain a tone of sweet reason.

She had had to learn that, although it was her nature to seethe, she must seethe discreetly. Unlike the average Pernese, dragonriders were apt to perceive strong emotional auras.

R'gul's heavy eyebrows drew together in a startled frown. He snapped his jaws together with exasperation. Lessa knew his answer before he uttered it.

'Queen's don't fly,' he said flatly.

'Except to mate,' S'lel amended. He had been dozing, a state he achieved effortlessly and frequently, although he was younger than the vigorous R'gul.

They are going to quarrel again, Lessa thought with an inward groan. She could stand about half an hour of that, and then her stomach would begin to churn. Their notion of instructing the new Weyrwoman in 'Duties to Dragon, Weyr, and Pern' too often deteriorated into extended arguments over minor details in the lessons she had to memorize and recite word-perfect. Sometimes, as now, she entertained the fragile hope that she might wind them up so tightly in their own inconsistencies that they would inadvertently reveal a truth or two.

'A queen flies only to mate,' R'gul allowed the correction.

'Surely,' Lessa said with persistent patience, 'if she can fly to mate, she can fly at other times.'

'Queens don't fly.' R'gul's expression was stubborn.

'Jora never did fly a dragon at all,' S'lel mumbled,

blinking rapidly in his bemusement with the past. His expression was vaguely troubled. 'Jora never left these apartments.'

'She took Nemorth to the feeding grounds,' R'gul snapped irritably.

Bile rose in Lessa's throat. She swallowed. She would simply have to force them to leave. Would they realize that Ramoth woke all too conveniently at times? Maybe she'd better rouse R'gul's Hath. Inwardly she permitted herself a smug smile as her secret ability to hear and talk to any dragon in the Weyr, green, blue, brown, or bronze, momentarily soothed her.

'When Jora could get Nemorth to stir at all,' S'lel muttered, picking at his underlip worriedly.

R'gul glared at S'lel to silence him and, succeeding, tapped pointedly on Lessa' slate.

Stifling her sigh, she picked up the stylus. She had already written this ballad out nine times, letter-perfect. Ten was apparently R'gul's magic number. For she had written every single one of the traditional Teaching Ballads, the Disaster Sagas, and the Laws, letter-perfect, ten times each. True, she had not understood half of them, but she knew them by heart.

'*Seas boil, and mountains move,*' she wrote.

Possibly. If there is a major inner upheaval of the land. One of Fax's guards at Ruath Hold had once regaled the Watch with a tale from his great-grandsire's days. A whole coastal village in East Fort had slid into the sea. There had been monumental tides that year and, beyond Ista, a mountain had allegedly emerged at the same time, its top afire. It had subsided years later. That might be to what the line referred. Might be.

'*Sands heat . . .*' True, in summer it was said that Igen Plain could be unendurable. No shade, no trees, no caves, just bleak sand desert. Even dragonmen eschewed that region in deep summer. Come to think of it, the sands of the Hatching Ground were always warm underfoot. Did those sands ever get hot enough to burn? And what warmed them, anyway? The same unseen internal fires that heated the water in the bathing pools throughout Benden Weyr?

'*Dragons prove . . .*' Ambiguous for half a dozen interpretations, and R'gul won't even suggest one as official. Does it mean that dragons prove the Red Star passes? How?

Coming out with a special keen, similar to the one they utter when one of their own kind passes to die *between*? Or did the dragons prove themselves in some other way *as* the Red Star passes? Besides, of course, their traditional function of burning the Threads out of the skies? Oh, all the things these ballads don't say, and no one ever explains. Yet there must originally have been a reason.

'Stones pile and fires burn/ Green withers, arm Pern.'

More enigma. Is someone piling the stones on the fires? Do they mean firestone? Or do the stones pile themselves as in an avalanche? The balladeer might at least have suggested the season involved – or did he, with *'green withers'*? Yet vegetation purportedly attracted Threads, which was the reason, traditionally, that greenery was not permitted around human habitations. But stones couldn't stop a Thread from burrowing underground and multiplying. Only the phosphine emissions of a firestone-eating dragon stopped a Thread. And nowadays, Lessa smiled thinly, no one, not even dragonmen – with the notable exceptions of F'lar and his wingmen – bothered to drill with firestone, much less uproot grass near houses. Lately hilltops, scoured barren for centuries, were allowed to burgeon with green in the spring.

'Guard all passes.'

She dug the phrase out with the stylus, thinking to herself: So no dragonrider can leave the Weyr undetected.

R'gul's current course of inaction as Weyrleader was based on the idea that if no one, Lord or holder, saw a dragonrider, no one could be offended. Even traditional patrols were flown now over uninhabited areas, to allow the current agitation about the 'parasitcal' Weyr to die down. Fax, whose open dissension had sparked that movement, had not taken the cause to his grave. Larad, the young Lord of Telgar, was said to be the new leader.

R'gul as Weyrleader. That rankled Lessa deeply. He was so patently inadequate. But his Hath had taken Nemorth on her last flight. Traditionally (and that word was beginning to nauseate Lessa for the sins of omission ascribable to its name) the Weyrleader was the rider of the queen's mate. Oh, R'gul looked the part – a big, husky man, physically vigorous and domineering, his heavy face suggesting a sternly disciplined personality. Only, to Lessa's thinking, the discipline was misdirected.

Now F'lar . . . he had disciplined himself and his wing-riders in what Lessa considered the proper direction. For he, unlike the Weyrleader, not only sincerely believed in the Laws and Traditions he followed, he understood them. Time and again she had managed to make sense of a puzzling lesson from a phrase or two F'lar tossed in her direction. But, traditionally, only the Weyrleader instructed the Weyrwoman.

Why, in the name of the Egg, hadn't Mnementh, F'lar's bronze giant, flown Nemorth? Hath was a noble beast, in full prime, but he could not compare with Mnementh in size, wingspread, or strength. There would have been more than ten eggs in that last clutch of Nemorth's if Mnementh had flown her.

Jora, the late and unlamented Weyrwoman, had been obese, stupid, and incompetent. On this everyone agreed. Supposedly the dragon reflected its rider as much as the rider the dragon. Lessa's thoughts turned critical. Undoubtedly Mnementh had been as repelled by the dragon as a man like F'lar would be by the rider – unrider, Lessa corrected herself, sardonically glancing at the drowsing S'lel.

But if F'lar had gone to the trouble of that desperate duel with Fax to save Lessa's life back in Ruath Hold to bring her to the Weyr as a candidate at the Impression, why had he not taken over the Weyr when she proved successful, and ousted R'gul? What was he waiting for? He had been vehement and persuasive enough in making Lessa relinquish Ruatha and come to Benden Weyr. Why, now, did he adopt such an aloof pose of detachment as the Weyr tumbled further and further into disfavor?

'To save Pern,' F'lar's words had been. From what if not R'gul? F'lar had better start salvation procedures. Or was he biding his time until R'gul blundered fatally? R'gul won't blunder, Lessa thought sourly, because he won't *do* anything. Most particularly he wouldn't explain what she wanted to know.

'*Star Stone watch, scan sky.*' From her ledge, Lessa could see the gigantic rectangle of the Star Stone outlined against the sky. A watch-rider always stood by it. One day she'd get up there. It gave a magnificent view of the Benden Range and the high plateau that came right up to the foot of the Weyr. Last Turn there had been quite a ceremony at

Star Stone, when the rising sun seemed to settle briefly on Finger Rock, marking the winter solstice. However, that only explained the significance of the Finger Rock, not the Star Stone. Add one more unexplained mystery.

'*Ready the Weyrs*,' Lessa wrote morosely. Plural. Not Weyr but Weyr*s*. R'gul couldn't deny there were five empty Weyrs around Pern, deserted for who knows how many Turns. She'd had to learn the names, the order of their establishment, too. Fort was the first and mightiest, then Benden, High Reaches, Hot Igen, Ocean Ista and plainland Telgar. Yet no explanation as to why five had been abandoned. Nor why great Benden, capable of housing five hundred beasts in its myriad weyr-caverns, maintained a scant two hundred. Of course, R'gul had fobbed their new Weyrwoman off with the convenient excuse that Jora had been an incompetent and neurotic Weyrwoman, allowing her dragon queen to gorge unrestrained. (No one told Lessa why this was so undesirable, nor why, contradictorily, they were so pleased when Ramoth stuffered herself.) Of course, Ramoth was growing, growing so rapidly that the changes were apparent overnight.

Lessa smiled, a tender smile that not even the presence of R'gul and S'lel could embarrass. She glanced up from her writing to the passageway that led from the Council Room up to the great cavern that was Ramoth's weyr. She could sense that Ramoth was still deeply asleep. She longed for the dragon to wake, longed for the reassuring regard of those rainbow eyes, for the comforting companionship that made life in the Weyr endurable. Sometimes Lessa felt she was two people: gay and fulfilled when she was attending Ramoth, gray and frustrated when the dragon slept. Abruptly Lessa cut off this depressing reflection and bent diligently to her lesson. It did pass time.

'*Red Star passes*.'

That benighted, begreened Red Star, and Lessa jammed her stylus into the soft wax with the symbol for a completed score.

There had been that unforgettable dawn, over two full Turns ago, when she had been roused by an ominous presentiment from the damp straw of the cheeseroom at Ruatha. And the Red Star had gleamed at her.

Yet here she was. And that bright, active future F'lar had so glowingly painted had not materialized. Instead of using

85

her subtle power to manipulate events and people for Pern's good, she was forced into a round of inconclusive, uninstructive, tedious days, bored to active nausea by R'gul and S'lel, restricted to the Weyrwoman's apartments (however much of an improvement that was over her square foot of the cheeseroom floor) and the feeding grounds and the bathing lake. The only time she used her ability was to terminate these sessions with her so-called tutors. Grinding her teeth, Lessa thought that if it weren't for Ramoth, she would just leave. Oust Gemma's son and take Hold at Ruatha as she ought to have done once Fax was dead.

She caught her lip under her teeth, smiling in self-derision. If it weren't for Ramoth, she wouldn't have stayed here a moment past Impression anyway. But, from the second in which her eyes had met those of the young queen on the Hatching Ground, nothing but Ramoth mattered. Lessa was Ramoth's and Ramoth was hers, mind and heart, irrevocably attuned. Only death could dissolve that incredible bond.

Ocassionally a dragonless man remained living, such as Lytol, Ruatha's Warder, but he was half shadow and that indistinct self lived in torment. When his rider died, a dragon winked into *between*, that frozen nothingness through which a dragon somehow moved himself and his rider, instantly, from one geographical position on Pern to another. To enter *between* held danger to the uninitiated, Lessa knew, the danger of being trapped *between* for longer than it took a man to cough three times.

Yet Lessa's one dragonflight on Mnementh's neck had filled her with an insatiable compulsion to repeat the experience. Naïvely she had thought she would be taught, as the young riders and dragonets were. But she, supposedly the most important inhabitant of the Weyr next to Ramoth, remained earthbound while the youngsters winked in and out of *between* above the Weyr in endless practice. She chafed at the intolerable restriction.

Female or not, Ramoth must have the same innate ability to pass *between* as the males did. This theory was supported – unequivocally in Lessa's mind – by 'The Ballad of Moreta's Ride.' Were not ballads constructed to inform? To teach those who could not read and write? So that the young Pernese, whether he be dragonman, Lord, or holder, might learn his duty toward Pern and rehearse Pern's bright history? These two arrant idiots might deny the existence of that Ballad, but how had Lessa learned it if it did not exist? No doubt, Lessa thought acidly, for the same reason queens had wings!

When R'gul consented – and she would wear him down till he did – to allow her to take up her 'traditional' responsibility as Keeper of the Records, she would find that Ballad. One day it was going to have to be R'gul's much delayed 'right time.'

Right time! she fumed. *Right time! I have too much of the wrong time on my hands. When will this particular right time of theirs occur? When the moons turn green? What are they waiting for? And what might the superior F'lar be waiting for? The passing of the Red Star he alone believes in?* She paused, for even the most casual reference to that phenomenon evoked a cold, mocking sense of menace within her.

She shook her head to dispel it. Her movement was injudicious. It caught R'gul's attention. He looked up from the Records he was laboriously reading. As he drew her slate across the stone Council table, the clatter roused S'lel. He jerked his head up, uncertain of his surroundings.

'Humph? Eh? Yes?' he mumbled, blinking to focus sleep-blurred eyes.

It was too much. Lessa quickly made contact with S'lel's Tuenth, himself just rousing from a nap. Tuenth was quite agreeable.

'Tuenth is restless, must go,' S'lel promptly muttered. He hastened up the passageway, his relief at leaving no less than Lessa's at seeing him go. She was startled to hear him greet someone in the corridor and hoped the new arrival would provide an excuse to rid herself of R'gul.

It was Manora who entered. Lessa greeted the headwoman of the Lower Caverns with thinly disguised relief. R'gul, always nervous in Manora's presence, immediately departed.

Manora, a stately woman of middle years, exuded an aura of quiet strength and purpose, having come to a difficult compromise with life which she maintained with serene dignity. Her patience tacitly chided Lessa for her fretfulness and petty grievances. Of all the women she had met in the Weyr, (When she was permitted by the dragonmen to meet any) Lessa admired and respected Manora most. Some instinct in Lessa made her bitterly aware that she would never be on easy or intimate terms with any of the women in the Weyr. Her carefully formal relationship with Manora, however, was both satisfying and satisfactory.

Manora had brought the tally slates of the Supply Caves. It was her responsibility as headwoman to keep the Weyr-woman informed of the domestic management of the Weyr. (One duty R'gul insisted she perform.)

'Bitra, Benden, and Lemos have sent in their tithes, but that won't be enought to see us through the deep cold this Turn.'

'We had only those three last Turn and seemed to eat well enough.'

Manora smiled amiably, but it was obvious she did not consider the Weyr generously supplied.

'True, but that was because we had stores of preserved and dried foods from more bountiful Turns to sustain us. That reserve is now gone. Except for those barrels and barrels of fish from Tillek ...' Her voice trailed off expressively.

Lessa shuddered. Dried fish, salted fish, fish, had been served all too frequently of late.

'Our supplies of grain and flour in the Dry Caves are very low, for Benden, Bitra, and Lemos are not grain producers.'

'Our biggests needs are grains and meat?'

'We could use more fruits and root vegetables for variety,' Manora said thoughtfully. 'Particularly if we have the long cold season the weather-wise predict. Now we did go to Igen Plain for the spring and fall nuts, berries ...'

'We? to Igen Plain?' Lessa interrupted her, stunned.

'Yes,' Manora answered, surprised at Lessa's reaction. 'We always pick there. And we beat out the water grains from the low swamplands.'

'How do you get there?' asked Lessa sharply. There could be only one answer.

'Why, the old ones fly us. They don't mind, and it gives the beasts something to do that isn't tiring. You knew that, didn't you?'

'That the women in the Lower Caverns fly with dragon-riders?' Lessa pursed her lips angrily. 'No. I wasn't told.' Nor did it help Lessa's mood to see the pity and regret in Manora's eyes.

88

'As Weyrwoman,' she said gently, 'your obligations restrict you where . . .'

'If I should ask·to be flown to . . . Ruatha, for instance,' Lessa cut in, ruthlessly pursuing a subject she sensed Manora wanted to drop, 'would it be refused me?'

Manora regarded Lessa closely, her eyes dark with concern. Lessa waited. Deliberately she had put Manora into a position where the woman must either lie outright, which would be distasteful to a person of her integrity, or prevaricate, which could prove more instructive.

'An absence for any reason these days might be disastrous. Absolutely disastrous,' Manora said firmly and, unaccountably, flushed. 'Not with the queen growing so quickly. You *must* be here.' Her unexpectedly urgent entreaty, delivered with a mounting anxiety, impressed Lessa far more than all R'gul's pompous exhortations about constant attendance on Ramoth.

'You must be here,' Manora repeated, her fear naked.

'Queens do not fly,' Lessa reminded her acidly. She suspected Manora was about to echo S'lel's reply to that statement, but the older woman suddenly shifted to a safer subject.

'We cannot, even with half-rations,' Manora blurted out breathlessly, with a nervous shuffling of her slates, 'last the full Cold.'

'Hasn't there ever been such a shortage before . . . in all Tradition?' Lessa demanded with caustic sweetness.

Manora raised questioning eyes to Lessa, who flushed, ashamed of herself for venting her frustrations with the dragonmen on the headwoman. She was doubly contrite when Manora gravely accepted her mute apology. In that moment Lessa's determination to end R'gul's domination over herself and the Weyr crystallized.

'No,' Manora went on calmly, 'traditionally,' and she accorded Lessa a wry smile, 'the Weyr is supplied from the first fruits of the soil and hunt. True, in recent Turns we have been chronically shorted, but it didn't signify. We had no young dragons to feed. They do eat, as you know.' The glances of the two women locked in a timeless feminine amusement over the vagaries of the young under their care. Then Manora shrugged. 'The riders used to hunt their beasts in the High Reaches or on the Keroon plateau. Now, however . . .'

She made a helpless grimace to indicate that R'gul's restrictions deprived them of that victual relief.

'Time was,' she went on, her voice soft with nostalgia, 'we would pass the coldest part of the Turn in one of the southern Holds. Or, if we wished and could, return to our birthplaces. Families used to take pride in daughters with dragonfolk sons.' Her face settled into sad lines. 'The world turns and times change.'

'Yes,' Lessa heard herself say in a grating voice, 'the world does turn, and times ... times will change.'

Manora looked at Lessa, startled.

'Even R'gul will see we have no alternative,' Manora continued hastily, trying to stick to her problem.

'To what? Letting the mature dragons hunt?'

'Oh, no. He's so adamant about that. No. We'll have to barter at Fort or Telgar.'

Righteous indignation flared up in Lessa.

'The day the Weyr has to buy what should be given ...' and she halted in midsentence, stunned as much by such a necessity as by the ominous echo of other words. 'The day one of my Holds cannot support itself *or* the visit of its rightful overlord ...' Fax's words rang in her head. Did those words again foreshadow disaster? For whom? For what?

'I know, I know,' Manora was saying worriedly, unaware of Lessa's shock. 'It goes against the grain. But if R'gul will not permit judicious hunting, there is no other choice. He will not like the pinch of hunger in his belly.'

Lessa was struggling to control her inner terror. She took a deep breath.

'He'd probably then cut his throat to isolate his stomach,' she snapped, her acid comment restoring her wits. She ignored Manora's startled look of dismay and went on. 'It is traditional for you as headwoman of the Lower Cavern to bring such matters to the attention of the Weyrwoman, correct?'

Manora nodded, unsettled by Lessa's rapid switches of mood.

'I, then, as Weyrwoman, presumably bring this to the attention of the Weyrleader who, presumably,' – she made no attempt to moderate her derision – 'acts upon it?'

Manora nodded, her eyes perplexed.

'Well,' Lessa said in a pleasant, light voice, 'you have

dutifully discharged your traditional obligation. It is up to me now to discharge mine. Right?'

Manora regarded Lessa warily. Lessa smiled at her reassuringly.

'You may leave it in my hands, then.'

Manora rose slowly. Without taking her eyes from Lessa, she began to gather up her records.

'It is said that Fort and Telgar had unusually good harvests,' she suggested, her light tone not quite masking her anxiety. 'Keroon, too, in spite of that coastal flooding.'

'Is that so?' Lessa murmured politely.

'Yes,' Manora continued helpfully, 'and the herds at Keroon and Tillek had good increase.'

'I'm happy for them.'

Manora shot her a measuring look, not at all assured by Lessa's sudden affability. She finished gathering up her Records, then set them down again in a careful pile.

'Have you noticed how K'net and his wingriders chafe at R'gul's restrictions?' she asked, watching Lessa closely.

'K'net?'

'Yes. And old C'gan. Oh, his leg is still stiff, and Tagath may be more gray with age than blue, but he was of Lidith's hatching. Her last clutch had fine beasts in it,' she remarked. 'C'gan remembers other days. . . .'

'Before the world turned and times changed?'

Lessa's sweet voice did not mislead Manora now.

'It is not just as Weyrwoman that you are attractive to the dragonmen, Lessa of Pern,' Manora said sharply, her face stern. 'There are several of the brown riders, for instance . . .'

'F'nor?' Lessa asked pointedly.

Manora drew herself up proudly. 'He is a man grown, Weyrwoman, and we of the Lower Caverns have learned to disregard the ties of blood and affection. It is as a brown rider, not the son I bore, that I recommend him. Yes, I'd recommend F'nor, as I would also recommend T'sum and L'rad.'

'Do you suggest them because they are of F'lar's wing and bred in the true traditions? Less apt to be swayed by my blandishments . . .'

'I suggest them because they believe in the tradition that the Weyr must be supplied from the Holds.'

'All right.' Lessa grinned at Manora, seeing the woman

could not be baited about F'nor. 'I shall take your recommendations to heart, for I do not intend . . .' She broke off her sentence. 'Thank you for apprising me of our supply problems. We need fresh meat most of all?' she asked, rising to her feet.

'Grains, too, and some of the southern root vegetables would be very welcome,' Manora replied formally.

'Very well,' Lessa agreed.

Manora left, her expression thoughtful.

Lessa reflected for long moments on that interview, sitting like a slim statuette in the capacious stony chair, her legs curled up under her on the padding.

Foremost was the disturbing knowledge that Manora was deeply afraid of the mere prospect of Lessa absent from the Weyr, from Ramoth's side, for any reason, for any length of time. Her instinctive fear reaction was a far more effective argument than any of R'gul's sententious mouthings. However, Manora had given no hint of the reason for that necessity. Very well, Lessa would not try to fly one of the other dragons, with or without the rider, as she had been beginning to think she could.

As for this matter of short supplies, on that Lessa would act. Especially since R'gul would not. And, since R'gul could not protest what he did not know, she would contrive, with the help of K'net or F'nor or however many she needed, to keep the Weyr decently supplied. Eating regularly had become a pleasant habit she did not wish to curtail. She did not intend being greedy, but a little judicious pilfering of a bountiful harvest would go unnoticed by the Hold Lords.

K'net, though, was young; he might be rash and indiscreet. Perhaps F'nor would be the wiser choice. But was he as free to maneuver as K'net, who was, after all, a bronze rider? Maybe C'gan. The absence of a retired blue rider, time heavy on his hands, might not be noticed at all.

Lessa smiled to herself, but her smile faded quickly.

'The day the Weyr has to barter for what should be given . . .' She thrust back the premonitory shudder, concentrated on the ignominy of that situation. It certainly emphasized the measure of her self-delusion.

Why had she thought being at the Weyr would be so different from Ruath Hold? Had her early childhood training instilled such a questionless reverence for the Weyr that life must alter its pattern because Lessa of Ruatha had been Impressed by Ramoth? How could she have been such a romantic little fool?

Look around you, Lessa of Pern, look around the Weyr with unveiled eyes. Old and hallowed is the Weyr? Yes, but shabby and worn – and disregarded. Yes, you were elated to sit in the Weyrwoman's great chair at the Council Table, but the padding is thin and the fabric dusty. Humbled to think your hands rest where Moreta's and Torene's had rested? Well, the stone is ingrained with dirt and needs a good scrubbing. And your rump may rest where theirs did – but that's not where you have your brains.

The shabby Weyr reflected the deterioration of its purpose in the scheme of life on Pern. Those handsome dragonriders, too, so brave in their wher-hide accoutrements, proud on the necks of their great beasts – they did not submit kindly to close examination without a few disappointing revelations. They were only men, with manlike lusts and ambitions, full of very human faults and frustrations, unwilling to disrupt their easy existence for the harsh exigencies that would reestablish the Weyr. They had settled too deeply in their isolation from the rest of their race; they did not realize they were little thought of. There was no real leader at their head ...

F'lar! What was he waiting for? For Lessa to see through R'gul's ineffectiveness? No, Lessa decided slowly, for Ramoth to grow up. For Mnementh to fly her when he can ... traditionalist that F'lar is, and Lessa thought this excuse to be specious ... when the mating dragon's rider became, traditionally, the Weyrleader. That rider!

Well, F'lar might just find events not turning out as *he* planned.

My eyes were dazzled by Ramoth's, but I can see around the rainbow now, Lessa thought, steeling herself against the tenderness that always accompanied any thought of the golden beast. Yes, I can see into the black and gray shadows now, where my apprenticeship at Ruatha should stand me in good stead. True, there's more to control than one small Hold and far more perceptive minds to influence. Perceptive but dense in their own way. A greater hazard if I lose. But how can I? Lessa's smile broadened. She rubbed her palms against her thighs in anticipation of the challenge. They can do nothing with Ramoth without me, and they must have Ramoth. No one can coerce Lessa of Ruatha, and they're as stuck with me as they were with Jora. Only, I'm no Jora!

Elated, Lessa jumped from the chair. She felt alive again And more powerful in herself than she felt when Ramoth was awake.

Time, time, time. R'gul's time. Well, Lessa had done with marking his time. She'd been a silly fool. Now she'd be the Weyrwoman F'lar had beguiled her to think she could be.

F'lar . . . her thoughts returned to him constantly. She'd have to watch out for him. Particularly when she started 'arranging' things to suit herself. But she had an advantage he couldn't know – that she could speak to all the dragons, not just Ramoth. Even to his precious Mnementh.

Lessa threw back her head and laughed, the sound echoing hollowly in the large, empty Council Room. She laughed again, delighted with an exercise she had had rare occasion to use. Her mirth roused Ramoth. The exultation of her decision was replaced by that of knowing the golden dragon was waking.

Ramoth stirred again and stretched restlessly as hunger pierced slumber. Lessa ran up the passage on light feet, eager as a child for the first sight of the glorious eyes and the sweetness that characterized the dragon's personality.

Ramoth's huge golden wedge-shaped head swiveled around as the sleepy dragon instinctively sought her Weyrmate. Lessa quickly touched her blunt chin, and the searching head was still, comforted. The several protecting lids parted over the many-faceted eyes, and Ramoth and Lessa renewed the pledge of their mutual devotion.

Ramoth had had those dreams again, she told Lessa, shuddering slightly. It was so cold *there!* Lessa caressed the soft down above her eye-ridge, soothing the dragon. Linked firmly to Ramoth as she had become, she was acutely aware of the dismay those curious sequences produced.

Ramoth complained of an itch by the left dorsal ridge.

'The skin is flaking again,' Lessa told her, quickly spreading sweet oil on the affected area. 'You're growing so fast,' she added with mock and tender dismay.

Ramoth repeated that she itched abominably.

'Either eat less so you'll sleep less or stop outgrowing your hide overnight.'

She chanted dutifully as she rubbed in the oil, 'The

dragonet must be oiled daily as the rapid growth in early development can overstretch fragile skin tissues, rendering them tender and sensitive.'

They itch, Ramoth corrected petulantly, squirming.

'Hush. I'm only repeating what I was taught.'

Ramoth issued a dragon-sized snort that blew Lessa's robe tightly around her legs.

'Hush. Daily bathing is compulsory, and thorough oiling must accompany these ablutions. Patchy skin becomes imperfect hide in the adult dragon. Imperfect hide results in skin ruptures that may prove fatal to a flying beast.'

Don't stop rubbing, Ramoth entreated.

'Flying beast indeed!'

Ramoth informed Lessa she was so hungry. Couldn't she bathe and oil later?

'The moment that cavern you call a belly is full, you're so sleepy you can barely crawl. You've gotten too big to be carried.'

Ramoth's tart rejoinder was interrupted by a low chuckle. Lessa whirled, hastily controlling the annoyance she felt at seeing F'lar lounging indolently against the archway to the ledge-corridor.

He had obviously been flying a patrol, for he still wore the heavy wher-hide gear. The stiff tunic clung to the flat chest, outlined the long, muscular legs. His bony but handsome face was still reddened by the ultra-cold of *between.* His curiously amber eyes glinted with amusement and, Lessa added, conceit.

'She grows sleek,' he commented, approaching Ramoth's couch with a courteous bow to the young queen.

Lessa heard Mnementh give a greeting to Ramoth from his perch on the ledge.

Ramoth rolled her eyes coquettishly at the wingleader. His smile of almost possessive pride in her doubled Lessa's irritation.

'The escort arrives in good time to bid the queen good day.'

'Good day, Ramoth,' F'lar said obediently. He straightened, slapping his heavy gloves against his thigh.

'We interrupted your patrol pattern?' asked Lessa, sweetly apologetic.

'No matter. A routine flight,' F'lar replied, undaunted. He sauntered to one side of Lessa for an unimpeded view of he queen. 'She's bigger than most of the browns. There have been high seas and flooding at Telgar. And the tidal swamps at Igen are dragon-deep.' His grin flashed as if this minor disaster pleased him.

As F'lar said nothing without purpose, Lessa filed that statement away for future reference. However irritating F'lar might be, she preferred his company to that of the other bronze riders.

Ramoth interrupted Lessa's reflections with a tart reminder: If she had to bathe before eating, could they get on with it before she expired from hunger?

Lessa heard Mnementh's amused rumble without the cavern.

'Mnementh says we'd better humor her,' F'lar remarked indulgently.

Lessa suppressed the desire to retort that she could perfectly well hear what Mnementh said. One day it was going to be most salutary to witness F'lar's stunned reaction to the knowledge that she could hear and speak to every dragon in the Weyr.

'I neglect her shockingly,' Lessa said, as if contritely.

She saw F'lar about to answer her. He paused, his amber eyes narrowing briefly. Smiling affably, he gestured for her to lead the way.

An inner perversity prompted Lessa to bait F'lar whenever possible. One day she would pierce that pose and flay him to the quick. It would take doing. He was sharp-witted.

The three joined Mnementh on the ledge. He hovered protectively over Ramoth as she glided awkwardly down to the far end of the long oval Weyr Bowl. Mist, rising from the warmed water of the small lake, parted in the sweep of Ramoth's ungainly wings. Her growth had been so rapid that she had no time to coordinate muscle and bulk. As F'lar set Lessa on Mnementh's neck for the short drop, she looked anxiously after the gawky, blundering queen.

Queens don't fly because they can't, Lessa told herself with bitter candor, contrasting Ramoth's grotesque descent with Mnementh's effortless drift.

'Mnementh says to assure you she'll be more graceful when she gets her full growth,' F'lar's amused voice said in her ear.

'But the young males are growing just as fast, and they're

not a bit . . .' She broke off. She wouldn't admit anything to that F'lar.

'They don't grow as large, and they constantly practice . . .'

'Flying! . . .' Lessa leaped on the word, and then, catching a glimpse of the bronze rider's face, said no more. He was just as quick with a casual taunt.

Ramoth had immersed herself and was irritably waiting to be sanded. The left dorsal ridge itched abominably. Lessa dutifully attacked the affected area with a sandy hand.

No, her life at the Weyr was no different from that at Ruatha. She was still scrubbing. And there was more of Ramoth to scrub each day, she thought as she finally sent the golden beast into the deeper water to rinse. Ramoth wallowed, submerging to the tip of her nose. Her eyes, covered by the thin inner lid, glowed just below the surface – watery jewels. Ramoth languidly turned over, and the water lapped around Lessa's ankles.

All occupations were suspended when Ramoth was abroad. Lessa noticed the women clustered at the entrance to the Lower Caverns, their eyes wide with fascination. Dragons perched on their ledges or idly circled overhead. Even the weyrlings, boy and dragonet, wandered forth curiously from the fledgling barracks of the training fields.

A dragon trumpeted unexpectedly on the heights by the Star Stone. He and his rider spiraled down.

'Tithings, F'lar, a train in the pass,' the blue rider announced, grinning broadly until he became disappointed by the calm way his unexpected good news was received by the bronze rider.

'F'nor will see to it,' F'lar told him indifferently. The blue dragon obediently lifted his rider to the wingsecond's ledge.

'Who could it be?' Lessa asked F'lar. 'The loyal three are in.'

F'lar waited until he saw F'nor on brown Canth wheel up and over the protecting lip of the Weyr, followed by several green riders of the wing.

'We'll know soon enough,' he remarked. He turned his head thoughtfully eastward, an unpleasant smile touching the corner of his mouth briefly. Lessa, too, glanced eastward where, to the knowing eye, the faint spark of the Red Star could be seen, even though the sun was full up.

'The loyal ones will be protected,' F'lar muttered under his breath, 'when the Red Star passes.'

How and why they two were in accord in their unpopular belief in the significance of the Red Star Lessa did not know. She only knew that she, too, recognized it as Menace. It had actually been the foremost consideration in all F'lar's arguments that she leave Ruatha and come to the Weyr. Why *he* had not succumbed to the pernicious indifference that had emasculated the other dragonmen she did not know. She had never asked him – not out of spite, but because it was so obvious that his belief was beyond question. He *knew*. And she *knew*.

And occasionally that knowledge must stir in the dragons. At dawn, as one, they stirred restlessly in their sleep – if they slept – or lashed their tails and spread their wings in protest if they were awake. Manora, too, seemed to believe. F'nor must. And perhaps some of F'lar's surety had infected his wingriders. He certainly demanded implicit obedience to tradition in his riders and received it, to the point of open devotion.

Ramoth emerged from the lake and half-flapped, half-floundered her way to the feeding grounds. Mnementh arranged himself at the edge and permitted Lessa to seat herself on his foreleg. The ground away from the Bowl rim was cold underfoot.

Ramoth ate, complaining bitterly over the stringy bucks that made her meal and resenting it when Lessa restricted her to six.

'Others have to eat, too, you know.'

Ramoth informed Lessa that she was queen and had priority.

'You'll itch tomorrow.'

Mnementh said she could have his share. He had eaten well of a fat buck in Keroon two days ago. Lessa regarded Mnementh with considerable interest. Was that why all the dragons in F'lar's wing looked so smug? She must pay more attention as to who frequented the feeding grounds and how often.

Ramoth had settled into her weyr again and was already drowsing when F'lar brought the train-captain into the quarters.

'Weyrwoman,' F'lar said, 'this messenger is from Lytol with duty to you.'

The man, reluctantly tearing his eyes from the glowing golden queen, bowed to Lessa.

'Tilarek, Weyrwoman, from Lytol, Warder of Ruath Hold,' he said respectfully, but his eyes, as he looked at Lessa, were so admiring as to be just short of impudence. He withdrew a message from his belt and hesitated, torn between the knowledge that women did not read and his instructions to give it to the Weyrwoman. Just as he caught F'lar's amused reassurance, Lessa extended her hand imperiously.

'The queen sleeps,' F'lar remarked, indicating the passageway to the Council Room.

Adroit of F'lar, Lessa thought, to be sure the messenger had a long look at Ramoth. Tilarek would spread the word on his return journey, properly elaborated with each retelling, of the queen's unusual size and fine health. Let Tilarek also broadcast his opinion of the new Weyrwoman.

Lessa waited until she saw F'lar offer the courier wine before she opened the skin. As she deciphered Lytol's inscription, Lessa realized how glad she was to receive news of Ruatha. But why did Lytol's first words have to be:

The babe grows strong and is healthy . . .

She cared little for that infant's prosperity. Ah . . .

Ruatha is green-free, from hill crown to crafthold verge. The harvest has been very good, and the beasts multiply from the new studs. Herewith is the due and proper tithe of Ruath Hold. May it prosper the Weyr which protects us.

Lessa snorted under her breath. Ruatha knew its duty, true, but not even the other three tithing holds had sent proper greetings. Lytol's message continued ominously:

A word to the wise. With Fax's death, Telgar has come to the fore in the growing sedition. Meron, so-called Lord of Nabol, is strong and seeks, I feel, to be first: Telgar is too cautious for him. The dissension strengthens and is more widespread than when I last spoke with Bronze Rider F'lar. The Weyr must be doubly on its guard. If Ruatha may serve, send word.

Lessa scowled at the last sentence. It only emphasized

the fact that too few Holds served in any way.

'. . . laughed at we were, good F'lar,' Tilarek was saying, moistening his throat with a generous gulp of Weyr-made wine, 'for doing as men ought.

'Funny thing, that, for the nearer we got to Benden Range the less laughing we heard. Sometimes it's hard to make sense of some things, being as how you don't do 'em much. Like if I were not to keep my sword arm strong and used to the weight of a blade,' and he made vigorous slashes and thrusts with his right arm, 'I'd be put to it to defend myself come a long-drawn fight. Some folk, too, believe what the loudest talker says. And some folk because it frightens them not to. However,' he went on briskly, 'I'm soldier-bred and it goes hard to take the gibes of mere crafters and holders. But we'd orders to keep our swords sheathed, and we did. Just as well,' he said with a wry grimace, 'to talk soft. The Lords have kept full guard since . . . since the Search . . .'

Lessa wondered what he had been about to say, but he went on soberly.

'There are those that'll be sorry when the Threads fall again on all that green around their doors.'

F'lar refilled the man's cup, asking casually about the harvests seen on the road here.

'Fine, fat and heavy,' the courier assured him. 'They do say this Turn has been the best in memory of living man. Why, the vines in Crom had bunches this big!' He made a wide circle with his two huge hands, and his listeners made proper response. 'And I've never seen the Telgar grain so full and heavy. Never.'

'Pern prospers,' F'lar remarked dryly.

'Begging your pardon' – Tilarek picked up a wizened piece of fruit from the tray – 'I've scooped better than this dropped on the road behind a harvest wagon.' He ate the fruit in two bites, wiping his hands on the tunic. Then, realizing what he had said, he added in hasty apology, 'Ruatha Hold sent you its best. First fruits as man ought. No ground pickings from us. You may be sure.'

'It is reassuring to know we have Ruatha's loyalty as well as its full measure,' F'lar assured him. 'Roads were clear?'

'Aye, and there's a funny thing this time of year. Cold, then suddenly warm like the weather couldn't remember the season. No snow and little rain. But winds! Like you'd never believe. They do say as how the coasts have been hit hard with high water.' He rolled his eyes expressively and then, hunching his shoulders, confidentially added, 'They do say Ista's smoking mountain that does appear and then ... *phffst* ... disappears ... has appeared again.'

F'lar looked properly skeptical, although Lessa did not miss the gleam of excitement in his eyes. The man sounded like one of R'gul's ambiguous verses.

'You must stay a few days for a good rest,' F'lar invited Tilarek genially, guiding him out past sleeping Ramoth.

'Aye and grateful. Man gets to the Weyr maybe once or twice in his life,' Tilarek was saying absently, craning his neck to keep Ramoth in sight as F'lar led him out. 'Never knew queens grew so big.'

'Ramoth is already much larger and stronger than Nemorth,' F'lar assured him as he turned the messenger over to the weyrling waiting to escort him to quarters.

'Read this,' Lessa said, impatiently shoving the skin at the bronze rider as soon as they were again in the Council Room.

'I expected little else,' F'lar remarked, unconcerned, perching on the edge of the great stone table.

'And ... ?' Lessa demanded fiercely.

'Time will tell,' F'lar replied serenely, examining a fruit for spots.

'Tilarek implied that not all the holders echo their Lords' seditious sentiments,' Lessa commented, trying to reassure herself.

F'lar snorted. 'Tilarek says "as will please his listeners," ' he said in a passable imitation of the man's speech.

'You'd better know, too,' F'nor said from the doorway, 'he doesn't speak for all his men. There was a good deal of grumbling in the escort.' F'nor accorded Lessa a courteous if absentminded salute. 'It was felt that Ruatha has been too long poor to give such a share to the Weyr its first profitable Turn. And I'll say that Lytol was more generous than he ought to be. We'll eat well ... for a while.'

F'lar tossed the messageskin to the brown rider.

'As if we didn't know that,' F'nor grunted after he had quickly scanned the contents.

'If you know that, what will you do about it?' Lessa

spoke up. 'The Weyr is in such disrepute that the day is coming when it can't feed its own.'

She used the phrase deliberately, noticing with satisfaction that it stung the memories of both dragonmen. The look they turned on her was almost savage. Then F'lar chuckled so that F'nor relaxed with a sour laugh.

'Well?' she demanded.

'R'gul and S'lel will undoubtedly get hungry,' F'nor said, shrugging.

'And you two?'

F'lar shrugged, too, and, rising, bowed formally to Lessa. 'As Ramoth is deep asleep, Weyrwoman, your permission to withdraw.'

'Get out!' Lessa shouted at them.

They had turned, grinning at each other, when R'gul came storming into the chamber, S'lel, D'nol, T'bor, and K'net close on his heels.

'What is this I hear? That Ruatha alone of the High Reaches sends tithes?'

'True, all too true,' F'lar conceded calmly, tossing the messageskin at R'gul.

The Weyrleader scanned it, mumbling the words under his breath, frowning at its content. He passed it distastefully to S'lel, who held it for all to read.

'We fed the Weyr last year on the tithings of three Holds,' R'gul announced disdainfully.

'*Last year*,' Lessa put in, 'but only because there were reserves in the supply caves. Manora has just reported that those reserves are exhausted. . . .'

'Ruatha has been very generous,' F'lar put in quickly. 'It should make the difference.'

Lessa hesitated a moment, thinking she hadn't heard him right.

'Not that generous.' She rushed on, ignoring the remanding glare F'lar shot her way.

'The dragonets require more this year, anyway. So there's only one solution. The Weyr must barter with Telgar and Fort to survive the Cold.'

Her words touched off instant rebellion.

'Barter? Never!'

'The Weyr reduced to bartering? Raid!'

'R'gul, we'll raid first. Barter never!'

That had stung all the bronze riders to the quick. Even

S'lel reacted with indignation. K'net was all but dancing, his eyes sparkling with anticipation of action.

Only F'lar remained aloof, his arms folded across his chest, glaring at her coldly.

'Raid?' R'gul's voice rose authoritatively above the noise. 'There can be no raid!'

Out of conditioned reflex to his commanding tone, they quieted momentarily.

'No raids?' T'bor and D'nol demanded in chorus.

'Why not?' D'nol went on, the veins in his neck standing out.

He was not the one, groaned Lessa to herself, trying to spot S'lan, only to remember that he was out on the training field. Occasionally he and D'nol acted together against R'gul in Council, but D'nol was not strong enough to stand alone.

Lessa glanced hopefully toward F'lar. Why didn't he speak up now?

'I'm sick of stringy old flesh, of bad bread, of wood-tasting roots,' D'nol was shouting, thoroughly incensed. 'Pern prospered this Turn. Let some spill over into the Weyr as it ought!'

T'bor, standing belligerently beside him, growled agreement, his eyes fixing on first one, then another of the silent bronze riders. Lessa caught at the hope that T'bor might act as substitute for S'lan.

'One move from the Weyr at this moment,' R'gul interrupted, his arm raised warningly, 'and all the Lords will move – against us.' His arm dropped dramatically.

He stood, squarely facing the two rebels, feet slightly apart, head high, eyes flashing. He towered a head and a half above the stocky, short D'nol and the slender T'bor. The contrast was unfortunate: the tableau was of the stern patriarch reprimanding errant children.

'The roads are clear,' R'gul went on portentously, 'with neither rain nor snow to stay an advancing army The Lords have kept full guards under arms since Fax was killed.' R'gul's head turned just slightly in F'lar's direction. 'Surely you all remember the scant hospitality we got on Search?' Now R'gul pinned each bronze rider in turn with a significant stare. 'You know the temper of the Holds, you saw their strength.' He jerked his chin up. 'Are you fools to antagonize them?'

103

'A good firestoning . . .' D'nol blurted out angrily and stopped. His rash words shocked himself as much as anyone else in the room.

Even Lessa gasped at the idea of deliberately using firestone against man.

'Something has to be done . . .' D'nol blundered on desperately, turning first to F'lar, then, less hopefully, to T'bor.

If R'gul wins, it will be the end, Lessa thought, coldly furious, and reacted, turning her thoughts toward T'bor. At Ruatha it had been easiest to sway angry men. If she could just . . . A dragon trumpeted outside.

An excruciatingly sharp pain lanced from her instep up her leg. Stunned, she staggered backward, unexpectedly falling into F'lar. He caught her arm with fingers like iron bands.

'You dare control . . .' he whispered savagely in her ear and, with false solicitude, all but slammed her down into her chair. His hand grasped her arm with vise-fingered coercion.

Swallowing convulsively against the double assault, she sat rigidly. When she could take in what had happened, she realized the moment of crisis had passed.

'*Nothing* can be done at this time,' R'gul was saying forcefully.

'At this time . . .' The words ricocheted in Lessa's ringing ears.

'The Weyr has young dragons to train. Young men to bring up in the proper Traditions.'

Empty Traditions, Lessa thought numbly, her mind seething with bitterness. And they will empty the very Weyr itself.

She glared with impotent fury at F'lar. His hand tightened warningly on her arm until his fingers pressed tendon to bone and she gasped again with pain. Through the tears that sprang to her eyes, she saw defeat and shame written on K'net's young face. Hope flared up, renewed.

With an effort she forced herself to relax. Slowly, as if F'lar had really frightened her. Slowly enough for him to believe in her capitulation.

As soon as she could, she would get K'net aside. He was ripe for the idea she had just conceived. He was young, malleable, attracted to her anyway. He would serve her purpose admirably.

'Dragonman, avoid excess,' R'gul was intoning. 'Greed will cause the Weyr distress.'

Lessa stared at the man, honestly appalled that he could clothe the Weyr's moral defeat with hypocritical homily.

Honor those the dragons heed
In thought and favor, word and deed.
Worlds are lost or worlds are saved
From the dangers dragon-braved.

'WHAT'S THE matter? Noble F'lar going against tradition?' Lessa demanded of F'nor as the brown rider appeared with a courteous explanation of the wingleader's absence.

Lessa no longer bothered to leash her tongue in F'nor's presence. The brown rider knew it was not directed at himself, so he rarely took offense. Some of his half brother's reserve had rubbed off on him.

His expression today, however, was not tolerant; it was sternly disapproving.

'He's tracing K'net,' F'nor said bluntly, his dark eyes troubled. He pushed his heavy hair back from his forehead, another habit picked up from F'lar, which added fuel to Lessa's grievance with the absent weyrman.

'Oh, is he? He'd do well to imitate him instead,' she snapped.

F'nor's eyes flashed angrily.

Good, thought Lessa. I'm getting to him, too.

'What you do not realize, Weyrwoman, is that K'net takes your instructions too liberally. A judicious pilfering would raise no protest, but K'net is too young to be circumspect.'

'My instructions?' Lessa repeated innocently. Surely F'nor and F'lar hadn't a shred of evidence to go on. Not that she cared. 'He's just too fed up with the whole cowardly mess!'

F'nor clamped his teeth down tightly against an angry rebuttal. He shifted his stance, clamped his hands around the wide rider's belt until his knuckles whitened. He returned Lessa's gaze coldly.

In that pause Lessa regretted antagonizing F'nor. He had tried to be friendly, pleasant, and had often amused her with anecdotes as she became more and more embittered. As the world turned colder, rations had gotten slimmer at the Weyr in spite of the systematic additions of K'net. Despair drifted through the Weyr on the icy winds.

Since D'nol's abortive rebellion, all spirit had drained out of the dragonmen. Even the beasts reflected it. Diet alone would not account for the dullness of their hide and their deadened attunement. Apathy could – and did. Lessa wondered that R'gul did not rue the result of his spineless decision.

'Ramoth is awake,' she told F'nor calmly, 'so you do not need to dance attendance on *me*.'

F'nor said nothing, and his continued silence began to discomfit Lessa. She rose, rubbing her palms on her thighs as if she could erase her last hasty words. She paced back and forth, glancing from her sleeping chamber into Ramoth's, where the golden queen, now larger than than any of the bronze dragons, lay in deep slumber.

If only she would wake, Lessa thought. When she's awake, everything's all right. As right as it can be, that is. But she's like a rock.

'So . . .' she began, trying to keep her nervousness out of her voice. 'F'lar is at last doing something, even if it is cutting off our one source of supply.'

'Lytol sent in a message this morning,' F'nor said curtly. His anger had subsided, but not his disapproval.

Lessa turned to face him, expectantly.

'Telgar and Fort have conferred with Keroon,' F'nor went on heavily. 'They've decided the Weyr is behind their losses. Why,' and his anger flared hot again, 'if you picked K'net, didn't you keep a close check on him? He's too green. C'gan, T'sum, *I* would have . . .'

'You? You don't sneeze without F'lar's consent,' she retorted.

F'nor laughed outright at her.

'F'lar did give you more credit than you deserve,' he replied, contemptuous in his own turn. 'Haven't you realized why he must wait?'

'No,' Lessa shouted at him. 'I haven't! Is this something I must divine, by instinct, like the dragons? By the shell of the first Egg, F'nor, no one *explains* anything to me!

'But it is nice to know that he has a reason for waiting. I just hope it's valid. That it is not too late already. Because I think it is.'

It was too late when he stopped me from reinforcing

T'bor, she thought, but refrained from saying. Instead, she added, 'It was too late when R'gul was too cowardly to feel the shame of . . .'

F'nor swung on her, his face white with anger. 'It took more courage than you'll ever have to watch that moment slide by.'

'Why?'

F'nor took a half step forward, so menacingly that Lessa steeled herself for a blow. He mastered the impulse, shaking his head violently to control himself.

'It is not R'gul's fault,' he said finally, his face old and drawn, his eyes troubled and hurt. 'It has been hard, hard to watch and to know you *had* to wait.'

'*Why?*' Lessa all but shrieked.

F'nor would no longer be goaded. He continued in a quiet voice.

'*I* thought you ought to know, but it goes against F'lar's grain to apologize for one of his own.'

Lessa bit back the sarcastic remark that rose to her lips, lest she interrupt this long-awaited enlightenment.

'R'gul is Weyrleader only by default. He'd be well enough, I suppose, if there hadn't been such a long Interval. The Records warn of the dangers . . .'

'Records? Dangers? What do you mean by Interval?'

'An Interval occurs when the Red Star does not pass close enough to excite the Threads. The Records indicate it takes about two hundred Turns before the Red Star swings back again. F'lar figures nearly twice that time has elapsed since the last Threads fell.'

Lessa glanced apprehensively eastward. F'nor nodded solemnly.

'Yes, and it'd be rather easy to forget fear and caution in four hundred years. R'gul's a good fighter and a good wingleader, but he has to see and touch and smell danger before he admits it exists. Oh, he learned the Laws and all the Traditions, but he never understood them in his bones. Not the way F'lar does or the way I have come to,' he added defiantly, seeing the skeptical expression on Lessa's face. His eyes narrowed, and he pointed an accusing finger at her. 'Nor the way you do, only you don't know why.'

She backed away, not from him but from the menace she *knew* existed, even if she didn't know why she believed.

'The moment F'lar Impressed Mnementh, F'lon began

training him to take over. Then F'lon got himself killed in that ridiculous brawl.' An expression comprised of anger, regret, and irritation passed over F'nor's face. Belatedly Lessa realized the man was speaking of his father. 'F'lar was too young to take over, and before anyone could intervene, R'gul got Hath to fly Nemorth and *we* had to wait. But R'gul couldn't control Jora's grief over F'lon, and she deteriorated rapidly. And he misinterpreted F'lon's plan for carrying us over the last of the Interval to mean isolation. Consequently' – F'nor shrugged expressively – 'the Weyr lost prestige faster all the time.'

'Time, time, time,' Lessa railed. 'It's always the wrong time. When is *now* the time?'

'Listen to me,' F'nor's stern words interrupted her tirade as effectively as if he had grabbed and shaken her. She had not suspected F'nor of such forcefulness. She looked at him with increased respect.

'Ramoth is full-grown, ready for her first mating flight. When she flies, all the bronzes rise to catch her. The strongest does not always get the queen. Sometimes it is the one everyone in the Weyr wants to have win her.' He enunciated his words slowly and clearly. 'That was how R'gul got Hath to fly Nemorth. The older riders wanted R'gul. They couldn't stomach a nineteen-year-old over them as Weyrleader, son though he was to F'lon. So Hath got Nemorth. And they got R'gul. They got what they wanted. And look what they've got!' His scornful gesture took in the threadbare weyr.

'It is too late, it is too late,' Lessa moaned, understanding a great deal, too well, too late.

'It may be, thanks to your prodding K'net into uncontrolled raiding,' F'nor assured her cynically. 'You didn't need him, you know. Our wing was handling it quietly. But when so much kept coming in, we cut our operations down. It's a case of too much too soon, since the Hold Lords are getting imprudent enough to retaliate. Think, Lessa of Pern,' and F'nor leaned toward her, his smile bitter, 'what R'gul's reaction will be. You didn't stop to think of that, did you? Think, now, what he will do when the well-armed Lords of the Hold appear, to demand satisfaction?'

Lessa closed her eyes, appalled at the scene she could picture all too clearly. She caught at her chair arm, limply sat down, undone by the knowledge she had miscalculated. Overconfident because she had been able to bring haughty Fax to his death, she was about to bring the Weyr to its ruin through that same arrogance.

There was suddenly noise enough for half the Weyr to be storming up the passageway from the ledge. She could hear the dragons calling excitedly to each other, the first outburst she had heard from them in two months.

Startled, she jumped up. Had F'lar failed to intercept K'net? Had K'net, by some horrible chance, been caught by the Lords? Together she and F'nor rushed out into the queen's weyr.

It was not F'lar and K'net and an angry Lord – or several – in tow who entered. It was R'gul, his cautious face distorted, his eyes wide with excitement. From the outside ledge Lessa could hear Hath generating the same intense agitation. R'gul shot a quick glance at Ramoth, who slumbered on obliviously. His eyes as he approached Lessa were coldly calculating. D'nol came rushing into the weyr at a dead run, hastily buckling on his tunic. Close on his heels came S'lan, S'lel, T'bor. They all converged in a loose semicircle around Lessa.

R'gul stepped forward, arm outstretched as if to embrace her. Before Lessa could step back, for there was something in R'gul's expression that revolted her, F'nor moved adroitly to her side, and R'gul, angry, lowered his arm.

'Hath is blooding his kill?' the brown rider asked ominously.

'Binth and Orth, too,' T'bor blurted out, his eyes bright with the curious fever that seemed to be affecting all the bronze riders.

Ramoth stirred restlessly, and everyone paused to watch her intently.

'Blood their kill?' Lessa exclaimed, perplexed but knowing that this was strangely significant.

'Call in K'net and F'lar,' F'nor ordered with more authority than a brown rider should use in the presence of bronzes.

R'gul's laugh was unpleasant.

'No one knows where they went.'

D'nol started to protest, but R'gul cut him off with a savage gesture.

'You wouldn't dare, R'gul,' F'nor said with cold menace.

Well, Lessa would dare. Her frantic appeal to Mnementh and Piyanth produced a faint reply. Then there was absolute blankness where Mnementh had been.

'She will wake,' R'gul was saying, his eyes piercing Lessa's. 'She will wake and rise ill-tempered. You must allow her only to blood her kill. I warn you she will resist. If you do not restrain her, she will gorge and cannot fly.'

'She rises to mate,' F'nor snapped, his voice edged with cold and desperate fury.

'She rises to mate with whichever bronze can catch her,' R'gul continued, his voice exultant.

And he means for F'lar not to be here, Lessa realized.

'The longer the flight, the better the clutch. and she cannot fly well or high if she is stuffed with heavy meat. She must not gorge. She must be permitted only to blood her kill. Do you understand?'

'Yes, R'gul,' Lessa said, 'I understand. For once I do understand you, all too well. F'lar and K'net are not here.' Her voice grew shrill. 'But Ramoth will never be flown by Hath if I have to take her *between*.'

She saw naked fear and shock wipe R'gul's face clear of triumph, and she watched as he got himself under control. A malevolent sneer replaced surprise at her threat. Did he think her defiance was empty?

'Good afternoon,' said F'lar pleasantly from the entrance. K'net grinned broadly at his side. 'Mnementh informs me that the bronzes blood their kill. How kind of you to call us in for the spectacle.'

Relief temporarily swept her recent antagonism for F'lar out of Lessa's mind. The sight of him, calm, arrogant, mocking, buoyed her.

R'gul's eyes darted around the semicircle of bronze riders, trying to pick out who had called in these two. And Lessa knew R'gul hated as well as feared F'lar. She could sense, too, that F'lar had changed. There was nothing passive or indifferent or detached about him now. Instead, there was tense anticipation. F'lar was done with waiting!

Ramoth roused, suddenly and completely awake. Her mind was in such a state that Lessa candidly realized F'lar and K'net had arrived none too soon. So intense were Ramoth's hunger pangs that Lessa hastened to her head to soothe her. But Ramoth was in no mood for placation. With unexpected agility she rose, making for the ledge.

Lessa ran after her, followed by the dragonmen. Ramoth hissed in agitation at the bronzes who hovered near the ledge. They scattered quickly out of her way. Their riders made for the broad stairs that led from the queen's weyr to the Bowl.

In a daze Lessa felt F'nor place her on Canth's neck and urge his dragon quickly after the others to the feeding grounds. Lessa watched, amazed, as Ramoth glided effortlessly and gracefully in over the alarmed, stampeding herd. She struck quickly, seizing her kill by the neck and furling her wings suddenly, dropping down on it, too ravenous to carry it aloft.

'Control her!' F'nor gasped, depositing Lessa unceremoniously to the ground.

Ramoth screamed defiance of her Weyrwoman's order. She sloughed her head around, rustling her wings angrily, her eyes blazing opalescent pools of fire. She extended her neck skyward to its full reach, shrilling her insubordination. The harsh echoes reverberated against the walls of the Weyr. All around, the dragons, blue, green, brown, and bronze, extended their wings in mighty sweeps, their answering calls brass thunder in the air.

Now indeed must Lessa call on the strength of will she had developed through hungry, vengeful years. Ramoth's wedge-shaped head whipped back and forth; her eyes glowed with incandescent rebellion. This was no amiable, trusting dragon child. This was a violent demon.

Across the bloody field Lessa matched wills with the transformed Ramoth. With no hint of weakness, no vestige of fear or thought of defeat. Lessa forced Ramoth to obey. Screeching protest, the golden dragon dropped her head to her kill, her tongue lashing at the inert body, her great jaws opening. Her head wavered over the steaming entrails her claws had ripped out. With a final snarl of reproach, Ramoth fastened her teeth on the thick throat of the buck and sucked the carcass dry of blood.

'Hold her,' F'nor murmured. Lessa had forgotten him. Ramoth rose, screaming, and with incredible speed landed on a second squealing buck. She made a second attempt to eat from the soft belly of her kill. Again Lessa exerted her authority and won. Shrilling defiance, Ramoth reluctantly blooded again.

She did not resist Lessa's orders the third time. The dragon had begun to realize now that irrestible instinct was upon her. She had not known anything but fury until she got the taste of hot blood. Now she knew what she needed: to fly fast, far, and long, away from the Weyr, away from these puny, wingless ones, far in advance of those rutting bronzes.

Dragon instinct was limited to here-and-now, with no ability to control or anticipate. Mankind existed in partnership with them to supply wisdom and order, Lessa found herself chanting silently.

Without hesitation, Ramoth struck for the fourth time, hissing with greed as she sucked at the beast's throat.

A tense silence had fallen over the Weyr Bowl, broken only by the sound of Ramoth's feeding and the high keening of the wind.

Ramoth's skin began to glow. She seemed to enlarge, not with gorging but with luminescence. She raised her bloody head, her tongue forking out to lick her muzzle. She straightened, and simultaneously a hum arose from the bronzes ringing the feeding ground in silent anticipation.

With a sudden golden movement Ramoth arched her great back. She sprang into the sky, wings wide. With unbelievable speed she was airborne. After her, in the blink of an eye, seven bronze shapes followed, their mighty wings churning buffets of sand-laden air into the faces of the watching weyrfolk.

Her heart in her mouth at the prodigious flight, Lessa felt her soul lifting with Ramoth.

'Stay with her,' F'nor whispered urgently. 'Stay with her. She must not escape your control now.'

He stepped away from Lessa, back among the folk of the Weyr, who, as one, turned their eyes skyward to the disappearing shining motes of the dragons.

Lessa, her mind curiously suspended, retained only enough physical consciousness to realize that she was in fact earthbound.

All other sense and feeling were aloft with Ramoth. And she, Ramoth-Lessa, was alive with limitless power, her wings beating effortlessly to the thin heights, elation surging through her frame, elation and – desire.

She sensed rather than saw the great bronze males pursuing her. She was contemptuous of their ineffectual efforts. For she was wingfree and unconquerable.

She snaked her head under one wing and mocked their puny efforts with shrill taunts. High above them she soared. Suddenly, folding her wings, she plummeted down, delighting to see them veer off in wing-crowding haste to avoid collision.

She soared quickly above them again as they labored to make up their lost speed and altitude.

So Ramoth flirted leisurely with her lovers, splendid in her newfound freedom, daring the bronze ones to outfly her.

One dropped, spent. She crowed her superiority. Soon a second abandoned the chase as she played with them, diving and darting in intricate patterns. Sometimes she was oblivious of their existence, so lost was she in the thrill of flight.

When, at last a little bored, she condescended to glance at her followers, she was vaguely amused to see only three great beasts still pursuing. She recognized Mnementh, Orth, and Hath. All in their prime; worthy, perhaps, of her.

She glided down, tantalizing them, amused at their now labored flights. Hath she couldn't bear. Orth? Now Orth was a fine young beast. She dropped her wings to slide between him and Mnementh.

As she swung past Mnementh, he suddenly closed his wings and dropped beside her. Startled, she tried to hover and found her wings fouled with his, his neck winding tightly about hers.

Entwined, they fell. Mnementh, calling on hidden reserves of strength, spread his wings to check their downward fall. Outmanoeuvred and startled by the terrific speed of their descent, Ramoth, too, extended her great wings. And then ...

Lessa reeled, her hands wildly grabbing out for any support. He seemed to be exploding back into her body, every nerve throbbing.

'Don't faint, you fool. Stay with her.' F'lar's voice grated in her ear. His arms roughly sustained her.

She tried to focus her eyes. She caught a startled glimpse of the walls of her own weyr. She clutched at F'lar, touching bare skin, shaking her head, confused.

'Bring her back.'

'How?' she cried, panting, unable to comprehend what could possibly entice Ramoth from such glory.

The pain of stinging blows on her face made her angrily

114

aware of F'lar's disturbing proximity. His eyes were wild, his mouth distorted.

'Think with her. She cannot go *between*. Stay with her.'

Trembling at the thought of losing Ramoth *between*, Lessa sought the dragon, still locked wing to wing with Mnementh.

The mating passion of the two dragons at that moment spiraled wide to include Lessa. A tidal wave rising relentlessy from the sea of her soul flooded Lessa. With a longing cry she clung to F'lar. She felt his body rock-firm against hers, his hard arms lifting her up, his mouth fastening mercilessly on hers as she drowned deep in another unexpected flood of desire.

'Now! *We* bring them safely home,' he murmured.

Dragonman, dragonman,
Between thee and thine,
Share me that glimpse of love
Greater than mine.

F'LAR CAME suddenly awake. He listened attentively,
heard and was reassured by Mnementh's gratified rumble.
The bronze was perched on the ledge outside the queen's
weyr. All was peacefully in order in the Bowl below.

Peaceful but different, F'lar, through Mnementh's eyes
and senses, perceived this instantly. There was an overnight
change in the Weyr. F'lar permitted himself a satisfied grin
at the previous day's tumultuous events. Something might
have gone wrong.

Something nearly did, Mnementh reminded him.

Who had called K'net and himself back? F'lar mused
again. Mnementh only repeated that he had been called
back. Why wouldn't he identify the informer?

A nagging worry intruded on F'lar's waking ruminations.
'Did F'nor remember to . . .' he began aloud.

F'nor never forgets your orders, Mnementh reassured him
testily. *Canth told me that the sighting at dawn today puts the
Red Star at the top of the Eye Rock. The sun is still off, too.*

F'lar ran impatient fingers through his hair. 'At the top
of the Eye Rock. Closer, and closer the Red Star came,'
just as the Old Records predicted. And that dawn when the
Star gleamed scarlet at the watcher *through* the Eye Rock
heralded a dangerous passing and . . . the Threads.

There was certainly no other explanation for that
careful arrangement of gigantic stones and special rocks on
Benden Peak. Nor for its counterpart on the eastern walls of
each of the five abandoned Weyrs.

First, the Finger Rock on which the rising sun balanced
briefly at dawn at the winter solstice. Then, two dragon
lengths behind it, the rectangular, enormous Star Stone,
chest-high to a tall man, its polished surface incised by two
arrows, one pointing due east toward the Finger Rock, the
other slightly north of due east, aimed directly at the Eye

Rock, so ingeniously and immovably set into the Star Stone.

One dawn, in the not too distant future, he would look through the Eye Rock and meet the baleful blink of the Red Star. And then . . .

Sounds of vigorous splashing interrupted F'lar's reflections. He grinned again as he realized it was the girl bathing. She certainly cleaned up pretty, and undressed . . . He stretched with leisurely recollection, reviewing what his reception from that quarter might be. She ought to have no complaints at all. What a flight! He chuckled softly.

Mnementh commented from the safety of his ledge that F'lar had better watch his step with Lessa.

Lessa, is it? thought F'lar back to his dragon.

Mnementh enigmatically repeated his caution. F'lar chuckled his self-confidence.

Suddenly Mnementh was alert to an alarm.

Watchers were sending out a rider to identify the unusually persistent dust clouds on the plateau below Benden Lake, Mnementh informed his wingleader crisply.

F'lar rose hastily, gathered up his scattered clothes, and dressed. He was buckling the wide rider's belt when the curtain to the bathing room was flipped aside. Lessa confronted him, fully clothed.

He was always surprised to see how slight she was, an incongruous physical vessel for such strength of mind. Her newly washed hair framed her narrow face with a dark cloud. There was no hint in her composed eyes of the dragon-roused passion they had experienced together yesterday. There was no friendliness about her at all. No warmth. Was this what Mnementh meant? What was the matter with the girl?

Mnementh gave an additional alarming report, and F'lar set his jaw. He would have to postpone the understanding they must reach intellectually until after this emergency. To himself he damned R'gul's green handling of her. The man had all but ruined the Weyrwoman, as he had all but destroyed the Weyr.

Well, F'lar, bronze Mnementh's rider, was now Weyrleader, and changes were long overdue.

Long overdue, Mnementh confirmed dryly. *The Lords of the Holds gather in force on the lake plateau.*

'There's trouble.' F'lar announced to Lessa by way of greeting. His announcement did not appear to alarm her.

'The Lords of the Hold come to protest?' she asked coolly.

He admired her composure even as he decried her part in this development.

'You'd have done better to let me handle the raiding. K'net's still boy enough to be carried away with the joy of it all.'

Her slight smile was secretive. F'lar wondered fleetingly if that wasn't what she had intended in the first place. Had Ramoth not risen yesterday, it would be a different story altogether today. Had she thought of that?

Mnementh forewarned him that R'gul was at the ledge. R'gul was all chest and indignant eye, the dragon commented, which meant he was feeling his authority.

'He has none,' F'lar snapped out loud, thoroughly awake and pleased with events, despite their precipitation.

'R'gul?'

She was quick-witted all right, F'lar admitted.

'Come, girl.' He gestured her toward the queen's weyr. The scene he was about the play with R'gul ought to redeem that shameful day in the Council Room two months back. He knew it had rankled in her as in him.

They had no sooner entered the queen's weyr than R'gul, followed by an excited K'net, stormed in from the opposite side.

'The watch informs me,' R'gul began, 'that there is a large body of armed men, with banners of many Holds, approaching the Tunnel. K'net here' – R'gul was furious with the youngster – 'confesses he has been raiding systematically – against all reason and most certainly against my orders. Of course, we'll deal with him later,' he informed the errant rider ominously, 'that is, if there is a Weyr left after the Lords are through with us.'

He turned back to F'lar, his frown deepening as he realized F'lar was grinning at him.

'Don't stand there,' R'gul growled. 'There's nothing to grin about. We've got to think how to placate them.'

'No, R'gul,' F'lar contradicted the older man, still grinning, 'the days of placating the Lords are over.'

'What? Are you out of your mind?'

'No. But *you* are out of order,' F'lar said, his grin gone, his face stern.

R'gul's eyes widened as he stared at F'lar as if he had never seen him before.

'You've forgotten a very important fact,' F'lar went on ruthlessly. 'Policy changes when the leader of the Weyr is replaced. *I*, F'lar, Mnementh's rider, am Weyrleader now.'

On that ringing phrase, S'lel, D'nol, T'bor, and S'lan came striding into the room. They stopped, shock-still, staring at the motionless tableau.

F'lar waited, giving them a chance to absorb the fact that the dissension in the room meant that authority had indeed passed to him.

'Mnementh,' he said aloud, 'call in all wingseconds and brown riders. We've some arrangements to make before our ... guests arrive. As the queen is asleep, dragonmen, into the Council Room, please. After you, Weyrwoman.'

He stepped aside to permit Lessa to pass, noticing the slight flush on her cheeks. She was not completely in command of her emotions, after all.

No sooner had they taken places at the Council Table than the brown riders began to stream in. F'lar took careful note of the subtle difference in their attitudes. They walked taller, he decided. And – yes, the air of defeat and frustration was replaced by tense excitement. All else being equal, today's events ought to revive the pride and purpose of the Weyr.

F'nor and T'sum, his own seconds, strode in. There was no doubt of their high, proud good humor. Their eyes flashed around daring anyone to defy their promotion as T'sum stood by the archway and F'nor marched smartly around to his position behind F'lar's chair. F'nor paused to make a deeply respectful bow to the girl. F'lar saw her flush and drop her eyes.

'Who's at our gate, F'nor?' the new Weyrleader asked affably.

'The Lords of Telgar, Nabol, Fort, and Keroon, to name the principal banners,' F'nor answered in a similar vein.

R'gul rose from his chair; the half-formed protest died on his lips as he caught the expression in the faces of the bronze riders. S'lel, beside him, started to mumble, picking at his lower lip.

'Estimated strength?'

'In excess of a thousand. In good order and well-armed,' F'nor reported indifferently.

F'lar shot his second a remonstrating look. Confidence was one thing, indifference preferable to defeat, but there was no wisdom in denying the situation was very tight.

'Against the Weyr?' S'lel gasped.

'Are we dragonmen or cowards?' D'nol snapped, jumping up, his fist pounding the table. 'This is the final insult.'

'Indeed it is,' F'lar concurred heartily.

'It has to be put down. We'll swallow no more,' D'nol continued vehemently, encouraged by F'lar's attitude. 'A few flaming . . .'

'That's enough,' F'lar said in a hard voice. 'We are dragonmen! Remember that, and remember also – never forget it – this fellowship is sworn to *protect*.' He enunciated that word distinctly, pinning each man with a fierce stare. 'Is that point clear?' He glared questioningly at D'nol. There were to be no private heroics today.

'We do not need firestone,' he continued, certain that D'nol had taken his meaning, 'to disperse these foolish Lords.' He leaned back and went on more calmly, 'I noticed on Search, as I'm sure you all did, that the common holder has not lost one jot of his . . . let us say . . . respect for dragonkind.'

T'bor grinned, and someone chuckled reminiscently.

'Oh, they follow their Lords quickly enough, incited with indignation and lots of new wine. But it's quite another matter to face a dragon, hot, tired, and cold sober. Not to mention on foot without a wall or Hold in sight.' He could sense their concurrence. 'The mounted men, too, will be too much occupied with their beasts to do any serious fighting,' he added with a chuckle, echoed by most of the men in the room.

'However consoling these reflections are, there are more powerful factors in our favor. I doubt the good Lords of the Hold have bothered to review them. I suspect' – he glanced around sardonically at his riders – 'they have probably forgotten them . . . as they have conveniently forgotten so much dragonlore . . . and tradition.

'It is now time to reeducate them.' His voice was steel. An affirming mutter answered him. Good, he had them.

'For instance, they are here at our gates. They've traveled long and hard to reach this remote Weyr. Undoubtedly some units have been marching for weeks. F'nor,' he said in a calculated aside, 'remind me to discuss patrol schedules later today. Ask yourselves this, dragonmen, if the Lords of the Holds are here, who is holding the Holds for the Lords? Who keeps guard on the Inner Hold, over all the Lords hold dear?'

He heard Lessa chuckling wickedly. She was quicker than any of the bronze riders. He had chosen well that day in Ruatha, even if it had meant killing while on Search.

'Our Weyrwoman perceives my plan. T'sum, implement it.' He snapped that order out crisply. T'sum, grinning broadly, departed.

'I don't understand,' S'lel complained, blinking in confusion.

'Oh, let me explain,' Lessa put in quickly, her words couched in the sweet, reasonable tone F'lar was learning to identify as Lessa at her worst. He couldn't blame her for wanting to get some of her own back from S'lel, but this taste of hers for vengeance could become pernicious.

'Someone ought to explain something,' S'lel said querulously. 'I don't like what's going on. Holders at the Tunnel Road. Dragons permitted firestone. I don't understand.'

'It's so simple,' Lessa assured him sweetly, not waiting for F'lar's permission. 'I'm embarrassed to have to explain.'

'Weyrwoman!' F'lar called her sharply to order.

She didn't look at him, but she did stop needling S'lel.

'The Lords have left their Holds unprotected,' she said. 'They appear not to have considered that dragons can move *between* in seconds. T'sum, if I am not mistaken, has gone to assemble sufficient hostages from the unguarded Holds to insure that the Lords respect the sanctity of the Weyr.' F'lar nodded confirmation. Lessa's eyes flashed angrily as she continued. 'It is not the fault of the Lords that they have lost respect for the Weyr. The Weyr has . . .'

'The Weyr,' F'lar cut in sharply. Yes, he would have to watch this slim girl very carefully and very respectfully. ' . . . the Weyr is about to insist on its traditional rights and prerogatives. Before I outline exactly how, Weyrwoman, would you greet our newest guests? A few words might be in order to reinforce the object lesson we will impress on all Pernese today.'

The girl's eyes sparkled with anticipation. She grinned with such intense pleasure that F'lar wondered if he was wise to let her instruct the defenseless hostages.

'I rely on your discretion,' he said emphatically, 'and intelligence to handle the assignment adroitly.' He caught her glance, held it until she briefly inclined her head in acknowledgement of his admonition. As she left, he sent a word ahead to Mnementh to keep an eye on her.

Mnementh informed him that that would be wasted effort. Hadn't Lessa shown more wit than anyone else in the Weyr? She was circumspect by instinct.

Circumspect enough to have precipitated today's invasion, F'lar reminded his dragon.

'But ... the ... Lords,' R'gul was sputtering.

'Oh, freeze up,' K'net suggested. 'If we hadn't listened to you for so long, we wouldn't be in this position at all. Shove *between* if you don't like it, but F'lar is Weyrleader now. And I say about time!'

'K'net! R'gul!' F'lar called them to order, shouting over the cheers K'net's impudent words produced. 'These are my orders,' he went on when he had their complete attention. 'I expect them to be followed exactly.' He glanced at each man to be sure there was no further question of his authority. Then he outlined his intentions concisely and quickly, watching with satisfaction as uncertainty was replaced with admiring respect.

Assured that every bronze and brown rider understood the plan perfectly, he asked Mnementh for the latest report.

The advancing army was streaming out across the lake plateau, the foremost units on the Tunnel Road, the one ground entrance to the Weyr. Mnementh added that the Holders' women were profiting from their stay in the Weyr.

'In what way?' F'lar demanded immediately.

Mnementh rumbled with the dragon equivalent of laughter. Two of the young greens were feeding, that was all. But for some reason such a normal occupation appeared to upset the women.

The woman was diabolically clever, F'lar thought privately, careful not to let Mnementh sense his concern. That bronze clown was as besotted with the rider as he was with the queen. What kind of fascination did the Weyr-woman have for a bronze dragon?

'Our guests are at the lake plateau,' he told the dragon-men. 'You have your positions. Order your wings out.' Without a backward look, he marched out, conquering an intense urge to hurry to the ledge. He absolutely did not want those hostages scared witless.

Down the valley by the lake, the women were lightly

attended by four of the smallest greens – big enough for the uninitiated – and the women were probably too scared at having been seized to notice that all four riders were barely out of adolescence. He spotted the slight figure of the Weyrwoman, seated to one side of the main group. A sound of muffled weeping drifted up to his ears. He looked beyond them, to the feeding grounds, and saw a green dragon single out a buck and run it down. Another green was perched on a ledge above, eating with typical messy, dragon greed. F'lar shrugged and mounted Mnementh, clearing the ledge for the hovering dragons who waited to pick up their own riders.

As Mnementh circled above the confusion of wings and gleaming bodies, F'lar nodded approvingly. A high, fast mating flight coupled with the promise of action improved everyone's morale.

Mnementh snorted.

F'lar paid him no attention, watching R'gul as he assembled his wing. The man had taken a psychological defeat. He would bear watching and careful handling. Once the Threads started to fall and R'gul's faith was restored, he'd come around.

Mnementh asked him if they should pick up the Weyr-woman.

'She doesn't belong in this,' F'lar said sharply, wondering why under the double moons the bronze had made such a suggestion. Mnementh replied that he thought Lessa would like to be there.

D'nol's wing and T'bor's rose in good formation. Those two were making good leaders. K'net took up a double wing to the Bow lip and winked out neatly, bound to re-appear behind the approaching army. C'gan, the old blue rider, had the youngsters organized.

F'lar told Mnementh to have Canth tell F'nor to proceed. With a final look to be sure the stones to the Lower Caverns were in place, F'lar gave Mnementh the signal to go *between.*

From the Weyr and from the Bowl,
Bronze and brown and blue and green,
Rise the dragonmen of Pern,
Aloft, on wing; seen, then unseen.

LARAD, LORD of Telgar, eyed the monolithic heights of
Benden Weyr. The striated stone looked like frozen water-
falls at sunset. And about as hospitable. A long moribund
awe squirmed at the back of his mind for the blasphemy
he and the army he led were about to commit. He stifled
that thought firmly.

The Weyr had outlived its usefulness. That was obvious.
There was no longer any need for the Holders to give up
the profits of their sweat and labor to the lazy weyrfolk.
The Holders had been patient. They had supported the
Weyr in good part out of gratitude for past services. But the
dragonmen had overstepped the borders of grateful
generosity.

First, this archaic Search foolishness. So a queen-egg
was laid. Why did the dragonmen need to steal away the
prettiest women among the Holders when they had women
of their own in the Weyr proper? No need to appropriate
Larad's sister, Kylara, eagerly awaiting a far different
alliance with Brant of Igen one evening and gone on
that ridiculous Search the next. Never heard from since,
either.

And killing Fax! Albeit the man had been dangerously
ambitious, he was of the Blood. And the Weyr had not been
asked to meddle in the affairs of the High Reaches.

But this steady pilfering. That was beyond enough. Oh,
a holder might excuse a few bucks now and again. But when
a dragon appeared out of nowhere (a talent that disturbed
Larad deeply) and snatched the best stud bucks from a herd
carefully protected and nurtured, that tore it!

The Weyr must be made to understand its subordinate
position in Pern. It would have to make other provision
to victual its people, for no further tithes would come from
anyone. Benden, Bitra, and Lemos would come around

soon. They ought to be pleased to end this superstitious domination by the Weyr.

Nevertheless, the closer they came to the gigantic mountain, the more doubts Larad experienced as to just how in the world the Lords would penetrate that massif. He signaled Meron, so-called Lord of Nabol (he didn't really trust this sharp-faced ex-Warder with no Blood at all) to draw his riding beast closer.

Meron whipped his mount abreast of Larad.

'There is no other way into the Weyr proper but the Tunnel?'

Meron shook his head. 'Even the locals are agreed.'

This did not dismay Meron, but he caught Larad's doubtful expression.

'I have sent a party on ahead, to the southern lip of the Peak,' and he indicated the area. 'There might be a low, scalable cliff, there where the brow dips.'

'You sent a party without consulting us? I was named leader . . .?'

'True,' Meron agreed, with an amiable show of teeth. 'A mere notion of mine.'

'A distinct possibility, I agree, but you'd have done better . . .' Larad glanced up at the Peak.

'They have seen us, have no doubt of that, Larad,' Meron assured him, contemptuously regarding the silent Weyr. 'That will be sufficient. Deliver our ultimatum and they will surrender before such a force as ours. They've proved themselves cowards over and over. I gave insult twice to the bronze rider they call F'lar, and he ignored it. What *man* would?'

A sudden rustling roar and a blast of the coldest air in the world interrupted their conference. As he mastered his plunging beast, Larad caught a confused panorama of dragons, all colors, sizes, and everywhere. The air was filled with the panic-stricken shrieks of plunging beasts, the cries of startled, terrified men.

Larad managed, with great effort, to drag his beast around to face the dragonmen.

By the Void that spawned us, he thought, struggling to control his own fear, I'd forgotten dragons are so big.

Foremost in that frightening array was a triangular formation of four great bronze beasts, their wings overlapping in a tremendous criss-cross pattern as they hovered just above the ground. A dragon's length above and beyond them, there ranged a second line, longer, wider, of brown beasts. Curving beyond them and higher up were blue and green and more brown beasts, all with their huge wings fanning cold air in great drafts on the terrified mob that had been an army moments before.

Where did that piercing cold come from, Larad wondered. He yanked down on his beast's mouth as it began to plunge again.

The dragonmen just sat there on their beasts' necks, watching, waiting.

'Get them off their beasts and the things away so we can talk,' Meron shouted to Larad as his mount cavorted and screamed in terror.

Larad signaled foot soldiers forward, but it took four men per mount to quiet them enough so the Lords could dismount.

Miscalculation number two, Larad thought with grim humor. We forgot the effect of dragons on the beasts of Pern. Man included. Settling his sword, pulling his gloves up onto his wrists, he jerked his head at the other Lords, and they all moved forward.

As he saw the Lords dismount, F'lar told Mnementh to pass the word to land the first three ranks. Like a great wave, the dragons obediently settled to the ground, furling their wings with an enormous rustling sigh.

Mnementh told F'lar that the dragons were excited and pleased. This was much more fun than Games.

F'lar told Mnementh sternly that this was not fun at all.

'Larad of Telgar,' the foremost man introduced himself, his voice crisp, his manner soldierly and confident for one relatively young.

'Meron of Nabol,'

F'lar immediately recognized the swarthy face with the sharp features and restless eyes. A mean and provocative fighter.

Mnementh relayed F'lar an unusual message from the Weyr. F'lar nodded imperceptibly and continued to acknowledge introductions.

'I have been appointed spokesman,' Larad of Telgar began. 'The Holder Lords unanimously agree that the Weyr has outlived its function. Consequently demands from the Weyr are out of order. There are to be no more Searches among our Holds. No more raiding on the herds and barns of any Hold by any dragonfolk.'

F'lar gave him courteous attention. Larad was well-spoken and succinct. F'lar nodded. He looked at each of the Lords before him carefully, getting their measure. Their stern faces expressed their conviction and righteous indignation.

'As Weyrleader, I, F'lar, Mnementh's rider, answer you. Your complaint is heard. Now listen to what the Weyrleader commands.' His casual pose was gone. Mnementh rumbled a menacing counterpoint to his rider's voice as it rang harshly metallic across the plateau, the words carried clearly back so that even the mob heard him.

'You will turn and go back to your Holds. You will then go into your barns and among your herds. You will make a just and equitable tithe. This will be on its way to the Weyr within three days of your return.'

'The Weyrleader is ordering the Lords to tithe?' Meron of Nabol's derisive laugh rang out.

F'lar signaled, and two more wings of dragonmen appeared to hover over the Nabolese contingent.

'The Weyrleader gives orders to the Lords to tithe,' F'lar affirmed. 'And until such time as the Lords send their tithings, we regret that the ladies of Nabol, Telgar, Fort, Igen, Keroon must make their homes with us. Also, the ladies of Hold Balan, Hold Gar, Hold . . .'

He paused, for the Lords were muttering angrily and excitedly among themselves as they heard this list of hostages. F'lar gave Mnementh a quick message to relay.

'Your bluff won't work,' Meron sneered, stepping forward, his hand on his sword hilt. Raiding among the herds could be credited; it had happened. But the Holds were sacrosanct! They'd not dare –

F'lar asked Mnementh to pass the signal, and T'sum's wing appeared. Each rider held a Lady on the neck of his dragon. T'sum held his group aloft but close enough so the Lords could identify each scared or hysterical woman.

Meron's face contorted with shock and new hatred.

Larad stepped forward, tearing his eyes from his own Lady. She was a new wife to him and much beloved. It was small consolation that she neither wept nor fainted, being a quiet and brave little person.

'You have the advantage of us,' Larad admitted bleakly.

'We will retire and send the tithe.' He was about to wheel when Meron pushed forward, his face wild.

'We tamely submit to their demands? Who is a dragon-man to order us?'

'Shut up,' Larad ordered, grabbing the Nabolese's arm.

F'lar raised his arm in an imperious signal. A wing of blues appeared, carrying Meron's would-be mountaineers, some bearing evidence of their struggle with the southern face of Benden Paek.

'Dragonmen do order. And nothing escapes their notice.' F'lar's voice rang out coldly.

'You will retire to your Holds. You will send proper tithing because we shall know if you do not. You will then proceed, under pain of firestone, to clear your habitations of green, croft and Hold alike. Good Gelgar, look to that southern outer Hold of yours. The exposure is acutely vulnerable. Clear all firepits on ridge defenses. You've let them become fouled. The mines are to be reopened and firestone stockpiled.'

'Tithes, yes, but the rest . . .' Larad interrupted.

F'lar's arm shot skyward.

'Look up, Lord. Look well. The Red Star pulses by day as well as night. The mountains beyond Ista steam and spout flaming rock. The seas rage in high tides and flood the coast. Have you all forgotten the Sagas and Ballads? As you've forgotten the abilities of dragons? Can you dismiss these portents that always presage the coming of Threads?'

Meron would never believe until he saw the silver Threads streaking across the skies. But Larad and many of the others, F'lar knew, now did.

'And the queen,' he continued, 'has risen to mate in her second year. Risen to mate and flown high and far.'

The heads of all before him jerked upward. Their eyes were wide. Meron, too, looked startled. F'lar heard R'gul gasp behind him, yet he dared not look, himself, lest it be a trick.

Suddenly, on the periphery of his vision, he caught the glint of gold in the sky.

Mnementh, he snapped, and Mnementh merely rumbled happily. The queen wheeled into view just then, a brave and glowing sight, F'lar grudgingly admitted.

Dressed in flowing white, Lessa was distinctly visible on

the curved golden neck. Ramoth hovered, her wingspan greater than even Mnementh's as she vaned idly. From the way she arched her neck, it was obvious that Ramoth was in good and playful spirits, but F'lar was furious.

The spectacle of the queen aloft had quite an effect on all beholders. F'lar was aware of its impact on himself and saw it reflected in the faces of the incredulous Holders, knew it from the way the dragons hummed, heard it from Mnementh.

'And, of course, our greatest Weyrwomen – Moreta, Torene, to name a only a few – have all come from Ruath Hold, as does Lessa of Pern.'

'Ruatha . . .' Meron grated out the name, clenched his jaw sullenly, his face bleak.

'Threads are coming?' asked Larad.

F'lar nodded slowly. 'Your harper can reinstruct you on the signs. Good Lords, the tithe is required. Your women will be returned. The Holds are to be put in order. The Weyr prepares Pern, as the Weyr is pledged to protect Pern. Your cooperation is expected –' he paused significantly – 'and will be enforced.'

With that, he vaulted to Mnementh's neck, keeping the queen always in sight. He saw her golden wings beat as the dragon turned and soared upward.

It was infuriating of Lessa to take this moment, when all his energy and attention ought to go to settling the Holder's grievance for a show of rebellion. Why did she have to flaunt her independence so, in full sight of the entire Weyr and all the Lords? He longed to chase immediately after her and could not. Not until he had seen the army in actual retreat, not until he had signaled for the final show of Weyr strength for the Holder's elucidation.

Gritting his teeth, he signaled Mnementh aloft. The wings rose behind him with spectacular trumpetings and dartings so that there appeared to be thousands of dragons in the air instead of the scant two hundred Benden Weyr boasted.

Assured that that part of his strategy was proceeding in order, he bade Mnementh fly after the Weyrwoman, who was now dipping and gliding high above the Weyr.

When he got his hands on that girl, he would tell her a thing or two . . . .

Mnementh informed him caustically that telling her a

thing or two might be a very good idea. Much better than flying so vengefully after a pair who were only trying their wings out. Mnementh reminded his irate rider that, after all, the golden dragon had flown far and wide yesterday, having blooded four, but had not eaten since. She'd be neither capable of nor interested in any protracted flying until she had eaten fully. However, if F'lar insisted on this ill-considered and completely unnecessary pursuit, he might just antagonize Ramoth into jumping *between* to escape him.

The very thought of that untutored pair going *between* cooled F'lar instantly. Controlling himself, he realized that Mnementh's judgment was more reliable than his at the moment. He'd let anger and anxiety influence his decisions, but . . .

Mnementh circled in to land at the Star Stone, the tip of Benden Peak being a fine vantage point from which F'lar could observe both the decamping army and the queen.

Mnementh's great eyes gave the appearance of whirling as the dragon adjusted his vision to its farthest reach.

He reported to F'lar that Piyanth's rider felt the dragon's supervision of the retreat was casuing hysteria among the men and beasts. Injuries were occurring in the resultant stampedes.

F'lar immediately ordered K'net to assume surveillance altitude until the army camped for the night. He was to keep close watch on the Nabolese contingent at all times, however.

Even as F'lar had Mnementh relay these orders, he realized his mind had dismissed the matter. All his attention was really on that high-flying pair.

You had better teach her to fly between, Mnementh remarked, one great eye shining directly over F'lar's shoulder. *She's quick enough to figure it out for herself, and then where are we?*

F'lar let the sharp retort die on his lips as he watched, breathless. Ramoth suddenly folded her wings, a golden streak diving through the sky. Effortlessly she pulled out at the critical point and soared upward again. Mnementh deliberately called to mind their first wildly aerobatic flight. A tender smile crossed F'lar's face, and suddenly he knew how much Lessa must have longed to fly, how bitter it must have been for her to watch the dragonets practice when she was forbidden to try.

Well, he was no R'gul, torn by indecision and doubt.

And she is no Jora, Mnementh reminded him pungently. *I'm calling them in,* the dragon added. *Ramoth has turned a dull orange.*

F'lar watched as the flyers obediently began a downward glide, the queen's wings arching and curving as she slowed her tremendous forward speed. Unfed or not, she could fly!

He mounted Mnementh, waving them on, down toward the feeding grounds. He caught a fleeting glimpse of Lessa, her face vivid with elation and rebellion.

Ramoth landed, and Lessa dropped to the ground, gesturing the dragon on to eat.

The girl turned then, watching Mnementh glide in and hover to let F'lar dismount. She straightened her shoulders, her chin lifted belligerently as her slender body gathered itself to face his censure. Her behavior was like that of any weyrling, anticipating punishment and determined to endure it, soundless. She was not the least bit repentant!

Admiration for this indomitable personality replaced the last trace of F'lar's anger. He smiled as he closed the distance between them.

Startled by his completely unexpected behavior, she took a half-step backward.

'Queens can, too, fly,' she blurted out, daring him.

His grin broadening to suffuse his face, he put his hands on her shoulders and gave her an affectionate shake.

'Of course they can fly,' he assured her, his voice full of pride and respect. 'That's why they have wings!'

Part III – Dust Fall

> The Finger points
> At an Eye blood-red.
> Alert the Weyrs
> To sear the Thread.

'You STILL doubt, R'gul?' F'lar asked, appearing slightly amused by the older bronze rider's perversity.

R'gul, his handsome features stubbornly set, made no reply to the Weyrleader's taunt. He ground his teeth together as if he could grind away F'lar's authority over him.

'There have been no Threads in Pern's skies for over four hundred Turns. There are no more!'

'There is always that possibility,' F'lar conceded amiably. There was not, however, the slightest trace of tolerance in his amber eyes. Nor the slightest hint of compromise in his manner.

He was more like F'lon, his sire, R'gul decided, than a son had any right to be. Always so sure of himself, always slightly contemptuous of what others did and thought. Arrogant, that's what F'lar was. Impertinent, too, and underhanded in the matter of that young Weyrwoman. Why, R'gul had trained her up to be one of the finest Weyrwomen in many Turns. Before he's finished her instruction, she'd known all the Teaching Ballads and Sagas letter-perfect. And then the silly child had turned to F'lar. Didn't have sense enough to appreciate the merits of an older, more experienced man. Undoubtedly she felt a first obligation to F'lar for discovering her on Search.

'You do, however,' F'lar was saying, 'admit that when the sun hits the Finger Rock at the moment of dawn, winter solstice has been reached?'

'Any fool knows that's what the Finger Rock is for,' R'gul grunted.

'Then why don't you, you old fool, admit that the Eye Rock was placed on Star Stone to bracket the Red Star when it's about to make a Pass?' burst out K'net.

R'gul flushed, half-starting out of his chair, ready to

take the young sprout to task for such insolence.

'K'net!' F'lar's voice cracked authoritatively. 'Do you really like flying the Igen patrol so much you want another few weeks at it?'

K'net hurriedly seated himself, flushing at the reprimand and the threat.

'There is, you know, R'gul, incontrovertible evidence to support my conclusions,' F'lar went on with deceptive mildness. ' "The Finger points/At an Eye blood-red. . . ." '

'Don't quote me verses I taught you as a weyrling,' R'gul exclaimed heatedly.

'Then have faith in what you taught,' F'lar snapped back, his amber eyes flashing dangerously.

R'gul, stunned by the unexpected forcefulness, sank back into his chair.

'You cannot deny, R'gul,' F'lar continued quietly, 'that no less than half an hour ago the sun balanced on the Finger's tip at dawn and the Red Star was squarely framed by the Eye Rock.'

The other dragonriders, bronze as well as brown, murmured and nodded their agreement to that phenomenon. There was also an undercurrent of resentment for R'gul's continual contest of F'lar's policies as the new Weyrleader. Even old S'lel, once R'gul's avowed supporter, was following the majority.

'There have been no Threads in four hundred Turns. There are no Threads,' R'gul muttered.

'Then, my fellow dragonman,' F'lar said cheerfully, 'all you have taught is falsehood. The dragons are, as the Lords of the Holds wish to believe, parasites on the economy of Pern, anachronisms. And so are we.

'Therefore, far be it from me to hold you here against the dictates of your conscience. You have my permission to leave the Weyr and take up residence where you will.'

Someone laughed.

R'gul was too stunned by F'lar's ultimatum to take offense at the ridicule. Leave the Weyr? Was the man mad? Where would he go? The Weyr had been his life. He had been bred up to it for generations. All his male ancestors had been dragonriders. Not all bronze, true, but a decent percentage. His own dam's sire had been a Weyrleader just as he, R'gul, had been until F'lar's Mnementh had flown the new queen.

But dragonmen never left the Weyr. Well, they did if they were negligent enough to lose their dragons, like that Lytol fellow at Ruath Hold. And how could he leave the Weyr *with* a dragon?

What did F'lar want of him? Was it not enough that he was Weyrleader now in R'gul's stead? Wasn't F'lar's pride sufficiently swollen by having bluffed the Lords of Pern into disbanding their army when they were all set to coerce the Weyr and dragonmen? Must F'lar dominate *every* dragonman, body and will, too? He stared a long moment, incredulous.

'I do not believe we are parasites,' F'lar said, breaking the silence with a soft, persuasive voice. 'Nor anachronistic. There have been long Intervals before. The Red Star does not always pass close enough to drop Threads on Pern. Which is why our ingenious ancestors thought to position the Eye Rock and the Finger Rock as they did . . . to confirm *when* a Pass will be made. And another thing" – his face turned grave – 'there have been other times when dragon-kind has all but died out . . . and Pern with it because of skeptics like you.' F'lar smiled and relaxed indolently in his chair. 'I prefer not to be recorded as a skeptic. How shall we record you, R'gul?'

The Council Room was tense. R'gul was aware of some-one breathing harshly and realized it was himself. He looked at the adamant face of the young Weyrleader and knew that the threat was not empty. He would either concede to F'lar's authority completely, though concession rankled deeply, or leave the Weyr.

And where could he go, unless to one of the other Weyrs, deserted for hundreds of Turns? And – R'gul's thoughts were savage – wasn't that indication enough of the cessa-tion of Threads? Five empty Weyrs? No, by the Egg of Faranth, he would practice some of F'lar's own brand of deceit and bide his time. When all Pern turned on the arrogant fool, he, R'gul, would be there to salvage some-thing from the ruins.

'A dragonman stays in his Weyr,' R'gul said with what dignity he could muster.

'And accepts the policies of the current Weyrleader?' The tone of F'lar's voice made it less of a question and more of an order.

So as not to perjure himself, R'gul gave a curt nod of his

head. F'lar continued to stare at him and R'gul wondered if the man could read his thoughts as his dragon might. He managed to return the gaze calmly. His turn would come. He'd wait.

Apparently accepting the capitulation, F'lar stood up and crisply delegated patrol assignments for the day.

'T'bor, you're weather-watch. Keep an eye on those tithing trains as you do. Have you the morning's report?'

'Weather is fair at dawning ... all across Telgar and Keroon ... if all too cold,' T'bor said with a wry grin. 'Tithing trains have good hard roads, though, so they ought to be here soon.' His eyes twinkled with anticipation of the feasting that would follow the supplies' arrival – a mood shared by all, to judge by the expressions around the table.

F'lar nodded. 'S'lan and D'nol, you are to continue an adroit Search for likely boys. They should be striplings, if possible, but do not pass over anyone suspected of talent. It's all well and good to present, for Impression, boys reared up in the Weyr traditions.' F'lar gave a one-sided smile. 'But there are not enough in the Lower Caverns. We, too, have been behind in begetting. Anyway, dragons reach full growth faster than their riders. We must have more young *men* to Impress when Ramoth hatches. Take the southern holds, Ista, Nerat, Fort, and South Boll where maturity comes earlier. You can use the guise of inspecting Holds for greenery to talk to the boys. And take along firestone and run a few flaming passes on those heights that haven't been scoured in – oh – dragon's years. A flaming beast impresses the young and arouses envy.'

F'lar deliberately looked at R'gul to see the ex-Weyr-leader's reaction to the order. R'gul had been dead set against going outside the Weyr for more candidates. In the first place, R'gul had argued that there were eighteen youngsters in the Lower Caverns, some quite young, to be sure, but R'gul would not admit that Ramoth would lay more than the dozen Nemorth had always dropped. In the second place, R'gul persisted in wanting to avoid any action that might antagonize the Lords.

R'gul made no overt protest, and F'lar went on.

'K'net, back to the mines. I want the dispositions of each firestone-dump checked and quantities available. R'gul, continue drilling recognition points with the weyrlings. They must be positive about their references. If they're

135

used as messengers and suppliers, they may be sent out quickly and with no time to ask questions.

'F'nor, T'sum' – F'lar turned to his own brown riders – 'you're clean-up squad today.' He allowed himself a grin at their dismay. 'Try Ista Weyr. Clear the Hatching Cavern and enough Weyrs for a double Wing. And, F'nor, don't leave a single Record behind. They're worth preserving.'

'That will be all, dragonmen. Good flying.' And with that, F'lar rose and strode from the Council Room up to the queen's weyr.

Ramoth still slept, her hide gleaming with health, its color deepening to a shade of gold closer to bronze, indicating her pregnancy. As he passed her, the tip of her long tail twitched slightly.

All the dragons were restless these days, F'lar reflected. Yet when he asked Mnementh, the bronze dragon could give no reason. He woke, he went back to sleep. That was all. F'lar couldn't ask a leading question for that would defeat his purpose. He had to remain discontented with the vague fact that the restlessness was some kind of instinctive reaction.

Lessa was not in the sleeping room, nor was she still bathing. F'lar snorted. That girl was going to scrub her hide off with this constant bathing. She'd had to live grimy to protect herself in Ruath Hold, but bathing twice a day? He was beginning to wonder if this might be a subtle Lessa-variety insult to him personally. F'lar sighed. That girl. Would she never turn to him of her own accord? Would he ever touch that elusive inner core of Lessa? She had more warmth for his half brother, F'nor, and for K'net, the youngest of the bronze riders than she had for F'lar who shared her bed.

He pulled the curtain back into place, irritated. Where had she gone to today when, for the first time in weeks, he had been able to get all the wings out of the Weyr just so he could teach her to fly *between?*

Ramoth would soon be too egg-heavy for such activity. He had promised the Weyrwoman, and he meant to keep that promise. She had taken to wearing the wherhide riding gear as a flagrant reminder of his unfulfilled pledge. From certain remarks she had dropped, he knew she would not wait much longer for his aid. That she should try it on her own didn't suit him at all.

He crossed the queen's weyr again and peered down the passage that led to the Records Room. She was often to be found there, poring over the musty skins. And that was one more matter that needed urgent consideration. Those, records were deteriorating past legibility. Curiously enough earlier ones were still in good condition and readable. Another technique forgotten.

That girl! He brushed his thick forelock of hair back from his brow in a gesture habitual to him when he was annoyed or worried. The passage was dark, which meant she could not be below in the Records Room.

'Mnementh,' he called silently to his bronze dragon, sunning on the ledge outside the queen's weyr. 'What is that girl doing?'

Lessa, the dragon replied, stressing the Weyrwoman's name with pointed courtesy, *is talking to Manora. She's dressed for riding,* he added after a slight pause.

F'lar thanked the bronze sarcastically and strode down the passage to the entrance. As he turned the last bend, he all but ran Lessa down.

You hadn't asked me where *she was,* Mnementh plaintively answered F'lar's blistering reprimand.

Lessa rocked back on her heels from the force of their encounter. She glared up at him, her lips thin with displeasure, her eyes flashing.

'Why didn't I have the opportunity of seeing the Red Star through the Eye Rock?' she demanded in a hard, angry voice.

F'lar pulled at his hair. Lessa at her most difficult would complete the list of this morning's trials.

'Too many to accommodate as it was on the Peak,' he muttered, determined not to let her irritate him today. 'And you already believe.'

'I'd've liked to see it,' she snapped and pushed past him toward the weyr. 'If only in my capacity as Weyrwoman and Recorder.'

He caught her arm and felt her body tense. He set his teeth, wishing, as he had a hundred times since Ramoth rose in her first mating flight, that Lessa had not been virgin, too. He had not thought to control his dragon incited emotions, and Lessa's first sexual experience had been violent. It had surprised him to be first, considering that her adolescent years had been spent drudging for lascivious warders and soldier-types. Evidently no one had bothered to penetrate the curtain of rags and the coat of filth she had carefully maintained as a disguise. He had been a considerate and gentle bedmate ever since, but, unless Ramoth and Mnementh were involved, he might as well call it rape.

Yet he knew someday, somehow, he would coax her into responding wholeheartedly to his lovemaking. He had a certain pride in his skill, and he was in a position to persevere.

Now he took a deep breath and released her arm slowly.

'How fortunate you're wearing riding gear. As soon as the wings have cleared out and Ramoth wakes, I shall teach you to fly *between*.'

The gleam of excitement in her eyes was evident even in the dimly lit passageway. He heard her inhale sharply.

'Can't put it off too much longer or Ramoth'll be in no shape to fly at all,' he continued amiably.

'You mean it?' Her voice was low and breathless, its usual acid edge missing. 'You will teach us today?' He wished he could see her face clearly.

Once or twice he had caught an unguarded expression on her face, loving and tender. He would give much to have that look turned on him. However, he admitted wryly to himself, he ought to be glad that melting regard was directed only at Ramoth and not at another human.

'Yes, my dear Weyrwoman, I mean it. I will teach you to fly *between* today. If only,' and he bowed to her with a flourish. 'to keep you from trying it yourself.'

Her low chuckle informed him his taunt was well-aimed.

'Right now, however,' he said, indicating for her to lead the way back to the weyr, 'I could do with some food. We were up before the kitchen.'

They had entered the well-lighted weyr, so he did not miss the trenchant look she shot him over her shoulder. She would not so easily forgive being left out of the group at the Star Stone this morning, certainly not with the bribe of flying *between*.

How different this inner room was now that Lessa was Weyrwoman, F'lar mused as Lessa called down the service shaft for food. During Jora's incompetent tenure as Weyrwoman, the sleeping quarters had been crowded with junk, unwashed apparel, uncleared dishes. The state of the Weyr and the reduced number of dragons were as much Jora's fault as R'gul's, for she had indirectly encouraged sloth, negligence, and gluttony.

If he, F'lar, had been just a few years older when F'lon, his father, had died ... Jora had been disgusting, but when dragons rose in mating flight, the condition of your partner counted for nothing.

Lessa took a tray of bread and cheese, and mugs of the stimulating *klah* from the platform. She served him deftly.

'You'd not eaten, either?' he asked.

She shook her head vigorously, the braid into which she had plaited her thick, fine dark hair bobbing across her shoulder. The hairdressing was too severe for her narrow face, but it did not, if that was her intention, disguise her femininity or the curious beauty of her delicate features. Again F'lar wondered that such a slight body contained so much shrewd intelligence and resourceful ... cunning – yes, that was the word, cunning. F'lar did not make the mistake, as others had, of underestimating her abilities.

'Manora called me to witness the birth of Kylara's child.'

F'lar maintained an expression of polite interest. He knew perfectly well that Lessa suspected the child was his, and it could have been, he admitted privately, but he doubted it. Kylara had been one of the ten candidates from the same Search three years ago which had discovered Lessa. Like others who survived Impression, Kylara had found certain aspects of Weyr life exactly suited to her temperament. She had gone from one rider's weyr to another's. She had even seduced F'lar – not at all against his will, to be sure. Now that he was Weyrleader, he found it wiser to ignore her efforts to continue the relationship. T'bor had taken her in hand and had had his hands full until he retired her to the Lower Caverns, well advanced in pregnancy.

Aside from having the amorous tendencies of a green dragon, Kylara was quick and ambitious. She would make a strong Weyrwoman, So F'lar had charged Manora and Lessa with the job of planting the notion in Kylara's mind. In the capacity of Weyrwoman ... of another Weyr ... her intense drives would be used to Pern's advantage. She had not learned the severe lessons of restraint and patience that Lessa had, and she didn't have Lessa's devious mind. Fortunately she was in considerable awe of Lessa, and F'lar suspected that Lessa was subtly influencing this attitude. In Kylara's case, F'lar preferred not to object to Lessa's meddling.

'A fine son,' Lessa was saying.

F'lar sipped his *klah*. She was not going to get him to admit any responsibility.

After a long pause Lessa added, 'She has named him T'kil.'

F'lar suppressed a grin at Lessa's failure get a rise from him.

'Discreet of her.'

'Oh?'

'Yes,' F'lar replied blandly. 'T'lar might be confusing if she took the second half of her name as is customary. T'kil,' however, still indicates sire as well as dam.'

'While I was waiting for Council to end,' Lessa said after clearing her throat, 'Manora and I checked the supply caverns. The tithing trains, which the Holds have been so gracious to send us' – her voice was sharp – 'are due within the week. There will shortly be bread fit to eat,' she added, wrinkling her nose at the crumbling gray pastry she was attempting to spread with cheese.

'A nice change,' F'lar agreed.

She paused.

'The Red Star performed its scheduled antic?'

He nodded.

'And R'gul's doubts have been wiped away in the en-lightening red glow?'

'Not at all,' F'lar grinned back at her, ignoring her sarcasm. 'Not at all, but he will not be so vocal in his criticism.'

She swallowed quickly so she could speak. 'You'd do well to cut out his criticism,' she said ruthlessly, gesturing with her knife as if plunging it into a man's heart. 'He is never going to accept your authority with good grace.'

'We need every bronze rider ... there are only seven, you know,' he reminded her pointedly. 'R'gul's a good wingleader. He'll settle down when the Threads fall. He needs proof to lay his doubts aside.'

'And the Red Star in the Eye Rock is not proof?' Lessa's expressive eyes were wide.

F'lar was privately of Lessa's opinion – that it might be wiser to remove R'gul's stubborn contentiousness. But he could not sacrifice a wingleader, needing every dragon and rider as badly as he did.

'I don't trust him,' she added darkly. She sipped at her hot drink, her gray eyes dark over the rim of her mug. As if, F'lar mused, she didn't trust him, either.

And she didn't, past a certain point. She had made that plain, and, in honesty, he couldn't blame her. She did recognize that every action F'lar took was toward one end ... the safety and preservation of dragonkind and weyrfolk and consequently the safety and preservation of Pern. To effect that end, he needed her full cooperation. When Weyr business or dragonlore were discussed, she suspended the antipathy he knew she felt for him. In conferences she supported him wholeheartedly and persuasively, but always he suspected the double edge to her comments and saw a speculative, suspicious look in her eyes. He needed not only her tolerance but her empathy.

'Tell me,' she said after a long silence, 'did the sun touch the Finger Rock before the Red Star was bracketed in the Eye Rock or after?'

'Matter of fact, I'm not sure, as I did not see it myself ... the concurrence lasts only a few moments ... but the two are supposed to be simultaneous.'

She frowned at him sourly. 'Whom did you waste it on? R'gul?' She was provoked, her angry eyes looked everywhere but at him.

'I am Weyrleader,' he informed her curtly. She was unreasonable.

She awarded him one long, hard look before she bent to finish her meal. She ate very little, quickly and neatly. Compared to Jora, she didn't eat enough in the course of an entire day to nourish a sick child. But then, there was no point in ever comparing Lessa to Jora.

He finished his own breakfast, absently piling the mugs together on the empty tray. She rose silently and removed the dishes.

'As soon as the Weyr is free, we'll go,' he told her.

'So you said.' She nodded toward the sleeping queen, visible through the open arch. 'We still must wait upon Ramoth.'

'Isn't she rousing? Her tail's been twitching for an hour.'

'She always does that about this time of day.'

F'lar leaned across the table, his brows drawn together

thoughtfully as he watched the golden-forked tip of the queen's tail jerk spasmodically from side to side.

'Mnementh, too. And always at dawn and early morning. As if somehow they associate that time of day with trouble ...'

'Or the Red Star's rising?' Lessa interjected.

Some subtle difference in her tone caused F'lar to glance quickly at her. It wasn't anger now over having missed the morning's phenomenon. Her eyes were fixed on nothing; her face, smooth at first, was soon wrinkled with a vaguely anxious frown as tiny lines formed between her arching, well-defined brows.

'Dawn ... that's when all warnings come,' she murmured.

'What kind of warnings?' he asked with quiet encouragement.

'There was that morning ... a few days before ... before you and Fax descended on Ruath Hold. Something woke me ... a feeling, like a very heavy pressure ... the sensation of some terrible danger threatening.' She was silent. 'The Red Star was just rising.' The fingers of her left hand opened and closed. She gave a convulsive shudder. Her eyes refocused on him.

'You and Fax did come out of the northeast from Crom,' she said sharply, ignoring the fact, F'lar noticed, that the Red Star also rises north of true east.

'Indeed we did,' he grinned at her, remembering that morning vividly. 'Although,' he added, gesturing around the great cavern to emphasize, 'I prefer to believe I served you well that day ... you remember it with displeasure?'

The look she gave him was coldly inscrutable.

'Danger comes in many guises.'

'I agree,' he replied amiably, determined not to rise to her bait. 'Had any other rude awakenings?' he inquired conversationally.

The absolute stillness in the room brought his attention back to her. Her face had drained of all color.

'The day Fax invaded Ruath Hold.' Her voice was a barely articulated whisper. Her eyes were wide and staring. Her hands clenched the edge of the table. She said nothing for such a long interval that F'lar became concerned. This was an unexpectedly violent reaction to a casual question.

'Tell me,' he suggested softly.

She spoke in unemotional, impersonal tones, as if she

were reciting a Traditional Ballad or something that had happened to an entirely different person.

'I was a child. Just eleven. I woke at dawn . . .' Her voice trailed off. Her eyes remained focused on nothing, staring at a scene that had happened long ago.

F'lar was stirred by an irresistible desire to comfort her. It struck him forcibly, even as he was stirred by this unusual compassion, that he had never thought that Lessa, of all people, would be troubled by so old a terror.

Mnementh sharply informed his rider that Lessa was obviously bothered a good deal. Enough so that her mental anguish was rousing Ramoth from sleep. In less accusing tones Mnementh informed F'lar that R'gul had finally taken off with his weyrling pupils. His dragon, Hath, however, was in a fine state of disorientation due to R'gul's state of mind. Must F'lar unsettle everyone in the Weyr . . .

'Oh, be quiet,' F'lar retorted under his breath.

'Why?' Lessa demanded in her normal voice.

'I didn't mean you, my dear Weyrwoman,' he assured her, smiling pleasantly, as if the entranced interlude had never occurred. 'Mnementh is full of advice these days.'

'Like rider, like dragon,' she replied tartly.

Ramoth yawned mightily. Lessa was instantly on her feet, running to her dragon's side, her slight figure dwarfed by the six-foot dragon head.

A tender, adoring expression flooded her face as she gazed into Ramoth's gleaming opalescent eyes. F'lar clenched his teeth, envious, by the Egg, of a rider's affection for her dragon.

In his mind he heard Mnementh's dragon equivalent of laughter.

'She's hungry,' Lessa informed F'lar, an echo of her love for Ramoth lingering in the soft line of her mouth, in the kindness in her gray eyes.

'She's always hungry,' he observed and followed them out of the weyr.

Mnementh hovered courteously just beyond the ledge until Lessa and Ramoth had taken off. They glided down the Weyr Bowl, over the misty bathing lake, toward the feeding ground at the opposite end of the long oval that comprised the floor of Benden Weyr. The striated, precipitous walls were pierced with the black mouths of single weyr entrances, deserted at this time of day by the few dragons who might otherwise doze on their ledges in the wintry sun.

As F'lar vaulted to Mnementh's smooth bronze neck, he hoped that Ramoth's clutch would be spectacular, erasing the ignominy of the paltry dozen Nemorth had laid in each of her last few clutches.

He had no serious doubts of the improvement after Ramoth's remarkable mating flight with his Mnementh. The bronze dragon smugly echoed his rider's certainty, and both looked on the queen possessively as she curved her wings to land. She was twice Nemorth's size, for one thing; her wings were half-a-wing again longer than Mnementh's, who was the biggest of the seven male bronzes. F'lar looked to Ramoth to repopulate the five empty Weyrs, even as he looked to himself and Lessa to rejuvenate the pride and faith of dragonriders and of Pern itself. He only hoped time enough remained to him to do what was necessary. The Red Star had been bracketed by the Eye Rock. The Threads would soon be falling. Somewhere, in one of the other Weyrs' Records, must be the information he needed to ascertain *when*, exactly, Threads would fall.

Mnementh landed. F'lar jumped down from the curving neck to stand beside Lessa. The three watched as Ramoth, a buck grasped in each of her forefeet, rose to a feeding ledge.

'Will her appetite never taper off'? Lessa asked with affectionate dismay.

As a dragonet, Ramoth had been eating to grow. Her full stature attained, she was, of course, now eating for her young, and she applied herself conscientiously.

F'nar chuckled and squatted, hunter fashion. He picked up shale-flakes, skating them across the flat dry ground, counting the dust puffs boyishly.

'The time will come when she won't eat everything in sight,' he assured Lessa. 'But she's young . . .'

'. . . and needs her strength,' Lessa interrupted, her voice, a fair imitation of R'gul's pedantic tones.

F'lar looked up at her, squinting against the wintry sun that slanted down at them.

'She's a finely grown beast, especially compared to Nemorth.' He gave a contemptuous snort. 'In fact, there *is* no comparison. However, look here,' he ordered peremptorily.

He tapped the smoothed sand in front of him, and she saw that his apparently idle gestures had been to a purpose. With a sliver of stone, he drew a design in quick strokes.

'In order to fly a dragon *between*, he has to know where to go. And so do you.' He grinned at the astonished and infuriated look of comprehension on her face. 'Ah, but there are certain consequences to an ill-considered jump. Badly visualized reference points often result in staying *between*.' His voice dropped ominously. Her face cleared of its resentment. 'So there are certain reference or recognition points arbitrarily taught all weyrlings. That," – he pointed first to his facsimile and then to the actual Star Stone with its Finger and Eye Rock companions, on Benden Peak – 'is the first recognition point a weyrling learns. When I take you aloft, you will reach an altitude just above the Star Stone, near enough for you to be able to see the hole in the Eye Rock clearly. Fix that picture sharply in your mind's eye, relay it to Ramoth. That will always get you home.'

'Understood. But how do I learn recognition points of places I've never seen?'

He grinned up at her. 'You're drilled in them. First by your instructor,' and he pointed the sliver at his chest, 'and then by going there, having directed your dragon to get the visualization from her instructor,' and he indicated Mnementh. The bronze dragon lowered his wedge-shaped head until one eye was focused on his rider and his mate's rider. He made a pleased noise deep in his chest.

Lessa laughed up at the gleaming eye and, with unexpected affection, patted the soft nose.

F'lar cleared his throat in surprise. He had been aware that Mnementh showed an unusual affection for the Weyrwoman, but he had had no idea Lessa was fond of the bronze. Perversely, he was irritated.

'However,' he said, and his voice sounded unnatural to himself, 'we take the young riders constantly to and from the main reference points all across Pern, to all the Holds, so that they have eyewitness impressions on which to rely. As a rider becomes adept in picking out landmarks, he gets additional references from other riders. Therefore, to go *between*, there is actually only one requirement: a clear picture of where you want to go. *And* a dragon!' He grinned

145

at her. 'Also, you should always plan to arrive above your reference point in clear air.'

Lessa frowned.

'It is better to arrive in open air' – F'lar waved a hand above his head – 'rather than underground,' and he slapped his open hand onto the dirt. A puff of dust rose warningly.

'But the wings took off within the Bowl itself the day the Lords of the Hold arrived,' Lessa reminded him.

F'lar chuckled at her uptake. 'True, but only the most seasoned riders. Once we came across a dragon and a rider entombed together in solid rock. They ... were ... very young.' His eyes were bleak.

'I take the point,' she assured him gravely. 'That's her fifth,' she added, pointing toward Ramoth, who was carrying her latest kill up to the bloody ledge.

'She'll work them off today, I assure you,' F'lar remarked. He rose, brushing off his knees with sharp slaps of his riding gloves. 'Test her temper.'

Lessa did so with a silent, *Had enough?* She grimaced at Ramoth's indignant rejection of the thought.

The queen went swooping down for a huge fowl, rising in a flurry of gray, brown and white feathers.

'She's not as hungry as she's making you think, the deceitful creature,' F'lar chuckled and saw that Lessa had reached the same conclusion. Her eyes were snapping with vexation.

'When you've finished the bird, Ramoth, do let us learn how to fly *between*,' Lessa said aloud for F'lar's benefit, 'before our good Weyrleader changes his mind.'

Ramoth looked up from her gorging, turned her head toward the two riders at the edge of the feeding ground. Her eyes gleamed. She bent her head again to her kill, but Lessa could sense the dragon would obey.

It was cold aloft. Lessa was glad of the fur lining in her riding gear, and the warmth of the great golden neck which she bestrode. She decided not to think of the absolute cold of *between* which she had experienced only once. She glanced below on her right where bronze Mnementh hovered, and she caught his amused thought.

F'lar tells me to tell Ramoth to tell you to fix the alignment of the Star Stone firmly in your mind as a homing. Then, Mnementh went on amiably, *we shall fly down to the lake. You will return from* between *to this exact point. Do you understand?*

Lessa found herself grinning foolishly with anticipation and nodded vigorously. How much time was saved because she could speak directly to the dragons! Ramoth made a disgruntled noise deep in her throat. Lessa patted her reassuringly.

'Have you got the picture in your mind, dear one?' she asked, and Ramoth again rumbled, less annoyed, because she was catching Lessa's excitement.

Mnementh stroked the cold air with his wings, greenish-brown in the sunlight, and curved down gracefully toward the lake on the plateau below Benden Weyr. His flight line took him very low over the rim of the Weyr. From Lessa's angle, it looked like a collision course. Ramoth followed closely in his wake. Lessa caught her breath at the sight of the jagged boulders just below Ramoth's wing tips.

It was exhilarating, Lessa crowed to herself, doubly stimulated by the elation that flowed back to her from Ramoth.

Mnementh halted above the farthest shore of the lake, and there, too, Ramoth came to hover.

Mnementh flashed the thought to Lessa that she was to place the picture of where she wished to go firmly in her mind and direct Ramoth to get there.

Lessa complied. The next instant the awesome, bone-penetrating cold of black *between* enveloped them. Before either she or Ramoth was aware of more than that biting touch of cold and impregnable darkness, they were above the Star Stone.

Lessa let out a cry of pure triumph.

It is extremely simple. Ramoth seemed disappointed.

Mnementh reappeared beside and slightly below them. *You are to return by the same route to the Lake,* he ordered, and before the thought had finished, Ramoth took off.

Mnementh was beside them above the lake, fuming with his own and F'lar's anger. *You did not visualize before transferring. Don't think a first successful trip makes you perfect. You have no conception of the dangers inherent in* between. Never *fail to picture your arrival point again.*

Lessa glanced down at F'lar. Even two wingspans apart, she could see the vivid anger on his face, almost feel the fury flashing from his eyes. And laced through the wrath, a terrible sinking fearfulness for her safety that was a more effective reprimand than his wrath. Lessa's safety, she wondered bitterly, or Ramoth's?

You are to follow us, Mnementh was saying in a calmer tone, *rehearsing in your mind the two reference points you have already learned. We shall jump to and from them this morning, gradually learning other points around Benden.*

They did. Flying as far away as Benden Hold itself, nestled against the foothills above Benden Valley, the Weyr Peak a far point against the noonday sky, Lessa did not neglect to visualize a clearly detailed impression each time.

This was as marvelously exciting as she had hoped it would be, Lessa confided to Ramoth. Ramoth replied: yes, it was certainly preferable to the time-consuming methods others had to use, but she didn't think it was exciting at all to jump *between* from Benden Weyr to Benden Hold and back to Benden Weyr again. It was dull.

They had met with Mnementh above the Star Stone again. The bronze dragon sent Lessa the message that this was a very satisfactory initial session. They would practice some distant jumping tomorrow.

Tomorrow, thought Lessa glumly, some emergency will occur or our hard-working Weyrleader will decide today's session constitutes keeping his promise and that will be that.

There was one jump she could make *between*, from anywhere on Pern, and not miss her mark.

She visualized Ruatha for Ramoth as seen from the heights above the Hold ... to satisfy that requirement. To be scrupulously clear, Lessa projected the pattern of the firepits. Before Fax invaded and she had had to manipulate its decline, Ruatha had been such a lovely, prosperous valley. She told Ramoth to jump *between*.

The cold was intense and seemed to last for many heartbeats. Just as Lessa began to fear that she had somehow lost them *between*, they exploded into the air above the Hold. Elation filled her. That for F'lar and his excessive caution! With Ramoth she could jump anywhere! For there was the distinctive pattern of Ruatha's fire-guttered heights. It was just before dawn, the Breast Pass between Crom and Ruatha, black cones against the lightening gray sky. Fleetingly she noticed the absence of the Red Star that now blazed in the dawn sky. And fleetingly she noticed a difference in the air. Chill, yes, but not wintry ... the air held that moist coolness of early spring.

Startled, she glanced downward, wondering if she could have, for all her assurance, erred in some fashion. But no, this was Ruath Hold. The Tower, the inner Court, the aspect of the broad avenue leading down to the crafthold were just as they should be. Wisps of smoke from distant chimneys indicated people were making ready for the day.

Ramoth caught the tenor of her insecurity and began to press for an explanation.

This is Ruatha, Lessa replied stoutly. *It can be no other. Circle the heights. See, there are the firepit lines I gave you . . . .*

Lessa gasped, the coldness in her stomach freezing her muscles.

Below her in the slowly lifting predawn gloom, she saw the figures of many men toiling over the breast of the cliff from the hills beyond Ruatha, men moving with quiet stealth like criminals.

She ordered Ramoth to keep as still as possible in the air so as not to direct their attention upward. The dragon was curious but obedient.

Who would be attacking Ruatha? It seemed incredible. Lytol was, after all, a former dragonman and had savagely repelled one attack already. Could there possibly be a thought of aggression among the Holds now that F'lar was Weyrleader? And what Hold Lord would be foolish enough to mount a territorial war in the winter?

No, not winter. The air was definitely springlike.

The men crept on, over the firepits to the edge of the heights. Suddenly Lessa realized they were lowering rope ladders over the face of the cliff, down toward the open shutters of the Inner Hold.

Wildly she clutched at Ramoth's neck, certain of what she saw.

This was the invader Fax, now dead nearly three Turns – Fax and his men as they began their attack on Ruatha nearly thirteen Turns ago.

Yes, there was the Tower guard, his face a white blot turned toward the Cliff itself, watching. He had been paid his bribe to stand silent this morning.

But the watch-wher, trained to give alarm for any intrusion – why was it not trumpeting its warning? Why was it silent?'

Because, Ramoth informed her rider with calm logic, *it*

senses your presence as well as mine, so how could the Hold be in danger?

No, No! Lessa moaned. *What can I do now? How can I wake them? Where is the girl I was? I was asleep, and then I woke. I remember. I dashed from my room. I was so scared. I went down the steps and nearly fell. I knew I had to get to the watch-wher's kennel. . . . I knew. . . .*

Lessa clutched at Ramoth's neck for support as past acts and mysteries became devastatingly clear.

She herself had warned herself, just as it was her presence on the queen dragon that had kept the watch-wher from giving alarm. For as she watched, stunned and speechless, she saw the small, gray-robed figure that could only be herself as a youngster, burst from the Hold Hall door, race uncertainly down the cold stone steps into the Court, and disappear into the watch-wher's stinking den. Faintly she heard it crying in piteous confusion.

Just as Lessa-the-girl reached that doubtful sanctuary, Fax's invaders swooped into the open window embrasures and began the slaughter of her sleeping family.

'Back – back to the Star Stone!' Lessa cried. In her wide and staring eyes she held the image of the guiding rocks like a rudder for her sanity as well as Ramoth's direction.

The intense cold acted as a restorative. And then they were above the quiet, peaceful wintry Weyr as if they had never paradoxically visited Ruatha.

F'lar and Mnementh were nowhere to be seen.

Ramoth, however, was unshaken by the experience. She had only gone where she had been told to go and had not quite understood that going where she had been told to go had shocked Lessa. She suggested to her rider that Mnement had probably followed them to Ruatha so if Lessa would give her the *proper* references, she'd take her there. Ramoth's sensible attitude was comforting.

Lessa carefully drew for Ramoth not the child's memory of a long-vanished, idyllic Ruatha but her more recent recollection of the Hold, gray, sullen,-at dawning, with a Red Star pulsing on the horizon.

And there they were again, hovering over the Valley, the Hold below them on the right. The grasses grew untended on the heights, clogging firepit and brickwork; the scene showed all the deterioration she had encouraged in her effort to thwart Fax of any profit from conquering Ruath Hold.

But, as she watched, vaguely disturbed, she saw a figure emerge from the kitchen, saw the watch-wher creep from its lair and follow the raggedly dressed figure as far across the Court as the chain permitted. She saw the figure ascend the Tower, gaze first eastward,. then northeastward. This was still not Ruatha of today and now! Lessa's mind reeled, disoriented. This time she had come back to visit herself of three Turns ago, to see the filthy drudge plotting revenge on Fax.

She felt the absolute cold of *between* as Ramoth snatched them back, emerging once more above the Star Stone. Lessa was shuddering, her eyes frantically taking in the reassuring sight of the Weyr Bowl, hoping she had not somehow shifted backward in time yet again. Mnementh suddenly erupted into the air a few lengths below and beyond Ramoth. Lessa greeted him with a cry of intense relief.

Back to your weyr! There was no disguising the white fury in Mnementh's tone. Lessa was too unnerved to respond in any way other than instant compliance. Ramoth glided swiftly to their ledge, quickly clearing the perch for Mnementh to land.

The rage on F'lar's face as he leaped from Mnementh and advanced on Lessa brought her wits back abruptly. She made no move to evade him as he grabbed her shoulders and shook her violently.

'How dare you risk yourself and Ramoth? Why must you defy me at every opportunity? Do you realize what would happen to all Pern if we lost Ramoth? Where did you go?' He was spitting with anger, punctuating each question that tumbled from his lips by giving her a head-wrenching shake.

'Ruatha,' she managed to say, trying to keep herself erect. She reached out to catch at his arms, but he shook her again.

'Ruatha? We were there. You weren't. Where did you go?'

'Ruatha!' Lessa cried louder, clutching at him distractedly because he kept jerking her off balance. She couldn't organize her thoughts with him jolting her around.

She was *at Ruatha*, Mnementh said firmly.

We were there twice, Ramoth added.

As the dragon's calmer words penetrated F'lar's fury, he stopped shaking Lessa. She hung limply in his grasp, her hands weakly plucking at his arms, her eyes closed, her face gray. He picked her up and strode rapidly into the queen's Weyr, the dragons following. He placed her upon the couch, wrapping her tightly in the fur cover. He called down the service shaft for the duty cook to send up hot *klah*.

'All right, what happened?' he demanded.

She didn't look at him, but he got a glimpse of her haunted eyes. She blinked constantly as if she longed to erase what she had just seen.

Finally she got herself somewhat under control and said in a low, tired voice. 'I did go to Ruatha. Only . . . I went *back* to Ruatha.'

'Back to Ruatha?' F'lar repeated the words stupidly; the significance momentarily eluded him.

It certainly does, Mnementh agreed and flashed to F'lar's mind the two scenes he had picked out of Ramoth's memory.

Staggered by the import of the visualization, F'lar found himself slowly sinking to the edge of the bed.

'You went *between* times?'

She nodded slowly. The terror was beginning to leave her eyes.

'*Between* times,' F'lar murmured. 'I wonder . . .'

His mind raced through the possibilities. It might well tip the scales of survival in the Weyr's favor. He couldn't think exactly how to use this extraordinary ability, but there *must* be an advantage in it for dragonfolk.

The service shaft rumbled. He took the pitcher from the platform and poured two mugs.

Lessa's hands were shaking so much that she couldn't get hers to her lips. He steadied it for her, wondering if going *between* times would regularly cause this kind of shock. If so, it wouldn't be any advantage at all. If she'd had enough of a scare this day, she might not be so contemptuous of his orders the next time; which would be to his benefit.

Outside in the weyr, Mnementh snorted his opinion on that. F'lar ignored him.

Lessa was trembling violently now. He put an arm

around her, pressing the fur against her slender body. He held the mug to her lips, forcing her to drink. He could feel the tremors ease off. She took long, slow, deep breaths between swallows, equally determined to get herself under control. The moment he felt her stiffen under his arm, he released her. He wondered if Lessa had ever had someone to turn to. Certainly not after Fax invaded her family Hold. She had been only eleven, a child. Had hate and revenge been the only emotions the growing girl had practiced?

She lowered the mug, cradling it in her hands carefully as if it had assumed some undefinable importance to her.

'Now. Tell me,' he ordered evenly.

She took a long deep breath and began to speak, her hands tightening around the mug. Her inner turmoil had not lessened; it was merely under control now.

'Ramoth and I were bored with the weyrling exercises,' she admitted candidly.

Grimly F'lar recognized that, while the adventure might have taught her to be more circumspect, it had not scared her into obedience. He doubted that anything would.

'I gave her the picture of Ruatha so we could go *between* there.' She did not look at him, but her profile was outlined against the dark fur of the rug. 'The Ruatha I knew so well – I accidentally sent myself backward in time to the day Fax invaded.'

Her shock was now comprehensible to him.

'And . . .' he prompted her, his voice carefully neutral.

'And I saw myself –' Her voice broke off. With an effort she continued. 'I had visualized for Ramoth the designs of the firepits and the angle of the Hold if one looked down from the pits into the Inner Court. That was where we emerged. It was just dawn' – she lifted her chin with a nervous jerk – 'and there was no Red Star in the sky.' She gave him a quick, defensive look as if she expected him to contest this detail. 'And I saw men creeping over the firepits, lowering rope ladders to the top windows of the Hold. I saw the Tower guard watching. Just watching.' She clenched her teeth at such treachery, and her eyes gleamed malevolently. 'And I saw myself run from the Hall into the watch-wher's lair. And do you know why' – her voice lowered to a bitter whisper – 'the watch-wher did not alarm the Hold?'

'Why?'

'Because there was a dragon in the sky, and *I*, Lessa of Ruatha, was on her.' She flung the mug from her as if she wished she could reject the knowledge, too. 'Because *I* was there, the watch-wher did not alarm the Hold, thinking the intrusion legitimate, with one of the Blood on a dragon in the sky. So I' – her body grew rigid, her hands clasped so tightly that the knuckles were white – '*I* was the cause of my family's massacre. Not Fax! If I had not acted the captious fool today, I would not have been there with Ramoth and the watch-wher would –'

Her voice had risen to an hysterical pitch of recimination. He slapped her sharply across the cheeks, grabbing her, robe and all, to shake her.

The stunned look in her eyes and the tragedy in her face alarmed him. His indignation over her willfulness disappeared. Her unruly independence of mind and spirit attracted him as much as her curious dark beauty. Infuriating as her fractious ways might be, they were too vital a part of her integrity to be exorcised. Her indomitable will had taken a grievous shock today, and her self-confidence had better be restored quickly.

'On the contrary, Lessa,' he said sternly, 'Fax would still have murdered your family. He had planned it very carefully, even to scheduling his attack on the morning when the Tower guard was one who could be bribed. Remember, too, it was dawn and the watch-wher, being a nocturnal beast, blind by daylight, is relieved of responsibility at dawn and knows it. Your presence, damnable as it may appear to you, was not the deciding factor by any means. It did, and I draw your attention to this very important fact, cause you to save yourself, by warning Lessa-the-child. Don't you see that?'

'I could have called out,' she murmured, but the frantic look had left her eyes and there was a faint hint of normal color in her lips.

'If you wish to flail around in guilt, go right ahead,' he said with deliberate callousness.

Ramoth interjected a thought that, since the two of them had been there that previous time as Fax's men had prepared to invade, it had already happened, so how could it be changed? The act was inevitable both that day and today. For how else could Lessa have lived to come to the

Weyr and impress Ramoth at the hatching?

Mnementh relayed Ramoth's message scrupulously, even to imitating Ramoth's egocentric nuances. F'lar looked sharply at Lessa to see the effect of Ramoth's astringent observation.

'Just like Ramoth to have the final word,' she said with a hint of her former droll humor.

F'lar felt the muscles along his neck and shoulders begin to relax. She'd be all right, he decided, but it might be wiser to make her talk it all out now, to put the whole experience into proper perspective.

'You said you were there twice?' He leaned back on the couch, watching her closely. 'When was the second time?'

'Can't you guess?' she asked sarcastically.

'No,' he lied.

'When else but the dawn I was awakened, feeling the Red Star was a menace to me? . . . Three days before you and Fax came out of the northeast.'

'It would seem,' he remarked dryly, 'that you were your own premonition both times.'

She nodded.

'Have you had any more of these presentiments . . . or should I say reinforced warnings?'

She shuddered but answered him with more of her old spirit.

'No, but if I should, *you* go. I don't want to.'

F'lar grinned maliciously.

'I would, however,' she added, 'like to know why and how it could happen.'

'I've never run across a mention of it anywhere,' he told her candidly. 'Of course, if you have done it – and you undeniably have,' he assured her hastily at her indignant protest, 'it obviously can be done. You say you thought of Ruatha, but you thought of it as it was on that particular day. Certainly a day to be remembered. You thought of spring, before dawn, no Red Star – yes, I remember your mentioning that – so one would have to remember references peculiar to a significant day to return *between* times to the past.'

She nodded slowly, thoughtfully.

'You used the same method the second time, to get to the Ruatha of three Turns ago. Again, of course, it was spring.'

He rubbed his palms together, then brought his hands down on his knees with an emphatic slap and rose to his feet.

'I'll be back,' he said and strode from the room, ignoring her half-articulated cry of warning.

Ramoth was curling up in the Weyr as he passed her. He noticed that her color remained good in spite of the drain on her energies by the morning's exercises. She glanced at him, her many-faceted eye already covered by the inner, protective lid.

Mnementh awaited his rider on the ledge, and the moment F'lar leaped to his neck, took off. He circled upward, hovering above the Star Stone.

You wish to try Lessa's trick, Mnementh said, unperturbed by the prospective experiment.

F'lar stroked the great curved neck affectionately. *You understand how it worked for Ramoth and Lessa?*

As well as anyone can, Mnementh replied with the approximation of a shrug. *When did you have in mind?*

Before that moment F'lar had had no idea. Now, unerringly, his thoughts drew him backward to the summer day R'gul's bronze Hath had flown to mate the grotesque Nemorth, and R'gul had become Weyrleader in place of his dead father, F'lon.

Only the cold of *between* gave them any indication that they had transferred; they were still hovering above the Star Stone. F'lar wondered if they had missed some essential part of the transfer. Then he realized that the sun was in another quarter of the sky and the air was warm and sweet with summer. The Weyr below was empty; there were no dragons sunning themselves on the ledges, no women busy at tasks in the Bowl. Noises impinged on his senses: raucous laughter, yells, shrieks, and a soft crooning noise that dominated the bedlam.

Then, from the direction of the weyrling barracks in the Lower Caverns, two figures emerged – a stripling and a young bronze dragon. The boy's arm lay limply along the beast's neck. The impression that reached the hovering observers was one of utter dejection. The two halted by the lake, the boy peering into the unruffled blue waters, then glancing upward toward the queen's weyr.

F'lar knew the boy for himself, and compassion for that younger self filled him. If only he could reassure that boy, so torn by grief, so filled with resentment, that he would one day become Weyrleader. . . .

Abruptly, startled by his own thoughts, he ordered Mnementh to transfer back. The utter cold of *between* was like a slap in his face, replaced almost instantly as they broke out of *between* into the cold of normal winter.

Slowly, Mnementh flew back down to the queen's weyr, as sobered as F'lar by what they had seen.

'I DON'T know why you insisted that F'nor unearth these ridiculous things from Ista Weyr,' Lessa exclaimed in a tone of exasperation. 'They consist of nothing but trivial notes on how many measures of grain were used to bake daily bread.'

F'lar glanced up at her from the Records he was studying. He sighed, leaned back in his chair in a bone-popping stretch.

'And I used to think,' Lessa said with a rueful expression on her vivid, narrow face, 'that those venerable Records would hold the total sum of all dragonlore and human wisdom. Or so I was led to believe,' she added pointedly.

F'lar chuckled. 'They do, but you have to disinter it.'

Lessa wrinkled her nose. 'Phew. They smell as if we had . . . and the only decent thing to do would be to rebury them.'

'Which is another item I'm hoping to find . . . the old preservative technique that kept the skins from hardening and smelling.'

'It's stupid, anyhow, to use skins for recording. There ought to be something better. We have become, dear Weyrleader, entirely too hidebound.'

While F'lar roared with appreciation of her pun, she regarded him impatiently. Suddenly she jumped up, fired by another of her mercurial moods.

'Well, you won't find it. You won't find the facts you're looking for. Because I know what you're really after, and it isn't recorded!'

'Explain yourself.'

'It's time we stopped hiding a rather brutal truth from ourselves.'

'Which is?'

'Our mutual feeling that the Red Star is a menace and that the Threads *will* come! *We* decided that out of pure conceit and then went back *between* times to particularly crucial points in our lives and strengthened that notion, in our earlier selves. And for you, it was when you decided you were destined' – her voice made the word mocking – 'to become Weyrleader one day.

'Could it be,' she went on scornfully, 'that our ultra-conservative R'gul has the right of it? That there have been no Threads for four hundred Turns because there are no more? And that the reason we have so few dragons is because the dragons sense they are no longer essential to Pern? That we *are* anachronisms as well as parasites?'

F'lar did not know how long he sat looking up at her bitter face or how long it took him to find answers to her probing questions.

'Anything is possible, Weyrwoman,' he heard his voice replying calmly. 'Including the unlikely fact that an eleven-year old, scared stiff, could plot revenge on her family's murderer and – against all odds – succeed.'

She took an involuntary step forward, struck by his unexpected rebuttal. She listened intently.

'I prefer to believe,' he went on inexorably, 'that there is more to life than raising dragons and playing spring games. That is not enough for me. And I have made others look further, beyond self-interest and comfort. I have given them a purpose, a discipline. Everyone, dragonfolk and Holder alike, profits.

'I am not looking in these Records for reassurance. I'm looking for solid facts.

'I can prove, Weyrwoman, that there have been Threads. I can prove that there have been Intervals during which the Weyrs have declined. I can prove that if you sight the Red Star directly bracketed by the Eye Rock at the moment of winter solstice, the Red Star will pass close enough to Pern to throw off Threads. Since I can prove those facts, I believe Pern is in danger. *I* believe . . . not the youngster of fifteen Turns ago. F'lar, the bronze rider, the Weyrleader, believes it!'

He saw her eyes reflecting shadowy doubts, but he

sensed his arguments were beginning to reassure her.

'You felt constrained to believe in me once before,' he went on in a milder voice, 'when I suggested that you could be a Weyrwoman. You believed me and ...' He made a gesture around the weyr as substantiation.

She gave him a weak, humorless smile.

'That was because I had never planned what to do with my life once I did have Fax lying dead at my feet. Of course, being Ramoth's Weyrmate is wonderful, but' – she frowned slightly – 'it isn't enough anymore, either. That's why I wanted so to learn to fly and ...'

'... that's how this argument started in the first place,' F'lar finished for her with a sardonic smile.

He leaned across the table urgently.

'Believe with me, Lessa, until you have cause not to. I respect your doubts. There's nothing wrong in doubting. It sometimes leads to greater faith. But believe with me until spring. If the Threads have not fallen by then ...' He shrugged fatalistically.

She looked at him for a long moment and then inclined her head slowly in agreement.

He tried to suppress the relief he felt at her decision. Lessa, as Fax had discovered, was a ruthless adversary and a canny advocate. Besides these, she was Weyrwoman: essential to his plans.

'Now, let's get back to the contemplation of trivia. They do tell me, you know, time, place, and duration of Thread incursions,' he grinned up at her reassuringly. 'And those facts I must have to make up my timetable?'

'Timetable? But you said you didn't know the time.'

'Not the day to the second when the Threads may spin down. For one thing, while the weather holds so unusually cold for this time of year, the Threads simply turn brittle and blow away like dust. They're harmless. However, when the air is warm, they are viable and ... deadly.' He made fists of both hands, placing one above and to one side of the other. 'The Red Star is my right hand, my left is Pern. The Red Star turns very fast and in the opposite direction from us. It also wobbles erratically.'

'How do you know that?'

'Diagram on the walls of the Fort Weyr Hatching Ground. That was the very first Weyr, you know.'

Lessa smiled sourly. 'I know.'

'So, when the Star makes a pass, the Threads spin off, down toward us, in attacks that last six hours and occur approximately fourteen hours apart.'

'Attacks last six hours?'

He nodded gravely.

'When the Red Star is closets to us. Right now it is just beginning its Pass.'

She frowned.

He rummaged among the skin sheets on the table, and an object dropped to the stone floor with a metallic clatter.

Curious, Lessa bent to pick it up, turning the thin sheet over in her hands.

'What's this?' She ran an exploratory finger lightly across the irregular design on one side.

'I don't know. F'nor brought it back from Fort Weyr. It was nailed to one of the chests in which the Records had been stored. He brought it along, thinking it might be important. Said there was a plate like it just under the Red Star diagram on the wall of the Hatching Ground.'

'This first part is plain enough: "Mother's father's father, who departed for all time *between*, said this was the key to the mystery, and it came to him while doodling: he said that he said: ARRHENIUS? EUREKA! MYCORRHIZA. ..." Of course, that part doesn't make any sense at all,' Lessa snorted. 'It isn't even Pernsese – just babbling, those last three words.'

'I've studied it, Lessa,' F'lar replied, glancing at it again and tipping it toward him to reaffirm his conclusions. 'The only way to depart for all time *between* is to die, right? People just don't fly away on their own, obviously. So it is a death vision, dutifully recorded by a grandchild, who couldn't spell very well either. "Doodling" as the present tense of dying!' He smiled indulgently. 'And as for the rest of it, after the nonsense – like most death visions, it "explains" what everyone has always known. Read on.'

' "Flamethrowing fire lizards to wipe out the spores. Q.E.D."?'

'No help there, either. Obviously just a primitive rejoicing that he is a dragonman, who didn't even know the right word for Threads.' F'lar's shrug was expressive.

Lessa wet one fingertip to see if the patterns were inked on. The metal was shiny enough for a good mirror if she could get rid of the designs. However, the patterns remained smooth and precise.

'Primitive or no, they had a more permanent way of recording their visions that is superior to even the well-preserved skins,' she murmured.

'Well-preserved babblings,' F'lar said, turning back to the skins he was checking for understandable data.

'A badly scored ballad?' Lessa wondered and then dismissed the whole thing. 'The design isn't even pretty.'

F'lar pulled forward a chart that showed overlapping horizontal bands imposed on the projection of Pern's continental mass.

'Here,' he said, 'this represents waves of attack, and this one,' – he pulled forward the second map with vertical bandings – 'shows time zones. So you can see that with a fourteen-hour break only certain parts of Pern are affected in each attack. One reason for spacing of the Weyrs.'

'Six full Weyrs,' she murmured, 'close to three thousand dragons.'

'I'm aware of the statistics,' he replied in a voice devoid of expression. 'It meant no one Weyr was overburdened during the height of the attacks, not that three thousand beasts must be available. However, with these timetables, we can manage until Ramoth's first clutches have matured.'

She turned a cynical look on him. 'You've a lot of faith in one queen's capacity.'

He waved that remark aside impatiently. 'I've more faith, no matter what your opinion is, in the startling repetitions of events in these Records.'

'Ha!'

'I don't mean how many measures for daily bread, Lessa,' he retorted, his voice rising. 'I mean such things as the time such and such a wing was sent out on patrol, how long the patrol lasted, how many riders were hurt. The brooding capacities of queens, during the fifty years a Pass lasts and the Intervals between such Passes. Yes, it tells that. By all I've studied here,' and he pounded emphatically on the nearest stack of dusty, smelly skins, 'Nemorth should have been mating twice a Turn for the last ten. Had she even kept to her paltry twelve a clutch, we'd have two hundred and forty more beasts. . . . Don't interrupt. But we had Jora as Weyrwoman and R'gul as Weyrleader, and we had fallen into planet-wide disfavor during a four hundred

Turn Interval. Well, Ramoth will brood over no measly dozen, and she'll lay a queen egg, mark my words. She will rise often to mate and lay generously. By the time the Red Star is passing closest to us and the attacks become frequent, we'll be ready.'

She stared at him, her eyes wide with incredulity. 'Out of Ramoth?'

'Out of Ramoth and out of the queens she'll lay. Remember, there are Records of Faranth laying sixty eggs at a time, including several queen eggs.'

Lessa could only shake her head slowly in wonder.

' "A strand of silver/In the sky.... With heat, all quickens/And all times fly,' F'lar quoted to her.

'She's got weeks more to go before laying, and then the eggs must hatch ...'

'Been on the Hatching Ground recently? Wear your boots. You'll be burned through sandals.'

She dismissed that with a guttural noise. He sat back, outwardly amused by her disbelief.

'And then you have to make Impression and wait till the riders –' she went on.

'Why do you think I've insisted on older boys? The dragons are mature long before their riders.'

'Then the system is faulty.'

He narrowed his eyes slightly, shaking the stylus at her.

'Dragon tradition started out as a guide... but there comes a time when man becomes too traditional, too – what was it you said? – too hidebound? Yes, it's traditional to use the weyrbred, because it's been convenient. And because this sensitivity to dragons strengthens where both sire and dam are weyrbred. That doesn't mean weybred is best. You, for example ...'

'There's Weyrblood in the Ruathan line,' she said proudly.

'Granted. Take your Naton; he's craftbred from Nabol, yet F'nor tells me he can make Canth understand him.'

'Oh, that's not hard to do,' she interjected.

'What do you mean?' F'lar jumped on her statement.

They were both interrupted by a high-pitched, penetrating whine. F'lar listened intently for a moment and then shrugged, grinning.

'Some green's getting herself chased again.'

'And that's another item these so-called all-knowing

Records of yours never mention. Why is it that only the gold dragon can reproduce?'

F'lar did not suppress a lascivious chuckle.

'Well, for one thing, firestone inhibits reproduction. If they never shewed stone, a green could lay, but at best they produce small beasts, and we need big ones. And, for another thing' – his chuckle rolled out as he went on deliberately, grinning mischievously – 'if the greens could reproduce, considering their amorousness and the numbers we have of them, we'd be up to our ears in dragons in next to no time.'

The first whine was joined by another, and then a low hum throbbed as if carried by the stones of the Weyr itself.

F'lar, his face changing rapidly from surprise to triumphant astonishment, dashed up the passage.

'What's the matter?' Lessa demanded, picking up her skirts to run after him. 'What does that mean?'

The hum, resonating everywhere, was deafening in the echo-chamber of the queen's weyr. Lessa registered the fact that Ramoth was gone. She heard F'lar's boots pounding down the passage to the ledge, a sharp *ta-ta-tat* over the kettledrum booming hum. The whine was so high-pitched now that it was inaudible, but still nerve-racking. Disturbed, frightened, Lessa followed F'lar out.

By the time she reached the ledge, the Bowl was a-whir with dragons on the wing, making for the high entrance to the Hatching Ground. Weyrfolk, riders, women, children, all screaming with excitement, were pouring across the Bowl to the lower entrance to the Ground.

She caught sight of F'lar, charging across to the entrance, and she shrieked at him to wait. He couldn't have heard her across the bedlam.

Fuming because she had the long stairs to descend, then must double back as the stairs faced the feeding grounds at the opposite end of the Bowl from the Hatching Ground, Lessa realized that she, the Weyrwoman, would be the last one there.

Why had Ramoth decided to be secretive about laying? Wasn't she close enough to her own weyrmate to want her with her?

A dragon knows what to do, Ramoth calmly informed Lessa. *You could have told me*, Lessa wailed, feeling much abused. Why, at the time F'lar had been going on largely about

164

huge clutches and three thousand beasts, that infuriating dragon-child had been doing it!

It didn't improve Lessa's temper to have to recall another remark of F'lar's – on the state of the Hatching Grounds. The moment she stepped into the mountain-high cavern, she felt the heat through the soles of her sandals. Everyone was crowded in a loose circle around the far end of the cavern. And everyone was swaying from foot to foot. As Lessa was short to begin with, this only decreased the likelihood of her ever seeing what Ramoth had done.

'Let me through!' she demanded imperiously, pounding on the wide backs of two tall riders.

An aisle was reluctantly opened for her, and she went through, looking neither to her right or left at the excited weyrfolk. She was furious, confused, hurt, and knew she looked ridiculous because the hot sand made her walk with a curious mincing quickstep.

She halted, stunned and wide-eyed at the mass of eggs, and forgot such trivial things as hot feet.

Ramoth was curled around the clutch, looking enormously pleased with herself. She, too, kept shifting, closing and opening a protective wing over her eggs, so that it was difficult to count them.

No one will steal them, silly, so stop fluttering, Lessa advised as she tried to make a tally.

Obediently Ramoth folded her wings. To relieve her maternal anxiety, however, she snaked her head out across the circle of mottled, glowing eggs, looking all around the cavern, flicking her forked tongue in and out.

An immense sigh, like a gust of wind, swept through the cavern. For there, now that Ramoth's wings were furled, gleamed an egg of glowing gold among the mottled ones. A queen egg!

'A queen egg!' The cry went up simultaneously from half a hundred throats. The Hatching Ground rang with cheers, yells, screams, and howls of exultation.

Someone seized Lessa and swung her around in an excess of feeling. A kiss landed in the vicinity of her mouth. No sooner did she recover her footing than she was hugged by someone else – she thought it was Manora – and then pounded and buffeted around in congratulation until she was reeling in a kind of dance between avoiding the celebrants and easing the growing discomfort of her feet.

She broke from the milling revelers and ran across the Ground to Ramoth. Lessa came to a sudden stop before the eggs. They seemed to be pulsing. The shells looked flaccid. She could have sworn they were hard the day she Impressed Ramoth. She wanted to touch one, just to make sure, but dared not.

You may, Ramoth assured her condescendingly. She touched Lessa's shoulder gently with her tongue.

The egg was soft to touch and Lessa drew her hand back quickly, afraid of doing injury.

The heat will harden it, Ramoth said.

'Ramoth, I'm so proud of you,' Lessa sighed, looking adoringly up at the great eyes that shone in rainbows of pride. 'You are the most marvelous queen ever. I do believe you will redragon all the Weyrs. I do believe you will.'

Ramoth inclined her head regally, then began to sway it from side to side over the eggs, protectingly. She began to hiss suddenly, raising from her crouch, beating the air with her wings, before settling back into the sands to lay yet another egg.

The weyrfolk, uncomfortable on the hot sands, were beginning to leave the Hatching Ground now that they had paid tribute to the arrival of the golden egg. A queen took several days to complete her clutch so there was no point to waiting. Seven eggs already lay beside the important golden one, and if there were seven already, this augured well for the eventual total. Wagers were being made and taken even as Ramoth produced her ninth mottled egg.

'Just as I predicted, a queen egg, by the mother of us all,' F'lar's voice said in Lessa's ear. 'And I'll wager there'll be ten bronzes at least.'

She looked up at him, completely in harmony with the Weyrleader at this moment. She was conscious now of Mnementh, crouching proudly on a ledge, gazing fondly at his mate. Impulsively Lessa laid her hand on F'lar's arm

'F'lar, I do believe you.'

'Only now?' F'lar teased her, but his smile was wide and his eyes proud.

Weyrman, watch; Weyrman, learn
Something new in every Turn.
Oldest may be coldest, too.
Sense the right; find the true!

IF F'LAR's orders over the next months caused no end of
discussion and muttering among the weyrfolk, they seemed
to Lessa to be only the logical outcomes of their discussion
after Ramoth had finished laying her gratifying total of
forty-one eggs.

F'lar discarded tradition right and left, treading on
more than R'gul's conservative toes.

Out of perverse distate for outworn doctrines against
which she herself had chafed during R'gul's leadership, and
out of respect for F'lar's intelligence, Lessa backed him
completely. She might not have respected her earlier
promise to him that she would believe with him until spring
if she had not seen his predictions come true, one after
another. These were based, however, not on the premonit-
tions she no longer trusted after her experience *between*
times, but on recorded facts.

As soon as the eggshells hardened and Ramoth had
rolled her special queen egg to one side of the mottled
clutch for attentive brooding, F'lar brought the prospective
riders into the Hatching Ground. Traditionally the candidates saw the eggs for the first time on the day of Impression. To this precedent F'lar added others: very few of the
sixty-odd were weyrbred, and most of them were in their
late teens. The candidates were to get used to the eggs,
touch them, caress them, be comfortable with the notion
that out of these eggs young dragons would hatch, eager
and waiting to be Impressed. F'lar felt that such a practice
might cut down on casualties during Impression when the
boys were simply too scared to move out of the way of the
awkward dragonets.

F'lar also had Lessa persuade Ramoth to let Kylara near
her precious golden egg. Kylara readily enough weaned her
son and spent hours, with Lessa acting as her tutor, beside

the golden egg. Despite Kylara's loose attachment to T'bor, she showed an open preference for F'lar's company. Therefore, Lessa took great pains to foster F'lar's plan for Kylara since it meant her removal, with the new-hatched queen, to Fort Weyr.

F'lar's use of the Hold-born as riders served an additional purpose. Shortly before the actual Hatching and Impression, Lytol, the Warder appointed at Ruath Hold, sent another message.

'The man positively delights in sending bad news,' Lessa remarked as F'lar passed the message skin to her.

'He's gloomy,' F'nor agreed. He had brought the message. 'I feel sorry for that youngster cooped up with such a pessimist.'

Lessa frowned at the brown rider. She still found distasteful any mention of Gemma's son, now Lord of her ancestral Hold. Yet . . . as she had inadvertently caused his mother's death and she could not be Weyrwoman and Lady Holder at the same time, it was fitting that Gemma's Jaxom be Lord of Ruatha.

'I, however,' F'lar said, 'am grateful for his warnings. I suspected Meron would cause trouble again.'

'He has shifty eyes, like Fax's,' Lessa remarked.

'Shifty-eyed or not, he's dangerous,' F'lar answered. 'And I cannot have him spreading rumors that we are deliberately choosing men of the Blood to weaken Family Lines.'

'There are more craftsmen's sons than Holders' boys, in any case,' F'nor snorted.

'I don't like him questioning that the Threads have not appeared,' Lessa said gloomily.

F'lar shrugged. 'They'll appear in due time. Be thankful the weather has continued cold. When the weather warms up and still no Threads appear, then I will worry.' He grinned at Lessa in an intimate reminder of her promise.

F'nor cleared his throat hastily and looked away.

'However,' the Weyrleader went on briskly. 'I can do something about the other accusation.'

So, when it was apparent that the eggs were about to hatch, he broke another long-standing tradition and sent riders to fetch the fathers of the young candidates from craft and Hold.

The great Hatching Cavern gave the appearance of being

almost full as Holder and Weyrfolk watched from the tiers above the heated Ground. This time, Lessa observed, there was no aura of fear. The youthful candidates were tense, yes, but not frightened out of their wits by the rocking, shattering eggs. When the ill-coordinated dragonets awkwardly stumbled – it seemed to Lessa that they deliberately looked around at the eager faces as though pre-Impressed – the youths either stepped to one side or eagerly advanced as a crooning dragonet made his choice. The Impressions were made quickly and with no accidents. All too soon, Lessa thought, the triumphant procession of stumbling dragons and proud new riders moved erratically out of the Hatching Ground to the barracks.

The young queen burst from her shell and moved unerringly for Kylara, standing confidently on the hot sands. The watching beasts hummed their approval.

'It was over too soon,' Lessa said in a disappointed voice that evening to F'lar.

He laughed indulgently, allowing himself a rare evening of relaxation now that another step had gone as planned. The Holder folk had been ridden home, stunned, dazed, and themselves impressed by the Weyr and the Weyrleader.

'That's because you were watching this time,' he remarked, brushing a lock of her hair back. It obscured his view of her profile. He chuckled again. 'You'll notice Naton . . .'

'N'ton,' she corrected him.

'All right, N'ton – Impressed a bronze.'

'Just as you predicted,' she said with some asperity.

'And Kylara is Weyrwoman for Pridith.'

Lessa did not comment on that, and she did her best to ignore his laughter.

'I wonder which bronze will fly her,' he murmured softly.

'It had better be T'bor's Orth,' Lessa said, bridling.

He answered her the only way a wise man could.

Crack dust, blackdust,
Turn in freezing air.
Waste dust, spacedust,
From Red Star bare.

LESSA WOKE abruptly, her head aching, her eyes blurred, her mouth dry. She had the immediate memory of a terrible nightmare that, just as quickly, escaped recall. She brushed her hair out of her face and was surprised to find that she had been sweating heavily.

'F'lar?' she called in an uncertain voice. He had evidently risen early. 'F'lar,' she called again, louder.

He's coming, Mnementh informed her. Lessa sensed that the dragon was just landing on the ledge. She touched Ramoth and found that the queen, too, had been bothered by formless, frightening dreams. The dragon roused briefly and then fell back into deeper sleep.

Disturbed her her vague fears, Lessa rose and dressed, forgoing a bath for the first time since she had arrived at the Weyr.

She called down the shaft for breakfast, then plaited her hair with deft fingers as she waited.

The tray appeared on the shaft platform just as F'lar entered. He kept looking back over his shoulder at Ramoth.

'What's gotten into her?'

'Echoing my nightmare. I woke in a cold sweat.'

'You were sleeping quietly enough when I left to assign patrols. You know, at the rate those dragonets are growing, they're already capable of limited flight. All they do is eat and sleep, and that's . . .'

' . . . what makes a dragon grow,' Lessa finished for him and sipped thoughtfully at her steaming hot *klah*. 'You are going to be extra-careful about their drill procedures, aren't you?'

'You mean to prevent an inadvertent flight *between* times? I certainly am,' he assured her. 'I don't want bored dragon-riders irresponsibly popping in and out.' He gave her a long, stern look.

'Well, it wasn't my fault no one taught me to fly early enough,' she replied in the sweet tone she used when she was being especially malicious. 'If I'd been drilled from the day of Impression to the day of my first flight, I'd never have discovered that trick.'

'True enough,' he said solemnly.

'You know, F'lar, if I discovered it, someone else must have, and someone else may. If they haven't already.'

F'lar drank, making a face as the *klah* scalded his tongue. 'I don't know how to find out discreetly. We would be foolish to think we were the first. It is, after all, an inherent ability in dragons, or you would never have been able to do it.'

She frowned, took a quick breath, and then let it go, shrugging.

'Go on,' he encouraged her.

'Well, isn't it possible that our conviction about the imminence of the Threads could stem from one of us coming back when the Threads are actually falling? I mean . . .'

'My dear girl, we have both analyzed every stray thought and action – even your dream this morning upset you, although it was no doubt due to all the wine you drank last night – until we wouldn't know an honest presentiment if it walked up and slapped us in the face.'

'I can't dismiss the thought that this *between* times ability is of crucial value,' she said emphatically.

'That, my dear Weyrwoman, *is* an honest presentiment.'

'But why?'

'Not why,' he corrected her cryptically. '*When.*' An idea stirred vaguely in the back of his mind. He tried to nudge it out where he could mull it over. Mnementh announced that F'nor was entering the weyr.

'What's the matter with you?' F'lar demanded of his half brother, for F'nor was choking and sputtering, his face red with the paroxysm.

'Dust . . .' he coughed, slapping at his sleeves and chest with his riding gloves. 'Plenty of dust, but no Threads,' he said, describing a wide arc with one arm as he fluttered his fingers suggestively. He brushed his tight wher-hide pants, scowling as a fine black dust drifted off.

F'lar felt every muscle in his body tense as he watched the dust float to the floor.

'Where did you get so dusty?' he demanded.

F'nor regarded him with mild surprise. 'Weather patrol in Tillek. Entire north has been plagued with dust storms lately. But what I came in for . . .' He broke off, alarmed by F'lar's taut immobility. 'What's the matter with dust?' he asked in a baffled voice.

F'lar pivoted on his heel and raced for the stairs to the Record Room. Lessa was right behind him, F'nor belatedly trailing after.

'Tillek, you said?' F'lar barked at his wingsecond. He was clearing the table of stacks for the four charts he then laid out. 'How long have these storms been going on? Why didn't you report them?'

'Report dust storms? You wanted to know about warm air masses.'

'How long have these storms been going on?' Flar's voice crackled.

'Close to a week.'

'*How close?*'

'Six days ago the first storm was noticed in upper Tillek. They have been reported in Bitra, Upper Telgar, Crom, and the High Reaches,' F'nor reported tersely.

He glanced hopefully at Lessa but saw she, too, was staring at the four unusual charts. He tried to see why the horizontal and vertical strips had been superimposed on Pern's land mass, but the reason was beyond him.

F'lar was making hurried notations, pushing first one map and then another away from him.

'Too involved to think straight, to see clearly, to understand,' the Weyrleader snarled to himself, throwing down the stylus angrily.

'You did say only warm air masses,' F'nor heard himself saying humbly, aware that he had somehow failed his Weyrleader.

F'lar shook his head impatiently.

'Not your fault, F'nor. Mine. I should have asked. I knew it was good luck that the weather held so cold.' He put both hands on F'nor's shoulders, looking directly into his eyes. 'The Threads have been falling,' he announced gravely. 'Falling into cold air, freezing into bits to drift on the wind' – F'lar imitated F'nor's finger-fluttering – 'as specks of black dust.'

' "Crack dust, blackdust," ' Lessa quoted. 'In "The

Ballad of Moreta's Ride," the chorus is all about black dust.'

'I don't need to be reminded of Moreta right now,' F'lar growled, bending to the maps. 'She could talk to any dragon in the Weyrs.'

'But I can do that!' Lessa protested.

Slowly, as if he didn't quiet credit his ears, F'lar turned back to Lessa. 'What did you just say?'

'I said I can talk to any dragon in the Weyr.'

Still staring at her, blinking in utter astonishment, F'lar sank down to the table top.

'How long,' he managed to say, 'have you had *this* particular skill?'

Something in his tone, in his manner, caused Lessa to flush and stammer like an erring weyrling.

'I . . . I always could. Beginning with the watch-wher at Ruatha.' She gestured indecisively in Ruatha's westerly direction. 'And I talked to Mnementh at Ruatha. And . . . when I got here, I could . . .' Her voice faltered at the accusing look in F'lar's cold, hard eyes. Accusing and, worse, contemptuous.

'I thought you had agreed to help me, to believe in me.'

'I'm truly sorry, F'lar. It never occurred to me it was of any use to anyone, but . . .'

F'lar exploded onto both feet, his eyes blazing with aggravation.

'The one thing I could not figure out was how to direct the wings and keep in contact with the Weyr during an attack, how I was going to get reinforcements and firestone in time. And you . . . you have been sitting there, spitefully hiding the . . .'

'I am NOT spiteful,' she screamed at him. 'I said I was sorry. I am. But you've a nasty, smug habit of keeping your own council. How was I to know you didn't have the same trick? You're F'lar, the Weyrleader, you can do *anything*. Only you're just as bad as R'gul because you never *tell* me half the things I ought to know . . .'

F'lar reached out and shook her until her angry voice was stopped.

'Enough. We can't waste time arguing like children.' Then his eyes widened, his jaw dropped. 'Waste time? That's it.'

'Go *between* times?' Lessa gasped.

'*Between* times!'

F'nor was totally confused. 'What are you two talking about?'

'The Threads started falling at dawn in Nerat,' F'lar said, his eyes bright, his manner decisive.

F'nor could feel his guts congealing with apprehension. At dawn in Nerat? Why, the rainforests would be demolished. He could feel a surge of adrenalin charging through his body at the thought of danger.

'So we're going *back* there, *between* times, and be there when the Threads started falling, two hours ago. F'nor, the dragons can go not only where we direct them but *when*.'

'Where? When?' F'nor repeated, bewildered. 'That could be dangerous.'

'Yes, but today it will save Nerat. Now, Lessa,' and F'lar gave her another shake, compounded of pride and affection, 'order out all the dragons, young, old, any that can fly. Tell them to load themselves down with firestone sacks. I don't know if you can talk across time . . .'

'My dream this morning . . .'

'Perhaps. But right now rouse the Weyr.' He pivoted to F'nor. 'If Threads are falling . . . were falling . . . at Nerat at dawn, they'll be falling on Keroon and Ista right now, because they are in that time pattern. Take two wings to Keroon. Arouse the plains. Get them to start the firepits blazing. Take some weyrlings with you and send them on to Igen and Ista. Those Holds are not in as immediate danger as Keroon. I'll reinforce you as soon as I can. And . . . keep Canth in touch with Lessa.'

F'lar clapped his brother on the shoulder and sent him off. The brown rider was too used to taking orders to argue.

'Mnementh says R'gul is duty officer and R'gul wants to know . . .' Lessa began.

'C'mon, girl,' F'lar said, his eyes brilliant with excitement. He grabbed up his maps and propelled her up the stairs.

They arrived in the weyr just as R'gul entered with T'sum. R'gul was muttering about this unusual summons.

'Hath told me to report,' he complained. 'Fine thing when your own dragon . . .'

'R'gul, T'sum mount your wings. Arm them with all the firestone they can carry, and assemble above Star Stone. I'll join you in a few minutes. We go to Nerat at dawn.'

'Nerat? I'm watch officer, not patrol . . .'

'This is no patrol,' F'lar cut him off.

'But, sir,' T'sum interrupted, his eyes wide, 'Nerat's dawn was two hours ago, the same as ours.'

'And that is *when* we are going to, brown rider. The dragons, we have discovered, can go *between* places temporally as well as geographically. At dawn Threads fell at Nerat. We're going back, *between* time, to sear them from the sky.'

F'lar paid no attention to R'gul's stammered demand for explanation. T'sum, however, grabbed up firestone sacks and raced back to the ledge and his waiting Munth.

'Go on, you old fool,' Lessa told R'gul irascibly. 'The Threads are here. You were wrong. Now be a dragonman! Or go *between* and stay there!'

Ramoth, awakened by the alarms, poked at R'gul with her man-sized head, and the ex-Weyrleader came out of his momentary shock. Without a word he followed T'sum down the passageway.

F'lar had thrown on his heavy wher-hide tunic and shoved on his riding boots.

'Lessa, be sure to send messages to all the Holds. Now, this attack will stop about four hours from now. So the farthest west it can reach will be Ista. But I want every Hold and craft warned.'

She nodded, her eyes intent on his face lest she miss a word.

'Fortunately, the Star is just beginning its Pass, so we won't have to worry about another attack for a few days. I'll figure out the next one when I get back.

'Now, get Manora to organize her women. We'll need pails of ointment. The dragons are going to be laced, and that hurts. Most important, if something goes wrong, you'll have to wait till a bronze is at least a year old to fly Ramoth . . .'

'No one's flying Ramoth but Mnementh,' she cried, her eyes sparkling fiercely.

F'lar crushed her against him, his mouth bruising hers as if all her sweetness and strength must come with him. He released her so abruptly that she staggered back against Ramoth's lowered head. She clung for a moment to her dragon, as much for support as for reassurance.

That is, if Mnementh can catch me, Ramoth amended smugly.

Wheel and turn
Or bleed and burn.
Fly *between*,
Blue and green.
Soar, dive down,
Bronze and brown
Dragonmen must fly
When Threads are in the sky.

As F'LAR raced down the passageway to the ledge, fire-sacks bumping against his thighs, he was suddenly grateful for the tedious sweeping patrols over every Hold and hollow of Pern. He could see Nerat clearly in his mind's eye. He could see the many-petaled vineflowers which were the distinguishing feature of the rainforests at this time of year. Their ivory blossoms would be glowing in the first beams of sunlight like dragon eyes among the tall, wide-leaved plants.

Mnementh, his eyes flashing with excitement, hovered skittishly over the ledge. F'lar vaulted to the bronze neck.

The Weyr was seething with wings of all colors, noisy with shouts and countercommands. The atmosphere was electric, but F'lar could sense no panic in that ordered confusion. Dragon and human bodies oozed out of opening around the Bowl walls. Women scurried across the floor from one Lower Cavern to another. The children playing by the lake were sent to gather wood for a fire. The weyrlings, supervised by old C'gan, were forming outside their barracks. F'lar looked up to the Peak and approved the tight formation of the wings assembled there in close flying order. Another wing formed up as he watched. He recognized brown Canth, F'nor on his neck, just as the entire wing vanished.

He ordered Mnementh aloft. The wind was cold and carried a hint of moisture. A late snow? This was the time for it, if ever.

R'gul's wing and T'bor's fanned out on his left, T'sum and D'nol on his right. He noted each dragon was well-laden with sacks. Then he gave Mnementh the visualization of the early spring rainforest in Nerat, just before dawn, the vineflowers gleaming, the sea breaking against the rocks of the High Shoal. . . .

He felt the searing cold of *between*. And he felt a stab of doubt. Was he injudicious, sending them all possibly to their deaths *between* times in this effort to outtime the Threads at Nerat?

Then they were all there, in the crepuscular light that promises day. The lush, fruity smells of the rainforest drifted up to them. Warm, too, and that was frightening. He looked up and slightly to the north. Pulsing with menace, the Red Star shone down.

The men had realized what had happened, their voices raised in astonishment. Mnementh told F'lar that the dragons were mildly surprised at their riders' fuss.

'Listen to me, dragonriders,' F'lar called, his voice harsh and distorted in an effort to be heard by all. He waited till the men had moved as close as possible. He told Mnementh to pass the information on to each dragon. Then he explained what they had done and why. No one spoke, but there were many nervous looks exchanged across bright wings.

Crisply he ordered the dragonriders to fan out in a staggered formation, keeping a distance of five wings' spread up or down.

The sun came up.

Slanting across the sea, like an ever-thickening mist, Threads were falling, silent, beautiful, treacherous. Silvery gray were those space-traversing spores, spinning from hard frozen ovals into coarse filaments as they penetrated the warm atmospheric envelope of Pern. Less than mindless, they had been ejected from their barren planet toward Pern, a hideous rain that sought organic matter to nourish it into growth. One Thread, sinking into fertile soil, would burrow deep, propagating thousands in the warm earth, rendering it into a black-dusted wasteland. The southern continent of Pern had already been sucked dry. The true parasites of Pern were Threads.

A stifled roar from the throats of eighty men and dragons broke the dawn air above Nerat's green heights – as if the Threads might hear this challenge, F'lar mused.

As one, dragons swiveled their wedge-shaped heads to their riders for firestone. Great jaws macerated the hunks. The fragments were swallowed and more firestone was demanded. Inside the beasts, acids churned and the poisonous

177

phosphines were readied. When the dragons belched forth gas, it would ignite in the air into ravening flame to sear the Threads from the sky. And burn them from the soil.

Dragon instinct took over the moment the Threads began to fall above Nerat's shores.

As much admiration as F'lar had always held for his bronze companion, it achieved newer heights in the next hours. Beating the air in great strokes, Mnementh soared with flaming breath to meet the down-rushing menace. The fumes, swept back by the wind, choked F'lar until he thought to crouch low on the lea side of the bronze neck. The dragon squealed as a Thread flicked the tip of one wing. Instantly F'lar and he ducked into *between*, cold, calm, black. The frozen Thread cracked off. In the flicker of an eye, they were back to face the reality of Threads.

Around him F'lar saw dragons winking in and out of *between*, flaming as they returned, diving, soaring. As the attack continued and they drifted across Nerat, F'lar began to recognize the pattern in the dragons' instinctive evasion-attack movements. And in the Threads. For, contrary to what he had gathered from his study of the Records, the Threads fell in patches. Not as rain will, in steady unbroken sheets, but like flurries of snow, here, above, there, whipped to one side suddenly. Never fluidly, despite the continuity their name implied.

You could see a patch above you. Flaming, your dragon would rise. You'd have the intense joy of seeing the clump shrivel from bottom to top. Sometimes, a patch would fall between riders. One dragon would signal he would follow and, spouting flame, would dive and sear.

Gradually the dragonriders worked their way over the rainforests, so densely, so invitingly green. F'lar refused to dwell on what just one live Thread burrow would do to that lush land. He would send back a low-flying patrol to quarter every foot. One Thread, just one Thread, could put out the ivory eyes of every luminous vineflower.

A dragon screamed somewhere to his left. Before he could identify the beast, it had ducked *between*. F'lar heard other cries of pain, from men as well as dragons. He shut his ears and concentrated, as dragons did, on the here-and-now. Would Mnementh remember those piercing cries later? F'lar wished he could forget them now.

He, F'lar, the bronze rider, felt suddenly superfluous. It

was the dragons who were fighting this engagement. You encouraged your beast, comforted him when the Threads burned, but you depended on his instinct and speed.

Hot fire dripped across F'lar's cheek, burrowing like acid into his shoulder ... a cry of surprised agony burst from F'lar's lips. Mnementh took them to merciful *between*. The dragonman battled with frantic hands at the Threads, felt them crumble in the intense cold of *between* and break off. Revolted, he slapped at injuries still afire. Back in Nerat's humid air, the sting seemed to ease. Mnementh crooned comfortingly and then dove at a patch, breathing fire.

Shocked at self-consideration, F'lar hurriedly examined his mount's shoulder for telltale score marks.

I duck very quickly, Mnementh told him and veered away from a dangerously close clump of Threads. A brown dragon followed them down and burned them to ash.

It might have been moments, it might have been a hundred hours later when F'lar looked down in surprise at the sunlit sea. Threads now dropped harmlessly into the salty waters. Nerat was to the east of him on his right, the rocky tip curling westward.

F'lar felt weariness in every muscle. In the excitement of frenzied battle, he had forgotten the bloody scores on cheek and shoulder. Now, as he and Mnementh glided slowly, the injuries ached and stung.

He flew Mnementh high and when they had achieved sufficient altitude, they hovered. He could see no Threads falling landward. Below him, the dragons ranged, high and low, searching for any sign of a burrow, alert for any suddenly toppling trees or disturbed vegetation.

'Back to the Weyr,' he ordered Mnementh with a heavy sigh. He heard the bronze relay the command even as he himself was *between*. He was so tired he did not even visualize where – much less, when – relying on Mnementh's instinct to bring him safely home through time and space.

Honor those the dragons heed,
In thought and favor, word and deed.
Worlds are lost or worlds are saved
From those dangers dragon-braved.

CRANING HER neck toward the Star Stone at Benden Peak, Lessa watched from the ledge until she saw the four wings disappear from view.

Sighing deeply to quiet her inner fears, Lessa raced down the stairs to the floor of Benden Weyr. She noticed that someone was building a fire by the lake and that Manora was already ordering her women around, her voice clear but calm.

Old C'gan had the weyrlings lined up. She caught the envious eyes of the newest dragonriders at the barracks windows. They'd have time enough to fly a flaming dragon. From what F'lar had intimated, they'd have Turns.

She shuddered as she stepped up to the weyrlings but managed to smile at them. She gave them their orders and sent them off to warn the Holds, checking quickly with each dragon to be sure the rider had given clear references. The Holds would shortly be stirred up to a froth.

Canth told her that there were Threads at Keroon, falling on the Keroon side of Nerat Bay. He told her that F'nor did not think two wings were enough to protect the meadowlands.

Lessa stopped in her tracks, trying to think how many wings were already out.

K'net's wing is still here, Ramoth informed her. *On the Peak.*

Lessa glanced up and saw bronze Piyanth spread his wings in answer. She told him to get *between* to Keroon, close to Nerat Bay. Obediently the entire wing rose and then disappeared.

She turned with a sigh to say something to Manora when a rush of wind and a vile stench almost overpowered her. The air above the Weyr was full of dragons. She was about to demand of Piyanth why he hadn't gone to Keroon when she realized there were far more beasts a-wing than K'net's twenty.

But you just left, she cried as she recognized the unmistakable bulk of bronze Mnementh.

That was two hours ago for us, Mnementh said with such weariness in his tone that Lessa closed her eyes in sympathy.

Some dragons were gliding in fast. From their awkwardness it was evident that they were hurt.

As one, the women grabbed salve pots and clean rags and beckoned the injured down. The numbing ointment was smeared on score marks where wings resembled black and red lace.

No matter how badly injured he might be, every rider tended his beast first.

Lessa kept one eye on Mnementh, sure that F'lar would not keep the huge bronze hovering like that if he'd been hurt. She was helping T'sum with Munth's cruelly pierced right wing when she realized the sky above the Star Stone was empty.

She forced herself to finish with Munth before she went to find the bronze and his rider. When she did locate them, she also saw Kylara smearing salve on F'lar's cheek and shoulder. She was advancing purposefully across the sands toward the pair when Canth's urgent plea reached her. She saw Mnementh's head swing upward as he, too, caught the brown's thought.

'F'lar, Canth says they need help,' Lessa cried. She didn't notice then that Kylara slipped away into the busy crowd.

F'lar wasn't badly hurt. She reassured herself about that. Kylara had treated the wicked burns that seemed to be shallow. Someone had found him another fur to replace the tatters of the Thread-bared one. He frowned – and winced because the frown creased his burned cheek. He gulped hurriedly at his *klah*.

Mnementh, what's the tally of able-bodied? Oh, never mind, just get 'em aloft with a full load of firestone.

'You're all right?' Lessa asked, a detaining hand on his arm. He couldn't just go off like this, could he?

He smiled tiredly down at her, pressed his empty mug into her hands, giving them a quick squeeze. Then he vaulted to Mnementh's neck. Someone handed him a heavy load of sacks.

Blue, green, brown, and bronze dragons lifted from the Weyr Bowl in quick order. A trifle more than sixty dragons hovered briefly above the Weyr where eighty had lingered so few minutes before.

So few dragons. So few riders. How long could they take such toll?

Canth said F'nor needed more firestone.

She looked about anxiously. None of the weyrlings were back yet from their messenger rounds. A dragon was crooning plaintively, and she wheeled, but it was only young Pridith, stumbling across the Weyr to the feeding grounds, butting playfully at Kylara as they walked. The only other dragons were injured or – her eye fell on C'gan, emerging from the weyrling barracks.

'C'gan, can you and Tagath get more firestone to F'nor at Keroon?'

'Of course,' the old blue rider assured her, his chest lifting with pride, his eyes flashing. She hadn't thought to send him anywhere, yet he had lived his life in training for this emergency. He shouldn't be deprived of a chance of it.

She smiled her approval at his eagerness as they piled heavy sacks on Tagath's neck. The old blue dragon snorted and danced as if he were young and strong again. She gave them the references Canth had visualized to her.

She watched as the two blinked out above the Star Stone.

It isn't fair. They have all the fun, said Ramoth peevishly. Lessa saw her sunning herself on the Weyr ledge, preening her enormous wings.

'You chew firestone and you're reduced to a silly green,' Lessa told her Weyrmate sharply. She was inwardly amused by the queen's disgruntled complaint.

Lessa passed among the injured then. B'fol's dainty green beauty moaned and tossed her head, unable to bend one wing that had been threaded to bare cartilage. She'd be out for weeks, but she had the worst injury among the dragons. Lessa looked quickly away from the misery in B'fol's worried eyes.

As she did the rounds, she realized that more men were injured than beasts. Two in R'gul's wing had sustained serious head damages. One man might los an eye completely. Manora had dosed him unconscious with numb-weed. Another man's arm had been burned clear to the bone. Minor though most of the wounds were, the tally dismayed

Lessa. How many more would be disabled at Keroon?

Out of one hundred and seventy-two dragons, fifteen already were out of action, some only for a day or two, however.

A thought struck Lessa. If N'ton had actually ridden Canth, maybe he could ride out on the next dragonade on an injured man's beast, since there were more injured riders than dragons. F'lar broke traditions as he chose. Here was another one to set aside – if the dragon was agreeable.

Presuming N'ton was not the only new rider able to transfer to another beast, what good would such flexibility do in the long run? F'lar had definitely said the incursions would not be so frequent at first, when the Red Star was just beginning its fifty-Turn long circling pass of Pern. How frequent was frequent? He would know, but he wasn't here.

Well, he *had* been right this morning about the appearance of Threads at Nerat, so his exhaustive study of those old Records had proved worthwhile.

No, that wasn't quite accurate. He had forgotten to have the men alert for signs of black dust as well as warming weather. As he had put the matter right by going *between* times, she would graciously allow him that minor error. But he did have an infuriating habit of guessing correctly. Lessa corrected herself again. He didn't guess. He studied. He planned. He thought and then he used common good sense. Like figuring out where and when Threads would strike according to entries in those smelly Records. Lessa began to feel better about their future.

Now, if he would just make the riders learn to trust their dragons' sure instinct in battle, they would keep casualties down, too.

A shriek pierced air and ear as a blue dragon emerged above the Star Stone.

Ramoth! Lessa screamed in an instinctive reaction, hardly knowing why. The queen was a-wing before the echo of her command had died. For the careening blue was obviously in grave trouble. He was trying to brake his forward speed, yet one wing would not function. His rider had slipped forward over the great shoulder, precariously clinging to his dragon's neck with one hand.

Lessa, her hands clapped over her mouth, watched

fearfully. There wasn't a sound in the Bowl but the flapping of Ramoth's immense wings. The queen rose swiftly to position herself against the desperate blue, lending him wing support on the crippled side.

The watchers gasped as the rider slipped, lost his hold, and fell – landing on Ramoth's wide shoulders.

The blue dropped like a stone. Ramoth came to a gentle stop near him, crouching low to allow the weyrfolk to remove her passenger.

It was C'gan.

Lessa felt her stomach heave as she saw the ruin the Threads had made of the old harper's face. She dropped beside him, pillowing his head in her lap. The weyrfolk gathered in a respectful, silent circle.

Manora, her face, as always, serene, had tears in her eyes. She knelt and placed her hand on the old rider's heart. Concern flickered in her eyes as she looked up at Lessa. Slowly she shook her head. Then, setting her lips in a thin line, she began to apply the numbing salve.

'Too toothless old to flame and too slow to get *between*,' C'gan, mumbled, rolling his head from side to side. 'Too old. But 'Dragonmen must fly/ when Threads are in the sky. . . .' His voice trailed off into a sigh. His eyes closed.

Lessa and Manora looked at each other in anguish. A terrible, ear-shattering note cut the silence. Tagath sprang aloft in a tremendous leap. C'gan's eyes rolled slowly open, sightless. Lessa, breath suspended, watched the blue dragon, trying to deny the inevitable as Tagath disappeared in mid-air.

A low moan sprang up around the Weyr, like the torn, lonely cry of a keening wind. The dragons uttered tribute.

'Is he . . . gone?' Lessa asked, although she knew.

Manora nodded slowly, tears streaming down her cheeks as she reached over to close C'gan's dead eyes.

Lessa rose slowly to her feet, motioning to some of the women to remove the old rider's body. Absently she rubbed her bloody hands dry on her skirts, trying to concentrate on what might be needed next.

Yet her mind turned back to what had just happened. A dragonrider had died. His dragon, too. The Threads had claimed one pair already. How many more would die this cruel Turn? How long could the Weyr survive? Even after Ramoth's forty matured, and the ones she soon would conceive, and her queen-daughters, too?

Lessa walked apart to quiet her uncertainties and ease her grief. She saw Ramoth wheel and glide aloft, to land on the Peak. One day soon would Lessa see those golden wings laced red and black from Thread marks? Would Ramoth ... disappear?

No, Ramoth would not. Not while Lessa lived.

F'lar had told her long ago that she must learn to look beyond the narrow confines of Hold Ruatha and mere revenge. He was, as usual, right. As Weyrwoman under his tutelage, she had further learned that living *was* more than raising dragons and Spring Games. Living was struggling to do something impossible – to succeed, or die, knowing you had tried!

Lessa realized that she had, at last, fully accepted her role: as Weyrwoman and as mate, to help F'lar shape men and events for many Turns to come – to secure Pern against the Threads.

Lessa threw back her shoulders and lifted her chin high.

Old C'gan had had the right of it.

Dragomen *must* fly
When Threads are in the sky!

Worlds are lost or worlds are saved
By those dangers dragon-braved.

As F'LAR had predicted, the attack ended by high noon, and weary dragons and riders were welcomed by Ramoth's high-pitched trumpeting from the Peak.

Once Lessa assured herself that F'lar had taken no additional injury, that F'nor's were superficial and that Manora was keeping Kylara busy in the kitchens, she applied herself to organizing the care of the injured and the comfort of the worried.

As dusk fell, an uneasy peace settled on the Weyr – the quiet of minds and bodies too tired or too hurtful to talk. Lessa's own words mocked her as she made out the list of wounded men and beasts. Twenty-eight men or dragons were out of the air for the next Thread battle. C'gan was the only fatality, but there had been four more seriously injured dragons at Keroon and seven badly scored men, out of action entirely for months to come.

Lessa crossed the Bowl to her Weyr, reluctant but resigned to giving F'lar this unsettling news.

She expected to find him in the sleeping room, but it was vacant. Ramoth was asleep already as Lessa passed her on the way to the Council Room – also empty. Puzzled and a little alarmed, Lessa half-ran down the steps to the Records Room, to find F'lar, haggard of face, poring over musty skins.

'What are you doing here?' she demanded angrily. 'You ought to be asleep.'

'So should you,' he drawled, amused.

'I was helping Manora settle the wounded . . .'

'Each to his own craft,' But he did lean back from the table, rubbing his neck and rotating the uninjured shoulder to ease stiffened muscles.

'I couldn't sleep,' he admitted, 'so I thought I'd see what answers I might turn up in the Records.'

'More answers? To what?' Lessa cried, exasperated with him. As if the Records ever answered anything. Obviously the tremendous responsibilities of Pern's defense against the Threads were beginning to tell on the Weyrleader. After all, there had been the stress of the first battle, not to mention the drain of the traveling *between* time itself to get to Nerat to forestall the Threads.

F'lar grinned and beckoned Lessa to sit beside him on the wall bench.

'I need the answer to the very pressing question of how one understrength Weyr can do the fighting of six.'

Lessa fought the panic that rose, a cold flood, from her guts.

'Oh, your time schedules will take care of that,' she replied gallantly. 'You'll be able to conserve the dragon-power until the new forty can join the ranks.'

F'lar raised a mocking eyebrow.

'Let us be honest between ourselves, Lessa.'

'But there have been Long Intervals before,' she argued, 'and since Pern survived them, Pern can again.'

'Before there were always six Weyrs. And twenty or so Turns before the Red Star was due to begin its Pass, the queens would start to produce enormous clutches. All the queens, not just one faithful golden Ramoth. Oh, how I curse Jora!' He slammed to his feet and started pacing, irritably brushing the lock of black hair that fell across his eyes.

Lessa was torn with the desire to comfort him and the sinking, choking fear in her belly that made it difficult to think at all.

'You were not so doubtful . . .'

He whirled back to her. 'Not until I had actually had an encounter with the Threads and reckoned up the numbers of injuries. That sets the odds against us. Even supposing we can mount other riders to uninjured dragons, we will be hard put to keep a continuously effective force in the air and still maintain a ground guard.' He caught her puzzled frown. 'There's Nerat to be gone over on foot tomorrow. I'd be a fool indeed if I thought we'd caught and seared every Thread in mid-air.'

'Get the Holders to to that. They can't just immure

themselves safely in their Inner Holds and let us do all. If they hadn't been so miserly and stupid . . .'

He cut off her complaint with an abrupt gesture. 'They'll do their part all right,' he assured her. 'I'm sending for a full Council tomorrow, all Hold Lords and all Craftmasters. But there's more to it than just marking where Threads fall. How do you destroy a burrow that's gone deep under the surface? A dragon's breath is fine for the air and surface work but no good three feet down.'

'Oh, I hadn't thought of that aspect. But the firepits . . .'

'. . . are only on the heights and around human habitations, not on the meadowlands of Keroon or on Nerat's so green rainforests.'

This consideration was daunting indeed. She gave a rueful little laugh.

'Shortsighted of me to suppose our dragons are all poor Pern needs to dispatch the Threads. Yet . . .' She shrugged expressively.

'There are other methods,' F'lar said, 'or there were. There must have been. I have run across frequent mention that the Holds were organizing ground groups and that they were armed with fire. What kind is never mentioned because it was so well-known.' He threw up his hands in disgust and sagged back down on the bench. 'Not even five hundred dragons could have seared all the Threads that fell today. Yet *they* managed to keep Pern Thread-free.'

'Pern, yes, but wasn't the Southern Continent lost? Or did they just have their hands too full with Pern itself?'

'No one's bothered with the Southern Continent in a hundred thousand Turns.' F'lar snorted.

'It's on the maps,' Lessa reminded him.

He scowled disgustedly at the Records, piled in uncommunicative stacks on the long table.

'The answer must be there. Somewhere.'

There was an edge of desperation in his voice, the hint that he held himself to blame for not having discovered those elusive facts.

'Half those things couldn't be read by the man who wrote them,' Lessa said tartly. 'Besides that, it's been your *own* ideas that have helped us most so far. You compiled the time maps, and look how valuable they have been already.'

'I'm getting too hidebound again, huh?' he asked, a

half smile tugging at one corner of his mouth.

'Undoubtedly,' she assured him with more confidence than she felt. 'We both know the Records are guilty of the most ridiculous omissions.'

'Well said, Lessa. So let us forget these misguiding and antiquated precepts and think up our own guides. First, we need more dragons. Second, we need them now. Third, we need something as effective as a flaming dragon to destroy Threads which have burrowed.'

'Fourth, we need sleep, or we won't be able to think of anything,' she added with a touch of her usual asperity.

F'lar laughed outright, hugging her.

'You've got your mind on one thing, haven't you?' he teased, his hands caressing her eagerly.

She pushed ineffectually at him, trying to escape. For a wounded, tired man, he was remarkably amorous. One with that Kylara. Imagine that woman's presumption, dressing his wounds.

'My responsibility as Weyrwoman includes care of you, the Weyrleader.'

'But you spend hours with blue dragonriders and leave me to Kylara's tender ministrations.'

'You didn't look as if you objected.'

F'lar threw back his head and roared. 'Should I open Fort Weyr and send Kylara on?' he taunted her.

'I'd as soon Kylara were Turns as well as miles away from here,' Lessa snapped, thoroughly irritated.

F'lar's jaw dropped, his eyes widened. He leaped to his feet with an astonished cry.

'You've said it!'

'Said what?'

'Turns away! That's it. We'll send Kylara back, *between* times, with her queen and the new dragonets.' F'lar excitedly paced the room while Lessa tried to follow his reasoning. 'No, I'd better send at least one of the older bronzes. F'nor, too . . . I'd rather have F'nor in charge. . . . Discreetly, of course –'

'Send Kylara back . . . where to? When to?' Lessa interrupted him.

'Good point.' F'lar dragged out the ubiquitous charts. 'Very good point. Where can we send them around here without causing anomalies by being present at one of the other Weyrs? The High Reaches are remote. No, we've found remains of fires there, you know, still warm, and no inkling as to who built them or why. And if we had already sent them back, they'd've been ready for today, and they weren't. So they can't have been in two places already. . . .' He shook his head, dazed by the paradoxes.

Lessa's eyes were drawn to the blank outline of the neglected Southern Continent.

'Send them there,' she suggested sweetly, pointing.

'There's nothing there.'

'They bring in what they need. There must be water, for Threads can't devour that. We fly in whatever else is needed, fodder for the herdbeasts, grain. . . .'

F'lar drew his brows together in concentration, his eyes sparkling with thought, the depression and defeat of a few moments ago forgotten.

'Threads wouldn't be there ten Turns ago. And haven't been there for close to four hundred. Ten Turns would give Pridith time to mature and have several clutches. Maybe more queens.'

Then he frowned and shook his head dubiously. 'No, there's no Weyr there. No Hatching Ground, no . . .'

'How do we know that?' Lessa caught him up sharply, too delighted with many aspects of this project to give it up easily. 'The Records don't mention the Southern Continent, true, but they omit a great deal. How do we know it isn't green again in the four hundred Turns since the Threads last spun? We do know that Threads can't last long unless there is something organic on which to feed and that once they've devoured all, they dry up and blow away.'

F'lar looked at her admiringly. 'Now, why hasn't someone wondered about that before?'

'Too hidebound.' Lessa wagged her finger at him. 'Besides, there's been no need to bother with it.'

'Necessity – or is it jealousy? – hatches many a tough shell.' There was a smile of pure malice on his face, and Lessa whirled away as he reached for her.

'The good of the Weyr,' she retorted.

'Furthermore, I'll send you along with F'nor tomorrow to look. Only fair, since it is your idea.'

Lessa stood still. 'You're not going?'

'I feel confident I can leave this project in your very capable, interested hands.' He laughed and caught her against his uninjured side, smiling down at her, his eyes glowing. 'I must play ruthless Weyrleader and keep the Hold Lords from slamming shut their Inner Doors. And I'm hoping' – he raised his head, frowning slightly – 'one of the Craftmasters may know the solution to the third problem – getting rid of Thread burrows.

'But . . .'

'The trip will give Ramoth something to stop her fuming.' He pressed the girl's slender body more closely to him, his full attention at last on her odd, delicate face. 'Lessa, you are my fourth problem.' He bent to kiss her.

At the sound of hurried steps in the passageway, F'lar scowled irritably, releasing her.

'At this hour?' he muttered, ready to reprove the intruder scathingly. 'Who goes there?'

'F'lar?' It was F'nor's voice, anxious, hoarse.

The look on F'lar's face told Lessa that not even his half brother would be spared a reprimand, and it pleased her irrationally. But the moment F'nor burst into the room, both Weyrleader and Weyrwoman were stunned silent. There was something subtly wrong with the brown rider. And as the man blurted out his incoherent message, the difference suddenly registered in Lessa's mind. He was tanned! He wore no bandages and hadn't the slightest trace of the Thread-mark along his cheek that she had tended this evening!

'F'lar, it's not working out! You can't be alive in two times at once!' F'nor was exclaiming distractedly. He staggered against the wall, grabbing the sheer rock to hold himself upright. There were deep circles under his eyes, visible despite the tan. 'I don't know how much longer we can last like this. We're all affected. Some days not as badly as others.'

'I don't understand.'

'Your dragons are all right,' F'nor assured the Weyrleader with a bitter laugh. 'It doesn't bother them. They keep all their wits about them. But their riders . . . all the weyrfolk . . . we're shadows, half alive, like dragonless men, part of us gone forever. Except Kylara.' His face contorted with intense dislike. 'All she wants to do is go back and watch herself. The woman's egomania will destroy us all, I'm afraid.'

His eyes suddenly lost focus, and he swayed wildly. His eyes widened, and his mouth fell open. 'I can't stay. I'm here already. Too close. Makes it twice as bad. But I had to warn you. I promise, F'lar, we'll stay as long as we can, but it won't be much longer . . . so it won't be long enough, but we tried. We tried!'

Before F'lar could move, the brown rider whirled and ran, half-crouched, from the room.

'But he hasn't gone yet!' Lessa gasped. 'He hasn't even gone yet!'

Part IV - The Cold Between

F'lar stared after his half brother, his brows contracting with the keen anxiety he felt.

'What can have happened?' Lessa demanded of the Weyrleader. 'We haven't even told F'nor. We ourselves just finished considering the idea.' Her hand flew to her own cheek. 'And the Thread-mark – I dressed it myself tonight – it's gone. Gone. So he's been gone a long while.' She sank down to the bench.

'However, he has come back. So he did go,' F'lar remarked slowly in a reflective tone of voice. 'Yet we now know the venture is not entirely successful even before it begins. And knowing this, we have sent him back ten Turns for whatever good it is doing.' F'lar paused thoughtfully. 'Consequently we have no alternative but to continue with the experiment.'

'But what could be going wrong?'

'I think I know and there is no remedy.' He sat down beside her, his eyes intent on hers. 'Lessa, you were very upset when you got back from going *between* to Ruatha that first time. But I think now it was more than just the shock of seeing Fax's men invading your own Hold or in thinking your return might have been responsible for that disaster. I think it has to do with being in two times at once.' He hesitated again, trying to understand this immense new concept even as he voiced it.

Lessa regarded him with such awe that he found himself laughing with embarrassment.

'It's unnerving under any conditions,' he went on, 'to think of returning and seeing a younger self.'

'That must be what he meant about Kylara,' Lessa gasped, 'about her wanting to go back and watch herself . . . as a child. Oh, that wretched girl!' Lessa was filled with anger for Kylara's self-absorption. 'Wretched, selfish creature. She'll ruin everything.'

'Not yet,' F'lar reminded her. 'Look, although F'nor warned us that the situation in his time is getting desperate, he didn't tell us how much he was able to accomplish. But you noticed that his scar had healed to invisibility – consequently some Turns must have elapsed. Even if Pridith lays only one good-sized clutch, even if just the forty of Ramoth's are mature enough to fight in three days' time, we have accomplished something. Therefore, Weyrwoman,' and he noticed how she straightened up at the sound of her title, 'we must disregard F'nor's return. When you fly to the Southern Continent tomorrow, make no allusion to it. Do you understand?'

Lessa nodded gravely and then gave a little sigh. 'I don't know if I'm happy or disappointed to realize, even before we get there tomorrow, that the Southern Continent obviously will support a Weyr,' she said with dismay. 'It was kind of exciting to wonder.'

'Either way,' F'lar told her with a sardonic smile, 'we have found only part of the answers to problems one and two.'

'Well, you'd better answer number four right now!' Lessa suggested. 'Decisively!'

Weaver, Miner, Harper, Smith,
Tanner, Farmer, Herdsman, Lord,
Gather, wingsped, listen well
To the Weyrman's urgent word.

THEY BOTH managed to guard against any reference to
his premature return when they spoke to F'nor the next
morning. F'lar asked brown Canth to send his rider to the
queen's weyr as soon as he awoke and was pleased to see
F'nor almost immediately. If the brown rider noticed the
curiously intent stare Lessa gave his bandaged face, he gave
no sign of it. As a matter of fact, the moment F'lar outlined
the bold benture of scouting the Southern Continent with
the possibility of starting a Weyr ten Turns back in time,
F'nor forgot all about his wounds.

'I'll go willingly only if you send T'bor along with Kylara.
I'm not waiting till N'ton and his bronze are big enough to
take her on. T'bor and she are as –' F'nor broke off with a
grimace in Lessa's direction. 'Well, they're as near a pair as
can be. I don't object to being . . . importuned, but there
are limits to what a man is willing to do out of loyalty to
dragonkind.'

F'lar barely managed to restrain the amusement he felt
over F'nor's reluctance. Kylara tried her wiles on every
rider, and, because F'nor had not been amenable, she was
determined to succeed with him.

'I hope two bronzes are enough. Pridith may have a mind
of her own, come matingtime.'

'You can't turn a brown into a bronze!' F'nor exclaimed
with such dismay that F'lar could no longer restrain himself.

'Oh, stop it!' And that touched off Lessa's laughter.
'You're as bad a pair,' F'nor snapped, getting to his feet.
'If we're going south, Weyrwoman, we'd better get started.
Particularly if we're going to give this laughing maniac a
chance to compose himself before the solemn Lords descend.
I'll get provisions from Manora. Well, Lessa? *Are* you
coming with me?'

Muffling her laughter, Lessa grabbed up her furred flying

cloak and followed him. At least the adventure was starting off well.

Carrying the pitcher of *klah* and his cup, F'lar adjourned to the Council Room, debating whether to tell the Lords and Craftmasters of this southern venture or not. The dragon's ability to fly *between* times as well as places was not yet well-known. The Lords might not realize it had been used the previous day to forestall the Threads. If F'lar could be sure that project was going to be successful – well, it would add an optimistic note to the meeting.

Let the charts, with the waves and times of the Thread attacks clearly visible, reassure the Lords.

The visitors were not long in assembling. Nor were they all successful in hiding their apprehension and the shock they had received now that Threads had again spun down from the Red Star to menace all life on Pern. This was going to be a difficult session, F'lar decided grimly. He had a fleeting wish, which he quickly suppressed, that he had gone with F'nor and Lessa to the Southern Continent. Instead, he bent with apparent industry to the charts before him.

Soon there were but two more to come, Meron of Nabol (whom he would have liked not to include, for the man was a troublemaker) and Lytol of Ruatha. F'lar had sent for Lytol last because he did not wish Lessa to encounter the man. She was still overly – and, to his mind, foolishly – sensitive at having had to resign her claim to Ruatha Hold for the Lady Gemma's posthumous son. Lytol, as Warder of Ruatha, had a place in this conference. The man was also an ex-dragonman, and his return to the Weyr was painful enough without Lessa's compounding it with her resentment. Lytol was, with the exception of young Larad of Telgar, the Weyr's most valuable ally.

S'lel came in with Meron a step behind him. The Holder was furious at this summons; it showed in his walk, in his eyes, in his haughty bearing. But he was also as inquisitive as he was devious. He nodded only to Larad among the Lords and took the seat left vacant for him by Larad's side. Meron's manner made it obvious that that place was too close to F'lar by half a room.

The Weyrleader acknowledged S'lel's salute and indicated the bronze rider should be seated. F'lar had given thought to the seating arrangements in the Council Room, carefully interspersing brown and bronze dragonriders with

Holders and Craftsmen. There was now barely room to move in the generously proportioned cavern, but there was also no room in which to draw daggers if tempers got hot.

A hush fell on the gathering, and F'lar looked up to see that the stocky, glowering ex-dragonman from Ruatha had stopped on the streshold of the Council. He slowly brought his hand up in a respectful salute to the Weyrleader. As F'lar returned the salute, he noticed that the tic in Lytol's left cheek jumped almost continuously.

Lytol's eyes, dark with pain and inner unquiet, ranged the room. He nodded to the members of his former wing, to Larad and Zurg, head of his own weavers' craft. Stiff-legged, he walked to the remaining seat, murmuring a greeting to T'sum on his left.

F'lar rose.

'I appreciate your coming, good Lords and Craftmasters. The Threads spin once again. The first attack has been met and seared from the sky. Lord Vincet,' and the worried Holder of Nerat looked up in alarm, 'we have dispatched a patrol to the rainforest to do a low-flight sweep to make certain there are no burrows.'

Vincet swallowed nervously, his face paling at the thought of what Threads could do to his fertile, lush holdings.

'We shall need your best junglemen to help –'

'Help? But you said . . . the Threads were seared in the sky?'

'There is no point in taking the slightest chance,' F'lar replied, implying that the patrol was only a precaution instead of the necessity he knew it would be.

Vincet gulped, glancing anxiously around the room for sympathy, and found none. Everyone would soon be in his position.

'There is a patrol due at Keroon and at Igen.' F'lar looked first at Lord Corman, then at Lord Banger, who gravely nodded. 'Let me say by way of reassurance that there will be no further attacks for three days and four hours.' F'lar tapped the appropriate chart. 'The Threads will begin approximately here on Telgar, drift westward through the southernmost portion of Crom, which is mountainous, and on, through Ruatha and the southern end of Nabol.'

'How can you be so certain of that?'

F'lar recognized the contemptuous voice of Meron of Nabol.

'The Threads do not not fall like a child's jackstraws, Lord Meron,' F'lar replied. 'They fall in a definitely predictable pattern; the attacks last exactly six hours. The intervals between attacks will gradually shorten over the next few Turns as the Red Star draws closer. Then, for about forty full Turns, as the Red Star swings past and around us, the attacks occur every fourteen hours, marching across our world in a time-able fashion.'

'So *you* say,' Meron sneered, and there was a low mumble of support.

'So the Teaching Ballads say,' Larad put in firmly.

Meron glared at Telgar's Lord and went on, 'I recall another of your predictions about how the Threads were supposed to begin falling right after Solstice.'

'Which they did,' F'lar interrupted him. 'As black dust in the Northern Holds. For the reprieve we've had, we can thank our lucky stars that we have had an unusually hard and long Cold Turn.'

'Dust?' demanded Nessel of Crom. 'That dust was Threads?' The man was one of Fax's blood connections and under Meron's influence: an older man who had learned lessons from his conquering relative's bloody ways and had not the wit to improve on or alter the original. 'My Hold is still blowing with them. They're dangerous?'

F'lar shook his head emphatically. 'How long has the black dust been blowing in your Hold? Weeks? Done any harm yet?'

Nessel frowned.

'I'm interested in your charts, Weyrleader,' Larad of Telgar said smoothly. 'Will they give us an accurate idea of how often we may expect Threads to fall in our own Holds?'

'Yes. You may also anticipate that the dragonmen will arrive shortly before the invasion is due,' F'lar went on. 'However, additional measures of your own are necessary, and it is for this that I called the Council.'

'Wait a minute,' Corman of Keroon growled. 'I want a copy of those fancy charts of yours for my own. I want to know what those bands and wavy lines really mean. I want . . .'

'Naturally you'll have a timetable of your own. I mean to

impose on Masterharper Robinton' – F'lar nodded respectfully toward that Craftmaster – 'to oversee the copying and make sure everyone understands the timing involved.'

Robinton, a tall, gaunt man with a lined, saturnine face, bowed deeply. A slight smile curved his wide lips at the now hopeful glances favored him by the Hold Lords. His craft, like that of the dragonmen, had been much mocked, and this new respect amused him. He was a man with a keen eye for the ridiculous, and an active imagination. The circumstances in which doubting Pern found itself were too ironic not to appeal to his innate sense of justice. He now contented himself with a deep bow and a mild phrase.

'Truly all shall pay heed to the master.' His voice was deep, his words enunciated with no provincial slurring.

F'lar, about to speak, looked sharply at Robinton as he caught the double barb of that single line. Larad, too, looked around at the Masterharper, clearing his throat hastily.

'We shall have our charts,' Larad said, forestalling Meron, who had opened his mouth to speak. 'We shall have the dragonmen when the Threads spin. What are these additional measures? And why are they necessary?'

All eyes were on F'lar again.

'We have one Weyr where six once flew.'

'But word is that Ramoth has hatched over forty more,' someone in the back of the room declared. 'And why did you Search out still more of your young men?'

'Forty-one as yet unmatured dragons,' F'lar said. Privately, he hoped that this southern venture would still work out. There was real fear in that man's voice. 'They grow well and quickly. Just at present, while the Threads do not strike with great frequency as the Red Star begins its Pass, our Weyr is sufficient . . . if we have your cooperation on the ground. Tradition is that' – he nodded tactfully toward Robinton, the dispenser of Traditional usage – 'you Holders are responsible for only your dwellings, which, of course, are adequately protected by firepits and raw stone. However, it is spring and our heights have been allowed to grow wild with vegetation. Arable land is blossoming with crops. This presents vast acreage vulnerable to the Threads which one Weyr, at this time, is not able to patrol without severely draining the vitality of our dragons and riders.'

At this candid admission, a frightened and angry mutter spread rapidly throughout the room.

'Ramoth rises to mate again soon,' F'lar continued in a matter-of-fact way. 'Of course, in other times, the queens started producing heavy clutches many Turns before the critical solstice as well as more queens. Unfortunately, Jora was ill and old, and Nemorth intractable. The matter –' He was interrupted.

'You dragonmen with your high and mighty airs will bring destruction on us all!'

'You have yourselves to blame,' Robinton's voice stabbed across the ensuing shouts. 'Admit it, one and all. You've paid less honor to the Weyr than you would your watch-wher's kennel – and that not much! But now the thieves are on the heights, and you are screaming because the poor reptile is nigh to death from neglect. Beat him, will you? When you exiled him to his kennel because he tried to warn you? Tried to get you to prepare against the invaders? It's on *your* conscience, not the Weyrleader's or the dragonriders' who have honestly done their duty these hundreds of Turns in keeping dragonkind alive . . . against your protests. How many of you' – his tone was scathing – 'have been generous in thought and favor toward dragonkind? Even since I became master of my craft, how often have my harpers told me of being beaten for singing the old songs as is their duty? You earn only the right, good Lords and Craftsmen, to squirm inside your stony Holds and writhe as your crops die aborning.'

He rose.

' "No Threads will fall. It's a harper's winter tale," ' he whined, in faultless imitation of Nessel. ' "These dragonmen leech us of heir and harvest," ' and his voice took on the constricted, insinuating tenor that could only be Meron's. 'And now the truth is as bitter as a brave man's fears and as difficult as mockweed to swallow. For all the honor you've done them, the dragonmen should leave you to be spun on the Threads' distaff.'

'Bitra, Lemos, and I,' spoke up Raid, the wiry Lord of Benden, his blunt chin lifted belligerently, 'have always done our duty to the Weyr.'

Robinton swung around to him, his eyes flashing as he gave that speaker a long, slow look.

'Aye, and you have. Of all the Great Holds, you three

have been loyal. But you others,' and his voice rose indignantly, 'as spokesmen for my craft, I know, to the last full stop in the score, your opinion of dragonkind. I heard the first whisper of your attempt to ride out against the Weyr.' He laughed harshly and pointed a long finger at Vincet. 'Where would you be today, good Lord Vincet, if the Weyr had *not* sent you packing back, hoping your ladies would be returned you? All of you,' and his accusing finger marked each of the Lords of that abortive effort, 'actually rode against the Weyr because ... "there ... were ... no ... more ... Threads!" '

He planted his fists on either hip and glared at the assembly. F'lar wanted to cheer. It was easy to see why the man was Masterharper, and he thanked circumstance that such a man was the Weyr's partisan.

'And now, at this critical moment, you have the incredible presumption to protest against any measure the Weyr suggests?' Robinton's supple voice oozed derision and amazement. 'Attend what the Weyrleader says and spare him your petty carpings!' He snapped those words out as a father might enjoin an erring child. 'You were,' and he switched to the mildest of polite conversational tones as he addressed F'lar, 'I believe, asking our cooperation, good F'lar? In what capacities?'

F'lar hastily cleared his throat.

'I shall require that the Holds police their own fields and woods, during the attacks if possible, definitely once the Threads have passed. All burrows which might land must be found, marked, and destroyed. The sooner they are located, the easier it is to be rid of them.'

'There's no time to dig firepits through all the lands ... we'll lose half our growing space,' Nessel exclaimed.

'There were other ways, used in olden times, which I believe our Mastersmith might know.' F'lar gestured politely toward Fandarel, the archetype of his profession if ever such existed.

The Smith Craftmaster was by several inches the tallest man in the Council Room, his massive shoulders and heavily muscled arms pressed against his nearest neighbors, although he had made an effort not to crowd against anyone. He rose, a giant tree-stump of a man, hooking thumbs like beast-horns in the thick belt that spanned his waistless midsection. His voice, by no means sweet after Turns of bellowing above roaring hearths and hammers, was, by comparison to Robinton's superb delivery, a diluted, unsupported light baritone.

'There were machines, that much is true,' he allowed in deliberate, thoughtful tones. 'My father, it was he, told me of them as a curiosity of the Craft. There may be sketches in the Hall. There may not. Such things do not keep on skins for long.' He cast an oblique look under beetled brows at the Tanner Craftmaster.

'It is our own hides we must worry about preserving,' F'lar remarked to forestall any intercraft disputes.

Fandarel grumbled in his throat in such a way that F'lar was not certain whether the sound was the man's laughter or a guttural agreement.

'I shall consider the matter. So shall all my fellow craftsmen,' Fandarel assured the Weyrleader. 'To sear Threads from the ground without damaging the soil may not be so easy. There are, it is true, fluids which burn and sear. We use an acid to etch design on daggers and ornamental metals. We of the Caft call it agenothree. There is also the black heavy-water that lies on the surface of pools in Igen and Boll. It burns hot and long. And if, as you say, the Cold Turn made the Threads break into dust, perhaps ice from the coldest northlands might freeze and break grounded Threads. However, the problem is to bring such to the Threads where they fall since they will not oblige us by falling where we want them. . . .' He screwed up his face in a grimace.

F'lar stared at him, surprised. Did the man realize how humorous he was? No, he was speaking with sincere concern. Now the Mastersmith scratched his head, his tough fingers making audible grating sounds along his coarse hair and heat-toughened scalp.

'A nice problem. A nice problem,' he mused, undaunted. 'I shall give it every attention.' He sat down, the heavy bench creaking under his weight.

The Masterfarmer raised his hand tentatively.

'When I became Craftmaster, I recall coming across a reference to the sandworms of Igen. They were once cultivated as a protective—'

'Never heard Igen produced anything useful except heat and sand,' quipped someone.

'We need every suggestion,' F'lar said sharply, trying to

identify that heckler. 'Please find that reference, Craft-master. Lord Banger of Igen, find me some of those sand-worms!'

Banger, equally surprised that his arid Hold had a hidden asset, nodded vigorously.

'Until we have more efficient ways of killing Threads, all Holders must be organized on the ground during attacks, to spot and mark burrows, to set firestone to burn in them. I do not wish any man to be scored, but we know how quickly Threads burrow deep, and no burrow can be left to multiply. You stand to lose more,' and he gestured emphatically at the Holder Lords, 'than any others. Guard not just yourselves, for a burrow on one man's border may grow across to his neighbor's. Mobilize every man, woman, and child, farm and crafthold. Do it now.'

The Council Room was fraught with tension and stunned reflection until Zurg, the Masterweaver, rose to speak.

'My craft, too, has something to offer ... which is only fair since we deal with thread every day of our lives ... in regard to the ancient methods.' Zurg's voice was light and dry, and his eyes, in their creases of spare, lined flesh, were busy, darting from one face in his audience to another. 'In Ruath Hold I once saw upon the wall ... where the tapestry now resides, who knows?' He slyly glanced at Meron of Nabol and then at Bargen of the High Reaches who had succeeded to Fax's title there. 'The work was as old as dragonkind and showed, among other things, a man on foot, carrying upon his back a curious contraption. He held within his hand a rounded, sword-long object from which tongues of flame ... magnificently woven in the orange-red dyes now lost to us ... spouted toward the ground. Above, of course, were dragons in close formation, bronzes predominating ... again we've lost that true dragon-bronze shade. Consequently I remember the work as much for what we now lack as for its subject matter.'

'A flame thrower?' the smith mumbled. A flame thrower,' he repeated with a falling inflection. 'A flame-thrower,' he murmured thoughtfully, his heavy brows drawn into a titanic scowl. 'A thrower of what sort of flame? It requires thought.' He lowered his head and didn't speak, so engrossed in the required thought that he lost interest in the rest of the discussion.

'Yes, good Zurg, there have been many tricks of every

trade lost in recent Turns,' F'lar commented sardonically. 'If we wish to continue living, such knowledge must be revived ... fast. I would particularly like to recover the tapestry of which Master Zurg speaks.'

F'lar looked significantly at those Lords who had quarreled over Fax's seven Holds after his death.

'It may save all of you much loss. I suggest that it appear at Ruatha. Or at Zurg's or Fandarel's crafthall. Whichever is most convenient.'

There was some shuffling of feet, but no one admitted ownership.

'It might then be returned to Fax's son, who is now Ruatha's Lord,' F'lar added, wryly amused at such magnanimous justice.

Lytol snorted softly and glowered around the room. F'lar supposed Lytol to be amused and experienced a fleeting regret for the orphaned Jaxom, reared by such a cheerless if honest guardian.

'If I may, Lord Weyrleader,' Robinton broke in, 'we might all benefit, as your maps prove to us, from research in our own Records.' He smiled suddenly, an unexpectedly embarrassed smile. 'I own I find myself in some disgrace for we Harpers have let slip unpopular ballads and skimped on some of the longer Teaching Ballads and Sagas ... for lack of listeners and, occasionally, in the interest of preserving our skins.'

F'lar stifled a laugh with a cough. Robinton was a genius.

'I must see that Ruathan tapestry,' Fandarel suddenly boomed out.

'I'm sure it will be in your hands very soon,' F'lar assured him with more confidence than he dared feel. 'My Lords, there is much to be done. Now that you understand what we all face, I leave it in your hands as leaders in your separate Holds and crafts how best to organize your own people. Craftsmen, turn your best minds to our special problems: review all Records that might turn up something to our purpose. Lords Telgar, Crom, Ruatha, and Nabol, I shall be with you in three days. Nerat, Keroon, and Igen, I am at your disposal to help destroy any burrow on your lands. While we have the Masterminer here, tell him your needs. How stands your craft?'

'Happy to be so busy at our trade, Weyrleader,' piped up the Masterminer.

Just then F'lar caught sight of F'nor, hovering about in the shadows of the hallway, trying to catch his eye. The brown rider wore an exultant grin, and it was obvious he was bursting with news.

F'lar wondered how they could have returned so swiftly from the Southern Continent, and then he realized that F'nor – again – was tanned. He gave a jerk of his head, indicating that F'nor take himself off to the sleeping quarters and wait.

'Lords and Craftmasters, a dragonet will be at the disposal of each of you for messages and transportation. Now, good morning.'

He strode out of the Council Room, up the passageway into the queen's weyr, and parted the still swinging curtains into the sleeping room just as F'nor was pouring himself a cup of wine.

'Success!' F'nor cried as the Weyrleader entered. 'Though how you knew to send just thirty-two candidates I'll never understand. I thought you were insulting our noble Pridith. But thirty-two eggs she laid in four days. It was all I could do to keep from riding out when the first appeared.'

F'lar responded with hearty congratulations, relieved that there would be at least that much benefit from this apparently ill-fated venture. Now all he had to figure out was how much longer F'nor had stayed south until his frantic visit the night before. For there were no worry lines or strain in F'nor's grinning, well-tanned face.

'No queen egg?' asked F'lar hopefully. With thirty-two in the one experiment, perhaps they could send a second queen back and try again.

F'nor's face lengthened. 'No, and I was sure there would be. But there are fourteen bronzes. Pridith out-matched Ramoth there,' he added proudly.

'Indeed she did. How goes the Weyr otherwise?'

F'nor frowned, shaking his head against an inner bewilderment. 'Kylara's ... well, she's a problem. Stirs up trouble constantly. T'bor leads a sad time with her, and he's so touchy everyone keeps a distance from him.' F'nor brightened a little. 'Young N'ton is shaping up into a fine wingleader, and his bronze may outfly T'bor's Orth when Pridith flies to mate the next time. Not that I'd wish Kylara on N'ton ... or anyone.'

'No trouble then with supplies?'

F'nor alughed outright. 'If you hadn't made it so plain we must not communicate with you here, we could supply you with fruits and fresh greens that are superior to anything in the north. We eat the way dragonmen should! F'lar, we must consider a supply Weyr down there. Then we shall never have to worry about tithing trains and . . .'

'In good time. Get back now. You know you must keep these visits short.'

F'nor grimaced. 'Oh, it's not so bad. I'm not here in this time, anyway.'

'True,' F'lar agreed, 'but don't mistake the time and come while you're still here.'

'Hmmm? Oh, yes, that's right. I forget time is creeping for us and speeding for you. Well, I shan't be back again till Pridith lays the second clutch.'

With a cheerful good-bye, F'nor strode out of the weyr. F'lar watched him thoughtfully as he slowly retraced his steps to the Council Room. Thirty-two new dragons, fourteen of them bronzes, was no small gain and seemed worth the hazard. Or would the hazard wax greater?

Someone cleared his throat deliberately. F'lar looked up to see Robinton standing in the archway that led to the Council Room.

'Before I can copy and instruct others about those maps, Weyrleader, I must myself understand them completely. I took the liberty of remaining behind.'

'You make a good champion, Masterharper.'

'You have a noble cause, Weyrleader,' and then Robinton's eyes glinted maliciously. 'I've been begging the Egg for an opportunity to speak out to so noble an audience.'

'A cup of wine first?'

'Benden grapes are the envy of Pern.'

'If one has the palate for such a delicate bouquet.'

'It is carefully cultivated by the knowledgeable.'

F'lar wondered when the man would stop playing with words. He had more on his mind than studying the time-charts.

'I have in mind a ballad which, for lack of explanation, I had set aside when I became the Master of my crafthall,' he said judiciously after an appreciative savoring of his wine. 'It is an uneasy song, both the tune and the words. One develops, as a harper must, a certain sensitivity for what will be received and what will be rejected . . . forcefully,' and he winced in retrospect. 'I found that this ballad unsettled singer as well as audience and retired it from use. Now, like that tapestry, it bears rediscovery.'

After his death C'gan's instrument had been hung on the Council Room wall till a new Weyrsinger could be chosen. The guitar was very old, its wood thin. Old C'gan had kept it well-tuned and covered. The Master-harper handled it now with reverence, lightly stroking the strings to hear the tone, raising his eyebrows at the fine voice of the instrument.

He plucked a chord, a dissonance. F'lar wondered if the instrument was out of tune or if the harper had, by some chance, struck the wrong string. But Robinton repeated the odd discord, then modulating into a weird minor that was somehow more disturbing than the first notes.

'I told you it was an uneasy song. And I wonder if you know the answers to the questions it asks. For I've turned the puzzle over in my mind many times of late.'

Then abruptly he shifted from the spoken to the sung tone.

> Gone away, gone ahead,
> Echoes roll unansweréd.
> Empty, open, dusty, dead,
> Why have all the Weyrfolk fled?
>
> Where have dragons gone together?
> Leaving Weyrs to wind and weather?
> Setting herdbeasts free of tether?
> Gone, our safeguards, gone, but whither?
>
> Have they flown to some new Weyr
> Where cruel Threads some others fear?
> Are they worlds away from here?
> Why, oh, why, the empty Weyr?

The last plaintive chord reverberated.

'Of course, you realize that the song was first recorded in the craft annals some four hundred Turns ago,' Robinton said lightly, cradling the guitar in both arms. 'The Red Star had just passed beyond attack-proximity. The people had ample reason to be stunned and worried over the sudden loss of the populations of five Weyrs. Oh, I imagine at the time they had any one of a number of explanations, but none ... not one explanation ... is recorded.' Robinton paused significantly.

'I have found none recorded, either,' F'lar replied. 'As a

matter of fact, I had all the Records brought here from the other Weyrs ... in order to compile accurate attack time-tables. And those other Weyr Records simply end—' F'lar made a chopping gesture with one hand. 'In Benden's Records there is no mention of sickness, death, fire, disaster – not one word of explanation for the sudden lapse of the usual intercourse between the Weyrs. Benden's Records continue blithely, but only for Benden. There is one entry that pertains to the mass disappearance ... the initiation of a Pernwide patrol routing, not just Benden's immediate responsibility. And that is all.'

'Strange,' Robinton mused. 'Once the danger from the Red Star was past, the dragons and riders may have gone *between* to ease the drain on the Holds. But I simply cannot believe that. Our craft Records do mention that harvests were bad and that there had been several natural catastrophes ... other than the Threads. Men may be gallant and your breed the most gallant of all, but mass suicide? I simply do not accept that explanation ... not for dragon-men.'

'My thanks,' F'lar said with mild irony.

'Don't mention it,' Robinton replied with a gracious nod.

F'lar chuckled appreciatively. 'I see we have been too weyrbound as well as too hidebound.'

Robinton drained his cup and looked at it mournfully until F'lar refilled it.

'Well, your isolation served some purpose, you know, and you handled that uprising of the Lords magnificently. I nearly choked to death laughing,' Robinton remarked, grinning broadly. 'Stealing their women in the flash of a dragon's breath!' He chuckled again, then suddenly sobered, looking F'lar straight in the eye. 'Accustomed as I am to hearing what a man does *not* say aloud, I suspect there is much you glossed over in that Council meeting. You may be sure of my discretion ... and ... you may be sure of my whole-hearted support and that of my not ineffectual craft. To be blunt, how may my harpers aid you?' and he strummed a vigorous marching air. 'Stir men's pulses with ballads of past glories and success?' The tune, under his flashing fingers, changed abruptly to a stern but determined rhythm. 'Strengthen their mental and physical sinews for hardship?'

'If all your harpers could stir men as you yourself do, I should have no worries that five hundred or so additional dragons would not immediately end.'

'Oh, then despite your brave words and marked charts, the situation is' – a dissonant twang on the guitar accented his final words – 'more desperate than you carefully did not say.'

'It may be.'

'The flame throwers old Zurg remembered and Fandarel must reconstruct – will they tip the scales?'

F'lar regarded this clever man thoughtfully and made a quick decision.

'Even Igen's sandworms will help, but as the world turns and the Red Star nears, the interval between daily attacks shortens and we have only seventy-two new dragons to add to those we had yesterday. One is now dead and several will not fly for several weeks.'

'Seventy-two?' Robinton caught him up sharply. 'Ramoth hatched but forty, and they are still too young to eat firestone.'

F'lar outlined F'nor and Lessa's expedition, taking place at that moment. He went on to F'nor's reappearance and warning, as well as the fact that the experiment had been successful in part with the hatching of thirty-two new dragons from Pridith's first clutch. Robinton caught him up.

'How can F'nore already have returned when you haven't heard from Lessa and him that there is a breeding place on the Southern Continent?'

'Dragons can go *between* times as well as places. They go as easily to a *when* as to a *where*.'

Robinton's eyes widened as he digested this astonishing news.

'That is how we forestalled the attack on Nerat yesterday morning. We jumped back two hours *between* time to meet the Threads as they fell.'

'You can actually jump backward? How far back?'

'I don't know. Lessa, when I was teaching her to fly Ramoth, inadvertently returned to Ruath Hold, to the dawn thirteen Turns ago when Fax's men invaded from the heights. When she returned to the present, I attempted a *between* times jump of some ten Turns. To the dragons it is a simple matter to go *between* times or spaces, but there appears to be a terrific drain on the rider. Yesterday, by the time we returned from Nerat and had to go on to Keroon, I felt as though I had been pounded flat and left to dry for a summer on Igen Plain.' F'lar shook his head. 'We have obviously succeeded in sending Kylara, Pridith, and the others ten Turns *between*, because F'nor has already reported to me that he has been there several Turns. The drain on humans, however, is becoming more and more marked. But even seventy-two more mature dragons will be a help.'

'Send a rider ahead in time to see if it is sufficient,' Robinton suggested helpfully. 'Save you a few days' worrying.'

'I don't know how to get to a *when* that has not yet happened. You must give your dragon reference points, you know. How can you refer him to times that have not yet occurred?'

'You've got an imagination. Project it.'

'And perhaps lose a dragon when I have none to spare? No, I must continue . . . because obviously I have, judging by F'nor's returns . . . as I decided to start. Which reminds me, I must give orders to start packing. Then I shall go over the time-charts with you.'

It wasn't until after the noon meal, which Robinton took with the Weyrleader, that the Masterharper was confident that he understood the charts and left to begin their copying.

Across a waste of lonely tossing sea,
Where no dragonwings had lately spread,
Flew a gold and a sturdy brown in spring,
Searching if a land be dead.

As RAMOTH and Canth bore Lessa and F'nor up to the Star Stone, they saw the first of the Hold Lords and Craftmasters arriving for the Council.

In order to get back to the Southern Continent of ten Turns ago, Lessa and F'nor had decided it was easiest to transfer first *between* times to the Weyr of ten Turns back which F'nor remembered. Then they would go *between* places to a seapoint just off the coast of the neglected Southern Continent which was as close to it as the Records gave any references.

F'nor put Canth in mind of a particular day he remembered ten Turns back, and Ramoth picked up the references from the brown's mind. The awesome cold of *between* times took Lessa's breath away, and it was with intense relief that she caught a glimpse of the normal weyr activity before the dragons took them *between* places to hover over the turgid sea.

Beyond them, smudged purple on this overcast and gloomy day, lurked the Southern Continent. Lessa felt a new anxiety replace the uncertainty of the temporal displacement. Ramoth beat forward with great sweeps of her wings, making for the distant coast. Canth gallantly tried to maintain a matching speed.

He's only a brown, Lessa scolded her golden queen.

If he is flying with me, Ramoth replied cooly, *he must stretch his wings a little.*

Lessa grinned, thinking very privately that Ramoth was still piqued that she had not been able to fight with her weyrmates. All the males would have a hard time with her for a while.

They saw the flock of wherries first and realized that there would have to be some vegetation on the Continent. Wherries needed greens to live, although they could subsist on little else besides occasional grubs if necessary.

Lessa had Canth relay questions to his rider. *If the Southern Continent was rendered barren by the Threads, how did new growth start? Where did the wherries come from?*

Ever notice the seed pods split open and the flakes carried away by the winds? Ever notice that wherries fly south after the autumn solstice?

Yes, but . . .

Yes, but!

But the land was Thread-bared!

In less than four hundred Turns even the scorched hilltops of our Continent begin to sprout in the springtime, F'nor replied by way of Canth, *so it is easy to assume the Southern Continent could revive, too.*

Even at the pace Ramoth set, it took time to reach the jagged shoreline with its forbidding cliffs, stark stone in the sullen light. Lessa groaned inwardly but urged Ramoth higher to see over the masking highlands. All seemed gray and desolate from that altitude.

Suddenly the sun broke through the cloud cover and the gray dissolved into dense greens and browns, living colors, the live greens of lush tropical growth, the browns of vigorous trees and vines. Lessa's cry of triumph was echoed by F'nor's hurrah and the brass voices of the dragons. Wherries, startled by the unusual sound, rose in squeaking alarm from their perches.

Beyond the headland, the land sloped away to jungle and grassy plateau, similar to mid-Boll. Though they searched all morning, they found no hospitable cliffs wherein to found a new Weyr. Was that a contributing factor in the southern venture's failure, Lessa wondered.

Discouraged, they landed on a high plateau by a small lake. The weather was warm but not oppressive, and while F'nor and Lessa ate their noonday meal, the two dragons wallowed in the water, refreshing themselves.

Lessa felt uneasy and had little appetite for the meat and bread. She noticed that F'nor was restless, too, shooting surreptitious glances around the lake and the jungle verge.

'What under the sun are we expecting? Wherries don't charge, and wild whers would come nowhere near a dragon. We're ten Turns before the Red Star, so there can't be any Threads.'

F'nor shrugged, grimacing sheepishly as he tossed his unfinished bread back into the food pouch.

'Place feels so empty, I guess,' he tendered, glancing around. He spotted ripe fruit hanging from a moonflower vine. 'Now that looks familiar and good enough to eat, without tasting like dust in the mouth.'

He climbed nimbly and snagged the orange-red fruit.

'Smells right, feels ripe, looks ripe,' he announced and deftly sliced the fruit open. Grinning, he handed Lessa the first slice, carving another for himself. He lifted it challengingly. 'Let us eat and die together!'

She couldn't help but laugh and saluted him back. They bit into the succulent flesh simultaneously. Sweet juices dribbled from the corners of her mouth, and Lessa hurriedly licked her lips to capture the least drop of the delicious liquid.

'Die happy – I will,' F'nor cried, cutting more fruit.

Both were subtly reassured by the experiment and were able to discuss their discomposure.

'I think,' F'nor suggested, 'it is the lack of cliff and cavern and the still, still quality of the place, the knowing that there are no other men or beasts about but us.'

Lessa nodded her head in agreement. 'Ramoth, Canth, would having no Weyr upset you?'

We didn't always live in caves, Ramoth replied, somewhat haughtily as she rolled over in the lake. Sizable waves rushed up the shore almost to where Lessa and F'nor were seated on a fallen tree trunk. *The sun here is warm and pleasant, the water cooling. I would enjoy it here, but I am not to come.*

'She is out of sorts,' Lessa whispered to F'nor. 'Let Pridith have it, dear one,' she called soothingly to the golden queen. 'You've the Weyr and all!'

Ramoth ducked under the water, blowing up a froth in disgruntled reply.

Canth admitted that he had no reservations at all about living Weyrless. The dry earth would be warmer than stone to sleep on, once a suitably comfortable hollow had been achieved. No, he couldn't object to the lack of the cave as long as there was enough to eat.

'We'll have to bring herdbeasts in,' F'nor mused. 'Enough to start a good-sized herd. Of course, the wherries here are huge. Come to think of it, I believe this plateau has no exits. We wouldn't need to pasture it off. I'd better check. Otherwise, this plateau with the lake and enough clear space for Holds seems ideal. Walk out and pick breakfast from the tree.'

'It might be wise to choose those who were not Hold-reared,' Lessa added. 'They would not feel so uneasy away from protecting heights and stone-security.' She gave a short laugh. 'I'm more a creature of habit than I suspected. All these open spaces, untenanted and quiet, seem ... indecent.' She gave a delicate shudder, scanning the broad and open plain beyond the lake.

'Fruitful and lovely,' F'nor amended, leaping up to secure more of the orange-red succulents. 'This tastes uncommonly good to me. Can't remember anything this sweet and juicy from Nerat, and yet it's the same variety.'

'Undeniably superior to what the Weyr gets. I suspect Nerat serves home first. Weyr last.'

They both stuffed themselves greedily.

Further investigation proved that the plateau was isolated, and ample to pasture a huge herd of foodbeasts for the dragons. It ended in a sheer drop of several dragonlengths into denser jungle on one side, the sea-side escarpment on the other. The timber stands would provide raw material from which dwellings could be made for the Weyrfolk. Ramoth and Canth stoutly agreed dragonkind would be comfortable enough under the heavy foliage of the dense jungle. As this part of the continent was similar, weatherwise, to Upper Nerat, there would be neither intense heat nor cold to give distress.

However, if Lessa was glad enough to leave, F'nor seemed reluctant to start back.

'We can go *between* time and place on the way back,' Lessa insisted finally, 'and be in the Weyr by late afternoon. The Lords will surely be gone by then.'

F'nor concurred, and Lessa steeled herself for the trip *between*. She wondered why the *when between* bothered her more than the *where*, for it had no effect on the dragons at all. Ramoth, sensing Lessa's depression, crooned encouragingly. The long, long black suspension of the utter cold of *between* where and when ended suddenly in sunlight above the Weyr.

Somewhat startled, Lessa saw bundles and sacks spread out before the Lower Caverns as dragonriders supervised the loading of their beasts.

'What has been happening?' F'nor exclaimed.

'Oh, F'lar's been anticipating success,' she assured him glibly.

Mnementh, who was watching the bustle from the ledge of the queen's weyr, sent a greeting to the travelers and the information that F'lar wished them to join him in the weyr as soon as they returned.

They found F'lar, as usual, bent over some of the oldest and least legible Record skins that he had had brought to the Council Room.

'And?' he asked, grinning a broad welcome at them.

'Green, lush, and livable,' Lessa declared, watching him intently. He knew something else, too. Well, she hoped he'd watch his words. F'nor was no fool, and this foreknowledge was dangerous.

'That is what I had so hoped to hear you say,' F'lar went on smoothly. 'Come, tell me in detail what you observed and discovered. It'll be good to fill in the blank spaces on the chart.'

Lessa let F'nor give most of the account, to which F'lar listened with sincere attention, making notes.

'On the chance that it would be practical, I started packing supplies and alerting the riders to go with you,' he told F'nor when the account was finished. 'Remember, we've only three days in this time in which to start you back ten Turns ago. *We* have no moments to spare. And we must have many more mature dragons ready to fight at Telgar in three days' time. So, though ten Turns will have passed for you, three days only will elapse here. Lessa, your thought that the farm-bred might do better is well-taken. We're lucky that our recent Search for rider candidates for the dragons Pridith will have come mainly from the crafts and farms. No problem there. And most of the thirty-two are in their early teens.'

'Thirty-two?' F'nor exclaimed. 'We should have fifty. The dragonets must have some choice, even if we get the candidates used to the dragonets before they're hatched.'

F'lar shrugged negligently. 'Send back for more. *You'll* have time, remember,' and F'lar chuckled as though he had started to add something and decided against it.

F'nor had no time to debate with the Weyrleader, for F'lar immediately launched on other rapid instructions.

F'nor was to take his own wingriders to help train the weyrlings. They would also take the forty young dragons of

Ramoth's first clutch: Kylara with her queen Pridith, T'bor and his bronze Piyanth. N'ton's young bronze might also be ready to fly and mate by the time Pridith was, so that gave the young queen two bronzes at least.

'Suppose we'd found the continent barren?' F'nor asked, still puzzled by F'lar's assurance. 'What then?'

'Oh, we'd've sent them back to, say, the High Reaches,' F'lar replied far too glibly, but quickly went on. 'I should send on other bronzes, but I'll need everyone else here to ride burrow-search on Keroon and Nerat. They've already unearthed several at Nerat. Vincet, I'm told, is close to heart attack from fright.'

Lessa made a short comment on that Hold Lord.

'What of the meeting this morning?' F'nor asked, remembering.

'Never mind that now. You've got to start shifting *between* by evening, F'nor.'

Lessa gave the Weyrleader a long hard look and decided she would have to find out what had happened in detail very soon.

'Sketch me some references, will you, Lessa?' F'lar asked.

There was a definite plea in his eyes as he drew clean hide and a stylus to her. He wanted no questions from her now that would alarm F'nor. She sighed and picked up the drawing tool.

She sketched quickly, with one or two details added by F'nor until she had rendered a reasonable map of the plateau they had chosen. Then, abruptly, she had trouble focussing her eyes. She felt light-headed.

'Lessa?' F'lar bent to her.

'Everything's . . . moving . . . circling . . .' and she collapsed backward into his arms.

As F'lar raised her slight body into his arms, he exchanged an alarmed look with his half brother.

'I'll call for Manora,' F'nor suggested.

'How do you feel?' the Weyrleader called after his brother.

'Tired but no more than that,' F'nor assured him as he shouted down the service shaft to the kitchens for Manora to come and for hot *klah*. He needed that, and no doubt of it.

F'lar laid the Weyrwoman on the sleeping couch, covering her gently.

'I don't like this,' he muttered, rapidly recalling what F'nor had said of Kylara's decline, which F'nor could not know was yet to come in his future. Why should it start so swiftly with Lessa?

'Time-jumping makes one feel slightly –' F'nor paused, groping for the exact wording. 'Not entirely ... whole. You fought *between* times at Nerat yesterday. . . .'

'I fought,' F'lar reminded him, 'but neither you nor Lessa battled anything today. There may be some inner ... mental ... stress simply to going *between* times. Look, F'nor, I'd rather only you came back once you reach the southern Weyr, I'll make it an order and get Ramoth to inhibit the dragons. That way no rider can take it into his head to come back even if he wants to. There is some factor that may be more serious than we can guess. Let's take no unnecessary risks.'

'Agreed.'

'One other detail, F'nor. Be very careful which times you pick to come back to see me. I wouldn't jump *between* too close to any time you were actually here. I can't imagine what would happen if you walked into your own self in the passageway, and I can't lose you.'

With a rare demonstration of affection, F'lar gripped his half brother's shoulder tightly.

'Remember, F'nor. I was here all morning and you did not arrive back from the first trip till midafternoon. And remember, too, *we* have only three days. You have ten Turns.'

F'nor left, passing Manora in the hall.

The woman could find nothing obviously the matter with Lessa, and they finally decided it might be simple fatigue; yesterday's strain when Lessa had to relay messages between dragons and fighters followed by the disjointing *between* times trip today.

When F'lar went to wish the southern venturers a good trip, Lessa was in a normal sleep, her face pale, but her breathing easy.

F'lar had Mnementh relay to Ramoth the prohibition he wished the queen to instill in all dragonkind assigned to the venture. Ramoth obliged, but added in an aside to bronze Mnementh, which he passed on to F'lar, that everyone else had adventures while she, the Weyr queen, was forced to stay behind.

No sooner had the laden dragons, one by one, winked out of the sky above the Star Stone than the young weyrling assigned to Nerat Hold as messenger came gliding down, his face white with fear.

'Weyrleader, many more burrows have been found, and they cannot be burned out with fire alone. Lord Vincet wants you.'

F'lar could well imagine that Vincet did.

'Get yourself some dinner, boy, before you start back. I'll go shortly.'

As he passed through to the sleeping quarters, he heard Ramoth rumbling in her throat. She had settled herself down to rest.

Lessa still slept, one hand curled under her cheek, her dark hair trailing over the edge of the bed. She looked fragile, childlike, and very precious to him. F'lar smiled to himself. So she was jealous of Kylara's attentions yesterday. He was pleased and flattered. Never would Lessa learn from him that Kylara, for all her bold beauty and sensuous nature, did not have one tenth the attraction for him that the unpredictable, dark, and delicate Lessa held. Even her stubborn intractableness, her keen and malicious humor, added zest to their relationship. With a tenderness he would never show her awake, F'lar bent and kissed her lips. She stirred and smiled, sighing lightly in her sleep.

Reluctantly returning to what must be done, F'lar left her so. As he paused by the queen, Ramoth raised her great, wedge-shaped head; her many-faceted eyes gleamed with bright luminescence as she regarded the Weyrleader.

'Mnementh, please ask Ramoth to get in touch with the dragonet at Fandarel's crafthall. I'd like the Mastersmith to come with me to Nerat. I want to see what his agenothree does to Threads.'

Ramoth nodded her head as the bronze dragon relayed the message to her.

She has done so, and the green dragon comes as soon as he can. Mnementh reported to his rider. *It is easier to do, this talking about, when Lessa is awake,* he grumbled.

F'lar agreed heartily. It had been quite an advantage yesterday in the battle and would be more and more of an asset.

Maybe it would be better if she tried to speak, across time, to F'nor ... but no, F'nor had come back.

F'lar strode into the Council Room, still hopeful that somewhere within the illegible portions of the old Records was the one clue he so desperately needed. There must be a way out of this impasse. If not the southern venture, then something else. Something!

Fandarel showed himself a man of iron will as well as sinew; he looked calmly at the exposed tangle of perceptibly growing Threads that writhed and intertwined obscenely.

'Hundreds and thousands in this one burrow,' Lord Vincet of Nerat was exclaiming in a frantic tone of voice. He waved his hands distractedly around the plantation of young trees in which the burrow had been discovered. 'These stalks are already withering even as you hesitate. Do something! How many more young trees will die in this one field alone? How many more burrows escaped dragon's breath yesterday? Where is a dragon to sear them? Why are you just standing there?'

F'lar and Fandarel paid no attention to the man's raving, both fascinated as well as revolted by their first sight of the burrowing stage of their ancient foe. Despite Vincet's panicky accusations, it was the only burrow on this particular slope. F'lar did not like to contemplate how many more might have slipped through the dragons' efforts and had reached Nerat's warm and fertile soil. If they had only had time enough to set out watchmen to track the fall of stray clumps. They could, at least, remedy that error in Telgar, Crom, and Ruatha in three days. But it was not enough. Not enough.

Fandarel motioned forward the two craftsmen who had accompanied him. They were burdened with an odd contraption: a large cylinder of metal to which was attached a wand with a wide nozzle. At the other end of the cylinder was another short pipe-length and then a short cylinder with an inner plunger. One craftsman worked the plunger vigorously, while the second, barely keeping his hands steady, pointed the nozzle end toward the Thread burrow. At a nod from this pumper, the man released a small knob on the nozzle, extending it carefully away from him and over the burrow. A thin spray danced from the nozzle and drifted down into the burrow. No sooner had the spray motes contacted the Thread tangles than steam hissed out of the burrow. Before long, all that remained of the pallid writhing tendrils was a smoking mass of blackened strands. Long after Fandarel had waved the craftsmen back, he stared at the grave. Finally he grunted and found himself a long stick with which he poked and prodded the remains. Not one Thread wriggled.

'Humph,' he grunted with evident satisfaction. 'However, we can scarcely go around digging up every burrow. I need another.'

With Lord Vincet a hand-wringing moaner in their wake, they were escorted by the junglemen to another undisturbed burrow on the sea-side of the rainforest. The Threads had entered the earth by the side of a huge tree that was already drooping.

With his prodding stick Fandarel made a tiny hole at the top of the burrow and then waved his craftsmen forward. The pumper made vigorous motions at his end, while the nozzle-holder adjusted his pipe before inserting it in the hole. Fandarel gave the sign to start and counted slowly before he waved a cutoff. Smoke oozed out of the tiny hole.

After a suitable lapse of time, Fandarel ordered the junglemen to dig, reminding them to be careful not to come in contact with the agenothree liquid. When the burrow was uncovered, the acid had done its work, leaving nothing but a thoroughly charred mass of tangles.

Fandarel grimaced but this time scratched his head in dissatisfaction.

'Takes too much time, either way. Best to get them still at the surface,' the Mastersmith grumbled.

'Best to get them in the air,' Lord Vincet chattered. 'And what will that stuff to to my young orchards? What will it do?

Fandarel swung around, apparently noticing the distressed Holder for the first time.

'Little man, agenothree in diluted form is what you use to fertilize your plants in the spring. True, this field has been burned out for a few years, but it is *not* Thread-full. It *would* be better if we could get the spray up high in the air. Then it would float down and dissipate harmlessly – fertilizing very evenly, too.' He paused, scratched his head gratingly. 'Young dragons could carry a team aloft. . . . Hmmm. A possibility, but the apparatus is bulky yet.' He turned his back on the surprised Hold Lord then and asked F'lar if the tapestry had been returned. 'I cannot yet discover how to make a tube throw flame. I got this mechanism from what we make for the orchard farmers.'

'Im still waiting for word on the tapestry,' F'lar replied, 'but this spray of yours is effective. The Thread burrow is dead.'

'The sandworms are effective too, but not really efficient,' F'lar grunted in dissatisfaction. He beckoned abruptly to his assistants and stalked off into the increasing twilight to the dragons.

Robinton awaited their return at the Weyr, his outward calm barely masking his inner excitement. He inquired politely, however, of Fandarel's efforts. The Mastersmith grunted and shrugged.

'I have all my craft at work.'

'The Mastersmith is entirely too modest,' F'lar put in. 'He has already put together an ingenious device that sprays agenothree into Thread burrows and sears them into a black pulp.'

'Not efficient. *I* like the idea of flamethrowers,' the smith said, his eyes gleaming in his expressionless face. 'A thrower of flame,' he repeated, his eyes unfocusing. He shook his heavy head with a bone-popping crack. 'I go,' and with a curt nod to the harper and the Weyrleader, he left.

'I like that man's dedication to an idea,' Robinton observed. Despite his amusement with the man's eccentric behavior, there was a strong undercurrent of respect for the smith. 'I must set my apprentices a task for an appropriate Saga on the Mastersmith. I understand,' he said, turning to F'lar, 'that the southern venture has been inaugurated.'

F'lar nodded unhappily.

'Your doubts increase?'

'This *between* times travel takes its own toll,' he admitted, glancing anxiously toward the sleeping room.

'The Weyrwoman is ill?'

'Sleeping, but today's journey affected her. We need another, less dangerous answer!' and F'lar slammed one fist into the other palm.

'I came with no real answer,' Robinton said then, briskly, 'but with what I believe to be another part of the puzzle. I have found an entry. Four hundred Turns ago the then Masterharper was called to Fort Weyr not long after the Red Star retreated away from Pern in the evening sky.'

'An entry? What is it?'

'Mind you, the Thread attacks had just lifted and the Masterharper was called one late evening to Fort Weyr. An unusual summons. However,' and Robinton emphasized the distinction by pointing a long, callous-tipped finger at F'lar, 'no further mention is ever made of that visit. There ought to have been, for all such summonses have a purpose. All such meetings are recorded, yet no explanation of this one is given. The record is taken up several weeks later by the Masterharper as though he had not left his crafthall at all. Some ten months afterward, the Question Song was added to compulsory Teaching Ballads.'

'You believe the two are connected with the abandonment of the five Weyrs?'

'I do, but I could not say why. I only feel that the events, the visit, the disappearances, the Question Song, are connected.'

F'lar poured them both cups of wine.

'I have checked back, too, seeking some indications.' He shrugged. 'All must have been normal right up to the point they disappeared. There are Records of tithing trains received, supplies stored, the list of injured dragons and men returning to active patrols. And then the Records cease at full Cold, leaving only Benden Weyr occupied.'

'And why that one Weyr of the six to choose from?' Robinton demanded. 'Island Ista would be a better choice if only one Weyr was to be left. Benden so far north is not a likely place to pass four hundred Turns.'

'Benden is high and isolated. A disease that struck the others and was prevented from reaching Benden?'

'And no explanation of it? They can't all – dragons, riders, weyrfolk – have dropped dead on the same instant and left no carcasses rotting in the sun.'

'Then let us ask ourselves, why was the harper called? Was he told to construct a Teaching Ballad covering this disappearance?'

'Well,' Robinton snorted, 'it certainly wasn't meant to reassure us, not with that tune – if one cares to call it a tune at all, and I don't – nor does it answer any questions! It poses them.'

'For us to answer?' suggested F'lar softly.

'Aye.' Robinton's eyes shone. 'For us to answer, indeed, for it is a difficult song to forget. Which means it was meant to be remembered. Those questions are important, F'lar!'

'Which questions are important?' demanded Lessa, who had entered quietly.

Both men were on their feet. F'lar, with unusual attentiveness, held a chair for Lessa and poured her wine.

'I'm not going to break apart,' she said tartly, almost annoyed at the excess of courtesy. Then she smiled up at F'lar to take the sting out of her words. 'I slept and I feel much better. What were you two getting so intense about?'

F'lar quickly outlined what he and the Masterharper had been discussing. When he mentioned the Question Song, Lessa shuddered.

'That's one I can't forget, either. Which, I've always been told,' and she grimaced, remembering the hateful lessons with R'gul, 'means it's important. But why? It only asked questions.' Then she blinked, her eyes went wide with amazement.

' "Gone away, gone ... *ahead!*" ' she cried, on her feet. 'That's it! All five Weyrs went ... *ahead*. But to when?'

F'lar turned to her, speechless.

'They came ahead to our time! Five Weyrs full of dragons,' she repeated in an awed voice.

'No, that's impossible,' F'lar contradicted.

'Why?' Robinton demanded excitedly. 'Doesn't that solve the problem we're facing? The need for fighting dragons? Doesn't it explain why they left so suddenly with no explanation except that Question Song?'

F'lar brushed back the heavy lock of hair that overhung his eyes.

'It would explain their actions in leaving,' he admitted, 'because they couldn't leave any clues saying where they went, or it would cancel the whole thing. Just as I couldn't tell F'nor I knew the southern venture would have problems. But how do they get here – if here is *when* they came? They aren't here now. How would they have known they were needed – or *when* they were needed? And this is the real problem – how can you conceivably give a dragon references to a *when* that has not yet occurred?'

'Someone here must go back to give them the proper references,' Lessa replied in a very quiet voice.

'You're mad, Lessa,' F'lar shouted at her, alarm written

on his face. 'You know what happened to you today. How can you consider going back to a *when* you can't remotely imagine? To a *when* four hundred Turns ago? Going back ten Turns left you fainting and half-ill.'

'Wouldn't it be worth it?' she asked him, her eyes grave. 'Isn't Pern worth it?'

F'lar grabbed her by the shoulders, shaking her, his eyes wild with fear.

'Not even Pern is worth losing you, or Ramoth. Lessa, Lessa, don't you dare disobey me in this.' His voice dropped to an intense icy whisper, shaking with anger.

'Ah, there may be a way of effecting that solution, momentarily beyond us, Weyrwoman,' Robinton put in adroitly. 'Who knows what tomorrow holds? It certainly is not something one does without considering every angle.'

Lessa did not shrug off F'lar's viselike grip on her shoulders as she gazed at Robinton.

'Wine?' the Masterharper suggested, pouring a mug for her. His diversionary action broke the tableau of Lessa and F'lar.

'Ramoth is not afraid to try,' Lessa said, her mouth set in a determined line.

F'lar glared at the golden dragon who was regarding the humans, her neck curled around almost to the shoulder joint of her great wing.

'Ramoth is young,' F'lar snapped and then caught Mnementh's wry thought even as Lessa did.

She threw her head back, her peal of laughter echoing in the vaulting chamber.

'I'm badly in need of a good joke myself,' Robinton remarked pointedly.

'Mnementh told F'lar that he was neither young nor afraid to try, either. It was just a long step,' Lessa explained, wiping tears from her eyes.

F'lar glanced dourly at the passageway, at the end of which Mnementh lounged on his customary ledge.

A laden dragon comes, the bronze warned those in the Weyr. *It is Lytol behind young B'rant on brown Fanth.*

'Now he brings his own bad news?' Lessa asked sourly.

'It is hard enough for Lytol to ride another's dragon or come here at all, Lessa of Ruatha. Do not increase his torment one jot with your childishness,' F'lar said sternly.

Lessa dropped her eyes, furious with F'lar for speaking so to her in front of Robinton.

Lytol stumbled into the queen's weyr, carrying one end of a large rolled rug. Young B'rant, struggling to uphold the other end, was sweating with the effort. Lytol bowed respectfully toward Ramoth and gestured the young brown rider to help him unroll their burden. As the immense tapestry uncoiled, F'lar could understand why Masterweaver Zurg had remembered it. The colors, ancient though they undoubtedly were, remained vibrant and undimmed. The subject matter was even more interesting.

'Mnementh, send for Fandarel. Here's the model he needs for his flamethrower,' F'lar said.

'That tapestry is Ruatha's,' Lessa cried indignantly. 'I remember it from my childhood. It hung in the Great Hall and was the most cherished of my Blood Line's possessions. Where has it been?' Her eyes were flashing.

'Lady, it is being returned to where it belongs,' Lytol said stolidly, avoiding her gaze. 'A masterweaver's work, this,' he went on, touching the heavy fabric with reverent fingers. 'Such colors, such patterning. It took a man's life to set up the loom, a craft's whole effort to complete, or I am no judge of true craftsmanship.'

F'lar walked along the edge of the immense arras, wishing it could be hung to afford the proper perspective of the heroic scene. A flying formation of three wings of dragons dominated the upper portion of half the hanging. They were breathing flame as they dove upon gray, falling clumps of Threads in the brilliant sky. A sky just that perfect autumnal blue, F'lar decided, that cannot occur in warmer weather. Upon the lower slopes of the hills, foliage was depicted as turning yellow from chilly nights. The slatey rocks suggested Ruathan country. Was that why the tapestry had hung in Ruatha Hall? Below, men had left the protecting Hold, cut into the cliff itself. The men were burdened with the curious cylinders of which Zurg had spoken. The tubes in their hands belched brilliant tongues of flame in long streams, aimed at the writhing Threads that attempted to burrow in the ground.

Lessa gave a startled exclamation, walking right onto the tapestry, staring down at the woven outline of the Hold, its massive door ajar, the details of its bronze ornamentation painstakingly rendered in fine yarns.

'I believe that's the design on the Ruatha Hold door,' F'lar remarked.

'It is . . . and it isn't,' Lessa replied in a puzzled voice.

Lytol glowered at her and then at the woven door. 'True. It isn't and yet it is, and I went through that door a scant hour ago.' He scowled down at the door before his toes.

'Well, here are the designs Fandarel wants to study,' F'lar said with relief, as he peered at the flamethrowers.'

Whether or not the smith could produce a working model from this woven one in time to help them three days hence F'lar couldn't guess. But if Fandarel could not, no man could.

The Mastersmith was, for him, jubilant over the presence of the tapestry. He lay upon the rug, his nose tickled by the nap as he studied the details. He grumbled, moaned, and muttered as he sat cross-legged to sketch and peer.

'Has been done. Can be done. Must be done,' he was heard to rumble.

Lessa called for *klah*, bread, and meat when she learned from young B'rant that neither he nor Lytol had eaten yet. She served all the men, her manner gay and teasing. F'lar was relieved for Lytol's sake. Lessa even pressed food and *klah* on Fandarel, a tiny figure beside the mammoth man, insisting that he come away from the tapestry and eat and drink before he could return to his mumbling and drawing.

Fandarel finally decided that he had enough sketches and disappeared, to be flown back to his crafthold.

'No point in asking him when he'll be back. He's too deep in thought to hear,' F'lar remarked, amused.

'If you don't mind, I shall excuse myself as well,' Lessa said, smiling graciously to the four remaining around the table. 'Good Warder Lytol, young B'rant should soon be excused, too. He's half asleep.'

'I most certainly am not, Weyrlady,' B'rant assured her hastily, widening his eyes with simulated alertness.

Lessa merely laughed as she retreated into the sleeping chamber. F'lar stared thoughtfully after her.

'I mistrust the Weyrwoman when she uses that particularly docile tone of voice,' he said slowly.

'Well, we must all depart,' Robinton suggested, rising.

'Ramoth is young but not that foolish,' F'lar murmured after the others had left.

Ramoth slept, oblivious of his scrutiny. He reached for the consolation Mnementh could give him, without response. The big bronze was dozing on his ledge.

Black, blacker, blackest,
And cold beyond frozen things.
Where is *between* when there is naught
To Life but fragile dragon wings?

'I JUST want to see that tapestry back on the wall at Ruatha,'
Lessa insisted to F'lar the next day. 'I want it where it
belongs.'

They had gone to check on the injured and had had one
argument already over F'lar's having sent N'ton along with
the southern venture. Lessa had wanted him to try riding
another's dragon. F'lar had preferred for him to learn to
lead a wing of his own in the south, given the Turns to
mature in. He had reminded Lessa, in the hope that it
might prove inhibiting to any ideas she had about going
four hundred Turns back, about F'nor's return trips, and
he had borne down hard on the difficulties she had already
experienced.

She had become very thoughtful, although she had said
nothing.

Therefore, when Fandarel sent word that he would like
to show F'lar a new mechanism, the Weyrleader felt
reasonably safe in allowing Lessa the triumph of returning
the purloined tapestry to Ruatha. She went to have the
arras rolled and strapped to Ramoth's back.

He watched Ramoth rise with great sweeps of her wide
wings, up to the Star Stone before going *between* to Ruatha.
R'gul appeared on the ledge just then, reporting that a
huge train of firestone was entering the Tunnel. Consequently, busy with such details, it was midmorning before
he could get to see Fandarel's crude and not yet effective
flamethrower ... the fire did not 'throw' from the nozzle
of the tube with any force at all. It was late afternoon before
he reached the Weyr again.

R'gul announces sourly that F'nor had been looking for
him – twice, in fact.

'Twice?'

'Twice, as I said. He would not leave a message with me

for you.' R'gul was clearly insulted by F'nor's refusal.

By the evening meal, when there was still no sign of Lessa, F'lar sent to Ruatha to learn that she had indeed brought the tapestry. She had badgered and bothered the entire Hold until the thing was properly hung. For upward of several hours she had sat and look at it, pacing its length occasionally.

She and Ramoth had then taken to the sky above the Great Tower and disappeared. Lytol had assumed, as had everyone at Ruatha, that she had returned to Benden Weyr.

'Mnementh,' F'lar bellowed when the messenger had finished. 'Mnement, where are they?'

Mnementh's answer was a long time in coming.

I cannot bear them, he said finally his mental voice soft and as full of worry as a dragon's could be.

F'lar gripped the table with both hands, staring at the queen's empty weyr. He knew, in the anguished privacy of his mind, where Lessa had tried to go.

Cold as death, death-bearing,
Stay and die, unguided.
Brave and braving, linger.
This way was twice decided.

BELOW THEM was Ruatha's Great Tower. Lessa coaxed Ramoth slightly to the left, ignoring the dragon's acid comments, knowing that she was excited, too.

That's right, dear, this is exactly the angle at which the tapestry illustrates the Hold door. Only when that tapestry was designed, no one had carved the lintels or capped the door. And there was no Tower, no inner Court, no gate. She stroked the surprisingly soft skin of the curving neck, laughing to hide her own tense nervousness and apprehension at what she was about to attempt.

She told herself there were good reasons prompting her action in this matter. The ballad's opening phrase, 'Gone away, gone ahead,' was clearly a reference to *between* times. And the tapestry gave the required reference points for the jump *between* whens. Oh, how she thanked the Masterweaver who had woven that doorway. She must remember to tell him how well he had wrought. She hoped she'd be able to. Enough of that. Of course, she'd be able to. For hadn't the Weyrs disappeared? Knowing they had gone ahead, knowing how to go back to bring them ahead, it was she, obviously, who must go back and lead them. It was very simple, and only she and Ramoth could do it. Because they already had.

She laughed again, nervously, and took several deep, shuddering breaths.

'All right, my golden love,' she murmured. 'You have the reference. You know when I want to go. Take me *between*, Ramoth, *between* four hundred Turns.'

The cold was intense, even more penetrating than she had imagined. Yet it was not a physical cold. It was the awareness of the absence of *everything*. No light. No sound. No touch. As they hovered, longer, and longer, in this nothingness, Lessa recognized full-blown panic of a kind that threatened to overwhelm her reason. She knew she sat on Ramoth's neck, yet she could not feel the great beast under her thighs, under her hands. She tried to cry out inadvertently and opened her mouth to . . . nothing . . . no sound in her own ears. She could not even feel the hands that she knew she had raised to her own cheeks.

I am here, she heard Ramoth say in her mind. *We are together,* and this reassurance was all that kept her from losing her grasp on sanity in that terrifying aeon of unpassing, timeless nothingness.

Someone had sense enough to call for Robinton. The Masterharper found F'lar sitting at the table, his face deathly pale, his eyes staring at the empty weyr. The craftmaster's entrance, his calm voice, reached F'lar in his shocked numbness. He sent the others out with a peremptory wave.

'She's gone. She tried to go back four hundred Turns,' F'lar said in a tight, hard voice.

The Masterharper sank into the chair opposite the Weyrleader.

'She took the tapestry back to Ruatha,' F'lar continued in that same choked voice. 'I'd told her about F'nor's returns. I told her how dangerous this was. She didn't argue very much, and I know going *between* times had frightened her, if anything could frighten Lessa.' He banged the table with an impotent fist. 'I should have suspected her. When she thinks she's right, she doesn't stop to analyze, to consider. She just does it!'

'But she's not a foolish woman,' Robinton reminded him slowly. 'Not even she would jump *between* times without a reference point. Would she?'

' "Gone away, gone ahead" – that's the only clue we have!'

'Now wait a moment,' Robinton cautioned him, then snapped his fingers. 'Last night, when she walked upon the tapestry, she was uncommonly interested in the Hall door. Remember, she discussed it with Lytol.'

F'lar was on his feet and halfway down the passageway. 'Come on, man, we've got to get to Ruatha.'

Lytol lit every glow in the Hold for F'lar and Robinton to examine the tapestry clearly.

'She spent the afternoon just looking at it,' the Warder said, shaking his head. 'You're sure she has tried this incredible jump?'

'She must have. Mnementh can't hear either her or Ramoth anywhere. Yet he says he can get an echo from Canth many Turns away and in the Southern Continent.' F'lar stalked past the tapestry. 'What is it about the door, Lytol? Think, man!'

'It is much as it is now, save that there are no carved lintels, there is no outer Court or Tower . . .'

'That's it. Oh, by the first Egg, it is so simple. Zurg said this tapestry is old. Lessa must have decided it was four hundred Turns, and she has used it as the reference point to go back *between* times.'

'Why, then, she's there and safe,' Robinton cried, sinking with relief in a chair.

'Oh, no, harper. It is not as easy as that,' F'lar murmured, and Robinton caught his stricken look and the despair echoed in Lytol's face.

'What's the matter?'

'There is nothing *between*,' F'lar said in a dead voice. 'To go *between* places takes only as much time as for a man to cough three times. *Between* four hundred Turns. . . .' His voice trailed off.

Who wills,
Can.
Who tries,
Does.
Who loves,
Lives.

THERE WERE voices that first were roars in her aching ears
and then hushed beyond the threshold of sound. She
gasped as the whirling, nauseating sensation apparently
spun her, and the bed which she felt beneath her, around
and around. She clung to the sides of the bed as pain
jabbed through her head, from somewhere directly in the
middle of her skull. She screamed, as much in protest at the
pain as from the terrifying, rolling, whirling, dropping lack
of a solid ground.

Yet some frightening necessity kept her trying to gabble
out the message she had come to give. Sometimes she felt
Ramoth trying to reach her in that vast swooping darkness
that enveloped her. She would try to cling to Ramoth's
mind, hoping the golden queen could lead her out of this
torturing nowhere. Exhausted, she would sink down, down,
only to be torn from oblivion by the desperate need to
communicate.

She was finally aware of a soft, smooth hand upon her
arm, of a liquid, warm and savory, in her mouth. She rolled
it around her tongue, and it trickled down her sore throat.
A fit of coughing left her gasping and weak. Then she
experimentally opened her eyes, and the images before her
did not lurch and spin.

'Who ... are ... you?' she managed to croak.

'Oh, my dear Lessa ...'

'Is that who I am?' she asked, confused.

'So your Ramoth tells us,' she was assured. 'I am Mardra
of Fort Weyr.'

'Oh, F'lar will be so angry with me,' Lessa moaned as
her memory came rushing back. 'He will shake me and
shake me. He always shakes me when I disobey him. But I
was right. I was right. Mardra? ... Oh, that ... awful ...

nothingness,' and she felt herself drifting off into sleep, unable to resist that overwhelming urge. Comfortingly, her bed no longer rocked beneath her.

The room, dimly lit by wallglows, was both like her own at Benden Weyr and subtly different. Lessa lay still, trying to isolate that difference. Ah, the weyrwalls were very smooth here. The room was larger, too, the ceiling higher and curving. The furnishings, now that her eyes were used to the dim light and she could distinguish details, were more finely crafted. She stirred restlessly.

'Ah, you're awake again, mystery lady,' a man said. Light beyond the parted curtain flooded in from the outer weyr. Lessa sensed rather than saw the presence of others in the room beyond.

A woman passed under the man's arm, moving swiftly to the bedside.

'I remember you. You're Mardra,' Lessa said with surprise.

'Indeed I am, and here is T'ton, Weyrleader at Fort.'

T'ton was tossing glows into the wallbasket, peering over his shoulder at Lessa to see if the light bothered her.

'Ramoth!' Lessa exclaimed, sitting upright, aware for the first time that it was not Ramoth's mind she touched in the outer weyr.

'Oh, that one,' Mardra laughed with amused dismay. 'She'll eat us out of the Weyr, and even my Loranth has had to call the other queens to restrain her.'

'She perches on the Star Stones as if she owned them and keens constantly,' T'ton added, less charitably. He cocked an ear. 'Ha. She's stopped.'

'You can come, can't you?' Lessa blurted out.

'Come? Come where, my dear?' Mardra asked, confused. 'You've been going on and on about our "coming," and Threads approaching, and the Red Star bracketed in the Eye Rock, and ... my dear, don't you realize the Red Star has been past Pern these two months?'

'No, no, they've started. That's why I came back *between* times ...'

'Back? *Between* times?' T'ton exclaimed, striding over to the bed, eyeing Lessa intently.

'Could I have some *klah*? I know I'm not making much sense, and I'm not really awake yet. But I'm not mad or still sick, and this is rather complicated.'

234

'Yes, it is,' T'ton remarked with deceptive mildness. But he did call down the service shaft for *klah*. And he did drag a chair over to her bedside, settling himself to listen to her.

'Of course you're not mad,' Mardra soothed her, glaring at her weyrmate. 'Or she wouldn't ride a queen.'

T'ton had to agree to that. Lessa waited for the *klah* to come; when it did, she sipped gratefully at its stimulating warmth.

Then she took a deep breath and began, telling them of the Long Interval between the dangerous passes of the Red Star: how the sole Weyr had fallen into disfavor and contempt, how Jora had deteriorated and lost control over her queen, Nemorth, so that, as the Red Star neared, there was no sudden increase in the size of clutches. How she had Impressed Ramoth to become Benden's Weyr-woman. How F'lar had outwitted the dissenting Hold Lords the day after Ramoth's first mating flight and taken firm command of Weyr and Pern, preparing for the Threads he knew were coming. She told her by now rapt audience of her own first attempts to fly Ramoth and how she had inadvertently gone back *between* time to the day Fax had invaded Ruath Hold.

'Invade . . . my family's Hold?' Mardra cried, aghast.

'Ruatha has given the Weyrs many famous Weyrwomen,' Lessa said with a sly smile at which T'ton burst out laughing.

'She's Ruathan, no question,' he assured Mardra.

She told them of the situation in which Dragonmen now found themselves, with an insufficient force to meet the Thread attacks. Of the Question Song and the great tapestry.

'A tapestry?' Mardra cried, her hand going to her cheek in alarm. 'Describe it to me!'

And when Lessa did, she saw – at last – belief in both their faces.

'My father has just commissioned a tapestry with such a scene. He told me of it the other day because the last battle with the Threads was held over Ruatha.' Incredulous, Mardra turned to T'ton, who no longer looked amused. 'She must have done what she has said she'd done. How could she possibly know about the tapestry?'

'You might also ask your queen dragon, and mine,' Lessa suggested.

'My dear, we do not doubt you now,' Mardra said sincerely, 'but it is a most incredible feat.'

'I don't think,' Lessa said, 'that I would ever try it again, knowing what I do know.'

'Yes, this shock makes a forward jump *between* times quite a problem if your F'lar must have an effective fighting force,' T'ton remarked.

'You will come? You will?'

'There is a distinct possibility we will,' T'ton said gravely, and his face broke into a lopsided grin. 'You said we left the Weyrs . . . abandoned them, in fact, and left no explanation. We went somewhere . . . somewhen, that is, for we are still here now. . . .'

They were all silent, for the same alternative occurred to them simultaneously. The Weyrs had been left vacant, but Lessa had no way of proving that the five Weyrs reappeared in her time.

'There must be a way. There must be a way,' Lessa cried distractedly. 'And there's no time to waste. No time at all!'

T'ton gave a bark of laughter. 'There's plenty of time at this end of history, my dear.'

They made her rest then, more concerned than she was that she had been ill some weeks, deliriously screaming that she was falling and could not see, could not hear, could not touch. Ramoth, too, they told her, had suffered from the appalling nothingness of a protracted stay *between*, emerging above ancient Ruatha a pale yellow wraith of her former robust self.

The Lord of Ruatha Hold, Mardra's father, had been surprised out of his wits by the appearance of a staggering rider and a pallid queen on his stone verge. Naturally and luckily he had sent to his daughter at Fort Weyr for help. Lessa and Ramoth had been transported to the Weyr, and the Ruathan Lord kept silence on the matter.

When Lessa was strong enough, T'ton called a Council of Weyrleaders. Curiously, there was no opposition to going . . . provided they could solve the problem of time-shock and find reference points along the way. It did not take Lessa long to comprehend why the dragonriders were so eager to attempt the journey. Most of them had been born during the present Thread incursions. They had now had close to four months of unexciting routine patrols and were bored with monotony. Training Games were pallid substitutes for the real battles they had all fought. The Holds, which once could not do dragonmen favors enough, were beginning to be indifferent. The Weyrleaders could see these incidents increasing as Thread-generated fears receded. It was a morale decay as insidious as a wasting disease in Weyr and Hold. The alternative which Lessa's appeal offered was better than a slow decline in their own time.

Of Benden, only the Weyrleader himself was privy to these meetings. Because Benden was the only Weyr in Lessa's time, it must remain ignorant, and intact, until her time. Nor could any mention be made of Lessa's presence, for that, too, was unknown in her Turn.

She insisted that they call in the Masterharper because her Records said he had been called. But when he asked her to tell him the Question Song, she smiled and demurred.

'You'll write it, or your successor will, when the Weyrs are found to be abandoned,' she told him. 'But it must be your doing, not my repeating.'

'A difficult assignment to know one must write a song that four hundred Turns later gives a valuable clue.'

'Only be sure,' she cautioned him, 'that it is a Teaching tune. It must *not* be forgotten, for it poses questions that I have to answer.'

As he started to chuckle, she realized she had already given him a pointer.

The discussions – how to go so far safely with no sustained sense deprivations – grew heated. There were more constructive notions, however impractical, on how to find reference points along the way. The five Weyrs had not been ahead in time, and Lessa, in her one gigantic backward leap, had not stopped for intermediate time marks.

'You did say that a *between* times jump of ten years caused no hardship?' T'ton asked of Lessa as all the Weyrleaders and the Masterharper met to discuss this impasse.

'None. It takes ... oh, twice as long as a *between* places jump.'

'It is the four hundred Turn leap that left you imbalanced. Hmmm. Maybe twenty or twenty-five Turn segments would be safe enough.'

That suggestion found merit until Ista's cautious leader, D'ram, spoke up.

'I don't mean to be a Hold-hider, but there is one

possibility we haven't mentioned. How do we know we made the jump *between* to Lessa's time? Going *between* is a chancy business. Men go missing often. And Lessa barely made it here alive.'

'A good point, D'ram,' T'ton concurred briskly, 'but I feel there is more to prove that we do – did – will – go forward. The clues, for one thing – they were aimed at Lessa. The very emergency that left five Weyrs empty sent her back to appeal for our help –'

'Agreed, agreed,' D'ram interrupted earnestly, 'but what I mean is can you be sure we reached Lessa's time? It hadn't happened yet. Do we know it can?'

T'ton was not the only one who searched his mind for an answer to that. All of a sudden he slammed both hands, palms down, on the table.

'By the Egg, it's die slow, doing nothing, or die quick, trying. I've had a surfeit of the quiet life we dragonmen must lead after the Red Star passes till we go *between* in old age. I confess I'm almost sorry to see the Red Star dwindle farther from us in the evening sky. I say, grab the risk with both hands and shake it till it's gone. We're dragonmen, aren't we, bred to fight the Threads? Let's go hunting . . . four hundred Turns ahead!'

Lessa's drawn face relaxed. She had recognized the validity of D'ram's alternate possibility, and it had touched off bitter fear in her heart. To risk herself was her own responsibility, but to risk these hundreds of men and dragons, the wreyfolk who would accompany their men . . .?

T'ton's ringing words for once and all dispensed with that consideration.

'And I believe,' the Masterharper's exultant voice cut through the answering shouts of agreement, 'I have your reference points.' A smile of surprised wonder illuminated his face. 'Twenty Turns or twenty hundred, you have a guide! And T'ton said it. As the Red Star dwindles in the evening sky . . .'

Later, as they plotted the orbit of the Red Star, they found how easy that solution actually was and chuckled that their ancient foe should be their guide.

Atop Fort Weyr, as on all the Weyrs, were great stones. They were so placed that at certain times of the year they marked the approach and retreat of the Red Star, as it orbited in its erratic two hundred Turn-long course around their sun. By consulting the Records which, among other morsels of information, included the Red Star's wanderings, it was not hard to plan jumps *between* of twenty-five Turns for each Weyr. It had been decided that the complement of each separate Weyr would jump *between* above its own base, for there would unquestionably be accidents if close to eighteen hundred laden beasts tried it at one point.

Each moment now was one too long away from her own time for Lessa. She had been a month away from F'lar and missed him more than she had thought possible. Also, she was worried that Ramoth would mate away from Mnementh. There were, to be sure, bronze dragons and bronze riders eager to do that service, but Lessa had no interest in them.

T'ton and Mardra occupied her with the many details in organizing the exodus, so that no clues, past the tapestry and the Question Song that would be composed at a later date, remained in the Weyrs.

It was with a relief close to tears that Lessa urged Ramoth upward in the night sky to take her place near T'ton and Mardra above the Fort Weyr Star Stone. At five other Weyrs great wings were ranged in formation, ready to depart their own times.

As each Weyrleader's dragon reported to Lessa that all were ready, reference points determined by the Red Star's travels in mind, it was this traveler from the future who gave the command to jump *between*.

The blackest night must end in dawn,
The sun dispel the dreamer's fear:
When shall my soul's bleak, hopeless pain
Find solace in its darkening Weyr?

THEY HAD made eleven jumps *between*, the Weyrleaders'
bronzes speaking to Lessa as they rested briefly between
each jump. Of the eighteen hundred-odd travelers, only
four failed to come ahead, and they had been older beasts.
All five sections agreed to pause for a quick meal and hot
klah before the final jump, which would be but twelve
Turns.

'It is easier,' T'ton commented as Mardra served the
klah, 'to go twenty-five Turns than twelve.' He glanced up
at the Red Dawn Star, their winking and faithful guide.
'It does not alter its position as much. I count on you,
Lessa, to give us additional references.'

'I want to get us back to Ruatha before F'lar discovers I
have gone.' She shivered as she looked up at the Red Star
and sipped hastily at the hot *klah*. 'I've seen the Star just
like that, once ... no, twice ... before at Ruatha.' She
stared at T'ton, her throat constricting as she remembered
that morning: the time she had decided that the Red Star
was a menace to her, three days after which Fax and F'lar
had appeared at Ruatha Hold. Fax had died on F'lar's
dagger, and she had gone to Bendon Weyr. She felt suddenly
dizzy, weak, strangely unsettled. She had not felt this way
as they paused between other jumps.

'Are you all right, Lessa?' Mardra asked with concern.
'You're so white You're shaking.' She put her arm around
Lessa, glancing, concerned, at her Weyrmate.

'Twelve Turns ago I was at Ruatha,' Lessa murmured,
grasping Mardra's hand for support. 'I was at Ruatha
twice. Let's go on quickly. I'm too many in this morning.
I must get back. I must get back to F'lar. He'll be so
angry.'

The note of hysteria in her voice alarmed both Mardra
and T'ton. Hastily the latter gave orders for the fires to be

240

extinguished, for the Weyrfolk to mount and prepare for the final jump ahead.

Her mind in chaos, Lessa transmitted the references to the other Weyrleaders' dragons: Ruatha in the evening light, the Great Tower, the inner Court, the land at springtime. . . .

A fleck of red in a cold night sky,
A drop of blood to guide them by,
Turn away, Turn away, Turn, be gone,
A Red Star beckons the travelers on.

BETWEEN THEM, Lytol and Robinton forced F'lar to eat, deliberately plying him with wine. At the back of his mind F'lar knew he would have to keep going, but the effort was immense, the spirit gone from him. It was no comfort that they still had Pridith and Kylara to continue dragonkind, yet he delayed sending someone back for F'nor, unable to face the reality of that admission: that in sending for Pridith and Kylara, he had acknowledged the fact that Lessa and Ramoth would not return.

Lessa, Lessa, his mind cried endlessly, damning her one moment for her reckless, thoughtless daring, loving her the next for attempting such an incredible feat.

'I said, F'lar, you need sleep now more than wine.' Robinton's voice penetrated his preoccupation.

F'lar looked at him, frowning in perplexity. He realized that he was trying to lift the wine jug that Robinton was holding firmly down.

'What did you say?'

'Come. I'll bear you company to Benden. Indeed, nothing could persuade me to leave your side. You have aged years, man, in the course of hours.'

'And isn't it understandable?' F'lar shouted, rising to his feet, the impotent anger boiling out of him at the nearest target in the form of Robinton.

Robinton's eyes were full of compassion as he reached for F'lar's arm, gripping it tightly.

'Man, not even this Masterharper has words enough to express the sympathy and honor he has for you. But you must sleep; you have tomorrow to endure, and the tomorrow after that you have to fight. The dragonmen must have a leader. . . .' His voice trailed off. 'Tomorrow you must send for F'nor . . . and Pridith.'

F'lar pivoted on his heel and strode toward the fateful door of Ruatha's great hall.

Oh, Tongue, give sound to joy and sing
Of hope and promise on dragonwing.

BEFORE THEM loomed Ruatha's Great Tower, the high
walls of the Outer Court clearly visible in the fading light.

The claxon rang violent summons into the air, barely
heard over the earsplitting thunder as hundreds of dragons
appeared, ranging in full fighting array, wing upon wing,
up and down the valley.

A shaft of light stained the flagstones of the Court as the
Hold door opened.

Lessa ordered Ramoth down, close to the Tower, and
dismounted, running eagerly forward to greet the men who
piled out of the door. She made out the stocky figure of
Lytol, a handbasket of glows held high above his head.
She was so relieved to see him that she forgot her previous
antagonism to the Warder.

'You misjudged the last jump by two days, Lessa,' he
cried as soon as he was near enough for her to hear him over
the noise of settling dragons.

'Misjudged? How could I' she breathed.

T'ton and Mardra came up beside her.

'No need to worry,' Lytol reassured her, gripping her
hands tightly in his, his eyes dancing. He was actually
smiling at her. 'You overshot the day. Go back *between*,
return to Ruatha of two days ago. That's all.' His grin
widened at her confusion. 'It is all right,' he repeated,
patting her hands. 'Take this same hour, the Great Court,
everything, but visualize F'lar, Robinton, and myself here
on the flagstones. Place Mnementh on the Great Tower and
a blue dragon on the verge. Now go.

Mnementh? Ramoth queried Lessa, eager to see her Weyrmate. She ducked her great head, and her huge eyes
gleamed with scintillating fire.

'I don't understand,' Lessa wailed. Mardra slipped a
comforting arm around her shoulders.

243

'But I do, I do – trust me,' Lytol pleaded, patting her shoulder awkwardly and glancing at T'ton for support. 'It is as F'nor has said. You cannot be several places in time without experiencing great distress, and when you stopped twelve Turns back, it threw Lessa all to pieces.'

'You know that?' T'ton cried.

'Of course. Just go back two days. You see, I *know* you have. I shall, of course, be surprised then, but now, tonight, I know you reappeared two days earlier. Oh, go. Don't argue. F'lar was half out of his mind with worry for you.'

'He'll shake me,' Lessa cried, like a little girl.

'Lessa!' T'ton took her by the hand and led her back to Ramoth, who crouched so her rider could mount.

T'ton took complete charge and had his Fidranth pass the order to return to the references Lytol had given, adding by way of Ramoth a description of the humans and Mnementh.

The cold of *between* restored Lessa to herself, although her error had badly jarred her confidence. But then there was Ruatha again. The dragons happily arranged themselves in tremendous display. And there, silhouetted against the light from the Hall, stood Lytol, Robinton's tall figure, and . . F'lar.

Mnementh's voice gave a brassy welcome, and Ramoth could not land Lessa quickly enough to go and twine necks with her mate.

Lessa stood where Ramoth had left her, unable to move. She was aware that Mardra and T'ton were beside her. She was conscious only of F'lar, racing across the Court toward her. Yet she could not move.

He grabbed her in his arms, holding her so tightly to him that she could not doubt the joy of his welcome.

'Lessa, Lessa,' his voice raggedly changed in her ear. He pressed her face against his, crushing her to breathlessness, all his careful detachment abandoned. He kissed her, hugged her, held her, and then kissed her with rough urgency again. Then he suddenly set her on her feet and gripped her shoulders. 'Lessa, if you ever . . .' he said, punctuating each word with a flexing of his fingers, then stopped, aware of a grinning circle of strangers surrounding them.

'I told you he'd shake me,' Lessa was saying, dashing tears from her face. 'But F'lar, I brought them all . . . all but

Benden Weyr. And that is why the five Weyrs were abandoned. I brought them.'

F'lar looked around him, looked beyond the leaders to the masses of dragons settling in the Valley, on the heights, everywhere, he turned. There were dragons, blue, green, brown, and a whole wingful of golden queen dragons alone.

'You brought the Weyrs?' he echoed, stunned.

'Yes, this is Mardra and T'ton of Fort Weyr, D'ram and . . .'

He stopped her with a little shake, pulling her to his side so he could see and greet the newcomers.

'I am more grateful than you can know,' he said and could not go on with all the many words he wanted to add.

T'ton stepped forward, holding out his hand, which F'lar seized and held firmly.

'We bring eighteen hundred dragons, seventeen queens, and all that is necessary to implement our Weyrs.'

'And they brought flamethrowers, too,' Lessa put in excitedly.

'But – to come . . . to attempt it . . .' F'lar murmured in admiring wonder.

T'ton and D'ram and the others laughed.

'Your Lessa showed the way . . .'

'. . . with the Red Star to guide us . . .' she said.

'We are dragonmen,' T'ton continued solemnly, 'as you are yourself, F'lar of Benden. We were told there are Threads here to fight, and that's work for dragonmen to do . . . in any time!'

Drummer, beat, and piper, blow,
Harper, strike, and soldier, go.
Free the flame and sear the grasses
Till the dawning Red Star passes.

EVEN AS the five Weyrs had been settling around Ruatha Valley, F'nor had been compelled to bring forward in time his southern weyrfolk. They had all reached the end of endurance in double-time life, gratefully creeping back to quarters they had vacated two days and ten Turns ago.

R'gul, totally unaware of Lessa's backward plunge, greeted F'lar and his Weyrwoman, on their return to the Weyr, with the news of F'nor's appearance with seventy-two new dragons and the further word that he doubted any of the riders would be fit to fight.

'I've never seen such exhausted men in my life,' R'gul rattled on, 'can't imagine what could have gotten into them, with sun and plenty of food and all, and no responsibilities.'

F'lar and Lessa exchanged glances.

'Well, the southern Weyr ought to maintained, R'gul. Think it over.'

'I'm a fighting dragonman, not a womanizer,' the old dragonrider grunted. 'It'd take more than a trip *between* times to reduce me like those others.'

'Oh, they'll be themselves again in next to no time,' Lessa said and, to R'gul's intense disapproval, she giggled.

'They'll have to be if we're to keep the skies Thread-free,' R'gul snapped testily.

'No problem about that now,' F'lar assured him easily.

'No problem? With only a hundred and forty-four dragons?'

'Two hundred and sixteen,' Lessa corrected him firmly.

Ignoring her, R'gul asked, 'Has that Mastersmith found a flamethrower that'll work?'

'Indeed he has,' F'lar assured R'gul, grinning broadly.

The five Weyrs had also brought forward their equipment. Fandarel all but snatched examples from their backs and, undoubtedly, every hearth and smithy through the continent would be ready to duplicate the design by morning. T'ton had told F'lar that, in his time, each Hold had ample flamethrowers for every man on the ground. In the course of the Long Interval, however, the throwers must have been either smelted down or lost as incomprehensible devices. D'ram, particularly, was very much interested in Fandarel's agenothree sprayer, considering it better than thrown-flame, since it would also act as a fertilizer.

'Well,' R'gul admitted gloomily, 'a flamethrower or two will be some help day after tomorrow.'

'We have found something else that will help a lot more,' Lessa remarked and then hastily excused herself, dashing into the sleeping quarters.

The sounds that drifted past the curtain were either laughter or sobs, and R'gul frowned on both. That girl was just too young to be Weyrwoman at such a time. No stability.

'Has she realized how critical our situation is? Even with F'nor's additions? That is, if they can fly?' R'gul demanded testily. 'You oughtn't to let her leave the Weyr at all.'

F'lar ignored that and began pouring himself a cup of wine.

'You once pointed out to me that the five empty Weyrs of Pern supported your theory that there would be no more Threads.'

R'gul cleared his throat, thinking that apologies – even if they might be due from the Weyrleader – were scarcely effective against the Threads.

'Now there was merit in that theory,' F'lar went on, filling a cup for R'gul. 'Not, however, as you interpreted it. The five Weyrs were empty because they . . . they came here.'

R'gul, his cup halfway to his lips, stared at F'lar. This man also was too young to bear his responsibilities. But . . . he seemed actually to believe what he was saying.

'Believe it or not, R'gul – and in a bare day's time you will – the five Weyrs are empty no longer. They're here, in the Weyrs, in this time. And they shall join us, eighteen hundred strong, the day after tomorrow at Telgar, with flamethrowers and with plenty of battle experience.'

R'gul regarded the poor man stolidly for a long moment. Carefully he put his cup down and, turning on his heel, left the weyr. He refused to be an object of ridicule. He'd better plan to take over the leadership tomorrow if they were to fight Threads the day after.

The next morning, when he saw the clutch of great bronze dragons bearing the Weyrleaders and their wingleaders to the conference, R'gul got quietly drunk.

Lessa exchanged good mornings with her friends and then, smiling sweetly, left the weyr, saying she must feed Ramoth. F'lar stared after her thoughtfully, then went to greet Robinton and Fandarel, who had been asked to attend the meeting, too. Neither Craftmaster said much, but neither missed a word spoken. Fandarel's great head kept swiveling from speaker to speaker, his deep-set eyes blinking occasionally. Robinton sat with a bemused smile on his face, utterly delighted by ancestral visitors.

F'lar was quickly talked out of resigning his titular position as Weyrleader of Benden on the grounds that he was too inexperienced.

'You did well enough at Nerat and Keroon. Well indeed,' T'ton said.

'You call twenty-eight men or dragons out of action good leadership?'

'For a first battle, with every dragonman green as a hatchling? No, man, you were on time at Nerat, however you got there,' and T'ton grinned maliciously at F'lar, 'which is what a dragonman must do. No, that was well flown, I say. Well flown.' The other four Weyrleaders muttered complete agreement with that compliment. 'Your Weyr is understrength, though, so we'll lend you enough odd-wing riders till you've gotten the Weyr up to full strength again. Oh, the queens love these times!' And his grin broadened to indicate that bronze riders did, too.

F'lar returned that smile, thinking that Ramoth was about ready for another mating flight, and this time, Lessa ... oh, that girl was being too deceptively docile. He'd better watch her closely.

'Now,' T'ton was saying, 'we left with Fandarel's crafthold all the flamethrowers we brought up so that the groundmen will be armed tomorrow.'

'Aye, and my thanks,' Fandarel grunted. 'We'll turn out new ones in record time and return yours soon.'

'Don't forget to adapt that agenothree for air spraying, too,' D'ram put in.

'It is agreed,' and T'ton glanced quickly around at the other riders, 'that all the Weyrs will meet, full strength, three hours after dawn above Telgar, to follow the Thread's attack across to Crom. By the way, F'lar, those charts of yours that Robinton showed me are superb. We never had them.'

'How did you know when the attacks would come?'

T'ton shrugged. 'They were coming so regularly even when I was a weyrling, you kind of knew when one was due. But this way is much, much better.'

'More efficient,' Fandarel added approvingly.

'After tomorrow, when all the Weyrs show up at Telgar, we can request what supplies we need to stock the empty Weyrs,' T'ton grinned. 'Like old times, squeezing extra tithes from the Holders.' He rubbed his hands in ancipitation. 'Like old times.'

'There's the southern Weyr,' F'nor suggested. 'We've been gone from there six Turns in this time, and the herd-beasts were left. They'll have multiplied, and there'll be all that fruit and grain.'

'It would please me to see that southern venture continued,' F'lar remarked, nodding encouragingly at F'nor.

'Yes, and continue Kylara down there, please, too,' F'nor added urgently, his eyes sparkling with irritation.

They discussed sending for some immediate supplies to help out the newly occupied Weyrs, and then adjourned the meeting.

'It is a trifle unsettling,' T'ton said as he shared wine with Robinton, 'to find that the Weyr you left the day before in good order has become a dusty hulk.' He chuckled. 'The women of the Lower Caverns were a bit upset.'

'We cleaned up those kitchens,' F'nor replied indignantly. A good night's rest in a fresh time had removed much of his fatigue.

T'ton cleared his throat. 'According to Mardra, no man can *clean* anything.'

'Do you think you'll be up to riding tomorrow, F'nor?' F'lar asked solicitously. He was keenly aware of the stress showing in his half brother's face, despite his improvement overnight. Yet those strenuous Turns had been necessary, nor had they become futile even in hindsight with the arrival of eighteen hundred dragons from past time. When F'lar had ordered F'nor ten Turns backward to breed the desperately needed replacements, they had not yet brought to mind the Question Song or known of the tapestry.

'I wouldn't miss that fight if I were dragonless,' F'nor declared stoutly.

'Which reminds me,' F'lar remarked, 'we'll need Lessa at Telgar tomorrow. She can speak to any dragon, you know,' he explained, almost apologetically, to T'ton and D'ram.

'Oh, we know,' T'ton assured him. 'And Mardra doesn't mind.' Seeing F'lar's blank expression, he added, 'As senior Weyrwoman, Mardra, of course, leads the queens' wing.'

F'lar's face grew blanker. 'Queens' wing?'

'Certainly,' and T'ton and D'ram exchanged questioning glances at F'lar's surprise. 'You don't keep your queens from fighting, do you?'

'Our *queens*? T'ton, we at Benden have had only *one* queen dragon – at a time – for so many generations that there are those who denounce the legends of queens in battle as black heresy!'

T'ton looked rueful. 'I had not truly realized till this instant how small your numbers were.' But his enthusiasms overtook him. 'Just the same, queens are very useful with flamethrowers. They get clumps other riders might miss. They fly in low, under the main wings. That's one reason D'ram's so interested in the agenothree spray. Doesn't singe the hair off the Holders' heads, so to speak, and is far better over tilled fields.'

'Do you mean to say that you allow your queens to fly – against Threads?' F'lar ignored the fact that F'nor was grinning, and T'ton, too.

'Allow?' D'ram bellowed 'You can't stop them. Don't you know your Ballads?'

' "Moreta's Ride?" '

'Exactly.'

F'nor laughed aloud at the expression on F'lar's face as he irritably pulled the hanging forelock from his eyes. Then, sheepishly, he began to grin.

'Thanks. That gives me an idea.'

He saw his fellow Weyrleaders to their dragons, waved cheerfully to Robinton and Fandarel, more lighthearted than he would have thought he'd be the morning before the second battle. Then he asked Mnementh where Lessa might be.

Bathing, the bronze dragon replied.

F'lar glanced at the empty queen's weyr.

Oh, Ramoth is on the Peak, as usual. Mnementh sounded aggrieved.

F'lar heard the sound of splashing in the bathing room suddenly cease, so he called down for hot *klah*. He was going to enjoy this.

'Oh, did the meeting go well?' Lessa asked sweetly as she emerged from the bathing room, drying-cloth wrapped tightly around her slender figure.

'Extremely. You realize, of course, Lessa, that you'll be needed at Telgar?'

She looked at him intently for a moment before she smiled again.

'I *am* the only Weyrwoman who can speak to any dragon,' she replied archly.

'True,' F'lar admitted blithely. 'And no longer the only queen's rider in Benden. . . .'

'I hate you!' Lessa snapped, unable to evade F'lar as he pinned her cloth-swathed body to his.

'Even when I tell you that Fandarel has a flamethrower for you so you can join the queens' wing?'

She stopped squirming in his arms and stared at him, disconcerted that he had outguessed her.

'And that Kylara will be installed as Weyrwoman in the south . . . in this time? As Weyrleader, I need my peace and quiet between battles. . . .'

The cloth fell from her body to the floor as she responded to his kiss as ardently as if dragon-roused.

From the Weyr and from the Bowl,
Bronze and brown and blue and green,
Rise the dragonmen of Pern,
Aloft, on wing; seen, then unseen.

RANGED ABOVE the Peak of Benden Weyr, a scant three hours after dawn, two hundred and sixteen dragons held their formations as F'lar on bronze Mnementh inspected their ranks.

Below in the Bowl were gathered all the weyrfolk and some of those injured in the first battle. All the weyrfolk, that is, except Lessa and Ramoth. They had gone on to Fort Weyr where the queens' wing was assembling. F'lar could not quite suppress a twinge of concern that she and Ramoth would be fighting, too. A holdover, he knew, from the days when Pern had had only one queen. If Lessa could jump four hundred Turns *between* and lead five Weyrs back, she could take care of herself and her dragon against Threads.

He checked to be sure that every man was well loaded with firestone sacks, that each dragon was in good color, especially those in from the southern Weyr. Of course, the dragons were fit, but the faces of the men still showed evidences of the temporal strains they had endured. He was procrastinating, and the Threads would be dropping in the skies of Telgar.

He gave the order to go *between*. They reappeared above, and to the south of Telgar Hold itself, and were not the first arrivals. To the west, to the north, and, yes, to the east now, wings arrived until the horizon was patterned with the great V's of several thousand dragon wings. Faintly he heard the claxon bell on Telgar Hold Tower as the unexpected dragon strength was acclaimed from the ground.

'Where is she?' F'lar demanded of Mnementh. 'We'll need her presently to relay orders . . .'

She's coming, Mnementh interrupted him.

Right above Telgar Hold another wing appeared. Even at this distance, F'lar could see the difference: the golden dragons shone in the bright morning sunlight.

A hum of approval drifted down the dragon ranks, and despite his fleeting worry, F'lar grinned with proud indulgence at the glittering sight.

Just then the eastern wings soared straight upward in the sky as the dragons became instinctively aware of the presence of their ancient foe.

Mnementh raised his head, echoing back the brass thunder of the war cry. He turned his head, even as hundreds of other beasts turned to receive firestone from their riders. Hundreds of great jaws masticated the stone, swallowed it, their digestive acids transforming dry stone into flame-producing gases, igniting on contact with oxygen.

Threads! F'lar could see them clearly now against the spring sky. His pulses began to quicken, not with apprehension, but with a savage joy. His heart pounded unevenly. Mnementh demanded more stone and began to speed up the strokes of his wings in the air, gathering himself to leap upward when commanded.

The leading Weyr already belched gouts of orange-red flame into the pale blue sky. Dragons winked in and out, flamed and dove.

The great golden queens sped at cliff-skimming height to cover what might have been missed.

Then F'lar gave the command to gain altitude to meet the Threads halfway in their abortive descent. As Mnementh surged upward, F'lar shook his fist defiantly at the winking Red Eye of the Star.

'One day,' he shouted, 'we will not sit tamely here, awaiting your fall. We will fall on you, where you spin, and sear you on your own ground.'

By the Egg, he told himself, if we can travel four hundred Turns backward and across seas and lands in the blink of an eye, what is travel from one world to another but a different kind of step?

F'lar grinned to himself. He'd better not mention that audacious notion in Lessa's presence.

Clumps ahead, Mnementh warned him.

As the bronze dragon charged, flaming, F'lar tightened his knees on the massive neck. Mother of us all, he was glad that now, of all times conceivable, he, F'lar, rider of bronze Mnementh, was a dragonman of Pern!

To be born as I was on April first imposes a challenge. In writing speculative fiction, I feel I have not failed the auspices of my natal day.

However, being 99 percent Irish indicates a certain perversity, so I tried out many other things before I settled down to write. I dabbled in the Theatre Arts, studied voice production for nine years before arriving at the horrifying conclusion that I was a better stage-director of opera than a singer. I capped off that facet with the production and stage-direction of the American premiere in Wilmington of Carl Orff's *Ludus de Nato Infante Mirificus*, which is not as far from speculative fiction as you might imagine.

I balance indifferent housekeeping with superb cooking; sew for anyone but myself, knit well, and (would you believe?) embroider; am currently raising three children, five cats, and a French poodle; swim, sail, ride horseback – western style by preference – collect Graustarkian romances, and resent being kept away from my typewriter by any one of the above-mentioned diversions.

My eyes are green, my hair is silver, and I freckle.

The rest is subject to change without notice.

ANNE McCAFFREY, 1969

DRAGONSONG BY ANNE MCCAFFREY

Menolly-Mistress of Music, Ward of Fire Lizards.

Every two hundred years or so, shimmering threads fall, raining black ruin on Pern. The great dragons of Pern hurl themselves through the beleaguered skies, flaming tongues of fire to destroy deadly Thread and save the Planet. It was not Threadfall that made Menolly unhappy. It was her father who betrayed her ambition to be a Harper, who thwarted her love of music. Menolly had no choice but to run away. She came upon a group of fire lizards, wild relatives of the fire-breathing dragons. Her music swirled about them; she taught nine to sing . . . Suddenly Menolly was no longer alone.

0 552 10661 5

DRAGONSDAWN BY ANNE MCCAFFREY

IN THE BEGINNING . . .

Before Thread, before the Dragons, before the Holds and the Weyrs and the elite Dragonriders of Pern, was just the great ship gliding through space with nearly three thousand colonists prepared to tackle the mighty task of beginning a new world on a strange planet.

It was a jewel of a planet – with rivers and seas and mountains, and breathable air and growing things. Then came the terror.

The strange, unidentifiable circles in the grass suddenly revealed a meaning, and every living thing was at risk. Many died – a horrible and consuming death. All resources, every man, woman and child had to fight the terrible nightmare of Thread.

But a new creature was about to save the planet. From the delicate fire lizards a new life was born – a new symbiosis between man and beast.

THE LEGEND OF PERN WAS ABOUT TO BEGIN.

0 552 13530 6